About the Author

Pamela Manresa currently lives in Colorado with her husband of forty-five years. They have four children and four grandchildren. They have traveled extensively both nationally and internationally and have lived in several cities around the United States. She worked in the corporate world for thirty years and as a victim advocate for five years. Having a diverse background, she likes to draw on her past experiences in much of her writing.

To Trap the Tortured Soul

Pam Manresa

Pamela Manresa

To Trap the Tortured Soul

Olympia Publishers
London

www.olympiapublishers.com
OLYMPIA PAPERBACK EDITION

ISBN: 978-1-80439-064-1

This is a work of fiction.
Names, characters, places and incidents originate from the writer's
imagination. Any resemblance to actual persons, living or dead, is
purely coincidental.

First Published in 2023

Olympia Publishers
Tallis House
2 Tallis Street
London
EC4Y 0AB

Printed in Great Britain

Dedication

To Mom, because I was listening.

Acknowledgments

I want to thank my husband for his support, for always believing in me and for being my biggest fan.

PROLOGUE

When they first met, he told her she was pretty, and it made her feel special. But after they were married, he told her she was rather ordinary, and she believed him.

On their wedding day, people gushed at what a beautiful bride she was so he showered her with passionate attention. But, on the wedding night he made her sleep on the hotel sofa telling her that she had embarrassed him and had acted vain, and she believed him.

One time he told her she had a unique way of looking at life and she was elated, but later, when he told her she was worthless and didn't have enough intelligence to have her own opinion, she believed him.

When their first child was born, he told her she was a good mother and it made her feel proud, but after child number three, he told her that her parenting skills were pathetic and she didn't deserve their respect. Her heart dropped to her feet, but she believed him.

Then one day, when he told her she was a good wife, she wanted to believe him. But later, when he berated her for being lethargic and lazy, telling her that if she was going to walk around half dead she should just give in to the impulse, she believed him that time, too.

SECTION ONE

FAMILY AND FRIENDS

Family and friends, friend or enemy,
You can't know one without knowing any.

CHAPTER ONE

THE FATHER

Sheriff Benjamin Callum was tired – so very tired. For the last week he had organized search parties, made phone calls, wrangled volunteers, and dealt with the family of a woman who, for lack of a better explanation, had simply vanished.

Jodee Warren, a thirty-six-year-old wife and mother on vacation with her husband and children, had disappeared four days into their family vacation in the uppermost western corner of Washington State.

Following the first twenty-four hours of searching by him and his staff, which proved fruitless, Callum had organized search parties with the help of other agencies in the state. One day later, her disappearance ended up in the local paper. After another day and a half her husband had informed his in-laws in St. Cloud, Minnesota. Thirty-six hours after that the search had been called off because of weather.

Sheriff Callum had been dealing with Mrs. Warren's husband, Doug Warren, for a week now and, putting professionalism aside, Callum felt that the man had proven to be about as much help as a tick on a dog's ass.

Doug Warren had provided an explanation of events that had made no sense, and then had given the authorities a description of his wife so vague that Callum was beginning to wonder if the man ever actually looked at his wife. His description was that she was short, maybe five-five, skinny but beginning to get on the pudgy side, blonde but not too blonde.

What the hell did that even mean, Callum had asked him, 'not too blonde?' And no one he knew would consider five foot five for a woman as being short.

Jodee Warren's kids had been of no more help than the husband. When asked for a description of their mother, one said she was 'super' skinny while the other said she was 'tall and kind of chubby.'

The oldest girl was the only one who seemed to be logical, but she was so stoic that an outsider would wonder if she didn't have a social affliction of some kind. The only way Callum knew for sure that there even was a Jodee Warren, was that the owners of the B and B they had stayed at had vouched to her authenticity. But even they seemed confused as to what she looked like: 'A nice looking woman; average height, average weight, dirty blonde, blue eyes, no, green eyes. Oh, maybe they were hazel… You know,' they'd said, 'average.'

While Callum had the Kokanee Bay Sheriff's Office work non-stop with every resource at their disposal, the missing woman's family wallowed in the tiny tourist town complaining of delays and sub-standard results. In the meantime, not one of them could describe what clothes she was wearing the day she disappeared or even remember the exact time any of them had seen her last. Stranger yet, after three days on vacation, not one of them had taken a picture of her.

They had pictures of each other, pictures of the wharf, pictures of the local museum, hell, even a picture of the front of the restaurant they had eaten dinner at the night before – but no pictures of a tall/short, skinny/fat average looking Jodee Warren with color-changing eyes.

Callum let these thoughts swirl around in his head while he filed the day's paperwork at nine in the evening and hoped he would finally be able to go home at least one night that week before midnight. He was so tired his bones hurt and was wondering if he'd even be able to drive home without falling asleep when a loud bang from the front office door jump-started his nervous system. Bending at the waist and looking around his office door like a floating head without a body, he saw a large, red-faced man standing just inside the vestibule. His arms were bowed at his side and his feet braced apart like he was challenging someone to a gunfight at high noon.

Taking immediate measure of the man, Callum guessed he stood around five foot ten, stout, and from the look in his eyes, really pissed-off. He had let the door slam behind him causing a loud bang and stood surveying the office obviously looking for signs of life. Seeing the floating head of Sheriff Callum peeking around the door at the far end of the room, he said loudly, "I want to talk to the sheriff." The heat of his impatience was evident.

"I'm Sheriff Callum," Callum announced as he straightened up his body and let his legs realign themselves with his torso as he came around the door. He was fifty-two years old and stood six foot one. His light-colored hair was just long enough to give an illusion of style but at the moment stood up in different directions like he'd tried to rub it off his head. His eyes were a light blue and carried an impressive amount of experience hidden behind layers of fatigue. In contradiction to the disarray of his hair, the shirt he wore was so crisp and white that the metal star pinned to it stood out like a bright sign advertising the message 'I'm the man in charge.'

The angry man stood facing straight ahead, unblinking. His

face was as red as the neon sign on the hardware store that could be seen through the large plate glass window at his back. His formidable bearing made him appear larger than he really was, and when he spoke his soft, saggy jowls jiggled, reminding Callum of a bulldog – a bulldog in overalls.

"I'm Joe Olson." He stated his name like it was supposed to be of some importance. "I'm Jodee Warren's father." He waited half a heartbeat before he continued. "I just came from the hotel where my son-in-law informed me that you've stopped looking for her. I want to know why."

Sheriff Callum expelled his breath in an audible sigh as his shoulders bent ever so slightly forward, like a balloon that had lost some of its air. Reaching to his right, he placed a file he was holding on top of the cabinet behind the door and stood in mirror image of Mr. Olson. He had learned long ago that to appear cooperative and gain someone's trust was to copy their mannerisms. But he also stood firm in front Mr. Olson because he didn't like to be intimidated. Especially in his own office by a belligerent man storming through the door at nine-goddamn-fifteen in the evening.

Resignation staining his tone he said, "Mr. Olson, why don't you come on back to my office and have a seat and we'll talk."

Mr. Olson walked the twenty feet from the front door to where the sheriff was waiting. He stomped across the room like a general in battle mode.

"Can I get you some coffee?" Callum offered as he indicated a chair in front of his desk.

"No, thanks, I'm here for one reason and one reason only, to find out why you've stopped looking for my daughter, 'sides that, I've been living off coffee for the past seventy-two hours. I'm so loaded up with coffee I may not sleep for a week."

"I can certainly understand that." Callum walked around his desk to sit in a large black leather chair that cradled an imprint of his backside from years of use.

"Sheriff, I'm not one who believes in beatin' round the bush. It took me two days to close up my glass shop, a day of flying from Minneapolis to Seattle and another day waiting around for a charter flight just to get here; which, by the way, is so far north in this country I thought we were flyin' into Canada. Now, I'm tired, broke, and dead on my feet and all I want to know is have you stopped looking for my daughter?"

"To begin with, Mr. Olson, I'm truly sorry about your daughter and I can understand you're upset, but like I told your son-in-law, we haven't been able to get one solid lead on where she is or even when she disappeared. In addition to that, neither Mr. Warren nor your grandchildren can even verify with any certainty the last time they remember seeing her. I have to tell you, I find that really odd. On top of that, a storm hit the area a couple days into the search which hindered our efforts even more. We have to wait for the storm out at sea to clear and hope it's before our resources completely dry up."

"Resources? Is this about money? My daughter is missing and you're concerned about money?" The bite of Mr. Olson's tone had Callum setting his jaw.

"No, it's not about money, Mr. Olson." Callum silently urged himself to be patient. "We've had people from all over the county in to help as well as the Coast Guard, but even they can't wait forever. Frankly, with or without the storm, the problem is we simply don't know where to look. As I understand it, your daughter and her family were on a ferry headed out to one of the outlying islands and when the ferry docked, she didn't get off. Mr. Warren went back on the ferry and looked for her but couldn't find her. He then talked to a couple of forest service personnel who maintain the island. They had a look around the island thinking maybe she had slipped by them and taken one of the trails that lead into the woods, but they couldn't find any evidence she had done this. After about four hours of looking, my office was called in."

Joe Olson sat and stared at the sheriff, confusion skewing his forehead as he worked his mouth around like he was slowly chewing taffy, defiance still in his eyes.

Callum continued, unfazed by the tight grip Mr. Olson had on the arms of his chair or the comical expression contorting his face. "There is a lot of forest in that area and we conducted searches for three days and found nothing. We then had to stop when the storm came on."

"So, you didn't find hide nor hair of her before the storm hit? Maybe she fell and is laying where you can't see her."

"We thought of that, but we didn't find any footprints around the trails or even down on the beach. And, frankly, the island just isn't that big. If she were on it I'm convinced we would have found her before then."

Mr. Olson swallowed noticeably hard as if that imaginary taffy had gotten stuck in his throat and he had just been able to force it down. His eyes softened around the edges, but he kept his mouth taut as he forced words between light lips. "She has to be somewhere."

Callum noticed the softening in Mr. Olson's eyes and added more sympathetically, "There is nothing I'd like more than to find your daughter, but we simply don't know where to look. And I don't mean to alarm you any more than I have to but there is speculation she might have fallen overboard."

Mr. Olson looked up sharply, his teeth biting together so hard it sounded like he was crunching bone.

Looking down as if lack of eye contact could soften the blow, Callum explained, "She wasn't wearing a life vest. We had the ferry company count them. The Coast Guard and some local fishermen searched the surrounding waters but found no trace of her either; no clothes, or hat, nothing she might have had on. If she had fallen overboard, they're convinced they would have found her on that stretch of water the ferry takes because it's a straight line between here and the island."

"There's no way she ended up in the water," Joe Olson bit out. "Doug told me the day had been clear and calm, no wind at all. Now, she may not be the brightest of my kids, but she knows how to stay on a damn boat."

Choosing to ignore Mr. Olson's biting statement, Callum continued, "Yes, it was calm that day, but even if the best case scenario is she did fall overboard and simply got disoriented in the water, without a vest on she would have been in serious trouble once the storm hit. Right now it's only speculation, mind you, but if that had happened we're convinced someone would have seen her. Besides, the ferries that run that route there are also small fishing boats that use that stretch of water, yet no one has come forward saying they saw anyone fall off a ferry or calling for help."

"See, there you go," Olson said, reiterating his point. "She didn't fall overboard. Now, I'm telling you here and now, she's out on that island or maybe got on the wrong ferry coming back. You just need to ask around."

Callum folded his hands before him on the desk and tapped his thumbs together like small cymbals. "Well, to tell you the truth, Mr. Olson, for the last week we haven't been able to get a lot of useful information from anyone. We even interviewed some of the other passengers and not one single person remembers her. And since they only run one ferry a day to that island, she couldn't have gotten on a different one. We just can't confirm at this point if she even got on *that* particular ferry."

Mr. Olson leaned forward in his chair. "Are you trying to convince me that she simply vanished into thin air?" Spittle sprayed from his lips. "I can tell you this right now, if she was told to get on that ferry then she was damn well on that ferry. Jodee knows her place."

Callum cocked his head back slightly, curiosity clouding his expression. The comment had him leaning his chest against the edge of his desk in direct response to Mr. Olson's aggressive behavior. "That may well be," he countered, "but I don't know what else to tell you. We have no leads and no clue where to look. Personally, I find the whole thing highly suspicious."

"Suspicious? Suspicious of who? Doug? There's no reason to be suspicious of Doug, he's a good husband and if he says he doesn't know where she is then he doesn't know."

"I didn't say I was suspicious of Mr. Warren. We vouched for his whereabouts and know he wasn't with her the whole time they were on the ferry. Seems your son-in-law was the life of the boat, so-to-speak. There were several people who remembered talking to him for the entire ride. But now that you bring him up, I do have to say I find it strange how he's responding to this whole thing. If my wife were missing, I wouldn't be as anxious to go back to Minnesota as he appears to be."

"It's not that he's anxious to go home, I know he's worried sick. But he has to get back to work. He's the vice president of a bank, you know, and he just can't put everything on hold forever."

"Yes, I know. He's told me several times. But we're not

giving up just yet. I do still have some volunteers continuing to look around the bay area and the surrounding woods outside of town just in case she did make it back to shore and is hurt somewhere. But that will have to be stopped by tomorrow morning if that other storm hits like they're predicting. I promise we'll continue to search as long as we can until weather tells us otherwise. But like I said, without any leads there's not a whole lot we can do."

Mr. Olson sat and stared at the sheriff, his furrowed brow demonstrating the difficulty his brain was having in absorbing the details. His body started to deflate as his shoulders slumped slightly and he leaned against the back of the chair. He lowered his eyes to the edge of Callum's desk staring at an unseen spot, worry overcoming his bravado.

Sheriff Callum released his own hold on his tensed-up muscles and leaned back in his chair. "I'm truly sorry, Mr. Olson."

With the change in the Sheriff's tone, Mr. Olson glanced up to see a look of pity aimed at him. Straightening up immediately, he said forcefully, "I can tell you now that something must have happened to her. Maybe she *is* hurt somewhere and got disoriented. Maybe she even made it as far as some hotel or something."

Callum reached up and scratched his head as he squeezed his eyes tightly closed, trying to hide his frustration. He scratched the top of his head so hard it looked like he was trying to dig an idea out of his brain but didn't want to look directly at it when he clawed it out. After a loud, tired sigh he said, "Okay, say that did happen. Say we somehow missed her on the island and the ferry when we searched them, and she *did* make it back to town to some hotel. If that were the case, why hasn't she contacted her family to let them know she's okay? This has been in the news for several days. She would have heard we're conducting a search for her and would have come forward before now, don't you think?"

"Well now, I just may have to disagree with you on that point." Sitting straight up in his chair, Olson's eyes darted from one corner of the room to the other like he was about to reveal a secret. "She may not know anyone is looking for her at all."

"I don't understand."

"I'm just saying that she's sometimes a little, I don't know, spacey, I guess you'd say. She doesn't always pay attention to her surroundings at times – sort of lives in her head."

Sheriff Callum gave a surprised humph. "Now that's interesting. This is something that might have been mentioned earlier?" Picking up a pen, he grabbed a manila folder lying on top of the stack of reports set on the corner of his desk, opened it to the first page and started making notes. "Okay now," he continued as he started writing without looking up, "are you saying she's forgetful or something. Does she have some kind of mental problem?"

"Listen now, I didn't say she's crazy. You're puttin' words in my mouth. I'm just saying she may have wandered off by herself and got lost."

"Why would she do that?"

"Wander off?"

"Yeah. Why would she just wander off without telling her family?"

"She likes being outdoors, that's all."

"Okay. So let me get this straight, you're saying she could have decided to take a hike around the island without letting anyone know she was going, somehow slipped by all the other passengers and the rangers, lost her bearings and simply got lost? Or better yet, somehow hid on the ferry until it got back to town and wondered off to do some exploring?"

"Well… Yeah, something like that. Maybe."

"But as I mentioned, no one even remembers seeing her *on* the ferry in the first place."

"Look, Sheriff, I'm just trying to help make sense of this whole thing. My wife is on the verge of a nervous breakdown, I've had to cancel jobs back home I can't afford to lose and now my grandkids are looking at me like I'm supposed to fix this whole thing. I'm at the end of my rope.

"And now what I'm hearing from you is I have to go back to the hotel and tell my wife that you don't have a clue as to where Jodee is or even where to keep looking."

Callum cocked his head, his patience wearing thinner than his exhaustion. "We're going to continue to search, but at this moment that's about the gist of it." Callum was truly wanting this man out of his office but maintained his professional demeanor and bit down on his waning patience.

"Then I'm just wasting my time here. But I know my wife's going to want to talk to you herself. Maybe it'll help her sleep some."

"Fine. I'd like to talk to your wife myself," Callum matched Mr. Olson's brusque tone. "Tell her she can come by around nine in the morning."

"Fine," Mr. Olson said roughly and rose abruptly from the chair. The metal tabs on the feet scraped the tiled floor as it slid backward a few inches causing Callum to cringe.

Mr. Olson turned and headed for the door without considering the social etiquette of shaking the sheriff's hand. As he turned his back he mumbled under his breath, "Missing and there's not a damn thing I can do about it… Makin' me lose work…"

Callum wasn't surprised at the man's quick departure, what surprised him were the caustic words he said with enough force that they were carried across the room. Callum wasn't sure if Mr. Olson knew he could hear him.

"…Troublesome girl… Been trouble since the day she was born."

Callum watched as the big man stomped from his office and once again let the front door shut with a loud bang.

Sitting still as he watched Mr. Olson leave, like the man's departure wasn't a direct slap of rudeness to his position, Callum crossed his hands over his chest and leaned back fully into the leather chair, letting the past twenty minutes wash over his over-worked memory.

After a few moments of contemplation, and with slow determination, Callum pulled himself to an upright position, grabbed a pencil from his desk drawer and turned the folder on Jodee Warren over to the back side. In the bottom left hand corner, in a spot he was sure no one would think to look, he wrote 'Prick.' He always wrote his opinion on the folder of everyone he interviewed as a reminder of how he felt about a person. It helped him remember how someone handled themselves during a crisis or a stressful situation in their life. It was his way of venting without saying a word and in all the years he'd been an officer, never once had he felt like he'd misjudged anyone. He was a good judge of character and from what he'd seen from one Mr. Joe Olson, his description of him, which was now written in small block letters on the back of the folder, was dead-on accurate. To be on the safe side though, he always wrote his opinion in pencil on the chance he had to erase it if a case went to trial. He didn't want to take the chance of someone seeing his opinion and jeopardizing a case.

Slowly, as if he'd just remembered he'd done it, his eyes drifted to the other corner of the folder, the corner he had reserved for Doug Warren, Jodee's husband. In the same block letters, he'd written his opinion of this man as well, 'Narcissist.'

Callum began to wonder what kind of family this woman had gone missing from and could only hope her mother would prove to be more… well…normal. Things with the case of Jodee Warren just didn't seem to add up.

CHAPTER TWO

THE MOTHER

Sheriff Callum walked to the front of the office where the coffee pot sat in a continuing state of burning grinds into a thick sludge. The machine was in such constant use that the glass pot had been stained brown years ago from lack of a good scrubbing. Deputy Robert Riley said it gave the coffee character. Callum always thought it made it taste old, but he'd grown accustomed to it, and with a recipe of his own, drank it nonetheless.

Going through his morning ritual before settling down to business, he propped open the office door that led to the street to let out the heat from a faulty furnace. He then grabbed his favorite cup that his son had given him on his birthday that read *World's Best Dad* and filled it three-quarters full of coffee, a quarter of milk, and two packets of sugar.

Standing holding the cup of black liquid to his nose he stared out the window that faced Main Street. Shielded by the glare of the morning sun bouncing off the plate glass, he appeared no more than a shadow.

Inhaling the pleasant aroma of the coffee, he looked over the rim of the cup through the steaming vapor that drifted skyward as a car pulled to a stop at the curb. He watched as a frail-looking woman got out of the beige compact car. Climbing out and turning around, she stood just inside the open car door listening obediently to the driver who remained partially hidden in the dark confines of the front seat. He noticed her only movement was her head as she nodded at whatever she was being told. He stood watching the scene, fascinated by an outdated straw hat she wore that bobbled on her head with each nod. She also held a matching straw purse that seemed as much a part of her as her arm.

When the driver leaned over to look up at her through the open door, Callum recognized Mr. Olson. It was straight up nine a.m.

Standing silent trying to enjoy the only semblance of calm he knew he would have all day, he listened to Mr. Olson's dictates which he could finally hear as the man leaned across the front seat of the car.

"Katie," Callum heard the man say, "I want you to get your questions asked and I'll be back to pick you up in twenty minutes. You understand?" The question was more of an order than an actual question.

"Yes, Joe." The woman's voice was so high pitched it was almost mouse-like.

"And don't prattle on. We don't have all day for you to finish up your business."

"I won't," came the woman's meek reply.

Callum's line of sight was blocked for a second when Deputy Riley walked past the window outside with their daily dose of pastry from Rose's Café down the street.

Riley entered the office and set their breakfast down on the desk. "Rose didn't have any Bear Claws this morning, so I got you a French cruller."

"That's okay," Callum responded, turning from the window. "Looks like Mrs. Olson is here." He turned to address his deputy as the squeal of tires caught their attention. As one, they turned to the window to see Mr. Olson swerve dangerously fast into traffic.

Riley straightened to his full height like someone had jabbed him with a poker and watched the car peel down the street. "What the hell?" The Mario Andretti racing move had him reaching for his ticket pad and start for the door to go after the driver. He pulled up short at the sight of the thin woman standing inside the door.

Rooted to a spot just across the threshold, the woman's eyes darted from one side of the room to the other like a cornered cat trying to find an escape route. With tentative movements, she approached Deputy Riley with shoulders slightly bent in submission – the metaphorical hat-in-hand, as if her normal disposition was to fear authority.

Callum watched as she walked to his deputy with a slow shuffle, her scuffed brown penny loafers scraping the floor like her feet were too heavy to pick up. She stopped in front of him, and keeping her face slightly down, she looked at Riley over the top of her eyes.

She stared at him without saying a word, her scrunched forehead illustrating her insecure quandary. As she waited for him to speak, she reached into her handbag without looking and pulled out a tissue to add to the many already bunched in her hand. Her eyes were red and swollen, like she'd had a sleepless night of crying. She was a stringy woman with leathery skin, thin and fragile as a piece of glass. Her hair was gray, lowlighted with the black she was born with and cut in a page-boy style which hinted at a personality that had been buried along with the fashion. She wore a dated blue seersucker dress, which hung limp on her frame, and held the faded yellow purse in front of her like a security blanket.

"Hello, ma'am, I'm Deputy Riley. Can I help you?" he said gently like he was trying to coax a timid child to his side.

Simply nodding her head, she stood in front of him in respectful compliance, intermittently dabbing her eyes with the wad of tissues. "I'm Katie Olson. Joe said the Sheriff wanted to talk to me."

"Yes. He's been expecting you," he said, tilting his head to the right to get a better look at her downturned face.

When she continued to stand unmoving, looking down at her feet, Riley reached out and touched her arm, "Ma'am, are you all right?"

As if he'd burned her arm, Katie Olson moved slightly out of his reach, but allowed her shell of uncertainty to lift long enough to respond, "Ya, ya, I'm fine. The Sheriff vants to see me," she reiterated.

Riley looked over at Callum as he drew his hand back from her and gave him a questioning look that hinted that he wasn't sure how to handle her. "Yes… Yes, ma'am. The Sheriff's been expecting you. He's right over there." He pointed to Callum standing at the window.

"Oh," the word came out on a tired breath as she dropped her eyes to his chest. "I vasn't sure who was in charge."

Callum came forward and reached to shake her hand. "I'm Sheriff Callum, ma'am."

Holding out her hand like she might not get it back, she shook Callum's hand. It was so quick and weak; he wasn't certain he'd even touched her. "Why don't you follow me back to my office and we'll have a seat." Callum stepped aside and gestured with his arm to the back room.

Riley had stepped to her side and attempted to air guide her by placing his hand behind her. She stayed unmoving.

It took a moment before it occurred to Callum she was expecting him to take the lead. He took a small step and waited for her to fall in line behind him. "Ma'am, if you'll follow me." He gave her a small smile hoping to relieve her tension.

Gravitating to the kind smile, Katie Olson followed Callum with steps so short and quick she looked like a geisha wrapped in a tight kimono. As Riley followed behind her, she resembled a prisoner being escorted to a cell instead of the mother of a missing woman.

Callum led her into his office and let her choose a seat in front of his desk. She sat down in the same chair that her husband had vacated the night before, the one closest to the door. She looked up into the face of Sheriff Callum and said in a quavering voice, "Joe said I could ask ya some questions maybe."

Callum went around his desk and sat in his chair as he spoke. "Yes. I mentioned to your husband last night that it might help if I spoke to you directly. I'll try and answer as best I can."

She hesitated a moment, careful to show her respect. Deputy Riley took the opportunity to offer her something to drink. He bent over at the waist to look her in the face as if he were addressing a shy child, "Can I get you something to drink, Mrs. Olson? Some hot tea or something?"

"No, thank ya kindly."

"All right then, ma'am. If you do need anything, you just let me know. I'll be waiting just outside the door." He left the room, carefully closing the door with a quiet click as if any sudden noise would have her running like a frightened deer.

Mrs. Olson waited for the door to close before she looked directly at Sheriff Callum and asked through fearful hiccups, "Has... Has there been any news of her?"

"No, ma'am, not yet."

"Vhat can I do, then? I'll do anything. Anything!" It was the only word she had used that was above a whisper. Mrs. Olson's thick Minnesotan accent had caught him off-guard and made him smile. Pretending to contemplate her response, Callum hid the grin behind his hand as he dragged it down his mouth and chin. He dipped his head quickly in the pretense of trying to find the file on Jodee Warren.

"Right now, we're still trying to piece together the why's, when's and what's of this whole thing," he answered, trying to take hold of his professionalism. "Mrs. Olson, if you don't mind, I do have some questions I'd like to ask you. Nothing serious, I'm just trying to get a handle on who your daughter is. Maybe it will help us find her."

"No, I dun mind, vhatever I can do."

"Thank you. To start with, can you tell me anything about your daughter's relationship with her husband?"

"Her relationship? With Doug?"

"I just want to know if she was unhappy or if there were any problems in the marriage."

"Her and Doug's marriage is solid and Doug has been a rock, you betcha. Why, if it weren't for Doug holdin' dat family together, I don't know vhat would'a happened."

"You mean with his children right now? Holding it together for them?"

"Ya, of course, but also at other times too, dun-cha-know?"

"What other times would that be, Mrs. Olson?"

"Well, my Jodee, she's a good girl, but sometimes she just seems a bit touched at times."

"No one can blame her, mind ya. But she's been acting strange for a while now. We just overlook it cause we don't want to alarm the children, and Doug is there besides to take care of her, yah?"

Callum's eyebrows rose in surprise. "How has she acted strange?"

The look on Callum's face had Katie Olson squirming. She sat up straighter in her chair as if repositioning herself would distract him from her comment. "Maybe I spoke out'a line. I don't mean strange, no, not t'all. She just has a different way of expressing herself. Ya know, a lot of very creative people express themselves in unique ways. I've read about it in books. Yah, my Jodee, she's just real unique."

"Hum, your husband referred to her as... Let me see here," Callum said. Flipping through his notes he paraphrased, 'not the brightest of his kids.'"

"Joe don't mean nothin' by that; he's just more the practical-minded kind and Jodee would be more of an artist if given the chance. Jodee is just different from her sisters and being the oldest; well, Joe might'a been a little harder on her but that's just cause he expected more of her than the other two girls. It's just hard for him to understand her, is all. He loves her. He loves all his girls far as that goes." Her tone had become high pitched and rapid.

"She was named after him," Mrs. Olson continued. "We took a female name of Joseph – Jodee Michelle Olson and Joseph Michael Olson, you see? But he's always gone by just plain Joe."

She mutilated the tissues in her hands as she rambled, and pieces fell unseen to the floor like blue confetti.

"That's real interesting, Mrs. Olson, but right now I need to ask you some specific questions about Jodee if you don't mind. For instance, was anything distressing her? Were there may be some family problems, financial troubles, anything along that nature?"

"Oh, no, no, nothing like that. Why I've never even seen Doug raise his voice at her. But, we raised her to be obedient and she never once gave him a reason to. And he's a real good provider. A bank executive, dun-cha-know."

"Yes, I know." He thought if he was told by one more member of that family that Doug Warren was a bank executive, he was going to take his gun out and shoot something. He continued without letting his irritation show. "What about other members of the family? How does she get along with them? Her sisters? How are their relationships?"

"She gets along fine with her sisters. Jodee has a real even temper, never says a harsh word to anyone; she never has liked confrontation. Why, there's been times I'd tell her, 'Jodee, you gotta stick up for yourself.' Of course, Joe never thought it vas lady-like for a girl to raise her voice and might'a been a little strict with her when she vas younger, but he calmed down when the other two came along."

Callum sat staring at her, his hands folded together, resting his chin on his thumbs. He let her talk but discreetly looked over her head at the clock on the wall.

"... But that's to be expected with your first. I mean, Joe sometimes may have gotten a little harsh with her, but she always understood it vasn't really about her. He just takes things awfully personal when they don't go right and Jodee always seemed to be underfoot at the wrong times. We haven't had the best couple of years with the business and he's been stressed..."

Sensing she was about to go into another round of accolades about her husband, he clenched his hands together until the knuckles were white and interrupted impatiently, "Mrs. Olson, I'm sure Mr. Olson is a fine man..."

"You know, he was so pleased vhen she married Doug..."

"… I'm sure he was, but…"

She continued as if not hearing him. "… He even gave 'em a car for a wedding present. Not a finer father anywhere, you betcha. Always provided for me and the girls for sure, no matter how tight times got."

Callum took the opportunity to make his point when lack of air forced her to stop. "That's nice to hear but I'm more concerned with why and how your daughter has disappeared right now."

"Oh, of course, of course. Joe always says I prattle on too much."

"That's okay, Mrs. Olson. But what I'm wondering is if you think there is any chance this may not have been an accident?"

"Not an accident? Of course it vas an accident, vhat else could it be?" She subconsciously pulled at the tissues in her hand until more pieces fell to the floor like feathers from a plucked chicken.

"We don't know, ma'am, but no one seems to be able to give me any definitive answers as to when they last saw her, what she was wearing, anything. Given the circumstances it seems like a plausible question. Your husband seems to think it was a waste of time for you to even come here since we had to call off the search. I have to say, it was the last reaction I expected to hear." Callum leaned forward as if to accentuate his point.

"Oh, for sure you misunderstood him." Mrs. Olson looked down, closing her eyes and mumbled the last few words as if in prayer. "He's worried sick, he is."

Callum rubbed his eyes with his thumb and forefinger, saying on a breath of tired air, "All right, Mrs. Olson, I just have a few more questions if you don't mind."

"Ya, ya, vhatever you need."

"When you said she'd been acting strangely lately, what exactly did you mean by that?"

"Nothing serious, really, and I don't mean strange. Like I said, she's unique."

"Okay, she's unique. What kind of unique things would she do?" Taking his eyes from her face, Callum flipped through the folder of Jodee Warren looking for a clue in the volume of notes, rapidly flipping the stabled sheets in the way a kid flipped the pages of a book to make a cartoon stick figure run across the blank horizon, hoping that somehow the words would magically materialize the answer.

"Nothing t'all that unusual," Mrs. Olson continued. "Oh, sometimes she'd go off on her own to think and forget to come in out'a the cold."

Callum sat up a little straighter in his chair, his forehead creasing from curiosity. "You don't think this is something that should have been mentioned earlier, Mrs. Olson?"

Startled by his quick movement, Mrs. Olson jerked slightly upright. "Like I said, it vasn't serious. Vhy I told Joe and Doug a thousand times to let her be and give her time to think. That's all she needed, some private time alone."

"How long had she been doing this?" Callum persisted, bending over the file to study a set of notes.

"Not long enough for anyone to even mention it. Everybody needs some time alone. And she never stayed out all that long. When it got too cold, she'd always come in. I just don't know why everyone vas always lookin' at her like she vasn't all there, you know? In the name of Job, she just needed time by herself. Why, I remember my great Aunt Hilde liked to go for walks to the point someone would hafta go hunt her down. I'm not saying Jodee did anything like that, of course. I mean, that would be impossible, wouldn't it, since they were on a ferry? I'm just saying that at times she needed to get away by herself."

Callum's slow intake of air made his nostrils flair, making it obvious his patience was wearing thin. He decided to do away with etiquette before his temper got the better of him. He asked her point blank. "Mrs. Olson, do you think your daughter is missing because she *wants* to be missing?"

"I don't even know vhat that means, Sheriff. How can someone vant to be missing?"

He noticed her accent was getting heavier the more uncomfortable the questions. "I mean, do you think your daughter wanted to intentionally leave her husband and has found a way to do it?" He questioned her like she was a slow-witted child.

"Now, how could she have found a vay to do dat? They were all out in the middle of a lake. That don't make no sense t'all, Sheriff."

Her evasive answers started making his head pound. Callum put the pen down and rubbed his temples. He could see Mrs. Olson was confused and becoming frustrated, much like himself. Obviously, this woman either would not or could not comprehend the circumstances. It had only been fifteen minutes and already Callum had had enough. He had spent the last five days interviewing every member of the family and had gotten nowhere. The husband was so self-absorbed that his only response to every question was how it would look for him in front of his peers. Her children were so dry-eyed and stoic, he wondered if *they* weren't a bit 'touched.' Her father was a brute and her mother now seemed to be more afraid of her husband than for her daughter's welfare. Yes, he'd had enough. He wondered where the line was between sympathy and just downright annoyance when it came to dealing with this family. He took a silent reflective moment and chided himself for missing the opportunity to show his true annoyance to Mr. Joseph Olson, and decided if anyone deserved his sympathy it was Mrs. Olson.

Callum continued. He was feeling slightly uneasy, as if he was forgetting to ask a key question. Mrs. Olson's ramblings were making him lose his concentration and he was becoming more and more frustrated by the minute. Trying to keep his patience in-check, he said, "Okay, Mrs. Olson, you're right, it would be impossible for her to intentionally walk away."

He rose from his chair, needing to end the conversation. Walking around his desk he attempted to help her out of his office without appearing too rude.

"You are goin' ta continue ta look fer her, aren't ya?" The glassy look of tears rimmed her eyes. Her English was now almost unrecognizable.

"Yes, ma'am, we're still going to do everything we can to find her." Callum was anxious to get her out of the office before she completely broke down and he had a situation on his hands he didn't want to deal with – consoling a weeping woman.

Mrs. Olson ignored his silent urging for her to leave and pulled out another tissue from her endless supply.

Callum gave her another moment to compose herself before asking, "Is there anything else I can do for you? If not, I really do need to see about some other matters this morning."

She continued to sit while she wiped her nose. Tears began falling onto her lap, turning her light blue dress into one with dark blue polka dots of wet heartache. He felt like he'd just kicked a puppy as he stared at her. She sat staring at her lap, like the answers would be found in the bumps of the material. She wiped her tears with the shredded tissue and left traces of paper behind on her lashes.

"Mrs. Olson, I know this is a hard time for you right now. We just want to find your daughter. I'm sorry if I've upset you." Callum reached down to put his hand on her shoulder.

She looked up at his face and saw the sincerity in his eyes. "Sheriff, I know ya dun mean ta upset me. I know dat. But my Jodee wouldn't do nothin like dat ta hurt her daddy or Doug."

Callum found it interesting how Mrs. Olson had put her husband at the top of the caste system of the wounded while leaving herself out altogether. He decided not to delve into that interesting fact, knowing it wouldn't do any good anyway.

"Yes, ma'am, I'm sure you're right." Callum reached down and gently grabbed her elbow and lifted her to her feet.

"Vell, thank ya sheriff fer talkin' to me." She rose from the chair. The remnants of the tissues slid from her dress onto the floor like dandruff. She didn't notice. "I hope I've been of some help."

"You have, ma'am, you have," he lied.

"Just please call me if ya hear anything." She sniffed and pulled the purse up with both hands and held it at her waist, reminding him of a child pushing a stroller.

Deputy Riley caught the desperate look on Callum's face as he peered through the large window in the office door. He stepped forward quickly to allow Mrs. Olson to exit.

As she and Riley walked down the hall, Sheriff Callum followed slowly, distracted by the thoughts pounding in his head. Something bothered him, something he'd wanted clarified, but which had slipped his mind due to his irritation with Mrs. Olson's answers. He was trying desperately to remember what it was.

They had gotten to the front door of the station when they saw Mr. Olson waiting at the curb in the rental car. Callum knew he must've simply driven to the edge of town and back to already be waiting for his wife so soon, leaving him with the impression the man didn't want to give his wife any more time than he thought she needed. Feeling indignant on behalf of her, Callum whispered under his breath, "What an asshole."

Mrs. Olson stepped through the glass doors into the soggy Washington weather. She walked the few feet to the car where her husband waited, impatiently drumming his fingers on the steering wheel.

Before Mrs. Olson could touch the car handle, Callum saw his deputy rush quickly forward to open the door for her. Reaching around her, he opened the door and helped her into the seat. As if he were a bull moose challenging a competitor, he leaned forward and gave a meaningful glare to Mr. Olson.

Callum got the distinct impression his dislike for Mr. Olson had rubbed off onto his deputy, as if it were dislike by association.

Mr. Olson scowled back at him with the piercing eyes of an angry man who was used to having his way. "Hurry up, Katie, and get in, we are going down to the bay where the volunteers are." He stressed the word 'we.'

It sounded like an accusation to Callum that perhaps Mr. Olson thought the sheriff's department was being neglectful in their duties and should have already been out there themselves, not knowing he had given the volunteers their orders the night before.

Mrs. Olson slid into the car as Riley closed the door. Callum realized that all Riley seemed to have done was piss off an already angry bear.

"Thank you both." Mrs. Olson touched Deputy Riley's hand resting on the car door as she looked at Sheriff Callum.

"Anytime, ma'am." Riley just couldn't seem to let Mr. Olson have the last word.

Callum had been watching this display of machismo from the door of the police station. He watched as Mrs. Olson fumbled clumsily with her dress and the seat belt as she settled into the passenger seat. As if the weight of not having to deal with the Olsons had taken some of the pressure off his memory, he remembered what he wanted to ask and marched toward the car's open window.

"Mrs. Olson, one more thing," he said quickly, leaning into the window as Riley stepped aside.

Giving Mr. Olson a cursory glance, he looked directly at Katie Olson and asked pointedly. "Can you think of anything that might have been troubling your daughter?"

"Uh, I'm not sure what you mean, Sheriff." Once again, her head was bent as she spoke.

"I mean, was your daughter depressed? I was wondering if something might have happened recently to cause her to be depressed?"

Like a priest giving solace, she reached her hand out and touched Callum's sleeve, "Well, she does miss Dougie J an awful lot, don't-cha-know."

"Dougie J? Who's Dougie J?"

"Douglas Junior, their youngest," she said matter-of-factly.

Suddenly, as if a piece of hope had jolted her suffering thoughts, she turned to her husband, "Joe, Dougie J." Excitement lighting up her face. "She's gone home to see Dougie J."

"Now, Katie," Mr. Olson said in a gentle tone that seemed out of character to Callum. "Minnesota is just too far for her to head off to on her own."

"But it's possible. She could have gotten on a bus."

"I'm sorry, Mrs. Olson," Callum interrupted. "I thought the Warrens only have three children. Are you saying they have a son at home that didn't come with them?"

Before she could answer him, Mr. Olson leaned over his wife and all but growled at Callum, "We've said all there is to say, we're wasting time. Now, we're going down to the bus station and start asking some questions, see if Katie might be right; it wouldn't hurt you none if you'd do your job as well." To emphasize his final word, he gunned the motor and pulled out into traffic with a squeal.

Callum jumped back from the open window so as not to be hit by the frame of the door, slowly straightening to his full height. He looked at Riley and turned back to watch the car round the corner. He and Riley stood stiffly staring at the retreating car.

"What the heck was that all about?" Riley finally asked.

"I don't know. But it looks like the Warrens must have left their youngest kid at home and they think maybe Jodee Warren misses him so much she may have gotten on a bus to go home."

"Why would they do that? Leave their youngest at home, I mean?"

"Don't know. Maybe he's too young to make a trip across country. You know how it is traveling with toddlers."

"Then why didn't Mr. Warren mention it when we talked to him?" Riley asked.

"Who knows? The guy's a little too into himself as it is and perhaps the kid just slipped his mind."

"You're telling me. You know, we never did get anything useful out of him. I couldn't tell if the whole situation made him upset or mad; like his wife going missing is more of an inconvenience than a tragedy. And the kids are just plain strange. Not showing a lot of emotion one way or the other. Damnedest thing if you ask me. If you ask me, the whole family seems a bit weird."

"Exactly what I was thinking," Callum said.

CHAPTER THREE

THE HUSBAND

Douglas Arthur Warren was a good-looking man, and depending on who was asked, he was the best looking of men, especially if the person asked was Doug Warren himself. He was a man who prided himself on being in control of any situation, whether the situation was his job, his family, or his downtime. He planned every event and action in his life with single-minded determination and didn't like having his plans interrupted, especially when those plans involved an expensive family vacation.

Now, two weeks after the incident that so mercilessly affected his life, he sat in the Seattle airport waiting to fly home to Minnesota. He realized, as he blindly stared out the airport window at the clouds rolling in over the Washington landscape, that his happiness was in jeopardy and he didn't know how to process it. His wife had gone missing on the very vacation he had painstakingly planned for weeks. His first thought upon the discovery of her disappearance had been 'how could she do this to me?'

It was this self-absorbed attitude he'd taken with him when he had been requested to talk to the local sheriff at the Kokanee Bay Sheriff's Office.

He had felt nothing but contempt for Sheriff Callum and his

minion, Deputy Riley, because he considered them beneath him and thought they didn't know what they were doing. He'd wanted them to call in more experienced men from Seattle, which they'd refused to do. Of course, the Coast Guard had been called in, but even they had stopped looking when the storm hit. It made him angry to think of their incompetence.

By the time the so-called sheriff's office personnel had finally gotten to the island, a forest service ranger and some local employees had already spent hours looking for Jodee. Doug had not been convinced anything serious had happened to her, like most people thought. He was sure she had simply wandered off into the woods and gotten turned around. Every time he'd tried to stress this opinion though, people had looked at him like he was a callous bastard not showing the right amount of concern for his wife. All he had tried to do was gain some control over a situation where he'd felt everyone was panicking for no reason and getting nothing accomplished.

The events of the last two weeks played over and over in his mind like a rerun of an old television show. Even now as he sat and blindly watched the planes come and go from the tarmac, the days replayed in his mind. If he'd admitted it to himself, he knew deep down that the authorities really hadn't had a choice but to call off the search; but that hadn't made it any better when he knew his life was going to be forever altered. He just wanted his wife found so he could return to his job and his well-ordered life.

If he was honest with himself, he knew that at first he was grateful the sheriff had been called in, somebody with authority who would rein in the chaos. But when all the sheriff wanted to do was ask questions, Doug began to feel he was dealing with a country bumpkin who didn't know his head from his ass. When Doug demanded to be put in charge of the search he was met with

45

derision, so he figured if it took him being contrite so something would get accomplished that's what he'd be.

Doug then took the tactic of applying the talent he'd practiced his whole life of drawing people into his confidence with his sincerity and natural intelligence. He decided that once he displayed the correct amount of contrition and answered the necessary questions, the local yocals would see how affected he was and they would start treating him with the courtesy and respect he deserved – although he thought it best not to mention the fact that Jodee had a habit of occasionally wandering off. He hadn't wanted everyone thinking he was married to some crazy woman. Lord knew he'd had enough of that from family over the last few months.

Now, as he looked out past the tarmac into the hazy hues of the Seattle landscape, thinking back on the questions from that yokel sheriff, he found himself fidgeting. There were questions thrown at him he hadn't been able to answer. Questions like when had he last seen her? What was she wearing? Where was she standing? Didn't his kids see her get on the ferry? Blah, blah, blah. God, he thought the questions would never end. By the time it was over he was exhausted, not from the constant barrage of questions but from having to keep up the pretense of being devastated when in reality he was beyond insulted at their treatment of him.

Then, after two hours of answering their questions, the sheriff had asked one that threw him for a loop. Why weren't he and his wife together on the ferry? He couldn't answer this one question and no matter how hard he thought, he honestly didn't know. He had been worn thin by her behavior over the last few months, but why *weren't* they together on the ferry?

"I was rounding up the kids," he'd offered as an explanation.

He remembered seeing her standing at the pier before the ferry departed just staring out at the water and had yelled at her that the ferry was leaving and for her to get on board. He had just taken it for granted she had obeyed him. Why wouldn't she? She always obeyed him; it was the basis of their marriage. But, then he remembered turning and walking on board without her and not looking back. Could it have really been the one time in their marriage she had defied him?

"But did you know for certain she had gotten on the ferry?" they had asked.

No, he didn't know.

"What was she doing before you boarded?" the Sheriff had persisted.

She was staring into space like she always did, he remembered – but this isn't what he told the sheriff. He told them she was looking out at the ocean and enjoying the view.

The façade of a concerned spouse had slipped in that moment when he realized he actually hadn't known what Jodee had been doing – because he never knew – and it made him angry. Fact was, he never knew what was on her mind any more and he wasn't a hundred percent sure she had gotten on the ferry at all. She knew better than to go against his orders, but she hadn't been herself for several months now.

Subconsciously, in a place he wouldn't allow himself to go, he knew he was angrier at being embarrassed in front of local authority than he was upset Jodee had turned up missing. He was certain she would eventually show up, but until she did, she was making him look the fool. He had inwardly seethed in that moment and for an instant he saw red.

He had looked up and noticed Callum and Deputy Riley staring at him, not saying a word. He quickly recovered from his silent condemnation into the look of the worried husband.

Then that no-excuse for a sheriff asked a question that truly offended him, he recalled. "Mr. Warren," he'd asked, "is it your wife's disappearance that's really troubling you or is it the inconvenience?"

"What kind of question is that?" Doug had wanted to know. "Of course, I'm concerned. My wife is missing, and it hurts. But really, would it be too much to ask of you to show a little understanding and sympathy for me since I'm the one having to go through this painful ordeal?"

The sheriff had simply looked at him with a blank expression on his face, an indication to Doug that he was dealing with a moron.

Doug silently continued to boil in outrage at the memory as he recounted the third meeting he'd had to endure several days later when they announced they didn't have any leads to continue the search. It was at that meeting the sheriff had issued the ultimate insult by asking if he thought Jodee may have gone missing on purpose.

He couldn't believe the Sheriff had the balls to suggest it was anything but an accident. The man obviously hadn't known who he was talking to. Why would anyone want to leave him? He was Doug Warren, Vice President of Mortgage Financing at one of the larger banks in Minnesota – a successful executive, great provider, the perfect husband and father.

By the end of the week, when they had finally ended with all the tedious questions and speculation, Doug had come to the conclusion that Sheriff Callum was nothing more than a low-paid civil servant who was bored from living in that Podunk town and was simply trying to make a name for himself by trying to create a scenario that didn't exist.

His temples pounded as he sat waiting for their flight to Minneapolis to be called over the airport intercom and the interviews went around and around in his head like an endless tilt-a-whirl. What could that sheriff have been thinking when he'd asked that final ludicrous question – did Jodee disappear on purpose? Doug knew for a fact any woman married to him would always feel lucky.

Although, he knew he'd lost his patience with her over the years because things were not always as smooth as he'd expected. Like when they were first married and he'd tried to train her in the proper decorum for an executive's wife – it was like trying to mold wood. And the times he'd had to remind her of the marriage vow of obedience so she'd show him the proper respect owed a husband. He admitted it had taken several years of marriage before he had eventually gotten her trained in what he considered her 'proper role' as his wife, but he'd finally succeeded.

Of course, he couldn't really blame her for being slow in learning her place and knew it wasn't all her fault. She simply lacked the proper education to comprehend the ways of the world. He'd married her a year out of high school and she simply didn't understand the fine nuances of society. Her childlike behavior was one of the reasons he'd noticed her in the first place. But as her husband, it was his job to correct her little eccentricities as soon as they were married; for example, stopping her from eating cold fried potato sandwiches or boiling that disgusting slimy vegetable, okra, which made the whole house smell. These things were cute when they had been dating, but as a successful executive's wife, it was something he just couldn't allow because it reeked of being poor.

Jodee had had the disadvantage of being born to inferior

people, who he despised. Although he had no respect for her parents, he never let it show to anyone. Both her parents had married right after high school, and even though his father-in-law built and owned his own glass company, Doug didn't consider it all that successful because profit was inconsistent from year to year and didn't even clear six figures in the best of times.

None of that mattered however because he knew he had them all fooled into believing he liked them. He knew, as sure as the sun shines that they thought their daughter couldn't have married better. Through their actions he'd known from the beginning they admired him for his education and his career. Over the years he became convinced without a doubt that he was their favorite son-in-law.

Yes, thinking back now over twenty years of marriage, it was ridiculous for anyone to think that Jodee would leave him intentionally. He resented the police for even hinting at such a thing. They obviously hadn't realized they'd been dealing with a superior, he'd reasoned. So he'd humored them in their naivety and answered their questions simply, so that they could understand his answers, all the while knowing Jodee would soon come strolling up – embarrassed but okay – and the whole ordeal would have been over and done with. They could have then gone back home and he could have dealt with her in private. But that hadn't happened.

He was convinced, now more than ever, she had been in a horrible accident that kept her from showing up. They hadn't found her and she hadn't come walking up by herself. The only thing he knew for sure was she was still missing and they were going home without her.

He knew he was going to have to resign himself to the fact that for the moment she was gone. It was something he might have to come to terms with. It made his mind go numb, which irritated him. Lack of rational thought was a lack of self-control and he wouldn't tolerate it. 'Damn her for making me feel this way,' he fumed.

When the airport finally called their flight number, he rounded up his children and boarded the plane as seat assignments were called. Random thoughts were still crowding his mind and pushing for dominance, jumping from the past to the present to the future. His inner focus had him moving on automatic pilot. It had been two days since he'd had to deal with that incompetent sheriff. They had forced him and his family to stay in that 'no-name' town far longer than he could tolerate. Order, he needed order in his life. All the random calls from concerned family members who had been notified, accusations from law enforcement, questions he couldn't answer that his family insisted on asking were all taking their toll. It was too much! He had to get home before the disruptions to his inner schedule made him go mad.

As they sat on the plane waiting for the other passengers to board, he found he was unable to fully concentrate on the next step he should take. Should he call his parents first when they landed? Should he talk to his boss and ask for a couple more days off? How was he going to handle the daily drudgery of dealing with the kids? Maybe he should contact a lawyer. For what, he had no idea, but it sounded good in his mind. What did they do with missing persons cases where the person missing lived hundreds of miles from where they went missing anyway?

All these unanswered questions made him feel like he was being buried alive, the dusty stain of the situation smothering his thoughts and suffocating his reasoning. The constant jumping of his thoughts from one thing to the next was doing damage to his structured life.

Nothing was working properly as he jerked angrily at his seat belt that refused to fasten. He could feel the blood veins in his head throbbing. It dawned on him suddenly, as if someone just opened the door to a very bright room, that it could take him months to get over Jodee's disappearance. This realization made his head hurt more. 'Damn her, damn her to hell for disrupting my life,' he silently cursed her.

The constant bumping of his elbow from the seat next to him, where his youngest daughter Dayla sat, finally caught his attention. He snapped at her when she stood up for the third time to get something out of the bag she had just stored in the overhead compartment.

"Dayla, what do you keep looking for?" He grabbed her arm to get her attention. He thought his head was going to explode.

"I want to get my iPod so I can listen to music on the ride home," she whimpered.

"You just got your book out, settle for that and sit still," he ground out at her.

"But I want to listen to some music." Tears started forming in her eyes.

God, when had she become such a whiner? he wondered. "Well you don't need it right now anyway, so just sit down and buckle up so they can get this damn plane in the air," he hissed at her as he roughly pulled her down by her forearm.

Dayla yelped in surprise as she half fell into the seat. He knew he had probably hurt her feelings with his rough behavior because he never treated his kids roughly and very rarely raised his voice, but his patience was at the breaking point.

Her small outcry caught the attention of the elderly woman across the aisle who raised an eyebrow at Doug, which irritated him more. He let Dayla's arm go and turned his head to look out the window of the plane, past the seat where Jodee was to have been seated. The empty seat had him catching his breath, which made his chest hurt. God, he needed a drink.

Audra turned around in her seat in front of them and looked over the headrest. "Dayla, go ahead and buckle up and I'll get it for you after the plane's in the air," she gently reassured her youngest sister.

"I want Mamma," Dayla whined.

"I know, sweetie, but Mom isn't here. Let's just try and make it home and maybe things will be better."

Audra's gentle whispering to Dayla started penetrating the farthest reaches of Doug's occupied mind. Like the curtain slowly rising before a play, he realized his oldest child had taken it upon herself during the whole calamity to try to console her siblings. When he thought of how she had stepped up to care for them he noticed the pain in his head wasn't quite so sharp. Her soft voice was like a welcome drug to his frazzled thoughts. Audra had been by his side the entire time and had run interference for him with his irritating in-laws. She had taken the chore of driving the almost two-hour trip from Kokanee Bay back to Seattle so he could sleep and was even now trying to prepare them for the flight home. She had remained in control and hadn't shed a tear but had stayed calm and watched over them all while he'd had to deal with the sheriff's department. She reminded him of him.

An idea suddenly took hold in his mind like a greedy leech latching onto a blood feast. Wasn't Audra nineteen now? Wasn't she old enough to handle the day-to-day child rearing of his younger kids until Jodee was found so he could stay focused on his job? He had noticed over the past few days how she made sure they had eaten and gotten to bed on time and answered their questions. If nothing else had proven she was up for the job of caring for them, the last few days certainly did. He knew she was enrolled for her first year of college and was supposed to be leaving home in a few weeks, but wasn't it her duty as his daughter to help him during this trying time? He knew she wouldn't mind staying home from school for a while. She could put off getting her degree for a few years, he decided. What was more important after all, his career and being the bread winner or a silly degree in fashion design. He sat and dwelled on the idea of it all, thankful for the reprieve of not having to think about the endless questions he couldn't answer. The more he thought about it, the better he felt. Yes, he liked the idea more and more. Like a glorious anesthetic that eased a searing wound, he had come up with a solution.

As he sat on the plane, cocooned in the hum of the metal shell, he began to feel his muscles relax and it slowly dawned on him that this tragedy could work to his advantage. Somewhere, in the inner realm of his mind, where guilt hid in the dark recesses of denial and empathy was smothered by his self-absorption, he had become aware of the attention this tragedy was gaining him. A flight attendant named Lucy had showed considerable kindness to him when he'd boarded the plane and had upgraded his family to better seats at the front of the cabin with more leg room. Lucy had learned of his situation from a fellow flight attendant who had been told by a co-worker who worked reservations. In addition to Lucy's kindness, the airline had graciously held seats for them on a last minute flight when Sheriff Callum's receptionist had called and explained their situation.

It also occurred to him that family and friends back home would be concerned for his well-being. He wouldn't have to deal with this mess by himself after all, he realized. He would have tons of help from his family, Jodee's family, friends, and sympathy from his employees. At this thought, he let out a much needed breath, feeling inner peace, and for the first time in days his mind started settling into its normal functioning mode of rational thought.

He settled back into the seat and stretched out his legs, relaxing – not enough to keep from garnering sympathy from the flight crew, but enough to give his much needed muscles a welcoming stretch. He put his head down and rested his forehead on the palm of his hand while his elbow rested on the armrest. He needed time to think. The flight attendant who passed him thought he was trying not to cry. He could hear her sympathetic sigh and inwardly smiled.

As the plane started gaining altitude, so did his spirits. It relieved him to know that he wouldn't have to deal with any more mundane questions and tedious details because there were people in his life who would want to come forward and do it for him – Audra for one.

He could feel the fatigue of the last few days being overcome by his excitement of impending attention. Maybe things wouldn't take as long to get back to normal as he thought. There was already attention coming his way from complete strangers so why not make use of family as well, he reasoned. He could make the situation work for him by having his mother take care of things at home until Audra could quit school. He'd also be able to take advantage of the attention at work from all the condolences his co-workers would throw his way. Who was he, after all, to keep family and friends from expressing their concern and willingness to comfort him? There was even the possibility the story could get in the local paper, he calculated, getting a little excited at the idea. Yes, as soon as the media learned who he was and who his friends were, they would definitely want to interview him. He made a mental note to call the paper as soon as they landed and started rehearsing his speech in his mind of what he was going to say to the reporters when they contacted him.

The first person he knew he had to call was Archer. No one had better connections to the media than his best friend. Not only was Archer a local celebrity because he played on the major league hockey team, but he was also a heartthrob – or so he'd been told over and over again by his sisters-in-law. Archer was a shoo-in to get him on TV, maybe even as early as the weekend, he marveled.

Yes, Doug decided. The minute they landed Archer would be his first call.

He leaned back in his seat as the plane found its flying altitude and for the first time in two weeks fell into a peaceful sleep.

CHAPTER FOUR

ARCHER

Archer Bayaud stood at his kitchen sink guzzling water after his afternoon run. He owned a condo on the sixth floor of one of the newer buildings in downtown Minneapolis. The condo was modest and homey, and though it was on the smaller side with only a thousand square feet, it was prime real estate because it connected its occupants to the skyway on the second floor, overlooked the Stone Arch Bridge, and sat along the bank of the Mississippi River – his favorite place to jog.

He stood trying to catch his breath after his run and ignored the first few rings of the phone. He finished his glass of water and wiped sweat from his face with a dish towel before reaching to answer the persistent ringing.

Fumbling for the receiver of his landline hanging on the wall without taking his eyes off the cabinet in front of him, he answered distractedly. "Yeah," was his only greeting.

"Archer... Archer? That you, man?"

"Doug? Yeah, of course it's me. What's up?"

"Listen, something happened. Something bad. I may need your help."

Archer set his glass on the granite countertop and focused his attention on the call. "What? What do you mean something happened? What's happened?"

"It's bad, man, really bad, and I'm not sure how to handle it."

"What is it?"

"Are you sitting down?"

"Doug, just tell me. Is it Jodee or one of the kids?"

"It's Jodee… She's missing."

Archer straightened unconsciously, his spine stiffening rigidly. He turned toward the base of the phone and stared at the receiver two feet in front of his face as if he were addressing a living being.

"What do you mean missing? How can she be missing?" A quickening fear started slowing his questions.

"We were out on a ferry going to some island while we were in Kokanee Bay and somewhere between the mainland and the island she just disappeared."

"Disappeared? Wait, hold on a minute, I'm not understanding you. How could she 'just disappear?'" he asked, mimicking Doug's tone. "Where are you, anyway?"

"We're in the airport here in town."

"We? Who's we?"

"Me and the kids. We just got in…"

"Hold it, hold it. Are you saying you came home without Jodee?"

"Aren't you listening? I told you, she's missing. We looked for days, man. Even her folks came out."

"So, you just left her there?"

"It's not like we just left her there… We don't know where she is. They searched for days but they finally gave up. That bum-fuck sheriff up there didn't have a clue as to what to do."

Archer's breathing slowed, building pressure in his chest until the pain made him remember to breathe.

"…We stayed as long as we could," Doug continued, "but nothing was progressing. I mean, everything seemed to be going great and then, boom, just like that, she was gone."

Archer's shoulders tensed. Fear caused a burning sensation at the top of his head before radiating down his face seeming to melt his skin as his mouth drooped in shock. A slow panic clawed out his insides making his back buckle at the waist as if the fear had dissolved his core muscles. Leaning over like a man about to expunge the contents of his stomach, he held himself up with his free hand on one knee.

He held the phone to his ear and could hear Doug on the other end but couldn't seem to comprehend the words as his friend went on describing the nightmare.

"…Then they had the audacity to suggest she may have done this on purpose. Can you believe that?"

The air was leaving Archer's throat so fast his face began to tingle. Still he listened, the phone attached to his ear like a growth.

"…But what is even more unbelievable is that Sheriff Taylor-wanna-be out there acted like I knew something I wasn't telling them, like I'd had something to do with her going missing."

The heaviness of the news bore down on Archer's muscles, he felt much like Atlas holding the weight of the world.

Unyielding, Doug continued, unaware of the effect the news was having on Archer.

"…Anyway, I was thinking maybe you can help me with the press. I mean, I'm thinking that if I can make a public announcement on TV or something, maybe I can keep them from dropping the case in Washington. What'd you think?"

Silence.

"Archer? Archer, are you still there?"

Archer raised his head from his bent position enough to see the wall in front of him and replied with what he hoped sounded rational. "Ycah, yeah, I'm still here. Uh… Whatever you think. I'll do what I can, you know that."

"Okay, thanks. Listen, I gotta go, the bags are coming down the carousel. I'll call you tomorrow."

With that, Doug hung up leaving Archer staring into space until the incessant beep, beep, beep of the phone in his ear made him realize he was holding a dead line. He reached up without standing straight and replaced the phone on its cradle.

The call had lasted twenty minutes and in that time Archer's insides had been ripped out by his best friend. His chest tight – his breathing came in quick, rapid bursts and he was having trouble drawing in a solid breath of air.

Momentarily he stood and leaned against the counter. Then slowly, like a rock dropped into mud sinking into a dark void, he slid down the counter, unaware of the bruises being carved into his back from the cabinet handles.

He slumped on the floor, his eyes fixated in space and began to murmur over and over like a mantra, "I'm sorry. I'm sorry. Oh, God, I didn't mean it. I'm so sorry."

With his back against the kitchen cabinet, he pulled his knees up to his chest, crossed his arms on top of his knees, laid his forehead on his arms, and wept.

SECTION TWO

THE DYNAMICS OF
A FRAGILE MIND

Sticks and stones can leave bones broken and the skin an ugly
blue,
but words forever haunt the mind and tear the soul in two.

CHAPTER FIVE

FEAR

Fourteen months earlier

Jodee Warren lived in a constant state of angst, an internal disquiet she'd lived with so long it had become her norm. On this particular morning, though, the dread had turned to an uneasy fear. She had found bruises on her daughter's back she suspected had been put there by her boyfriend Travis. He was a problem she didn't know how to handle. She wanted to go running into the street screaming and shouting and cause Travis severe physical pain, but she knew Doug would never allow such outwardly egregious behavior. Besides, Jodee had no real proof it was Travis and Audra had been avoiding her for over a week, ever since she had inadvertently walked in on her daughter standing in front of the bathroom mirror in panties and a bra. Audra had screamed at her mother to get out. She did, but not before seeing the fading purple bruises across her daughter's neck and shoulders.

Jodee inwardly debated talking to Doug about what she'd seen, but he had always stressed to her that all household problems were hers to deal with and he did not like being bothered by trivial matters. Those were the words he used, 'trivial household matters.' He considered anything to do with their kids to fall under this category: school issues like teacher conferences, doctor and dental appointments, and 'silly childhood squabbles.'

She had lain awake for a third night in a row pondering if Audra's bruises went beyond the realm of household problems. Did it compare to a broken water pipe that Doug would insist on knowing about because it would require money to fix, or would he consider it a silly squabble between two infatuated teenagers?

Weighing her concern for her daughter against breaking one of Doug's many dictates was what had kept her awake at night worrying. This problem with Audra wouldn't cost any money but there was definitely something broken.

As the sun forced its outstretched arms of light through the crack in her bedroom curtains and blared its optical alarm into her eyes, Jodee wearily climbed out of bed, her head sore from lack of sleep, thankful the night was finally over.

With her mind on her oldest child, and hoping for a moment alone with her before the rest of the family woke up, Jodee grabbed her robe off the end of the bed, careful not to wake Doug. She slipped into her robe and headed for the door.

Walking briskly, but quietly, down the hall, she peeked her head around the door of Audra's room. Before she could wake her daughter with a timid 'good morning,' she realized she was too late when she saw that Audra was already out of bed and the shower in the Jack and Jill bathroom she shared with her sisters was running.

Jodee slowly withdrew her head and resigned herself to another day of worry. Feeling defeated, she walked down the hall to the kitchen like a wounded soldier too tired to care about an impending danger.

As she stood at the kitchen counter in her immaculate kitchen preparing the coffee, Doug came into the room holding a blue dress shirt. She hadn't realized he had been awake when she had left their bedroom and knew her senses were slow because of her exhausted state.

Holding the shirt in front of him like a matador's cape, he scolded her. "Jodee, I told you that when you iron my shirts to make sure you concentrate on the sleeves. Just look at these wrinkles. I wanted to wear this today and now I can't."

"I'm sorry, Doug. It must have gotten wrinkled hanging next to the other shirts in the closest. Won't your suit jacket cover it?

"Oh, that's your answer for everything, isn't it? Instead of doing it right, you just expect me to keep my jacket on all day. Doesn't matter if its ninety degrees outside," he mocked in a high-pitched voice. "Just keep your jacket on 'cause Jodee doesn't have time to do things right."

"If you let me get the kids off to school first I'll iron it real fast." She reached for the shirt but he jerked it out of her reach.

"Oh, don't bother. You wouldn't get it done right anyway." He flung the shirt on the back of a kitchen chair and headed to a cabinet for a cup. "I hope the coffee is ready at least."

"It's almost done. I had a hard night so I'm moving a little slow this morning." Jodee stepped to one side in a subjugating move as Doug reached around her. He had never touched her in anger, but his words slapped her harder than any hand ever could and it always made her cringe.

"Listen to me," Doug scolded the back of her head, "I don't care how hard your night was. You know I have to be at work at eight and I don't like having my morning routine disrupted because you can't sleep. You know that. So I expect breakfast to be on the table and you to pull yourself together by the time I get out of the shower. Understand?"

"Yes. I'm sorry." Jodee turned to face him as she slipped like a clumsy ice skater to the other side of the kitchen to the stove, hoping action would allay his anger. "It really will only take me a minute to iron your shirt."

"Don't bother, I said." His snappish response had Jodee surreptitiously look to the kitchen door hoping none of the kids would walk in. Doug never allowed the children see them argue, and if they did, he always found a way to blame her.

Like a premonition of bad occurrences, Jodee looked at the kitchen door just as Lexie walked in. Stopping dead in her tracks, Lexie eyed her parents as they both saw her enter the room at the same time. Unmoving, they watched her with the look of two thieves caught in the beam of a police searchlight.

Recovering quickly, Doug reached for the discarded shirt and handed it to Jodee in a gesture sweet with gratitude. "Now, Jodee, I already said not to bother yourself. You know I've told you to not make such a fuss over minor details. Once again, you've made a mountain out of a mole hill. I'll just wear a different shirt."

Bending at the waist, he air-kissed his wife on her cheek. To an observer, the kiss looked like an affectionate peck. To Jodee, the recipient of this so-called kiss, it felt as if Doug had simply spit air at her face while making a smacking sound.

"You just worry about getting the kids to school. They're your first priority, not me. You should try to remember that." Doug walked out of the room past his daughter and gave her a wink, "Mornin', Pumpkin, did you sleep well?"

"Morning, Daddy. I guess." Giving her mother a cursory glance, she added, "Morning, Mom."

"Morning, honey. Can I get you something to eat?" Jodee stood beside the stove holding the blue dress shirt next to her breast like a shield that would deflect the impending fault that would be hurled at her come evening.

"No, I'm not hungry. I'll just have some juice." Lexie walked past her mother and opened the refrigerator door with a pull so hard it made the condiments inside the door rattle like fragile bells.

Jodee stood still waiting for Lexie to make her choice, her daughter's obvious anger apparent in her movements.

Before Jodee could find her voice and ask Lexie what was bothering her, she heard Audra come out of her bedroom and run down the hall.

"I'm meeting with the college counselor after school today so I won't be home 'til about five. Bye," Audra yelled the instructions to whoever wanted to listen as she slammed the front door.

Breakfast moved fast and messy after that. Jodee moved on autopilot getting breakfast on the table and her other three children out the door.

Thirty minutes later, Doug pulled out of the driveway waving at them as they headed down the sidewalk to their appropriate schools.

Fortunately for Jodee, Brooklyn Park Elementary was in the same direction as the high school, so Lexie always dropped her younger siblings off before continuing on to her own school.

Jodee watched the morning departure of her family from the plate glass window of her living room. She was finally alone and was hoping to catch a quick nap before starting on the list of chores Doug wrote out for her each day.

She stood lost in thought and watched Dougie J swing from his two sisters' hands as the three of them walked down the block for their last six weeks of school. She could see Dayla scold him with the little jerk she gave his arm. In his usual fashion, Dougie J ignored his sister and continued to swing and skip down the sidewalk, reminding Jodee of a jumping bean she'd seen once while on vacation.

Staring out the window long after her kids had disappeared around the corner, Jodee's thoughts battled her tired body for dominance as she lost herself in the predicament of uncertainty: should she nap or should she start on her housework? Should she tell Doug about Audra or shouldn't she?

Her groggy thoughts tumbled around each other like clothes in a washing machine.

Without realizing, she had begun to squint against the morning sun as it had glided over the house and entered the window like an accusatory task master. She'd lost track of time as she stared into space, not knowing how long she had stood there thinking and worrying.

She was brought out of her reverie by the tapping on the glass in front of her. She came out of her trance with embarrassment and waved back at her neighbor, Toni, who was staring at her and holding up two paper cups and giving them a slight jiggle as if saying, 'hey, sleepyhead, wake up, let me in.'

Jodee turned from the window, shocked at how long she'd stood there, and opened the door.

Toni came in with her usual friendly forcefulness and handed Jodee one of the cups of coffee she'd bought. Taking a sip of her own brew, she shook off the morning chill like a shivering mastiff. "Jodee, where were you?" she asked. "I must have stood outside your window for five minutes before I finally got your attention."

"Sorry, I guess I was just lost in thought. Are you just coming home?"

"Yes. After stopping a Jus Beans. I was on call last night, but I brought you a latté and thought I'd come by and vent a little."

"It's really nice of you. I can really use this, this morning." Jodee took the hot cup from her friend and took a tentative sip, glad for the distraction Toni offered.

Antonia Louisa Cavallo, known to everyone she knew as Toni, had been a neighbor of Doug and Jodee's for over five years. A transplant from New York's little Italy, she had the spunk and vocabulary of someone from the wrong side of Manhattan. Reaching all of five foot six when her top-knot bun was at its peak, she had hair so black it was almost purple, dark eyes, and the plump body of a manicotti-loving donna. And inside her spice-laden interior were the complexities and fiery substance of any proud Italian American.

Being a first generation American, her parents were still steeped in their customs from the old country regarding marriage and family. So in order to escape a bad marriage that had been designed to specifically fit her parents' religious beliefs, Toni packed up her belongings one hot Autumn day, rented a U-Haul, and tried to find a place as different from New York as she could find. That place happened to be Minnesota. On her sight-seeing trip to Los Angeles, her car broke down on the northern border of the country's bible belt when she discovered a clean, cold, family-oriented state. The upside was it had very few Italians with archaic notions.

Now, five years later, she had a house in the suburbs, a good job as a marketing rep and a next-door neighbor she could confide in when the disturbing traits of human behavior invaded her nightmares from her volunteer work as a Victim Advocate made it difficult to sleep.

Besides being a good friend, Jodee had become Toni's own personal therapist when she needed someone to talk to. Jodee was unlike anyone Toni had ever met; sweet-tempered, unassuming, modest, and most importantly – normal.

And even though Toni was sure Jodee probably cringed every time cuss words followed one of her horrific tales of abuse that came along with being a Victim Advocate, Jodee never judged.

"Did you have a lot of calls last night?" Jodee's concern for her friend was only slightly hidden behind her curiosity with Toni's job as a volunteer.

"Yeah. Why can't people ever hurt each other at a decent hour?" Her response was said jokingly but reflected a note of truth as Toni walked through the living room into the kitchen and sat at the table, making herself at home. "I didn't leave the hospital until about an hour ago. I had to stay with a woman who didn't have a ride home."

"Was there a game last night or something?" Jodee asked Toni's retreating back as she followed her friend into the kitchen. Pulling a chair out for herself, she sat across from Toni as if she were the guest and not the hostess.

"Had to have been." Sitting her cup of coffee down, Toni reached her arms over her head and arched backward, surprisingly flexible for her size. "It never fails, either. The Vikings lose, or the Twins miss a fly ball, or there's a full moon, or whatever excuse these men want to use and some woman is gonna get it."

"I've never understood that," Jodee said with a furrowed brow. "Why do men take sports so seriously it causes them to beat up someone they love?" She had taken the lid off the latté and began to stir a packet of sugar into the hot liquid.

"I don't think it's so much the game," Toni answered, "as it is a way for them to blame their low self-esteem and jackass characters on someone else. Fortunately, last night was only a couple of domestic violence cases and no deaths."

"That's really a shame, isn't it? Sometimes I think being hit all the time would be worse than death," Jodee commented while absently stirring the coffee.

"Sometimes you'd be right. But that's why I like coming over here. I need to see a normal family to keep everything in perspective."

This statement gave Jodee pause. An instinct like a fleeting whisper crossed her mind that she couldn't grab on to and caused her to silence her movements in mid stir.

Toni noticed the silence enter the room like someone had opened all the windows and let a frigid air in. Watching her friend for a moment, the silence becoming uncomfortable. Toni asked, "Did I say something wrong?"

Jodee looked up quickly, "What?" she asked hesitantly. "Oh…oh, no. You didn't say anything wrong."

"I just meant that I need to see a happy marriage like yours and Doug's to help keep me sane. You know?"

"Oh, sure, I understand," Jodee slowly added, staring at her coffee as if the swirling mocha colors could reveal the answer to her illusive thoughts like a gypsy's tea leaves.

"Is anything wrong, Jodee?" Toni had leaned forward against the table and cupped her coffee with both hands and looked at her friend in a way that said, 'You can tell me anything.'

"What? Oh, no, nothing's wrong. Just tired I guess," Jodee responded a little too quickly. "I mean, it's just really, sad isn't it? Girls being hit and yet they seem to want to stay rather than leave. I guess I'm just having a hard time figuring that out. And then how can you tell if a girl is really being hit? I remember you telling me lots of times that women claim they've run into doors or fallen down or something."

"That's true. But women do this because they're scared. Most times, if a woman rats out her husband or boyfriend, or whoever, then the next time he goes around the bend and gets mad at her, she's going to get it even worse. That's why a lot of women don't press charges. I remember this one time where the wife was swearing up and down that her and her husband had just been having a small disagreement. That she didn't need help and hadn't meant to call the cops. She was saying this while in an ambulance heading to the hospital with a broken arm. She was going to defend him no matter what because she knew next time it happened, he'd really beat her if she told."

"How do you know she wasn't telling the truth? That maybe she really did break her arm by falling. How do you know she didn't want to accuse her husband of something he didn't really do?"

"Not to belittle your questions, Jodee, but that is exactly the mentality of a lot of abused people – they try to rationalize their excuses through denial. Most of them usually do defend their abusers, but you can tell by the look in their eyes they're scared when they're doing it." Toni was drinking and talking as if they were just having a nice chat at a dinner party, trying to keep her instincts at bay.

But Jodee's questions were making Toni squirm in her seat as if the chair had suddenly turned to rock and wouldn't allow her to find a comfortable position. Tentatively, she pushed her cup aside as if it were blocking her path and looked Jodee directly in the eyes.

"Jodee, is something wrong? Are you maybe trying to ask how I know if someone is being abused on a regular basis?"

"Yes, that's it. Like that." Jodee's eyes blinked rapidly as she spoke. A habit that greatly annoyed her family.

Toni continued, ignoring her friend's telltale sign of stress. "Sometimes it's hard to tell," she said, "because these women become experts at covering it up. Most of the time they wear long sleeves and pants to cover up the bruises on their arms and legs. If there are bruises on their face, they apply heavy make-up. It's usually the meanest assholes who hit their wives and girlfriends in the face, though. But these men know their wives will never press charges, so they just don't care if the marks show. The law usually can't do a whole lot with them either. The ones you really have to watch out for are the men who are smart enough to hit their wives where the bruises don't show, like on their arms and legs and back. These are the men who get away with it for years because other people can't see the abuse and the women are too scared to come forward – or too ashamed."

After a few seconds of watching Jodee's reaction to this news, Toni asked, "Jodee, this is making me very uncomfortable. Is someone you know being abused?"

Jodee jerked her head up at Toni's question. "What? Oh, no, no, of course not," she added a little too quickly. "I was just lost in thought, thinking about what you do. You know? Just interested." She gave herself a mental shake, trying to clear the befuddlement of her mind.

"Because you know you can talk to me if there's anything wrong." Toni tried to hide the anxiety in her eyes under a tone of nonchalance.

Jodee knew she had overstepped. Doug would be furious if he ever found out she had talked to Toni. Her blinking became more pronounced.

Trying to hide her embarrassment with a unconvincing disguise of confidence, Jodee started stacking the paper cups from the table. "I should let you get home. I know you're probably exhausted from being on call last night. You should go right home and go to bed."

Toni, taking the hint, nodded her head. Sitting back with a heavy sigh, she resignedly said, "Yes, I am tired. I should get going." She got up and slowly headed for the front door.

Jodee caught up to walk her friend out, standing slightly behind her as she waited for Toni to open the door, aggressively wringing her hands as if trying to scrub off caked-on mud.

Toni, her hand on the doorknob, her head bent, spoke to the floor. "You will tell me if anything is ever wrong, won't you?"

"Of course, I would. If there was anything wrong, you'd be the first person I'd call. But don't worry, everything is fine," she lied.

Toni hesitantly walked out the door. Once outside, she turned and looked through the Warren's plate glass window to give Jodee one last wave.

Jodee waved back at Toni and watched her walk away. Once she was out of sight, Jodee sat down on the armchair by the door and stared at her hands. The wringing had turned them red and she had actually hurt her left wrist from bending it forward.

She sat for several minutes trying to compose herself. She could feel a strong pressure in her chest like someone was sitting on it. The anxiety started clawing its way to the surface of her conscience. She shuddered. She mentally went over her conversation with Toni, furtively hoping she hadn't revealed anything that would cause Doug to become angry if he found out. But she couldn't remember everything that had been said. Fact was, she couldn't remember the few moments between Toni explaining how to recognize abuse to the moment she had asked if anything was wrong.

She wrapped her arms around herself and slowly started

rocking back and forth. She sat for a few moments willing her system to return to normal. Her mind played a litany of *'if Doug were to find out, if Doug were to find out…"*

She continued to sway, feeling her own apprehension, wanting desperately to understand the root of it, its creation. But being strong enough to understand her own truths, her inner self, was not one of Jodee's strong points. That had been trained out of her long ago.

Afraid to utter what her soul knew to be the truth, to give it life by uttering its name, she denied what was easily recognizable to anyone else, she was sure if she said its name aloud it would overtake her senses and consume her. It, the word that described its own meaning and took strength from simply being acknowledged – fear.

CHAPTER SIX

VERBAL WOUNDS

"Jodee, what are you doing? I've got to get going or I'm going to be late." Irritated, Doug pulled his golf bag from the hall closet. "Archer is waiting and if I'm late you know we'll miss our tee time."

"He's almost ready," Jodee yelled over her shoulder as she tugged Dougie J's sweater over his head. "Now listen, you behave yourself at the party, okay, sweetie? And make sure you say thank you to Mrs. Johnson for inviting you."

"Are we going to have cake?" Dougie J inquired about the issue that was most important in his five-year-old mind.

"Oh, you're going to have cake and play games and there'll be balloons," Jodee responded as she put his gift in a plastic bag so it would be easier for him to carry.

"Jodee, for God's sake, what's the hold up?" Doug was standing at the garage door, clutching his car keys at his side so tightly, his knuckles were white.

"He's ready. Come on, Dougie. Your daddy's waiting."

Doug held the door open for his son. "Get in the car, buddy, and I'll be right there."

"'Kay. Bye, Mom." Dougie J bounced to the car while the plastic-enclosed gift dragged on the cement behind him.

"What time are you going to pick him up?" Doug wanted to

know, checking his watch. Monitoring Jodee's time and activity was a duty he took seriously.

"The girls are going to pick him up this afternoon at four. I don't think I'll be back from Mother and Dad's until around five."

"Where are the girls anyway?"

Monitoring his daughter's behavior was in direct contrast to the amount of energy he expelled on watching his wife's. In his mind, the children were Jodee's responsibility, but Jodee was his – as long as he approved of her directives with the children, of course.

"Audra and Lexie are shopping for prom dresses and Dayla is spending the day with Amanda."

"Dayla was at Amanda's last weekend. Don't you think the Fergusons may be getting tired of always having her at their house?"

His question held an edge she was all too familiar with. It told her she had forgotten a rule. She just wasn't sure which one it was.

Quick to alleviate his temper, Jodee tried to soften the situation with the only excuse she had at her disposal. "They asked me last weekend when I picked her up if they could take her to the zoo this weekend because there is a special exhibit of baby animals, and I told her she could go. Since I knew I was going to have to be at Mother and Dad's this weekend anyway, and I knew you'd be golfing, I thought it would be okay." Still trying desperately to lighten Doug's mood, she explained offhandedly, if not a little too fast, "I know they're together a lot, but girls that age think they can't go one day without seeing their best friends."

"Don't patronize me, Jodee. I'm not so stupid that you have

to explain my own daughter to me. And I know Audra has a date with Travis tonight, so I doubt she's going to want to stay home and babysit." Doug was anxiously pacing, weighing his need to leave for his golf date with his need to correct Jodee's decisions.

Jodee hesitated, trying to decide if she should voice her concerns for their oldest daughter. Quietly she said, "I, uh, was thinking of asking her to postpone her date tonight."

Doug asked in a dismissing tone as he counted his clubs, "Why would you want to do that?"

"I'm, uh, just a little worried about her is all. I don't think she and Travis are getting along right now and I think it might be good for her to take a break."

"Oh, I'm sure she'd like that, right before prom," Doug condescendingly retorted. "You just leave those two alone. They probably had some kind of little tiff over some insignificant teenage crap. It's normal at their age. Sometimes, Jodee, you can be so over-dramatic."

Deciding his already immaculate clubs were all there, he straightened slowly and like a six-year-old boy fascinated by a scab, he picked at the one issue that always led to an argument – her over-the-top sense of obligation to her parents.

"Tell me again why you are going all the way to St. Cloud to water your parent's plants when your sister lives right there in town? Why do you always feel that you're the only one who can help them out?"

Jodee knew it was Doug's way of showing his displeasure at her 'catering to her parents,' as he liked to call it. She also felt it gave him some kind of perverted pleasure to always start a fight right before she would have to go. As if the enjoyment of his day was in direct relation to how miserable he could make hers. But even understanding this, his words cut into the open wound of her unfounded guilt toward her parents and split the scar a little deeper each time.

In her usual fashion, Jodee tried to diffuse the conversation with explanations that excused her sisters. "Nora can't make it because she has a teacher's conference. And Brigid has to work at the Mall of America."

All of this was true. The problem was, however, that it was true the last time their parents were out of town, too. To Jodee, it was easier to tell a couple of little white lies than to listen to Doug berate her. In truth, Jodee didn't know why Nora couldn't go to their parents' house to help out when she only lived three miles away from them. As for Brigid, she was always excused from helping because she lived in south Minneapolis and it was just too far for her to travel. But being the baby of the family, Brigid had always been excused whenever there were extra duties, as Jodee's dad always made a point to tell her.

Since the day Brigid was born and their Swedish grandmother had dubbed her a 'lilla prinsessan,' she had forever remained daddy's little princess. For twenty-six years, Brigid had always been exempt from just about anything she didn't like to do.

In the secret corners of Jodee's mind, a place she seldom let herself explore, her sisters' indifference toward their parents' needs was something she envied, but not something she would allow herself to feel. Ingrained into her psyche from the delicate age of four, her unworthiness of having been born a girl had been drilled into her mind by a father who resented the fact that his oldest child had not been born a boy. This guilt had been passed to her like she had purposely usurped the position and prevented the son that could have been.

Jodee continued her explanation to Doug to assuage his

anger, "Besides, I don't mind. I'm just going to water their plants, pick up their mail and maybe do a little yard work. I thought it would be a nice welcome home gift for them."

"You not minding is not the point. They've only been gone a week. It's not like they went on a world cruise. Besides, if you'd take a more active role in your own children's lives and stop acting like a whimpering child when it comes to your parents, maybe your kids wouldn't feel so neglected by you. You should have been the one to take Dayla and Amanda to the zoo. And right this moment you should be with your oldest daughters helping them pick out their prom dresses."

Neglected? Her girls felt neglected? This statement made her lungs compress and made it hard for her to draw in a breath of air. "But, Doug," she tried to explain over the instantaneous pressure in her chest. "I didn't know about the zoo exhibit, and Audra and Lexie are shopping with a bunch of their friends. They're making a day of it. I don't think they wanted any of the mothers to go."

"You really do live in an alternate reality, don't you?" His question was rhetorical. "It's not that they didn't want you tagging along, it's that they didn't want to be embarrassed by you knowing you don't know the first thing about today's fashion."

"But they told me it was to be girls only, today," she squeaked out, not understanding why it was so important to her that he understand. She secretly wished she hadn't sent Dougie J to wait in the car. Doug never criticized her in front of other people, even their kids.

"Fine, I don't have time to argue with you. Just make sure you're home in time to fix dinner." His final command was emphasized with a slam of the garage door.

"I will, I promise," she said to his retreating back.

As Doug drove away to take their son to his third birthday party that month, Jodee stood transfixed in the kitchen. She didn't know what to focus on: her husband's accusation that she was neglectful, that her girls may be embarrassed of her, or the constant necessity to please her parents.

Mentally shaking herself free of the heaviness Doug's words had left her feeling, she started moving quickly, knowing she had to get going in order to get back in time to fix dinner. She picked up her car keys, slipped on her coat and headed for the car... All the while reliving Doug's words in her mind. Those words, those harsh words that continued to swirl through her brain like a whirlpool – circling, colliding, confusing, sucking her self-worth down to the dark depths to join her slowly fading identity, her children felt neglected.

Jodee always enjoyed driving and the hour and ten-minute drive to her parents' home was no exception. She had a ritual for any long trip; first she would stop at the McDonalds in the small strip mall next to the highway for a large diet Coke, then she would set her car radio to the soft rock station, adjust the back of her car seat to a slight incline, then sit back and enjoy the scenery as she drove. It was her chance to let her mind relax.

She was hoping that her confrontation with Doug would not spoil the drive she had looked forward to and she could get into the rhythm she needed to enjoy it. She wished she could ease her mind by talking to the girls, to see if they needed anything and a way to prove to herself that she was not neglectful. But she knew calling them while they were with their friends was an unforgivable sin.

As if fate had intervened, her cell phone rang as she hit the highway. She took her eyes off the road long enough to hit answer. "Hello," she answered.

"Mom, it's me." Audra sounded out of breath.

"Oh, Audra, I'm glad you called. Are you having a good time? Do you need anything?" Jodee could hear a gaggle of giggles in the background and knew her daughters were enjoying their shopping day.

"Lexie wants to know how much Daddy is letting us spend on shoes."

Ignoring Audra's need to get her daddy's approval, Jodee took a chance of making the decision herself. "I don't think you should go over sixty."

Jodee could tell Audra had failed in her attempt to cover the mouthpiece of her phone as she shouted over the noise of the mall to her sister. "Lexie, mom says you can spend up to sixty."

Lexie's high squeal could be heard over the phone. "Yea, I'm running back to DSW to get the black ones I saw."

"Mom, are you sure it's okay with Dad for both of us to spend sixty? Maybe I should call him." Audra's practicality was one of the traits that made Jodee proud; but at the same time her daughter's constant second guessing any of her decisions always hurt just a bit.

"Yes, I'm sure it's all right and there's no need to bother him while he's golfing."

"Okay, if you're sure. Gotta go. See you later."

"Audra, wait," Jodee rapidly yelled, "don't forget to pick up Dougie J at four."

"I know, Mom. God, you've only told me twice already. Do you think I'm so irresponsible that I'd forget my own brother?"

"No, I'm sorry, honey, of course not. Listen, you two have fun and I'll see you later this afternoon."

"Fine," Audra responded snappishly. "I gotta go." Audra hung up the phone before Jodee could say her good-bye.

Jodee shut off her phone and dismissed her daughter's rude tone as typical teenage attitude. She turned up the radio and forced herself to relax back into the driver's seat ready to enjoy the drive north to her hometown of St. Cloud.

Twenty minutes down Highway 94, the open space and colored scenery of Minnesota's byways had its usual calming effect on Jodee's nerves, as if she was wrapped in the warmth of a soft winter sweater.

It was early May, but the snow in Minnesota could linger late into the month as the fragile heads of baby plants fought their way to the surface, hungry to be nourished by the sun like baby birds in a brittle nest. The colors of sparse wildflowers mingled with the spring golds of the prairie grasses. Early-awakened leaves shimmered in the sun as the trees competed with each other to be closest to its heat.

The various greens of the trees combined with the dark purples and maroons of leafy shrubs protected the creamy mounds of white snow that lay beneath them. This last visage of winter refusing to melt and surrender to summer reminded Jodee of huge bouquets of flowers sitting on fragile lace doilies.

She never tired of marveling at all the different colors of green that Mother Nature provided; from the dark hunter green of the spruce trees, the apple greens of early blossoms from the fruit trees, to the Kelly and alpine greens that intermingled with the browns of bare limbs and the sunflower yellows of rebirth as new trees yearned for dominance like sentries that cordoned off the highway from the fields and farmland tiered into the hillside like a green wedding cake.

Passing the rural stretches of land and scattered houses put her at ease and she let her mind drift into a much-needed peace. The highway to St. Cloud was never busy in the middle of the morning and she could relax enough to scan the open spaces of multicolored landscape that melded together. Out of the corner of her eye, the colors blurred together as she sped by creating a fusion of watercolor as if Monet himself had painted the scenery. It was soothing, beautiful and comfortable.

Bright sunshine and brisk air made a day that had started out hurtful into a day of hope.

Sweet Dreams by the Eurythmics came on the radio and had Jodee's mind remembering the words that Doug had accused her of earlier – 'living in an alternate reality,' a dream. Surprisingly, the idea did not disturb her. In truth, it was a pleasant thought. 'An alternate reality,' she mused; one where angry words did not exist and feelings were treated like spun sugar – too delicate to be handled roughly. The image ran through her head helping her calm down.

Driving up to her parents' house she noticed a fine layer of snow still covered their driveway. Being that their front door faced north, cold weather hovered in their entrance longer than anywhere else. Ironically, it was synonymous with the way the house made her feel whenever she entered it – cold and isolated.

As she got out of her car and walked across the drive to the front door, she noticed that the snow was more ice than snow. It crunched beneath her feet and made a crackling sound. It had snowed and then had frozen because of the lack of sunshine. She knew that a standard snow shovel would not remove the snow and would simply leave the cement an icy slope. As a favor to her aging parents, and a nice surprise on their return home, she decided she would get out the snow blower and clear the hard-packed danger before she left.

She spent the first part of the visit collecting mail and sorting it, watering house plants, gathering up the recycling bins and putting them on the curb, doing a load of laundry and shoveling up dog poo from their back yard. Eddie, her dad's pride and joy was a mean muscular little bulldog named after Ed Asner, the boss on the 1970s *The Mary Tyler Moore Show*. Her dad spoiled Eddie relentlessly and took him everywhere. All through the winter, the dog would do his business along the edging that lined the flower beds along the back fence. Due to the recent snow melt, it became apparent that the task of picking up after the dog would be necessary as she walked out back to empty the trash. She thought happily that her dad would particularly appreciate her doing this unpleasant job for him.

With just over an hour before she had to leave for home, Jodee went over in her mind again about clearing the driveway. She knew handling the big snow blower would be a challenge for her, but her parents were getting older and it would be safer for them to get their luggage inside the house if the walk was clear. She made the conscientious decision to try and maneuver the machine in what she hoped would be a much-appreciated gesture. She thought how happy her dad would be to see it done when they got home, knowing he wouldn't have to do it.

The snow blower was buried in the garage behind the barbeque grill and some tools. She wondered why her dad had put it in such an inconvenient place. It took a lot of tugging and lifting for Jodee to drag the blower out from behind the items and then it took her several minutes to get it started. She finally positioned herself behind the blower as she walked it over the cement letting it eat away at the ice-encrusted snow. The snow blower was a ten year old monstrosity that was a little heavy for her to use, but one her dad refused to replace. It took all her strength to keep it directed in a straight line.

After twenty-five grueling minutes, she was finally finished. Sweating, with her back aching, she began reversing the process of getting the blower back into its place in the garage. She hadn't thought to bring gloves and her hands had become cold and raw, but she was pleased with her effort and just knew it was going to make her dad proud of her.

As Jodee bent down to lift a heavy toolbox back into place, she heard a car drive up behind her. Smiling, she turned around just as her parents were getting out of the car. Eddie was the first to jump from the car, running toward her and snarling like he'd never seen her before. Secretly, she really hated that dog.

She laid the toolbox down to put a barricade between herself and Eddie. Smiling, she greeted her parents. "Mother, Dad, you're home early. I thought you weren't getting back until tomorrow."

"Yah, we were going to, but your Uncle Gunther's gout flared up. Dulut is hard on him dis time of year, don't-cha-know?" Jodee knew her mother meant the town of Duluth. Her mother's Minnesota accent always became more apparent whenever she was tired and she recalled that the trip up north was always a long one.

Katie Olson walked up to her daughter and gave her a hug. "Whaddaya doing here?"

"I thought I'd come and check on the house and do a few errands for you." Hope apparent in her eyes, she continued, "I just wanted your first day home to be relaxing without you having to think of doing any chores."

Joe Olson walked into the garage eyeing the toolbox Jodee had set down. "What are you doing with the toolbox? Is something broken?" His tone reflected a panicked worry.

"No, nothing's broken. I was putting it back. I got out the snow blower and got the snow off the driveway for you. It had turned to ice and I didn't want you to slip on it."

"You used the snow blower?"

"Yes. Wasn't that okay?" Jodee's hopeful mood was slowly sliding down her spleen.

"Didn't you have trouble getting it started?" Her dad's voice was rising in pitch with each sentence.

"Well, a little, but I always have trouble getting blowers started."

"You didn't check to see if there was any oil in it, did you?" Joe's tone was accusatory.

"Uh, oil?"

"Now, Joe," Katie tried to intervene. "She couldn't have known."

"She ran the blower without oil in it." He was eyeing Jodee like she was a convict just escaped prison.

Barking at her, he asked, "Do you know what you've done, girl? You've broken my blower!"

"I didn't," Jodee tried to say. "It still runs."

"Running it without oil in it breaks it. Don't you know that?"

"Daddy, I'm sorry, I didn't know. But I'm sure it's not broken. It was working fine." Jodee started working her way around her father to the front of the garage, giving him a wide berth as if distance could diffuse her guilt.

"Of course, you'd think it was working fine because you don't know your head from a hole in the ground. You should know by now that blowers always have to be emptied of its oil before storing them for the summer. You've seen me do it a million times." He reached down and shoved the toolbox to the side and started yanking at the grill to get to the snow blower.

"I was only trying to help, really. I didn't know you had already decided to put it away for the summer." Jodee looked at her mother for support.

Joe continued his tirade. "What have I told you about her, Katie? What? She's always making trouble. Do you know what it's going to cost to get this fixed?" The question was rhetorical.

"Joe, calm down. Ya know she di'n't mean it."

Jodee began to shake, her father's temper frightened her. Eddie came toward her and made an attempt to nip her ankle.

"Daddy, if it *is* broken, I'll pay to get it fixed."

"Really, girl, you'll pay?" he snarled sarcastically. "You mean your husband will pay."

Getting her courage up, Jodee came forward to help her dad dig out the machine. "Let's try and start it, okay? Just to see."

"Don't touch it. Haven't you done enough?" He jerked the toolbox she had grabbed from her hand. "Go home. You've done enough damage," he shouted.

"Jodee, baby," her mother said carefully, "maybe you should go on home now."

"Mother," Jodee turned toward her mother with tears in her eyes. "I really am sorry. I was just trying to help."

"I know, I know, but it's best if you go on home now."

Jodee backed away, looking from her mother's pleading face to her dad's bulging back. Finally, she turned and started slowly walking toward her car.

Deliberately, as if he knew she hadn't yet reached her car, her father said, "She's always been nothing but trouble. I wish you'd never given birth to that girl!"

Jodee stopped dead in her tracks, the pain from her father's words felt like a scalpel opening her chest and letting the life flow out of her body in a sharp bitter sting that paralyzed her.

Katie flinched at her husband's harsh words. "Joe?" She turned toward her daughter's hunched back, knowing she had heard the words herself.

The tone of his wife's voice made Joe turn. He saw Jodee standing still in the middle of the drive. Jodee heard his reply to his wife saying his name. "Humph," was his only reply.

Katie ran into the house, grabbed Jodee's car keys and purse and quickly walked back to her daughter. Wrapping one arm around her shoulders and handing Jodee her belongings, she said, "Ya know he doesn't really mean it, Jodee. He's just upset is-t'all." She walked Jodee to her car. "You go on home now and I'll give ya a jingle later in da week."

Jodee got in her car like a rubber doll. She started the engine and slowly made a U-turn in the street. She looked in her rearview mirror as she drove away and saw her mother trying to placate her father. Strangely, as if the sky had suddenly turned dark, the things in her world slowly became lost in shadows. By the time she had reached the highway, her mind was numb.

Her father wished she'd never been born! The words kept going around and around in her head, but she couldn't cry. If only she could cry. She'd always felt that he didn't like her, but never hated. Now she knew the truth because he'd been able to say it without the least sign of regret.

The drive back down Highway 94 was made in a surreal state. The bright spring trees she had passed coming up, the ones that had given her so much pleasure with their growth and colors, seemed strangely large and ominous. They were no longer the normal sized trees but had grown fifty feet taller in the short time she'd seen them last. In fact, the whole world seemed to have gotten bigger.

Suddenly, with frightening clarity, she realized it wasn't the world that had grown but it was she who was smaller. The fear overtook her. It was a panic attack, but more intense than she'd ever felt before. She'd had feelings of severe nervousness before and what her mom called 'the jitters' sometimes when she was away from her kids too long. Those attacks always had her afraid that if she didn't get home something terrible would happen, and had the nursery rhyme, 'ladybug, ladybug fly away home, your house is on fire and your children are gone' playing around and around in her head. But this attack was different – more intense, more real, scaring her.

She began to feel she was shrinking away, slowly sliding from life like ink on a wet page – no meaning, no substance, no existence. Soon she would be gone, giving reality to those words her father had so callously said.

CHAPTER SEVEN

INSECURITY

How she had gotten home, she couldn't quite remember. What she did remember was racing down the highway praying she made it home before she totally shrunk away below the windshield into a tiny speck of nothingness. Her panic attack had hit its peak.

The miles flew by and the car seemed to have a mind of its own. In her surreal state, she swore the car was floating above the highway. The wheels weren't touching the asphalt and the car seemed to drive itself. It dawned on her that she didn't need to drive at all; the car knew its way home. She clung to the steering wheel only from fear that if the car floated away, she wanted to float with it. It was a white-knuckled drive that made her arms ache and her heart pound painfully against her ribs. Her temples throbbed and fear had her crying.

She was dying, she could feel it.

The car took the off-ramp at a dangerously higher speed than she ever would have normally. The tires squealed. By the time the car was inside the garage she was covered in sweat and on the verge of hyperventilating. She rolled out of the car the second the garage door hit the floor, bent at the waist and took several deep breaths trying to calm herself down.

It was a quarter after four and Doug's order that she have

dinner on the table on time made her shake with alarm. She quickly let herself into the house and stumbled into the kitchen. Dropping her purse on the floor, she made her way down the hall, bumping into the walls, to her bathroom.

Ripping off her clothes, tearing her blouse in the process, she climbed into the shower and let the cold water run over her head and body. She stayed in the water until her skin puckered and goose bumps covered her body, but eventually her breathing slowed down and the tingling of hyperventilation subsided.

Ten minutes later, her breathing now back to normal, she crawled out of the shower, dried off, dressed in clean clothes, and went to the kitchen to start dinner. Her hurt and panic hidden behind a mask of normalcy.

She could hear the roaring in the far reaches of her silent mind. She had bent down to retrieve the sponge from under the sink when the running water grabbed her attention like a child's is grabbed by the twinkling of carnival lights.

She had looked up to see the sun invade the window and shoot through the domestic waterfall as colors cascaded down the length of the liquid crystal and create a rainbow that bounced around the porcelain sink.

She stayed crouched with her hands on the edge of the counter, mesmerized as the display of dancing colors awakened her mind once more to a world that was becoming more and more familiar. A place where there was no criticism and hateful words. A world of color and laughter and light. Hypnotized by the sparkling colors, she sat and stared, letting the water run, her sanity slipping away with each drop from the faucet, one coherent thought after another being swallowing by the drain.

Somewhere, in the far reaches of her conscience, she could

hear the clatter of her family coming in the door. The noise was there, but so distant it was like hearing the clamoring of traffic from blocks away.

"What are you doing, Mommy?" Dougie J had appeared and was standing by her side, interrupting her musings.

She was startled by him, surprised to see him there. She looked over at him with a dazed look in her eyes. Speaking as if from a dream, she said, "I'm watching the rainbows in the sink and waiting for the fairies to appear. Can you see them?"

Taking a look from the water to his mom, he answered innocently, "I can see the rainbows."

"Well, if you look real close, you can see the fairies because they're the ones who make the rainbow. Just like in your storybooks."

"Jodee," Doug snapped coming up behind her, "I've asked you to stop filling that boy's head with nonsense!"

Doug's reprimand brought her fiercely out of her reverie. With a suddenness that startled her, she mentally shook herself trying to reclaim reality, like a drunk trying to concentrate through an alcoholic fuzz. With disappointment clear on her face, she snapped to and that bright cheerful world was gone – she was home, in her kitchen.

Jodee cringed from the sudden intrusive bark of her husband and quickly ducked her head inside the cabinet to reach the sponge she'd been looking for, pretending she was simply playing a game. "I, uh, was just wanting him to see the colors that the running water was making around the sink. It's just make-believe," she stammered as she let the lie hide in a secluded part of her mind.

Turning around, she saw Audra and Lexie standing in the doorway next to their father with quizzical looks on their faces.

Gathering her thoughts, she tried desperately to force reality to come quicker into focus to stop her children from looking at her like she was an out-patient from a mental ward. Noticing Lexie holding a long white plastic garment bag, she asked as normally as she could muster, "What do you have there? Is that your prom dress?"

The excitement of her new dress had Lexie exclaim with excitement, breaking the standoff. "Oh, yes, wait till you see! I'm going to try it on right now." She went skipping down the hall and into her room. The rest of the family heard her door close loudly.

Audra stood transfixed, confusion on her face.

Doug bristled openly with impatience.

Dougie J, watching his father, shyly ducked behind Jodee's legs.

Doug put down his golf bag and said just above a sneer, "You need to stop telling him that fairies exist. He's a boy and it doesn't interest him. Does it, son?"

Grabbing Jodee's hand, Dougie J bowed his head and shook it slightly.

Jodee felt her son's tiny fingers give her hand a squeeze. She looked down and forced her mind to focus, her eyes softening.

Looking up at his mother's face, wanting to please both his parents obvious on his face, he said timidly, "I like the fairies, too, though, mommy. They're like Tinker Bell in Peter Pan, huh?"

"Oh, uh… Yes, that's right," Jodee said just as timidly as she snuck a peek in Doug's direction. "I was thinking that I could see Tinker Bell."

Doug watched the exchange between his wife and son. "Peter Pan is one thing, Dougie J, because I know it's your favorite story, but you know you can't really see Tinker Bell in the water, right?"

Dougie stared at his father and simply shrugged his shoulders. To break his father's stare, he finally said, "I like Peter Pan the bestest."

"I know you do, son. Say, why don't you go in your room and play with your Peter Pan sword?"

Jodee, trying desperately to quell the panic she was feeling, and wanting to hide it from her five-year-old, agreed with her husband. "Yes, sweetie, why don't you let Audra take you to your room and help you get ready for dinner. Then I'll read you Peter Pan before bed." Her voice had a slight quiver she couldn't completely hide.

"Okay, Mommy," Dougie said reluctantly as he slowly started for the hall, tiny crease lines across his little forehead.

Audra, trying to lighten his mood, took hold of his hand. "Come on, Dougie J, let's go to your room and you can show me what you got at the party."

Doug watched his son and oldest daughter reach the hall before he turned his attention back to Jodee. "What's wrong with you?" he snapped.

Jodee could see the kids slowly entering the hall, not quite out of earshot of Doug's waspishness. Knowing Audra was old enough to understand the disagreements between adults, Jodee always tried to shield her son from seeing and hearing Doug's anger, and so she lied and said, "Nothing. I was just playing pretend with Dougie J that's all."

"Is that what you're calling it now? Jodee, really, this dazed look you seem to always have has got to stop."

"I've had a bad day," she said in an attempt to explain and yet not wanting to reveal the cruelty of her father earlier that had caused her to slide into fantasy.

"Well, you're not the only one whose day was bad because mine was rotten." Doug continued, purposely ignoring the vacant look in his wife's eyes and not wanting to hear what was obviously bothering her. Self-pitying sob stories always irritated him.

As Doug's explanation of his bad golf day spun on ad nauseam, Jodee let her mind slide back into her mental haze with relief. She could hear her husband's voice, but the words were far away.

Doug, noticing the vacant look once again in Jodee's eyes, became annoyed that she seemed to be ignoring him. Giving a loud sigh, he relented, ending his story, and asked her what was wrong.

As if someone had pulled an invisible string on her back, she turned her eyes to him and recited the confrontation with her father, emotionlessly. The cruelty from her dad told just above a whisper. She ended the retelling of what happened with the truth of her dad's feelings for her – the wish that she'd never been born.

"Oh, for God's sake, is that all? He was just mad. Besides, you shouldn't have messed with his stuff. You know how he is. Your little tiff with your dad still doesn't beat the day I had. Did you hear me tell you that Archer told me he and Nicole are getting a divorce? It completely threw him off his game and just ruined our golf day."

The anxiety attack had left Jodee drained and feeling disconnected from her body. The news of Archer's divorce couldn't seem to penetrate farther than the outer layer of her anxiety to give the reaction Doug so evidently expected. It irritated him. "Jodee, snap out of it! Did you hear me? My best friend is getting divorced."

"What? Oh, I'm sorry, Doug. It just…it hurt so much to hear Daddy say that."

"Yeah, well your dad will get over it but Archer is not going to be himself for a long time and I'm going to have to be there to help him through it." Doug picked up his golf clubs and headed for the garage. "Everything isn't always about you, you know. Stop acting so bloody wounded. You've always been so hyper-sensitive about everything." With this final insult he walked into the garage and let the door slam behind him.

The bang of the door made her jump and reverberated through her system. The biting remark made her visibly stoop and bend inward as if he had physically punched her in the chest. It couldn't have hurt more if she'd been hit with a whip.

CHAPTER EIGHT

OBEDIENCE

"Jodee, I'm going after work to look at the playsets for Dougie J's birthday so I'll be home late."

"All right," she said in her usual meekness. Five days after the incident with the snow blower, Jodee still had not mentally come to terms with her father's admission. She was having trouble concentrating on day-to-day tasks, forever reliving in her head the cruel words he had thrown in her direction, 'I wish you'd never given birth to that girl!' It was a cycle she couldn't escape and causing dreams where she ran throughout the night, not being able to find her way home and searching for something, something that was just out of reach – something that needed her. The dream was the same every night, except the paths she ran were always different and treacherous. And like a record stuck on a scratched groove, her whirling mind would repeat the phrase over and over in her dreams 'never been born, never been born,' to the point her head would start to pound and she would wake in a sweat. At other times she could hear a baby crying, only to wake and find herself whimpering. She would then awaken feeling exhausted and melancholy and harboring a slight headache.

Doug continued to talk over his shoulder as he poured himself a cup of coffee, not noticing her quiet tone. "Listen, I was talking to a guy at work who says I can get a good deal on one of those real big sets. You know the kind you see on TV. He says his kids have one with a climbing wall, three swings, a rope ladder, the works. I think it's something Dougie J will really like."

The words climbing wall brought Jodee's meandering mind back into focus like the slow shutter of a camera. Her maternal protection for her son had her mentally shaking herself and she turned to confront her husband. It was the catalyst she needed to snap her out of the depression she'd been in for days. "Doug," she said unusually forcefully. "You know I think he's too young for something that elaborate. I think we should just get him something small, like a simple swing set with a slide and maybe a teeter-totter or something. I think he's too young right now to be on a climbing wall or trying to go across a rope ladder."

"For crying out loud, Jodee, if it were left up to you he would stay a toddler for the rest of his life. Besides, this is something he'll get a lot more use out of than just a simple swing set." He mimicked her. "This is something he'll be able to play on for years. He only turns six once."

Trying to reason with his frugal side, Jodee said, "I just want to remind you that we spoke about this in the fall and you said they were too expensive."

"We've discussed this till I'm blue in the face. It's noted, you don't agree, but if Carl can get me a big set for the same price as one of those small ones, then that's what I'm going to do."

The one issue that could over-ride any earlier decision Doug had made was if he thought someone had bought something bigger and better than he had. Keeping up with the Joneses may have been a cliché with some people but for Doug Warren it was a lifestyle. It wasn't something he would ever consciously admit to doing, but it was still a way of life he couldn't help but follow. He continued, "Jim Harper also bought one a couple of years ago and his kids still play on it. I also figure that Dayla is still young enough to play on it too so it will really be for both of them."

"But aren't they something like a thousand dollars? I thought we were going to use any extra money to put into Audra's college fund for next year?" Jodee reasoned.

"Jodee, I'm tired of talking about this. I've made up my mind and it's final. When you get a job then you'll get to make the decision as to how we spend the money. As I remember, my name is on those checks and this is what I've decided to do."

His remark was like a hard slap across her confidence and he always used it whenever they argued about money.

"Now I'm going to go look after work, so I'll be home later than normal. This is your night off so you can brood about it later." He picked up his car keys, leaned forward for the customary cheek kiss as if to say, 'case closed,' and hurried to his car.

When he turned around, Jodee used the tips of her fingers to wipe off the wetness of his kiss on her cheek, thankful that it was her night off.

She knew his comment about her not having a job was unfair since it was his decision for her not to work. But having a night off made up for his tiresome comment. Having a night off for Jodee Warren did not mean it was a night where she didn't have to cook. No, having a night off was Doug's way of saying it was her night that she didn't have to have sex. It was his rationale of fair play regarding their sex life. It was a bargain she had agreed to after her second baby, she had begun to dread having sex because it had become a chore trying to keep up with two babies and still satisfy her husband's constant demands. He came up with the deal that they would have sex every other night as a way to be fair to both of them – his night on, her night off, so to speak.

No matter the circumstances, whether they had had a fight, she had a cold, he'd had a bad day at work, it didn't matter; this deal had been made like a contract and had been adhered to for the past fifteen years.

Doug thought sex was something that kept his mind focused and his body relaxed so he endured any unpleasantness between him and Jodee to have sex when it was his night on, as long as it kept him 'on his game.' For Jodee, sex had become a tiresome part of their marriage. Doug's love making had always been quick and selfish and had never gotten better. He always left her frustrated. She began to view it more an act of necessity to keep her husband from nagging her than an act of passion. After five years of marriage, she started viewing Doug as a big sweaty animal who grunted over her, released himself with a loud groan and then quickly fell asleep; leaving her dissatisfied and angry. It became no more an act of love than her seeing him off to work every day, something she needed to do to get him to leave her alone.

After nineteen years of marriage, Jodee seeing Doug off to work had slowly transformed from an idyllic scene from a 1950s sitcom to a mindless obligation. It was indicative of their entire marriage that she never questioned, and he didn't notice. She was required to kiss his cheek and see him out the door in order to keep him happy, and he needed to be escorted to the door by his wife as a sign of reverence. It was no more important than changing the bed sheets – an unpleasant necessity that kept life tidy and unsoiled. Appearances were everything to Doug.

The change in their life would sadden her if she allowed herself to think about it, but it was a place she never allowed herself to go. To remember back when she was twenty and freshly married, how she would kiss him goodbye at the door like a man going off to war who might never return. She had wanted her love to follow him throughout the day. After a few years passed, her 'soldier-husband' acted more like a man who fought the war on a daily basis and began to treat her like his station outranked hers. Her goodbye kisses became a little more reserved. Ten years into the marriage, the morning ritual became a required chore because the soldier had turned into a sergeant who returned affection as a matter of regulation. Slowly, and ever so slightly, she stopped initiating the kisses all together and wondered if he ever noticed. The sergeant had promoted himself to general with Patton-esque rigidity. It was at this time that the farewell kisses became his request and he expected her to comply as a sort of salute to his status.

Jodee stood still and listened for the garage door to hit its final descent on the concrete slab as Doug backed his silver BMW out of the drive. When she knew she was finally alone, her shoulders came down a good three inches as she visibly relaxed and let out the breath she always seemed to be holding in his presence. Her posture went from ramrod stiff to a slumped hunchback that replicated an old woman from a storybook, as if the pressure in her lungs had been the only thing that kept her upright. She stayed like this for several minutes as if to gather the strength to stand straight again.

It was at this time of day, the time that her husband went to his job at the bank that Jodee was finally able to take a deep breath of air and fill her body with the minute bit of relief that seemed to constantly elude her. Not that this physical relief and mental respite was anything she would ever admit to herself she needed. To do that would be going against everything her mother had ever drilled into her on how to be the dutiful wife – 'obey your husband and always have a cheery disposition.'

Well, she knew she had failed years ago on the cheery disposition thing, but obeying was something she was an expert at.

Jodee knew, without ever having to analyze it, that her mother and her mother-in-law had been cut from the same cloth. Maybe it had been the time in which they were raised, she wasn't sure, but being the obedient wife was like an unbreakable covenant for them both. The only difference was that her mother-in-law was adored by her husband, the Major, so being obedient to this sweet man was no real hardship. As for her mother, she was treated more like a possession by her father and being obedient to him was a necessity.

Jodee's mother-in-law, Grace Angela Warren, was a woman of strong beliefs in how a woman conducted herself at all times and in every situation. She and her brother Daniel had been raised in the heart of Georgia by very stark parents, three aunts, and a strong southern grandmother who all lived within a mile of each other. Being inundated on a daily basis with manners was a way of life. Daniel's education had been left to their father, and although Grace's father had been a strong influence in her life, it had been the women in the family who took it upon themselves to teach Grace how to be a proper southern woman. She had so much southern estrogen guiding her life that at times Jodee thought Grace would forget she was no longer living in the days of white gloves and seasoned cotillions.

Jodee had always been fascinated by her mother-in-law and the stories of her growing up in the south and thought how the southern woman was an interesting concept, especially during Grace's teen years of the 1950s. With rules of etiquette preached like it was the Bible, Grace had learned how to be the perfect wife: a wife never raises her voice, she smiles no matter the circumstances, she never makes a fuss in public, she must always look her best for her husband, cleanliness was next to Godliness, and above all a wife should succumb to the wisdom of her husband and obey him in household affairs. The only flaw in all these well-meaning dictates was they forgot to pass on to Grace that all these rules of wifely femininity were really more a romantic notion of the past than actual rules.

If the southern woman was nothing else, she was her own woman and knew when to exert her authority and when not to. Every strong southern wife knew that in order to control the home, she had to obtain the skills of knowing when situations required her to step back and let the southern male step forward. It was a delicate balancing act between control and acquiescence, but one that was necessary in keeping peace in the home and the illusion of male dominance alive, an art that had been perfected over generations. Grace, however, was not taught this one very fine detail and grew to believe that to disobey her husband was the ultimate sin. She therefore passed this same philosophy onto the only daughter she could claim, her very young eighteen-year-old daughter-in-law, Jodee.

When Doug and Jodee were first married, Doug had just graduated college and had not yet obtained a job that paid well enough for them to buy a home. To make ends meet, they lived with his parents for the first three years of their marriage and the birth of their first child. It was during this very vulnerable time of Jodee's life that her lessons in wifely obedience were taught to her by her very enthusiastic mother-in-law.

Jodee was fine tuned to the southern style of marriage by Grace with all the discipline of a fine finishing school. Grace, along with Doug's aunts and grandmother who would visit twice a year, kept her up to date of every fine little detail of how to be a proper wife. At times, Jodee felt she was in a continuous episode of *Leave It To Beaver*.

Not once, in those three years of living with her in-laws, did she ever see her mother-in-law raise her voice or complain. Doug's aunts, whenever they visited, practiced decorum like breaking form was against the law. And never once had Jodee ever seen Doug's grandmother without her pearls around her neck, including the day she was laid to rest. In short, Jodee came to believe they were the epitomes of perfect wives and women.

During this time, Jodee's own mother would take every opportunity to remind her that her new husband was the head of the house – even if they didn't have their own home. It was the symbolism that mattered.

Born Katherine Irene Hansen, Jodee's mother had been raised on a farm outside of Moorhead, Minnesota. It had been a modest-sized farm that had been in their family almost since the Norwegian immigrants decided to make Minnesota their new home at the end of the nineteenth century. Having been raised on a farm where work was equivalent to having a full belly, Katie was used to hard work. She had learned early that surviving on a farm meant knowing how to take orders. It was her father who ran the farm and the help – meaning her along with her four brothers, two sisters and their mother. It was also this part of the farm Katie resented the most. By the time she had met Joseph Olson, the family farm had had several hard years of poor crops from severe frosts that would precede dry summers causing too little food for too many mouths. Being the seventh child in a family of nine, Katie decided meeting and marrying Joe was the answer to her prayers. Escaping her impoverished family and moving to a bigger city had always been in her plans. Getting pregnant three months into their relationship hadn't been.

Joseph Olson had been a young man with dreams of a military career. During his senior year of high school, he spent every spare moment outside of classes to run and get in shape. He had planned to enlist into the military as soon as he graduated and wanted to be in tiptop shape to prove his dedication.

It was at the end of Katie's senior year at the annual Sock Hop they met. Joe had been a year older than she and had graduated with her brother Paul, but he had never taken notice of Paul's younger sister until he decided to go to the dance on a lark and saw her standing across the room in her pale pink dress and white ankle socks. The band was playing their version of *Cry* by Johnny Ray. Her face was soft and she was transfixed with the words of the song when she looked over and saw him staring at her. They had felt an immediate attraction to each other.

The summer following that dance, they spent almost all their time together. Throughout the weeks that followed, he would drive out to her family's farm to pick her up and take her into Fargo for a burger and a movie. They teased and flirted the entire summer until the flirting became more passionate. Then, the day before he was to go to Minneapolis with his dad to talk to an army recruiter, a very scared yet excited Katie met him at the park to inform him she was pregnant.

This news had given Joe's parents the excuse they needed to keep him from enlisting. His father had been in one war and he had vowed that none of his own kids would ever experience it, even if the country wasn't at war at the time he couldn't take the chance that one day they would be. So, after first giving Joe a stern reprimand for being irresponsible, they played on his sense of decency and guilt to marry the girl and give the baby a home. Joe listened with an ever-growing dread as he watched his dreams being brutally ripped out by the roots. His strong sense of responsibility won over – there would be no military career.

Resigning himself to the fact that his military dream was gone, Joe married Katie and they moved into a small apartment in Fargo while he worked for his dad as a glass cutter. He loved Katie and he began to believe that life wouldn't be so bad. Katie was a hard worker and as she got bigger with child he began to dream of her giving birth to a son, him taking over his dad's business, and then passing that business onto his boy as they worked side by side.

Once again, however, life pulled a bad joke on Joe when the son he had been expecting ended up being a girl. They named her Jodee. And as unfair as he knew it was, his resentment toward this pink little twist of fate was deep.

The family history of her birth lived in Jodee's mental makeup like a wart, sometimes itching her conscience and getting in the way, and other times just an annoyance she knew was there and could ignore.

Today she was determined not to focus on her failures. Ever so slowly she straightened her resolve along with her spine and tried not to think about the two women in her life she would never measure up to.

Jodee calmly walked to the radio and turned it on to her favorite station, deciding to enjoy the small respite of quiet solitude, and went about doing the daily chores Doug had written out for her.

CHAPTER NINE

SELF-DOUBT

Toni had had a hard night. She'd been working overtime to finish a project for a client when she'd been called out to assist the police on two difficult cases: a suicide and domestic abuse case. She'd spent the first part of the night consoling a grieving widow whose husband decided that drinking himself to death was cleaner than a gun. Then she'd spent five hours waiting in the emergency room of the hospital for the doctors to stitch up a woman's head where she'd been hit with a bottle by her irate husband, answering question upon question by the detective on duty, and trying to convince the badly injured woman to file charges. When she'd finally left the hospital, she had to run her project over to the client in downtown Minneapolis before she could call it a day and go home.

She was so tired she couldn't even gather the strength to voice it out loud. It wasn't so much the physical fatigue as the mental, and it wasn't so much dealing with a grieving widow as it was dealing with women who put up with abusive men. Once again she wondered if she was getting burnt out on being an advocate. The thought passed through her mind like it always did when she was too tired to care where her mind wandered.

At eleven the next morning she finally drove into her driveway, thankful it was Saturday so she could sleep the day away. Getting out of her car, she walked to the trunk to retrieve her briefcase, computer, and a bag of groceries she had purchased on the way home. When she reached the rear of her car, she saw Jodee's teenage daughter, Audra, standing with her boyfriend Travis in front of the Warren house. Audra was standing facing Travis, leaning into him as he leaned against his faded red Ford that was parked at the curb. His hands on her shoulders. From a distance, they looked like two sweethearts staring into each other's eyes with their foreheads touching while he caressed her neck and rubbed her shoulders.

Toni gave the young couple a quick glance as she leaned forward into her trunk. As she stood, her hands full, she looked over at them again. Hoping they would be willing to help her with her things and getting them into the house, she started to wave to get their attention when something in Audra's posture stopped her. Audra wasn't leaning toward Travis, she looked more like a turtle that was trying to tuck its neck into its shell. Toni stopped what she was doing and faced the couple.

Toni didn't know if her senses were simply on overload or her exhaustion had her imagining things, but something seemed off. Going unnoticed, she faced Audra and Travis full on and watched them, curious.

It only took a minute for Toni to realize that this wasn't a couple in the throes of young love. This was something else. Something she had already seen too much of for one day. She saw that Travis had a hard grip on Audra's shoulders. As he pulled her toward him, he pressed his forehead against hers forcing her head back as if giving her a subtle head-butt.

Even though she stood yards away, Toni heard the sharp intake of Audra's breath when Travis moved his hands from her shoulders to around her neck. She watched as Travis jutted his jaw forward and whispered something in a harsh tone in Audra's ear. Taking a moment to compose herself, Toni started across her yard determined to find out what was going on. Remembering her talk with Jodee from a couple of weeks before, it looked to Toni that Jodee may have been right – Travis was mistreating Audra.

Knowing she had to be careful to not let the situation get out of hand, Toni swallowed her misgivings and started across the lawn. Past experience had taught her that confronting an abusive man head-on usually made the woman retreat into the typical mode of defending her man. Making excuses for him and taking the blame for the abuse was the norm, then once everyone had left the man would take it out on the woman, making things worse, which was exactly what had happened the night before with her latest victim. The husband and wife had argued over a cold piece of meatloaf, he had slapped her and commenced to yelling at her loud enough to attract the neighbors. When the cops showed up and saw the red mark on the woman's face, they went to arrest the husband for assault. The wife did the typical song and dance of saying she had run into a cabinet door. There was not a lot the cops could do but leave.

Once they had left, the husband was so incensed that the cops had been called, he threw a beer bottle at his wife's head cutting her left temple. It took a full hour of verbal abuse and bleeding before the woman finally got angry enough to fight back. By the time a second call had come into the cops from the neighbors, the broken bottle on the floor and the bleeding wife on the couch, it was obvious what had happened and the cops knew this time they could make an arrest; but, they wanted the wife to file formal charges. When the man heard this, he got angry again and called his wife a lazy slut, blaming her for the cops having to be at their house in the first place. This had been when Toni arrived.

The tension between the cops and the husband was only slightly less important to Toni than the woman with the bleeding head. Toni's attention to the wife seemed to be making the man angrier as he accused them of taking his wife's side because they hadn't seen what really happened, saying she attacked him first. Toni saw a look pass between the man and the wife and, as if on cue, the wife started defending her husband. Toni knew at this point that she had to get the wife away from the husband without making it look like she was blaming him. She knew from past cases that when the couple was alone again, the beating would probably be worse the next time.

Toni was able to back the cops off long enough to talk to the husband. She gently explained to him that his wife probably needed stitches and it would be best for him if she took his wife to the hospital. Toni knew that confronting the man in a hostile way and outright blaming him in front of the cops would only anger him more. Her first priority was the wife. Once she got her out of the house, the cops could do whatever they wanted with the husband, while she tried to convince the wife to file charges. Toni had learned that to keep an abusive man from escalating the situation out of control, it had to look like she wasn't taking sides. This was how she planned to approach Travis and Audra, friendly and without accusation.

Trying to keep her anger from showing, Toni knew she would have to carefully diffuse the situation without making Travis suspicious, so he wouldn't blame Audra later on. She also had to make certain that Jodee was right and not simply being an overprotective mother – although Toni doubted it. She had to make sure the situation today was not simply a lover's quarrel.

Taking a deep breath, Toni made a beeline for the couple, walking a little faster than she had intended.

Audra and Travis were so focused on their conversation they didn't see or hear Toni approaching. Travis was pushing his forehead hard against Audra's as he dug his fingers into her shoulders. In a low firm tone he said, "I told you to stay away from him, damn it. What is it you don't understand about that?"

"Travis, he's just a friend. I've been friends with Ryan since first grade. You know that."

"Don't tell me what I know. And what have I said about keeping your voice down?"

"I'm sorry, I forgot. But you're hurting me."

"I don't give a good goddamn. You are so stupid, you know that? Guys can't be friends with girls. All he wants from you is to get in your pants." He squeezed her shoulders a little harder for emphasis, making her cringe.

"Brad told me he saw the two of you in the cafeteria sitting alone. I think you are purposely trying to embarrass me in front of my friends."

"I would never do that, Travis. Ryan and I were talking over our science project that's due next week, that's all."

In a quick shift of tone, he said in a quiet forceful way meant to intimidate. "Well, I don't know if I want to go to prom tonight with someone who doesn't respect my feelings."

"Travis," she pleaded, "you don't mean that. My parents bought me a new dress and all our friends will be there."

"You have no one to blame but yourself." The disappointment in Audra's eyes made Travis smile with the obvious knowledge that he was in control. The fear in her eyes had him smirking as he reveled in her distress.

"Miss Cavlo, Miss Cavlo!" Dougie J came bounding out the

front door with a wide smile just before Toni reached the Travis'
car.

Travis and Audra heard Dougie J running down the walkway
and jumped apart like two people guilty of a crime.

Toni stopped and turned toward the child as he continued to
run toward her. "Dougie J, hello there. What are you up to?" Toni
took an instant to turn and eye Travis.

With a startled expression, Audra stared at her neighbor. The
look Toni had given Travis was full of malice, and suspicion.
Toni could see the worry on Audra's face and watched as she
made an exaggerated display of enthusiasm at seeing her little
brother as if her ruse would distract Toni from the obvious.

"Dougie, what are you doing here!" She bent down to look
at Dougie J on his level and held her arms out to him.

Ignoring his sister, Dougie J ran around her to their neighbor.
"Miss Cavlo, come and see what I got for my birthday!" Toni
thought it was cute how the little six-year-old always
mispronounced her name.

"Oh, my goodness, is it your birthday?" Toni tried to convey
happiness at Dougie's news while still maintaining vigilance on
Travis.

"Huh, uh, tomorrow, but I'm getting my present today!" He
grabbed her hand to drag her toward the house.

"Oh, okay, okay," she said. "Just a second there though, I
want to say hello to your sister."

Turning toward the young couple, Toni addressed them, "Hi,
Audra. Travis."

Toni watched Travis retreat into the stereotypical act of the
meek and innocent. She'd seen that play too many times not to
recognize it – the I-don't-know-what's-going-on look that the
guilty always thought fooled authority. "Hello, Ms. Cavallo. How

113

are you?" His pretense of respect could not hide the guilt around his eyes.

"Is everything all right?" Toni asked dubiously, inwardly thinking 'you don't fool me, kid.'

"Oh, yes," Audra said a little too quickly. "We were just talking about prom tonight, weren't we, Travis?"

Looking directly at Travis to let him know she knew what he'd been doing, Toni said, "Yeah, I did hear something about prom being tonight."

"Yes, ma'am, we were talking about who all is going to be there tonight," Travis said with sticky sweetness.

Ignoring Travis, Toni asked, "Audra, what happened to your forehead, honey? You've got a big red mark on it?"

"Oh… oh, really?" Audra stammered, as she immediately proceeded to rub her forehead with the heel of her hand. "Oh, I… I, uh, don't know. How funny. I must have gotten too much sun."

"Miss Cavlo," Dougie yanked on her hand impatiently. "Come and see my present, now."

Shocked by how much strength her little six-year-old neighbor had, she pulled back just a little to give one last warning remark, looking directly at Travis. "Well, you kids have fun tonight, and be nice to each other. Now, I guess I'd better go see Dougie's present before he pulls my arm off."

"Yeah, thanks, Ms. Cavallo." Turning toward his car he said over his shoulder to Audra, "I'd better go. See you later, Audra."

With a pleading look at Travis, Audra said in a pathetic tone, "Really, you mean it?" As if she knew she had given something away, she added quickly, "I mean, yeah, of course. I'll be ready at seven."

"Yeah, yeah." Travis offhandedly threw the words at her as

he got in his car and sped away.

"Now, Miss Cavlo. Come on," pleaded Dougie J.

With the aid of a small boy, the tense situation was diffused as he pulled Toni toward the house, followed by Audra. Turning back to look at Audra, Toni saw a look of relief cross her face, as if she was grateful for the interruption. Toni began to wonder how far Travis' jealousy and control had gone when it came to Audra. She decided she needed to make a point of talking to Jodee.

Being pulled through the front door, Toni said, "I think I'd better let your mom know I'm here, Dougie. Don't you?"

"Naw, she's with Lexie doing girl stuff or somethin'. Come on."

Audra walked through the front door behind her brother and Toni. Ignoring her excited brother's squeals, she immediately turned right to go down the hall and escape to her room.

Noticing Audra was trying to get to her room Toni tried to stop her so the mark on her forehead would be obvious when her parents saw her. Quickly Toni asked, "Audra, don't you want to come and see Dougie's present with us?"

Without turning fully around, Audra said in profile, "No, that's okay. I've seen it." She continued to half run, half walk to her room.

Watching Audra retreat, bothered she wasn't going to be able to talk her, Toni turned to Dougie. "Well, I guess it's just you and me, little man. Take me to your present."

Letting go of her hand, convinced she would finally follow him, Dougie J ran through the kitchen and out the back door. Bouncing up and down, he yelled, "Look, look, I'm getting a swing set!"

Toni stepped through the screen door before it could slam. In the middle of a rather sizeable back yard, two men in matching blue work shirts were busy assembling a rather impressive playset.

"My goodness, look at that. Aren't you a lucky little boy," she stated with what she thought would be an impressive enough excitement to make Dougie J happy.

Even though it looked like the two workmen had a long way to go before finishing the set, Toni could tell it was going to be big.

"Yeah, but I don't get to play on it till tomorrow cause it's my birthday."

"Well, that's good because I don't think it will be finished before tomorrow."

"Look, look," Dougie chimed as he ran over to a toolbox sitting on the ground and grabbed the brochure of his birthday present, handing it to Toni.

"Oh, yes, let me see," Toni said as she took the brochure. Scanning the paperwork, she could see what the set was going to look like. The main body was a sturdy Redwood square that resembled a small fort with an upper deck that stood seven feet off the ground and was protected by a peaked roof. On one side, jutting from the top deck, was a long support bar where two yellow swings hung. Directly opposite the swings, on the other side of the fort, was a matching yellow slide. The side of the set farthest from the house was a cargo chain ladder leading up to the top deck from the ground. Inside the little square platform was a red plastic steering wheel mounted to one side, resembling a boat's helm. On the side facing the kitchen window was a faux rock wall with rubber, multi-colored hand grips. Underneath the upper deck hung a green tire swing supported by heavy chains.

Toni sat down on the back step of the house to study the brochure. Dougie came and sat by her and chatted excitedly near her shoulder explaining the intricacies of his present and pointing to the pictures in the brochure "…And this here is a ladder made of rope and this is going to have a wheel like a real boat that can be my hideout. I'm going to play Peter Pan and make people climb the sides of my ship to get up to see me and everything."

"That sounds very exciting. When is your party?"

"It's tomorrow and Mommy says we're having ice cream cake and everything."

Toni was happy to sit and listen to her youngest neighbor. He was in the middle of telling her about the new plastic sword he wanted so he could play his favorite storybook character when a loud scream came from inside the house.

"Arrgghhh! Mother, what have you done? It'll never be ready in time now!" Toni could tell by the tone of voice that Jodee's middle daughter was having a fit about something.

Somewhere in the house a door slammed followed by heavy footsteps and a second door. The yelling match continued.

"I haven't done anything to it yet, Lexie!" Jodee yelled back, her statement more pleading than angry. "And why didn't you tell me before the day of the prom that this dress was too big? I could have sworn it fit you when you bought it. Now, get out here so we can fit it or it won't be done in time for sure!"

"No, you'll ruin it. And it did fit until you decided to *fix it*," Lexie snidely remarked as she made air quotes with her fingers.

"Lexie, all I did was take in the sides. It isn't ruined, but it will be if I have to rush to fix the rest of it."

"What is that all about?" Toni asked Dougie J.

"My stupid sisters are going to a pom tonight," Dougie explained in a pout.

"You mean prom?"

"Yeah, and they're being all stupid about it."

117

"Oh." Toni wasn't sure what to say to her little friend to make him feel better. She opted for, "Well, girls can sometimes be silly about stuff like that."

"I guess. But they been yelling all day." Toni could tell Dougie was upset by the way he kept his eyes on the ground. He reached into the pocket of his jeans and brought out a little doll.

"What do you have there, Dougie?" Toni wanted to get his attention off the chaos going on in the house.

"It's Peter Pan. My Grandpa George got it for me at Disneyland."

"Well, it's very nice. Did he and your grandma go to Disneyland just to get this for you?"

With a little less enthusiasm than he'd shown earlier, Dougie responded, "Yeah. And see, I also have Tinker Bell." He pulled out a little Tinker Bell doll from his other pocket.

He put the two dolls in his lap and stared down at them with a soft sadness on his face.

Toni felt sorry for him, so she simply let him hold his dolls without saying anything. They sat together in silence as she rubbed his back.

After watching Dougie for a few moments, as the two of them listened to the fighting behind them, she thought it would help if she could get him to talk. "It's hard to hear your sisters and Mommy yelling sometimes, isn't it?"

"Uh-huh." He sat in silence. Then said, "It makes mommy sad."

His remark took Toni by surprise. So that was it. He was worried about his mom. For only being six, she thought it was awfully sensitive of him. It puzzled her. Kids who were overly sensitive to in-family fighting usually were personally bothered by the overall yelling. But Dougie seemed more concerned for his mother's feelings.

From directly behind them, Dayla came stomping through the kitchen as she fumed at the top of her lungs. Toni could hear her through the open door. "Mom, you didn't answer me. Why can't I go?"

"Dayla, please, not now," Jodee implored as she carried a light pink formal dress into the kitchen draped across her arms like a baby and headed for the laundry room as Dayla dogged her heels. "I have to deal with your sisters right now. Have you seen Audra come in the house yet?"

"How would I know if she's in the house or not?" Dayla replied in a snotty tone. "She's probably still outside sucking face with Travis."

Toni thought Dayla's tone bordered on disrespectfulness as she sat uncomfortably on the step listening.

"Well, I think I heard her come in. Go see if she's in her room, please. I have to make sure she gets to the hairdresser on time and then I have to finish Lexie's dress."

"Then can I go to Amanda's?"

"No, Dayla. I already told you, you can't go over to her house this weekend. Your dad and I think you've been over there enough for one month."

"You always think of everybody but me," Dayla whined. "You don't care about anything I want!"

"Dayla, I said enough." Jodee pleaded, exasperated.

"Daddy would let me go."

"No, he wouldn't. You've been at Amanda's every weekend and it's time you stayed home. Now why don't you go find Audra while I finish fixing Lexie's dress?" Jodee begged tiredly.

It was only eleven-thirty in the morning but when Toni snuck a peek inside the house, she could see the tired blue circles of exhaustion that surrounded Jodee's eyes.

"I want to take the dress to a tailor or something," Lexie continued the disagreement with her mother.

"Lexie, stop. I can fix it. You just have to give me time."

"But you don't know how to sew good enough. Allison said her mom would fix it for me. Let me take it to her."

Dayla interrupted Jodee's answer to Lexie, "Audra won't open her door, Mom. And I'm going to Amanda's whether you like it or not."

Lexie screamed, "Dayla, shut up! Mom is working on my dress!"

"You shut up. I don't care about your stupid dress. Besides, you just said she can't fix it."

Toni couldn't take any more. She felt guilty sitting on the stoop listening to her friend arguing with her daughters and stood up to leave. "Maybe I'd better go," Toni said to Dougie.

As she reached for the door, prepared for the consequences of letting the three women know she was there and that she had heard everything, she looked through the dark shadows of the screen door and saw a transformation come over Jodee.

Standing as if frozen, Jodee's habitual nervous blinking began to increase rapidly as she slowly turned her head from side to side between her yelling daughters like she was watching a tennis match as the two girls totally ignored their mother.

Toni watched as a blank expression came over Jodee's face as she looked down at the dress in her arms. Acting like she'd never seen it before, she gave the material a little bounce as if trying to gauge the weight of it. Continuing to stare at the downy object, she let the bottom of the formal slide from her cradled arms and land on the floor in a crumple of pink taffeta. She blinked more as her eyes glazed over. Holding up the bodice to face level she stared at it as if she couldn't quite make out what it was – blinking, blinking. She started rubbing the material between her fingers as if the texture and substance were foreign to her.

Unsure of what she was seeing, whether Jodee was going to faint or if it was a break from reality like none she'd ever seen, Toni opened the door and made a quick move toward Jodee.

At the same time as Toni pulled the screen door open, Lexie yelled in outrage. "Mom, you're dragging my dress on the floor!"

Snapping out of the trance she was in, Jodee looked up like she'd been slapped and saw Lexie, Dayla and Toni staring at her. The vacant look in her eyes had Lexie responding in a tone heavy with annoyance, "Mom! What's wrong with you?"

As Jodee stayed silent, Toni could tell she was trying desperately to recognize her surroundings by willing herself to concentrate. The emotions that ran across her face were so fast and fleeting they reminded Toni of images being flipped on consecutive sheets of paper showing a moving caricature of perplexed lunacy.

Jodee blinked, blinked, blinked as if trying to bring the world into focus as her eyebrows stayed in a fixed question mark position.

"Oh, great," Dayla said sarcastically. "She's blinking again."

Jodee cocked her head at the sound of her girls talking, not unlike a dog listening for a command. Her eyes took on a far away look as if she were seeing something in the distance. A slow sign of panic crossed Jodee's face, and Toni could tell she was trying harder and harder to focus.

As soon as Toni reached out and took hold of her upper arm, Jodee came back to the room like Toni had pinched her instead of giving her arm a comforting squeeze. With a suddenness that shocked everyone, she said firmly, "Alexis Jane, stop. I will get it finished in time. I promise. Dayla, for the last time, I said no!"

Toni had never seen anyone change so quickly. It startled and confused her in equal measure. She let go of Jodee's arm and stepped back.

Lexie stepped toward her mother, reaching for the dress. "Mother, what happened to you? Your eyes were all glassy."

"Nothing," Jodee lied. "I'm just getting a headache." Her feigned bravado was a façade and Toni knew it.

"Seriously, Mom, that was totally spooky." Lexie was gathering her dress off the floor, more concerned for the dress than her mother's strange behavior.

Jodee blinked some more with a quickness that made her look like an old-fashioned flirt. Standing with arms crossed in front of her, Dayla said in disgust, "Oh gawd, Mom, stop blinking. You have no idea how dumb it makes you look."

"Dayla, for all that's holy, will you shut up!" Lexie screamed at her sister.

Toni watched as the fighting continued, concentrating on Jodee and seeing her react like she had never lost track of the moments.

"I don't have to. And I'm going to Amanda's. I'm not falling for whatever mind game Mom is playing," Dayla replied apathetically.

"I don't think she's playing," Lexie said.

"Whatever."

"Dayla Louise, go to your room," Jodee ordered. Turning her head she looked at Toni with a mix of humiliation and embarrassment.

Toni tried to cover the awkwardness by smiling compassionately. Before she could form a reply, she was halted mid-step by Dayla's final words as she stomped from the room.

"Oh! You're the meanest mom ever! I hate you!" A bedroom door slammed a few seconds later.

Dayla's words reverberated around the room like a sledgehammer against a bell. Toni heard Jodee gasp and watched the apparent shock and hurt cross her face like a dark cloud.

Jodee stood still and stared at Toni as if silently apologizing. When she spoke, it was in a whisper. "She's never said that to me before. Even when she was smaller and threw temper tantrums."

Toni knew kids always said they hated their parents, but they never meant it. But the force behind Dayla's words had been powerful and she could feel Jodee's devastation because her eyes were brimming with unshed tears. Toni had the feeling that Jodee had actually believed the thirteen-year-old.

"She didn't mean it, honey."

"Oh, please, mother. Dayla is such a brat. Don't be so sensitive. You know she didn't mean it." Lexie was trying with little success to free the upper part of her dress Jodee still had a death grip on.

Toni stepped over to Jodee and hugged her around the shoulders.

Lexie was pleading, "Mom, please let go of the dress."

The front door banged open as Doug came in with Archer in tow. Walking with purposeful strides across the living room into the kitchen, he took in the scene with blistering eyes.

"What the heck is going on in here? We can hear the yelling from the front yard!"

Everyone turned toward the loud booming voice as the two men stood in the archway to the kitchen.

Jodee jumped back from Toni's touch as if it stung.

With a quickness that surprised Toni, Lexie ran to Doug.

"Daddy, prom is tonight and my dress doesn't fit." She had turned into a whining daddy-I-need-you spoiled child right before Toni's eyes.

"Lexie." He opened his arms and folded her into a hug, ever the doting father. "Don't worry, honey, I'm sure we can do something about it."

While Doug was catering to Lexie, Toni whispered to Jodee. "Jodee, are you all right?"

Jodee simply stood rooted to the spot looking at Toni, blinking heavily, like she was trying to clear smoke from her eyes.

Archer, going around Doug and Lexie, walked shyly into the kitchen. "Hello, Jodee. It's nice to see you." He stood looking at her with his hands in the back pockets of his jeans.

Toni stayed focused on Jodee, not seeing the look on Archer's face as he continued to stare at her.

Wringing her hands tightly, Jodee gave a shy glimpse up at Archer.

"Hi, Archer." Stumbling a little, Jodee confessed, "I'm so embarrassed you had to hear any of this."

Toni gave a quick glance at Archer while also trying to take in the dynamics of Doug and Lexie.

Releasing Lexie, Doug walked a few feet further into the kitchen to stand next to Archer.

"Now, Jodee, what the heck is going on in here?" He addressed her with his hands on his hips and the tone of a school principal in disciplinary mode.

Before Jodee could explain, Dayla came out of her room at a run, adding to the cacophony in the kitchen. "Daddy, you're home!" She ran up behind him and wrapped her arms around his waist. "I thought I heard you come in."

As if nothing out of the norm had happened, Toni watched Jodee go from the confused hurt mother to the responsible wife in a matter of seconds. Taking a step back against the counter, she could do nothing but watch. Jodee's transformation had her furrowing her forehead until two deep lines formed between her eyebrows.

"Oh, it's just been one of those mornings," Jodee explained calmly. "Prom is tonight, and Lexie and Audra need to get to the hair salon, I'm working on Lexie's dress, the workmen are outside putting Dougie's birthday present together. You know, the usual chaos." Her nonchalant words did not match the shadow behind her eyes.

"Daddy, Mom won't let me go to Amanda's." Dayla buried her face into her father's back as she continued to squeeze him around the middle.

Trying to extract himself from Dayla's hold, Doug gave Toni a cursory greeting as if he'd just noticed her. "Oh, hi, Toni."

"Hello, Doug." She'd always liked Doug but there was something about him she couldn't put her finger on, not unlike a puzzle where a couple of major pieces were missing and she couldn't see the full picture without them.

Looking down over his shoulder at Dayla as he tugged at her arms, Doug asked, "Now, what's this? Mom won't let you go to Amanda's?"

Whining like a two year old, Dayla pouted out her lower lip, "Nooo."

"I told her she'd been spending enough time at Amanda's like we talked about," Jodee said.

Watching Archer from the corner of his eye, Doug said, "I never said any such thing. Really, Jodee, I don't know where you get these things. Of course, you can go to Amanda's, Dayla. I don't know where your mother gets these ideas."

A look of betrayal crossed Jodee's face and Toni watched her slip inside herself again. Toni stood in place, observing, and began to believe she could actually see Jodee crumble by the way she curled ever so slightly toward her center, like a blowup doll slowly deflating.

Realizing she was being watched, Jodee gave Toni a dismissive glance and turned toward the countertop in the pretense of staying busy. It was then that Dayla added to Jodee's mental wound.

"I knew you wouldn't be as mean as Mom, Daddy. Thank you, thank you. I'm going to call her now." She ran out of the kitchen to the phone in the living room.

"Jodee, you've really got to stop being so strict with the girls." Turning to Archer he added with a shake of his head. "Women? Right, Archer?" It wasn't really a question. "I swear I have to keep an eye on her every minute."

Archer simply looked at Doug without responding.

Toni watched the exchange between man and wife and her confusion deepened. It was a side of Doug she'd never seen before, his purposeful attempt to undermine Jodee. Maybe she was just tired and was reading something into the situation that wasn't there because Jodee continued to act as if everything was normal.

Giving Archer a slight pat on the shoulder, Doug said, "Come on out back, Archer, and let me show you what we bought Dougie J for his birthday tomorrow."

On his way out the door, Doug turned, "Oh, by-the-way, Jodee, Archer will be staying for dinner."

"That is if it's okay with you, Jodee?" Archer politely inquired.

"Oh, uh, of course. That's fine," Jodee replied without turning around, never taking her eyes off of the cabinet while she rummaged around as if looking for something she couldn't find.

"Of course it's not a problem. She's happy to have you." Doug responded quickly, blocking Jodee's right to the respect she was entitled to as his wife. "Now, come on out back and take a look."

The two men disappeared out the door into the back yard as Archer gave Jodee one last quick glance.

"Jodee, I can see you're really busy and I'm gonna go." Toni wasn't sure if leaving was the right thing to do.

Jodee gave a polite "bye" to her friend with a nod of the head. Toni saw the little smile Jodee gave her but the haunted look behind her eyes contradicted it.

Toni walked through the living room heading for the front door and caught one last trailing remark from Lexie to her mother as she stepped aside to let Lexie leave ahead of her.

"Mom, I'm taking my dress to Allison's. I'd rather have her mom work on it." Lexie turned sharply and walked out the front door ahead of Toni. She carried her pink formal like it was a fragile child.

At the same time, Dayla's conversation with Amanda over the phone was a snippet of mangled words that Toni caught out of the corner of her ear. She was sure Jodee could hear them as well since it was apparent Dayla was purposefully talking louder than need be.

"Yeah, I'll be over soon... My brother's birthday... Oh, they always give him whatever he wants cause he's the baby... I don't care about any stupid playset... My birthday? A necklace, whatever... I don't care, he's mom's favorite... I wish I had your mom... Nah... Who cares... Okay, see you soon."

Dayla hung up and ran around Toni behind her sister.

Just as Toni moved to follow the two girls out of the house, she heard Dougie J from the kitchen, "It's okay, Mommy. I love you."

Touched by this little boy's sensitivity, Toni leaned slightly to the left and looked at the scene in the other room. She watched as Dougie J put his tiny arms around his mother's hips.

He looked up and saw his mom looking down at him. He then reached behind him and pulled something out of his back pocket and handed it up to Jodee. It was one of the little dolls he had shown Toni earlier. "Here, you can hold Tinker Bell if you want. She'll make you feel better."

Toni heard Jodee say, "Oh, thank you, honey, I think that would really help." Taking the small doll, Jodee studied the little fairy with her green dress and yellow hair like she'd never seen it before.

Ashamed at herself for spying, Toni turned to quietly exit the house. Turning back one last time to make sure she hadn't been seen, she saw Dougie J run out the backdoor as she saw Jodee squeeze the Tinker Bell doll and hold it to her heart as if it was the greatest gift she'd ever received.

Puzzled, Toni left the house and softly closed the door behind her. Am I just really tired, she wondered, or is something terribly out of proportion in the Warren household?

It was a question that would haunt her over the weeks to come.

CHAPTER TEN

HUMILIATION

"Douglas Junior, don't you dare go outside and get dirty. We have to leave for the church in fifteen minutes." Jodee was putting the final touches on her makeup as she stood facing the mirror.

"I'm just gonna get my sword, Mom!" Dougie yelled, already heading for the backyard.

"Doug, can you please explain to your son he can't take a sword to the church?" she yelled from their open bedroom door.

Straightening his tie in the foyer's mirror, Doug absently responded to Jodee's plea. "Dougie, buddy, you're not going to be able to play with the sword today. We're going to your Uncle Robert's wedding, remember? You're going to be carrying a pillow with their rings on it and that's going to be much more fun. Why don't you go see if your sisters are ready to go?"

"Ahhh." Dougie stomped back into the kitchen and down the hall yelling. "Audie, Lexie, Dayla! Come on, Dad says it's time to go!"

"Dougie J, stop yelling, we're coming," Dayla screamed back, walking into the room followed by her sisters.

"Girls, don't you look nice," Doug said mechanically. "Where's your mother?"

"She's still in your room," Audra said.

"Take your brother and go get in the car. We'll be there in a minute," Doug ordered.

As her girls started gathering purses and sweaters and their little brother to head for the car as they'd been told, Jodee walked into the room wearing a peach, V-neck, knee length, sleeveless shift with a complimentary belt, cream pumps and a fashionable rollup brim hat with a matching floral band. The color of the dress offset her eyes and favored her coloring. She looked like spring personified. She was lovely.

Catching Audra as she walked to the kitchen with Dougie J in tow, Jodee off-handedly asked, "Audra, don't you think that sweater is going to be too hot for today?"

"Oh, no, no not really. I think I heard it might get cold later in the day." Audra gripped Dougie J's hand a little tighter and all but ran to the garage.

Jodee gave her daughter a small smirk, knowing this to be a lie, but distracted by the chaos of getting to the church on time, she didn't have time to reason Audra's choice. Ever since the night of the prom when Travis had been two hours late to pick her up, embarrassing her, Audra had tiptoed around her parents, refusing to talk. This simple lie about the weather had been the most words she had said in three weeks.

Doug interrupted Jodee's thoughts as he tugged on his suit jacket. "Make sure your brother is buckled up."

"Okay, Dad," Lexie answered as she, too, headed for the garage through the kitchen.

Doug waited until the last of his kids were in the garage before he turned to Jodee. With an appraising glare he asked her, "Jodee, what is on your head?"

Straightening the hat on her head in the hall mirror, she offhandedly answered, "It's a hat. Why?"

"I know it's a hat." His sarcasm caught her attention. "I want to know what makes you think you should wear it?"

"It's a spring wedding and I thought it went nice with the dress." The subtle halting of her arms adjusting the hat contradicted her confidence when she answered.

"You look like an old lady going to church."

"But hats are really in this spring."

"Jodee, hats haven't been in since the turn of the century. And even if they are, some women just can't pull them off and I'm afraid you're one of them."

The look in Jodee's eyes betrayed her hurt. "It cost quite a bit of money. I'd hate not to wear it," she stammered.

"Just take it back to the store next week, but you need to take it off because we've got to get going." Doug turned and headed for the car, not noticing the wounded look in his wife's eyes.

"And you'd better hope they take it back because it's coming out of your clothing allowance."

Jodee regretfully, but obediently, removed the hat. She had saved three months of her clothing allowance to buy her outfit for the wedding. The hat had cost a third of it. Doug had always estimated what he felt she needed for clothes and controlled her monthly budget with a firm hand. When she had found the hat, she'd had to forego a new pair of shoes because she was too afraid to ask Doug for more money. Whenever she had asked him for additional money in the past, he would lecture her for days on her frivolousness. Once he'd even chastised her in a department store for squandering his income. She'd been mortified when the reprimand had gotten heated enough to catch the attention of the store security guard, but Doug had convinced the man that he was simply having to put the 'little woman in her place.' With a wink and a nod of understanding, the guard had let them pass. She had put back the twenty-dollar pair of gloves she'd wanted for winter and slid out the door behind Doug in total humiliation.

Now, with a final look at the pretty little hat, and giving one final touch to the soft brim, she turned and followed her husband out the door in her new peach dress, her two year old pumps, and her out-of-date purse.

Robert Lee was the youngest of the Warren brothers and it was his wedding day. His wife to be, Marcy Ottoson, was a beauty four years his senior and happened to be the same age as his sister-in-law, Jodee.

The wedding was sophisticated and subdued in the local Lutheran church. The reception was held in the very large yard of the country club, with a party tent serving as shelter for dinner and dancing. At four in the afternoon, with the lights already lit up to welcome in the evening activities, the day had turned out to be unusually warm for a Minnesota spring. The crisp air helped awaken the early flowers and a warm easy breeze soothed the heat from the sun as it slid down the individual bodies of guests.

Doug and Jodee roamed the landscaped lawns, cheerfully greeting the guests. Since Doug had been a groomsman, he'd not had time before the wedding to talk to anyone. Feeling it was his duty as the oldest brother he walked around with an air of privilege, shaking hands and kissing babies like a politician in the middle of a campaign.

"Jodee, Doug, wasn't it a beautiful wedding?" Brigid greeted them enthusiastically as she walked over to them, holding her glass of champagne high in a toast.

"Brigid, I'm so glad you could make it." Doug greeted her with an embrace that was held a little too tightly and a little too long. In usual fashion, Jodee ignored the display by taking a sip of champagne and turned to scan the crowd.

Brigid slid smoothly from his grasp with just enough body contact to hint at flirting. "It was so nice of your parents to invite our whole family."

"Nonsense," Doug said. "Family is family."

"Well, I'll have to thank them all the same. Wasn't it a gorgeous wedding?"

"Yes, yes it was. And don't you look stunning," Doug was barely on this side of appropriate as he looked her up and down. She was wearing a two-piece light wool pink suit with a herringbone pattern. The skirt was a mid-calf pencil skirt that complimented her thin calves. The look was set off by a cream-colored felt porkpie hat with a black band perched above a stylish ponytail.

"Thank you, thank you," Brigid said jauntily. "And you're not so bad yourself."

"The hat really compliments your face. You know, I don't know why more women don't wear hats." Doug's slurred compliment was being helped along by three glasses of champagne and one large double scotch.

Jodee, aware of the exchange between her husband and her sister, pretended not to notice by continuing to casually nod at passing guests. Doug's last statement, however, had her looking over suddenly, hurt and confusion apparent in her eyes.

"I so agree," Brigid said with a wave of her hand. "But a lot of women just are not up with the current trends."

Looking at her sister, Brigid saw the confused look on her face. "What's the matter, Jo-Jo?"

Using the pet name she'd always called her sister. "Don't you like my hat? You know, if you had come to the mall I could have helped you find one that matched your dress, too."

Jodee was too upset to answer as Doug swayed on his feet,

oblivious to her stare.

Noticing the exchange between husband and wife, Brigid said in her usual unabashed style, "Well, we can't all outshine the bride, now can we?" Brigid had a unique talent for always being able to bring the conversation back to herself, no matter the topic being discussed. It was her main mission in life to be the center of attention. Being told as a small child she was pretty – first by her parents, then her grandparents, and then verified by the many boyfriends and dates she'd always had – Brigid had always believed it. In her heart of hearts, she believed other women envied her and all men wanted her. She wore this trait in her personality like a warm fur, cloaked in pretension and accepted it without the self-consciousness that might attack a more modest woman. So without the bothersome energy of expending humility, she accepted her brother-in-law's flirting as just another day of being admired.

"I'm sorry, I, uh, yes, I like your hat. I had a hat I was going to wear, but…" Uncharacteristically Jodee started slowly, yet defiantly, to explain the situation when she was interrupted from behind.

"Hello, everyone." Archer had stepped to Jodee's side, brushing her arm lightly with his sleeve.

"Archer, buddy, how you doing?" Doug slurred as he took a whiskey sour from the passing waiter.

"Good. Good. It was a nice ceremony, wasn't it?"

"Yes, it was. Did you get a drink, or maybe three?" joked Doug.

"Yeah, but I'm sticking to beer. I've got a game tomorrow." Turning to Jodee he said, "Jodee, you look very pretty today."

"Thank you, Archer. You look very handsome yourself."

"I wanted to thank you again for dinner the other night. It

was very good." He was engrossed in how the sun kissed her shoulders, making them look particularly soft and glowing.

"It's my pleasure. You know you're always welcome."

Brigid eyed Archer with bedroom eyes so obvious, it would have had to have been censored for children. He was the true reason why she had come to the wedding alone. Becoming impatient for him to notice her, she started pursing her lips in a pout that rivaled Marilyn Monroe.

Archer, unaware of his slight, continued to focus on Jodee. "Well, I very much appreciate it none the less. Particularly now. To tell you the truth, I needed this day with friends."

"Don't be silly, Archer. You're family, you know that."

Archer showed appreciation for her comment with a slight tilt of his smile as he stood in his habitual stance with his hands in his pockets, staring at her.

Jodee, uncomfortable with his stare, looked down at the drink in her hand.

Brigid, loudly sighing at being ignored, glided over to Archer's side. Like a hungry cat sliding between its owner's legs, she cunningly grabbed his attention by hooking her arm through the crook of his, making sure her breast brushed his forearm, and all but purred, "Archer, aren't you even going to say hello?"

A slight reddening of his face betrayed his embarrassment of not noticing Jodee's younger sister. He looked down with a sincere apology. "Oh, Brigid, I didn't see you standing there. I'm sorry. How are you?"

Truly confused at his admission, Brigid cocked her head back like she'd never conceived of such a thing. Stammering slightly, she replied, "Fine, thank you." Whether it was a form of punishment for him ignoring her, or true interest in his well-being couldn't be determined when she said, "I'm so sorry to hear about your divorce."

Bringing up his divorce on a day that had already reminded him of his own failed marriage made Archer square his shoulders. "Uh, well, I guess sometimes things just don't work out like you'd hope," he replied as he subtly tried to extract himself from her arm by standing straighter and pulling his arm close to his side.

"I totally agree, but you know you'll always have friends you can come to if you need to." Brigid held onto his arm like a weed with burrs. Her innuendo was becoming embarrassingly obvious as she then grabbed his hand and held it between her breasts so tightly her cleavage sandwiched his pinkie finger.

Jodee could feel Archer's ire rising, which seemed to be completely missed by Brigid as she continued to ramble on about friends of hers who had also divorced. Wanting to diffuse the situation before Archer lost his temper altogether, Jodee interrupted Brigid, "Um, would anyone like something to drink? The waiter is heading in the opposite direction if you do."

Pulling his hand from Brigid's stronghold, Archer turned to Jodee. "Jodee, your drink is empty. Let me get you something." He turned from the group so quickly, he practically ran in the opposite direction, forgetting to ask Brigid or Doug if they needed a drink too.

Archer's quick exit and dismissal of her had Brigid refocusing her attention on her sister. Staring at Jodee like she was studying a bug under a microscope, her mental analysis quietly popped from her mouth unheeded, "It's because you're blonde."

Before Jodee could ask Brigid what she meant by her remark, the head caterer stepped up to the front of the tent and announced dinner was being served.

Within the short hour between the ceremony and being seated for dinner, Doug had had enough drinks to heighten his already limited inhibitions. He was feeling every ounce of the alcohol that coursed through his bloodstream. He put his arms around the waist of Jodee and Brigid and half guided, half stumbled his way to their reserved tables.

Since he and his brother, Bill, were groomsmen, the tables directly in front of the head table were reserved for them and their families. Each round table held eight guests. The bride and groom, their parents, the maid of honor and best man, the bride and groom's best friends, were also seated at the main table at the front of the large white tent.

As the oldest brother, Doug purposely took the seat closest to the head table facing the guests so that everyone could see him when he gave the toast he felt was his right to give.

Doug and Jodee were joined by Dougie J, and Bill's family. Audra, Lexie, and Dayla had been seated with their Grandpa and Grandma Olson at the next table with Aunt Brigid and their Aunt Nora's family, who had to be squeezed in with a couple of extra chairs.

Drinks continued to be handed out by the bar staff on silver trays during dinner and Doug snagged one with every passing. His face had become a blotchy red and his words were showing signs of a heavy tongue.

Dinner was proceeding festively with talk of the dresses and flowers and songs when Nora decided she needed to play mother to her niece who seemed to be flush from the heat.

She reached her arm around Audra's shoulders and asked, "Sweetie, it is so warm, why don't you take off that sweater?"

The touch of her aunt's arm at the base of her neck had Audra flinching. Her sudden movement startled Nora and caught

Jodee's attention.

"Audra, honey, what's wrong? Did I hurt you or something?"

Jodee stared at her daughter, waiting for an answer. Her fear of what she suspected had alarm building at her feet and working its way up her body in a cold chill.

"Oh, no, it's nothing. I just slept wrong and have a crick in my neck, that's all. It's kind-of tender. I get one all the time. I think my pillow is too old or something. I thought if I left my sweater on the heat will help it, you know? I just need to stretch it." Her overly excessive explanation only made her lie more obvious to her mother.

Jodee couldn't stand her daughter's constant excuses any more. With unaccustomed force, she was determined to get to the bottom of her daughter's strange behavior once and for all. As she pushed back her chair to stand so she could walk the four feet to Audra's side, the soft tapping of a spoon on a wine glass next to her redirected her focus and she slowly sat back down.

It was Doug. "Ladies and gentlemen," he began as he stood with a slight wobble. "I'd like your attention, please." His voice was firm with an apparent slur as he concentrated on each syllable. He dragged each word out as if he were trying to overcome a lisp. The alcohol had taken its toll on his senses. The audience slowly quieted down, and all heads turned his way.

He continued, "I'd like to…to congratulate the wedding, uh, I mean the new couple and welcome Marcy, into, uh, the family. Look at this be-u-tee-ful couple. Are they not great together?" The crowd turned their faces to Rob and Marcy with smiles as Doug kept speaking. "Marriage is a sacred constitution; oh sorry, I mean institution." He chuckled.

The crowd shared his mishap with nervous laughter.

He took a second to gain his composure and get control of

his tongue by hiding his drunkenness with a sip from his water glass. It was a trait of Doug's to never appear out of control or vulnerable. Setting down the glass, he tugged on the vest of his tux, and like some magical force pulled himself together with the will of strength uncommon for someone with so much alcohol in his system.

"As everyone who knows me knows I've been married for a lonnng time, over twenty years in fact. Feels more like fifty, right honey?" He turned his glass to Jodee with a laugh. The crowd laughed with him.

Jodee looked up as Doug turned toward her, unsure of what her response should be but hearing the laughter around her, she smiled uneasily.

Feeling he had the full attention of the audience, he turned back to the bride and groom with a glass of champagne in his hand. "Marriage is a challenge. It's something you have to work on daily. To me, it's like the meeting of two cultures coming together to form a village. A village with children, responsibilities, traditions, and laws. Homes that need to be built, farms with seeds that need to be planted, and a new unified culture that needs to be cultivated."

The crowd was enthralled by his metaphors and the more experienced couples nodded their heads in agreement.

Feeling especially proud of himself, he preached, "Sometimes, the two cultures that meet are equal in their experience, intelligence, and politics. These are the villages that succeed and thrive. Looking at my brother and his new wife, I believe that they have just such unification..."

There were ahs from the crowd and a light applause.

"...I want you to know how happy I am you have found each other. Looking at your new bride though, I can see that there will not need to be much cultivating for you, Rob. She is beautiful, and intelligent. I envy you your success in your choice of a wife."

Rob raised his glass in salute to his new wife.

Marcy gave a slight nod of her head to Doug as a thank you.

"It's something not all of us find in a wife," Doug said pointedly.

Some of the crowd turned their attention to Jodee while others were simply focused on the speech and its meaning for the new couple.

Jodee sat with a smile plastered on her face, seeing the stares from the corner of her eyes and growing more uncomfortable with each word, not sure what direction Doug's speech was going.

"When I married Jodee, well, you could say it was like the Roman Empire making an alliance with Nebraska. She was very young and inexperienced. I didn't even give her a chance to finish her education but wanting her all to myself." He smiled broadly and the crowd followed his lead.

"Yes, I've had to groom her over the years since she was not blessed with her sister's brain." He looked at Nora with a raised glass and she returned the compliment with her own. "And I may not have gotten the pick of the litter when it came to looks." He then turned his attention to Brigid. Brigid beamed with knowing superiority.

Jodee's stomach was beginning to drop and the old feeling of dread was slowly sneaking up her backbone. She blinked rapidly a couple of times. Those looking her way gave uncomfortable chuckles and looks.

To keep from having tears form in her eyes, Jodee batted them and looked down coyly. This movement was misinterpreted by the crowd thinking she was in on the toast, and it eased their momentary apprehension.

Doug's speech seemed unending. "...But all-in-all, she's been a good child bearer and has helped me build my village with strong, healthy children and a solid foundation."

Not knowing what else to do, Jodee looked up, plastered a fake smile on her mouth and sat frozen in place, keeping her hands folded in her lap and her back straight. She looked up and watched Doug finish his speech, but her eyes were blinded by humiliation.

"...So, let us all raise our glass to the new couple and wish them a solid foundation while they build their own little village and sow their own seeds, so to speak." Doug laughed as he raised his glass.

The crowd all lifted their glasses in salute.

Just as everyone was finishing their drinks, Doug added one more stone to Jodee's stomach.

"Oh, and Marcy, do me a favor would you? Don't go to seed like my wife, it makes it hard to want to plow the fields, if you know what I mean."

While everyone applauded and laughed, Doug stepped forward and hugged his brother and new sister-in-law. As he walked back to his seat, the older gentlemen patted him on the back with mock understanding of the speech they were convinced was all in good fun as their wives playfully swatted their husband's arms.

Jodee sat drowning in embarrassment, knowing Doug's speech was not in jest. She gave a mechanical smile to those who were congratulating her on how clever her husband was. She turned stiffly in her chair, trying to hide the pain.

Not sure how to react, her eyes slowly roamed the crowd while she tried to keep them from their intermittent blinking. She found Audra staring at her with open humiliation. She looked at Lexie who was looking down at her plate and pushing the food back and forth with her fork like it was the enemy. Dayla simply looked confused, not sure why some people were laughing but her sisters seemed angry.

Jodee gave her daughters a shaky smile and continued to discreetly look around the tables when her eyes fell on Archer, who looked fit to kill. She was confused by his reaction. Was he angry at her for her inept ability of being a satisfying wife to his best friend?

Then, with painful trepidation, Jodee's eyes fell on her mother's face. It had turned a sickly paleness and her eyes were downcast, as if she were too ashamed to look at anyone.

Slowly and reluctantly, like a child preparing herself for punishment, Jodee looked at her father. He did not have the same reaction as her mother. He did not hide from the shame he felt for her. He simply looked at her with contempt in his eyes and nodded in understanding, as if to say, "I knew Doug was embarrassed of you, girl."

Jodee stared at her father but really didn't see him. Her blinking had returned with renewed force and her breathing became labored. An odd sensation came over her as she watched her father slowly fade into a cloud – a dark cloud that had engulfed his head and was working itself down his body in misty calmness.

The cloud mesmerized her, and she felt herself begin to float. The familiar tingling sensation in her face and hands started to elevate with her body. She knew if she just let herself go, she'd be able to float above the crowd and disappear. It seemed like such a nice thing to do. She started to let her mind go to see how far she'd fly when a strong, gentle hand cemented her in place.

"Well, look who I found under our table?" The Colonel said as he touched Jodee on the shoulder with one hand as his other hand held Dougie J's.

Jodee could hear her father-in-law speaking but it seemed as if he were talking to her from another room, distant and quiet.

"Mommy, I was playing submarine." Dougie J looked up at his grandfather with a smile.

Dougie J. Her son. Her son was talking to her, but his voice sounded muffled like she had cotton in her ears. She looked at him and forced herself to concentrate on his words while she stared at his mouth.

The Colonel squeezed her shoulder and his touch was warm and comforting, seeming to ground her.

"Grandpa said it was okay." His little face had a look of concern on it as he watched his mother's eyes look at him as if she didn't quite recognize him.

"Yes, I did. All little boys should have a submarine all their own."

Jodee looked up at the Colonel and saw his eyes were filled with a kind of softness she didn't understand. She looked at Dougie J, confused to why his face was so close but his voice seemed so far away. Was she already too far above the ground? she wondered. If so, how could she feel the Colonel's hand on her shoulder?

Her mind was swirling trying to make sense of her surroundings.

"Jodee, are you all right, dear?" The Colonel asked sympathetically when she hadn't responded to Dougie's excited playfulness.

"What?" She looked up into the Colonel's face. Her eyes blinking rapidly. She felt herself slowly floating down. Her body returning to the solid foundation of her chair.

"Jodee, dear, don't you worry about that ridiculous speech of Doug's. We all know he has a bad sense of humor when he's been drinking. As far as I'm concerned, you are the pick of any litter."

He knows. This sweet, sweet man understands, she thought as her mind became one with her body again.

How she loved her father-in-law. He always made her feel beautiful – and worthy.

"Mommy." Dougie J let go of his grandfather's hand and threw his tiny arms around his mother's neck. "Mommy, I love you. You're the best mommy in the world."

"Well, of course she is," he confirmed as he smiled down at his grandson. "Don't you worry, Jodee, dear." The Colonel turned his attention back to her. "I'll have a talk with him." He tried to soothe the wounds he'd seen in her eyes.

"Oh, no, no that's all right, Colonel," Jodee replied as she hugged Dougie around his middle. "I'm all right. Really, I am. I know he was joking," she lied. "All I need is a hug from my two favorite men." She reached over and squeezed the Colonel's hand.

Dougie J turned his head and kissed Jodee on the cheek.

The Colonel watched mother and son for a moment then nodded and walked away.

Jodee continued to hold her son like a lifeline that kept her tethered to Earth. She looked past her tiny son's shoulder, out the opening of the tent and into the fading blue of the sky – that sky that beckoned her. She yearned for that freedom.

No, she chided herself. She couldn't be tempted by the freedom the feeling offered her. Her son needed her.

So, she simply stared at the clouds that floated slowly past in the distance and sat Dougie J in her lap with her arms around his middle. In a few seconds, the feeling of his breathing against her chest calmed her yearnings. She was fully back in the reality of the moment and things were going to be okay, she reminded herself, but still feeling she had almost made it – made it past the ugliness to freedom. But not now. Later, she thought. When her children no longer needed her. So, she would wait.

CHAPTER ELEVEN

CONTROL

"But, Doug, I told you the hat was expensive. That was why I wanted to wear it so badly," Jodee pleaded.

"Yeah, well I didn't know it was that expensive. You're just going to have to take it back." Doug was flipping the credit card statement from front to back as if the numbers would change before his eyes like magic if he did it hard enough.

"It's been beyond the thirty days. I don't know if they'll take it back."

"Then it's definitely coming out of your clothing allowance. I was thinking of letting you keep it out of the goodness of my heart, but not now. I think you manipulated this whole thing. Waiting past the grace period so you'd get to keep it. Well, just consider it your birthday present."

His logic was so convoluted she couldn't follow it. If she had to pay for it out of her clothing budget, then how could he make it a birthday present? It would be like she was buying her own present. On top of that, her birthday was still months away.

"I swear, Jodee, you can spend money faster than anyone I know."

Doug's remark was cut short as Dougie J bounded into the kitchen from the backyard. Doug tamped down his temper with the sight of his son and his demeanor changed so fast it always astounded Jodee how he could do it. It was like watching a barking bulldog become a mewing kitten in a heartbeat. It was also the only time Doug watched what he said to his wife. If one of their children ever did catch them having words, Doug wanted to make sure it looked like it was never his fault but that he was the one taking the metaphorical beating.

"Hey, buddy, having fun outside?" Doug's tone was easy-going and playful.

"Uh-huh," he responded timidly, looking between parents. "Mom, I'm hungry," he said. "Can I have a peanut butter sandwich?"

Turning quickly so her son couldn't see the distress in her eyes, knowing she couldn't turn her emotions off as quickly as Doug could, she pretended to be looking for something in a utensil drawer. "But you know Audra is going to watch you tonight so your Daddy and I can go out, and you're going to get to order pizza and have breadsticks? How about an apple?"

"I just want a little sandwich and apples make me more hungry," he begged.

"For God's sake, Jodee, give the kid a sandwich," Doug snapped.

Jodee flinched at Doug's unaccustomed tone of voice in front of Dougie J.

Dougie J gave his dad a quick, fearful look, startled by his tone.

In order to continue to be the reasonable parent in his son's eyes, Doug bent down to Dougie's level. Cradling the invoices and budget book in his arms, he calmly said, "Hey, kiddo, you eat your sandwich and maybe before your mom and I have to leave, we'll play catch. Okay?"

"'Kay," Dougie J answered.

"Fine. Let me get these things put away, you eat, and I'll meet you in the backyard." He stood up and without looking in Jodee's direction, headed for the home office.

Half an hour later Doug walked into the bedroom as Jodee stepped out of the shower.

"I want you to wear the navy blue dress," he stated definitively as he rummaged in his closet for his suit.

"But Doug, that dress is wool. It will be too hot for tonight."

"Jodee, do we have to do this every time we go out? I'm wearing my brown suit and your blue dress will go better with the tie I'm wearing. Besides, you know you look best in blue."

His compliments always caught Jodee by surprise. They were so infrequent she lapped them up, the same way a dying man would lap up muddy water from a hole in the desert.

Hoping his playing with Dougie J had soothed his mood, she was willing to do anything to keep him calm, even if it meant sweating throughout a dinner.

"Really? You think so? If you really think it looks best on me then I will wear it. If it gets too hot, I'll just stand under the ceiling fan or something."

"That's a good girl. You just leave it to me; I know what looks best on you. This evening is important to me and I want to make sure you dress the part since you know you don't have the same sense of flair as your sister."

The insult was a little more subtle than his normal remarks, but still potent enough to have Jodee's mood sink to the bottom of her chest as quickly as water disappears into desert sand.

Jodee hated the annual employee appreciation dinners held every July. The food was always plentiful and delicious, but it also meant she had to spend the evening sitting through the boredom

148

of dry speeches and making small talk with other wives she hardly knew. She always felt they were judging her, and she always fell short. After arriving at the function, she decided to stay by Doug's side hoping she could avoid talking to them as long as possible.

As they stood around waiting for the dinner to commence, she tried hard to look interested in the ever-persistent shoptalk between Doug and his co-workers of prime rates, stock prices, and financial quotas. Fortunately, it only took half an hour of pretending to be engaged before the CFO approached the podium and announced over a microphone that dinner was being served and asked everyone to please find their seats. The crowd followed his instructions and found their assigned tables.

It took a few moments for Doug to locate the table where he and Jodee were to sit. He had automatically approached the table where his boss was sitting with the other upper executives. Assuming it was where their assigned seats would be, he was confused to instead find the name of Mark Wilkenson – a young up-and-comer as his boss had called him. Upon discovering where they were seated, which was at a table a row over, Doug's mood went from professional courtesy to ill-hidden resentment. And he aimed this resentment toward Jodee.

Twenty minutes into the dinner, the typical speeches for the evening began. Earlier than anyone expected and interrupting people eating their salads. Doug had been pushing the food around on his plate and tried to act as if the insult of sitting with people he considered his inferiors didn't affect him. Jodee tried to lighten his mood by commenting on trivial aspects of the party, but animosity leeched through his skin like sweat.

"Just look how beautiful the flowers are," she tried.

Doug murmured a response.

Next to Jodee a woman overly made up caught her attention. "I just love your dress. The color really suits you."

"Thank you. I thought it might be too warm but fortunately they've got the air conditioner just right."

"They always have the room too cold in here every year. I know they want to accommodate the massive body heat this party stirs up, but every year I have to bring a wrap."

Another woman across from the made-up matron decided to join in. "Last year I actually had to borrow my husband's suit jacket."

"Well, I guess it was good I wore wool then because I honestly can't remember it being cold last year," Jodee laughed.

The three women talked and laughed and Jodee found herself having a really good time, forgetting Doug's sour disposition and the reason behind it.

At one point, one of the women leaned forward to address Doug. "Are you having a good time, Mr. Warren?"

Doing all but completely ignoring her, he groaned out an obligatory response gruffly, looking over her head in a form of deliberate dismissal as he said, "Yes, it's fine."

The woman's eyes took on a look of confusion and insult as she jerked her head back like a surprised chicken. "Well!" she said under her breath.

Jodee was never so happy to have the conversation interrupted as the bank president took the podium and made a polite request for silence. He proceeded to give the welcoming introduction and congratulatory comments expected of him. He thanked everyone on a successful year, announced that the evening was meant to be spent enjoying the successes of the individual departments, and for the managers – at least for the evening – to ignore the current economic downturn and the effects it could have on their business.

The underlying meaning was obvious to only the managers who knew that their promotions were directly linked to the success of their departments. The year had proved to be particularly difficult for some since their financial goals had not been met. They tried to pretend the night wasn't about the bottom line, but the not-so-sly remark by the president and sideways looks between department heads made the individual department managers nervous.

Doug's face took on an ashen pallor, but Jodee, trying desperately to ignore the obvious competitiveness between the managers, returned to the camaraderie of her new friends. As the bank president sat back down, giving the party a short break before the next speaker, Jodee nibbled on the last of the green beans on her plate.

"You know, this is a really good meal this year. Don't you think so?" she asked Doug, hoping to diffuse his obvious ire.

"Yeah, yeah, sure." His dismissal of her wasn't lost on Jodee.

"You're not eating your beans, though. Don't you like them?"

"I do. I'm just taking my time," he responded as he once again looked over at the head table.

"They're coming around to pick up the plates. You should try and finish."

"I will, I will," he said ignoring his fellow tablemates.

Jodee set her fork down and turned to see the wait staff picking up the plates at the next table. Leaning over slightly, Jodee said to Doug, "If you don't want your beans, can I have them?"

Turning abruptly back to Jodee, Doug snapped, "Leave my meal alone, I'll eat them when I'm ready. When you make the money in this family, then you can make the decision on the food. Understand?"

To make his point, he picked up his plate and over his right shoulder snapped his fingers at the waiter. "You can take my plate now." Wiping his mouth with his napkin, he put it on the table with a slap, turned in his seat with his back to Jodee, and feigned anticipation of the upcoming speeches. The green beans untouched on the plate.

Jodee turned back to the heavily made-up woman hoping no one had heard Doug's outburst and pretended his comment didn't cut her to the quick.

Throughout the endless array of speeches, Doug kept sneaking glances in the direction of his boss as he sat talking to the president and CFO, and the much younger, less experienced man sitting with them, Mark Wilkenson. The story was that Mark had a joint master's in finance and economics, but rumor had it he was the nephew of one of the executives in the home office. Whatever the reason didn't matter, someone had intentionally replaced Doug with Mark at the elite table. It was a deliberate snub to Doug, and to add insult to injury, he and Jodee had ended up sitting with people he didn't even know.

As dessert was handed out, Doug fumed more to himself than to Jodee but loud enough for her to hear him. "I'm going to find out who made up the seating assignments if it's the last thing I do."

Jodee cringed inside, knowing where the rest of the evening was going.

As the speeches wore on with the tediousness of a toothache, Jodee decided to make the best of what was left of the evening, knowing nothing she did would lighten Doug's mood. She tried to enjoy her dessert and coffee and not let the overbearing competitiveness of the people around her ruin one of the few nights out she got a year, even if it was this particular event. She would listen politely and applaud when necessary and ignore her husband's surliness with hopeful determination that it would all end soon.

As the long-winded executives finally decided they had spoken long enough, music started up and dishes were quickly being removed from the tables. Jodee turned her head to ask Doug if they were staying for the dancing when she watched his assistant walk up to them and stop behind Doug's chair.

"Hello, Mrs. Warren."

"Leona, hi. How are you?"

"Fine, thank you. Hi, Mr. Warren." Leona had adroitly slipped between the two chairs and situated herself between Doug and Jodee, slightly turning her back to Jodee.

Doug turned his head when he heard his name. Leona was standing so close to his side his face almost brushed her right breast when he turned to look up at her. The hint of roses wafted across the table whenever she moved.

"Hello, Leona."

"The music is starting up and I wondered if I could have the first dance with you?" She had a girlish little voice that always reminded Jodee of a twelve-year-old.

"I'm not much of a dancer, I'm afraid. I don't think I'd be able to keep up with you."

"Oh, come on Mr. Warren, it'll be fun. If you like, we can dance to something a little slower." The syrup in her voice was thick with innuendo.

Turning her head slightly to her left, Leona addressed Jodee over her shoulder, never taking her eyes off Doug. "You don't mind if I steal your husband from you do you Mrs. Warren?"

"No, of course not. Doug, you should dance. I'm going to get a glass of wine and I'll find you when the dance is over."

Downing the last of his red wine, Doug stood and with his hand at the base of her back, he escorted Leona to the dance floor where a large majority of people were already heading.

Leona was wearing a short, tight-fitting white capped-sleeve dress with an unusual amount of sequins that reminded Jodee of a dress out of a Vegas nightclub. The back had a diamond cutout that was so low that Doug's hand touched the bare skin at the curve right above her butt.

Jodee entered the ballroom with a glass of white wine a few moments later and spotted Doug and Leona dancing to a song by *Prince*. She stood against a wall drinking her wine and watched them dance. It felt good to have a moment to herself.

As the song finished, another one started up immediately on the last chord and Leona grabbed Doug by the arm as he started to walk off the dance floor. Jodee smiled at Doug's look of apprehension. Jodee thought it was good for him to dance. Besides, as long as Leona kept him dancing, he couldn't drink. Thinking of how he was such an unpleasant drunk made her shudder a little as she tried to keep her mind from dredging up the night of Rob and Marcy's wedding. She had to admit, there was a portion of the wedding she couldn't remember, but she did remember feeling disconnected and ashamed and the feeling had lasted for days.

Jodee watched Doug and Leona continue to dance as she let the anxiety of the green bean incident slide down her body along with the Pinot Grigio.

The young administrative assistant was a petite twenty-seven-year-old with thick hair the color of a rusty bucket and boobs that seemed equivalent to her IQ. She had gotten the job at the bank after getting an associate degree at the community college in some sort of administrative training. She had been Doug's assistant for just over a year and Jodee had gotten to know her from brief phone calls and company get-togethers like the one they were at tonight.

As Jodee watched Doug and Leona on the dance floor, she noticed with each sway of the music Leona's hips got a little closer to Doug, and Doug appeared to be a little less uncomfortable with each gyration. Strangely, Jodee didn't mind.

The wine was beginning to work its soothing effects on her system, and she decided to find a seat against a far wall to just sit and watch people dance. Deciding to sit next to a large potted Ficus that half hid her from the other guests, she sat and listened to the music, fascinated by the swirl of colored dresses of the women and the vibration from the music reverberating off the walls. She watched in silence and pretended she was camouflaged with the plant which kept her protected from the chaos of the scene.

With a relaxed calm, Jodee leaned her head against the wall and closed her eyes as she let the rhythms from the band float around her like frantic snowflakes. Her left arm lay across her stomach and supported her right hand that held her wine. The position was natural and comfortable. The warmth of her blue wool dress and the wine were beginning to engulf her in heat as if she were wrapped in a soft blanket, and the secluded spot in the room made her feel safe. In a few moments she drifted into a peaceful, welcomed nap with quick dreams darting in and out of her mind.

She woke with a sudden little jerk, just before her wine glass fell from her hand. She didn't know how long she'd been asleep, but the music had ended. The band was on a break and she looked up to see Doug surrounded by co-workers with what looked to be a Tequila Sunrise in his hand. She was worried he might have been looking for her, so she stood up from her chair to get a better look at his face. As she stood to survey the situation, Leona appeared at her side.

"Mrs. Warren, are you enjoying the party?" The question seemed to come out of her mouth in slow motion and Jodee could tell her speech was altered by what smelled like gin.

"Yes, thank you. Are you having fun?"

"Oh, yes. I just love parties and dancing. I'd dance every night if I could."

"You're still young enough that you should go out dancing as much as you can."

"Oh, I know, and I want to thank you for letting me dance with Mr. Warren all night. He's really better than he thinks he is."

"That's good to hear." Jodee was responding without really paying attention to the conversation.

"You know, everyone thinks he's just the best boss. He's always fair to everyone and never gets mad at anything. I mean, the other day, last Tuesday I think it was, we found out that our department hadn't met our yearly goal and it could affect everyone's raises, especially Mr. Warren's. We were all kind of worried and walking on eggshells all day, but you know, Mr. Warren didn't get mad or anything. In fact, he never said a word about it. We think he doesn't blame anyone in particular and that was why he didn't get upset, 'cause he knows we all work as hard as we can."

Jodee turned and finally looked at Leona's face, not sure what to say. She remembered last Tuesday. Doug had come home in a foul mood. He had snapped at her all evening and complained about the veal she'd made for dinner. And in a rare moment of temper he had yelled at Lexie for being on the phone too long. She'd been glad it had been her night off for having sex. She hated having sex with him when he was in a bad temper. The sex was always rushed and unpleasant.

With a slight clearing of her throat to hide the pause in the conversation, Jodee responded to Leona in the only way she knew how. "Oh, uh, well, I'm sorry about the goal problem and I'm sure you're right, Doug doesn't blame anyone. I'm sure it will be better next year."

"Oh, sure, I know it will."

Jodee had turned her eyes back to Doug as she listened out of the corner of her ear to Leona's prattling. Suddenly, like a shadow passing before her eyes, Doug turned and gave her a look letting her know he'd seen her asleep. A slight shiver of misgiving scampered down Jodee's skin. At the same moment, Leona finished her sentence.

"You must feel so lucky to be married to such a good man."

'Lucky to be married' – Leona's choice of words had conjured up a memory that had been buried deep in Jodee's subconscious, one she thought she'd forgotten. Slowly, as if the lights had been dimmed in the room, Jodee's eyes went from the scene in front of her to a dark past only she could see.

It had been her wedding day. She and Doug had had a day of dancing and laughing, the guests were all happy and wishing them well, then, right before they left the reception for the downtown Hyatt where they'd spend their first night as husband and wife, her father had taken her aside. In the pretense of giving her a loving hug, he told her in her ear, 'Don't mess this up, girl. You know you don't have a lot going for you and it's taken all your mother and I've got to make sure you're settled well, so you just make sure you abide by those vows you just spoke – to obey your husband, you hear me? You just consider yourself lucky to be married to such a good man and mind your step.' With that he gave her a hard squeeze while the on-looking guests gave an audible 'ahh,' thinking he was hugging her out of love. Jodee had just stared at her dad as her mood went from one of happy optimism to self-loathing and doubt. Her father had just told her she had nothing going for her and if this very good man hadn't married her, then what else did she have? It was the beginning of a vow she made to herself at that moment, to always obey her husband, always, so she would give him no reason to be disappointed in her like her father was.

Leona was still talking as Jodee slowly came back into herself. "Well, the band is starting up again and I'm going to find a new partner."

"Oh, oh, yes. Well, I think Doug is probably looking for me. It was nice talking to you, Leona."

"Yes, you too, Mrs. Warren. Talk to you later, bye." Leona was already making a beeline to a handsome young man in a pinstriped suit by the time she'd said her goodbye to Jodee.

Jodee tentatively walked over to Doug. As she approached him, he turned his attention from the man he was speaking to.

"Oh, Jodee, there you are. I want to introduce you to Mr. Petersen. He's the director of sales in the downtown office." He gave her a look to let her know he wasn't happy with her.

She hid her unease at his look by turning her attention to the man beside him. "Hello, Mr. Petersen. It's nice to meet you."

"Mrs. Warren, it's nice to meet you. Aren't you lovely in blue."

Jodee was dubious but hid it behind a polite remark. "Thank you. How very kind of you. Are you here with your wife?"

"Sadly, no, she couldn't make it."

"Oh, that's a shame. I hope you're enjoying yourself anyway."

"I would enjoy myself more if I had a dancing partner and Doug tells me you're quite the dancer. Would you mind giving me the honor?"

Dance? Jodee thought. Doug knew she wasn't a very good dancer. "Oh, well, I assure you he flatters me more than I deserve."

"Well, I'll take my chances if you will."

After slight hesitation she joked, "All right then, I'd be happy to dance with you; but don't say I didn't warn you."

"Yes, go ahead and dance with him, honey. I'm going to go get myself another drink." Jodee noticed Doug's voice was on the razor edge of being slurred and she noticed his eyes were red.

"Of course." Jodee hid her concern behind a mask of pleasantry. "Do you mind holding my glass?" She looked Doug directly in the eye to try and gauge his mood.

Mr. Petersen took Jodee's hand and led her onto the dance floor, "And please, call me Derek."

Jodee let herself be led onto the floor while her mind fretted over Doug seeing her asleep against the wall.

When the dance ended, and Jodee had thanked Mr. Petersen, she found Doug at the edge of the dance floor talking to his boss, John Erickson.

"I'm sorry about the mix up with the tables, Doug. The caterer had gotten the names from my assistant and mixed up the envelopes. I had wanted you sitting with me at the table so I could discuss next year's plan with you. I just want you to know, you have nothing to worry about. Everybody's numbers are low this year, but you've been doing a great job. Your bonus should reflect that."

As if a spotlight had been directed to frame Doug's face, Jodee watched the light in his eyes go from apprehension to relief and then joy.

Speaking casually, Doug responded with the professional lying he had mastered, "I didn't give it a thought, John. Really, I didn't even notice. But I do appreciate you telling me."

"Yes, well, I thought you should know. In fact, I'd like you in San Francisco next week to help get the new branch in order. Can you do that?"

"You bet. Anything I can do." Doug's happy change of demeanor reminded Jodee of a puppy wagging its tail when getting a treat.

"Now, enough shop talk. You should dance with your wife and enjoy the rest of the party."

Turning to Jodee, John Erickson took her left hand, cradled it softly in both of his and said, "Mrs. Warren, nice to see you again. Doug is one lucky man. Have a good evening." With that, he slid his hand across the top of hers and disappeared into the crowd as Jodee blushed.

"Did you hear that?" Doug asked rhetorically. "Man, he just made my year." Doug's enthusiasm had reversed the sour disposition he'd carried all night like Atlas throwing off the weight of the world.

Doug was in such a good mood after his talk with Mr. Erickson, he closed down the party with enough drinks to fuel several people and danced every song with whatever woman was close enough to agree, which most of the time was Leona.

CHAPTER TWELVE

SHAME

At one in the morning, Jodee convinced Doug to give her the keys to the car so she could drive home. She was exhausted, her feet hurt, and she just wanted to go home. She had perspired through her dress from all the dancing so that the fabric was sticking to her back. She wanted nothing more than to take a quick shower and go to bed.

On the drive home, Doug laid his head against the headrest in the car and hummed tunes from the evening. He was in a pleasant stupor of drink, perfume, music, and thoughts of a huge bonus.

As they turned into their driveway, Doug looked over at Jodee. Her face was bathed in light from the streetlamp in the corner of their yard. "You're pretty the way the light hits your face."

Jodee looked over at him cautiously as she waited for the garage door to open. "Thank you," she said timidly.

"No, I mean it. You were really good tonight. John was really impressed with you." His words tumbled over each other with just enough coherence to be understood. But while his eyes stayed on her face, his words betrayed his thoughts. "Boy, that Leona sure can dance. She has some moves I've never seen before. At one point I thought she was going to fall out of that dress."

Jodee was focused on pulling the car into the garage and didn't notice him staring at her. "Yes, she's very good," she answered absently.

Jodee put the car in park and turned off the engine. Grabbing her handbag and shifting to get out the door, she said over her shoulder, "Doug, you go on in and get into bed. I'll lock up."

Doug mumbled some kind of response as he swaggered into the house and down the hall to their bedroom. Jodee locked the backdoor, kicked her shoes off in the hall, and headed straight to their master bath to rinse off.

After a few minutes of standing under tepid water, Jodee toweled off, put on the cotton T-shirt she always wore and walked out of the bathroom, glad that her bed was waiting. She was so tired. The good thing about Doug having a little too much to drink, she thought, was he'd already be asleep. She knew she'd probably have to remove his clothes and push him over to his side of the bed, but it was the least of her cares. She just wanted to go to sleep.

As she stood in the door of the bathroom with the light framing her body, she looked up to see Doug lounging on the bed like a centerfold model. He was naked.

"Doug?" She wasn't sure she was seeing what she was seeing.

"I don't want you to wear anything to bed, Jodee." He raised his eyebrows as he said words he was certain would turn her on.

He wasn't asleep. In fact, he was horny! Jodee cringed. She hesitated at the door of the bathroom.

"Uh, Doug, don't you think you should get some sleep? Don't you have a golf game in the morning?" She said the first thing that came to her mind, hoping he'd take the hint.

"I'm never too tired to make love to my wife. Besides, it always calms me down. Now, come here."

Jodee turned off the light to the bathroom in slow motion. She walked to the bed in the soft glow of light shining in the window from the outside streetlamp. She tried again.

"I'm just a little tired is all. It was such a long evening and I know you must be tired, too. I don't want your game to be off since you have to get up so early."

"Don't worry about me... Oh, I know what your problem is, you think it's your night off. But I just thought of something, since it's almost one in the morning technically it's my night on." He said this with a chuckle that grated on Jodee's nerves.

Jodee stood at the side of the bed, reluctant to remove her shirt.

"Or don't you want to make love to me?" The hardness in his tone belied his drunken state as the crease between his eyes grew into a deep crevice.

Jodee could tell Doug's mood was beginning to sour and quickly stripped down as she crawled into bed next to him. "Of course, I do," she lied.

He climbed on top of her with the speed and grace of a dog smelling a bitch in heat.

His weight as he landed on her forced the air from her lungs with startled pressure and made her utter a surprised groan. Doug mistook the noise for passion. As he started kissing her neck, he grabbed her wrists and swung them above her head in a tight and painful grip. She wriggled beneath him trying to get air into her lungs. The more she wriggled, the more turned-on he became. Then, with his weight on his hands and shoulders, he raised himself above her, placed his knees between her legs, and forced them open. He entered her so swiftly it caused pain, like a sharp scrape on a raw wound.

His love making was fast and sweaty with no regard for her readiness. His grunting reminded her of a pig rooting for food. She turned her head away from him on the pillow and tried to distance herself from the situation by thinking of other things – the party, tomorrow's chores, the wish that she was far away. She prayed it would be over quickly.

Doug had buried his face in the pillow beside her head, unaware that she'd turned away, that she had stopped moving, or that she was silently crying. He continued to hump her up and down with furious pleasure. He was half passed-out from the alcohol but glad it had slowed down his orgasm. Then, with a sudden shudder of release he fell on top of her with all his weight, a small sound of contentment expelled from his throat. He lay there, slowly letting his system take him into the realm of sweet satisfied unconsciousness.

Jodee lay for a moment, she heard his breathing slow into a gargled snore. She carefully pulled her wrists out from his slackened grasp. When she thought he was fully asleep, she slowly pushed his shoulder and rolled him off her. As she squirmed out from under him, he fell on to his back beside her. She reached down to pull the covers over him when she heard him softly mumble, "Maybe you should get a boob job, it's like making love to a board." The words were spoken so quietly Jodee knew he was saying them in his sleep, which hurt more than if he'd been awake because she knew it was how he truly felt.

She left the sheet tangled around his calves, pulled the comforter from the foot of the bed and covered her naked form. She rolled over onto her side, glad that the sex was over but hurt to realize that he'd been thinking of Leona and her bountiful curves. She heard him start snoring again. She felt ashamed and didn't know why. She buried her face into her pillow as the tears slid across her nose and down the side of her face. To hide her grief-filled hiccups so she wouldn't wake Doug, she placed her hands deeper under the pillow to pull up around her mouth when her fingers brushed against something hard. The surprise of feeling something under her pillow temporarily distracted her from the pain. She lifted enough to pull out whatever had stemmed the flow of tears.

"Oh, my sweet baby," she said to herself. She slowly held up the tiny plastic Tinker Bell doll and watched the glittered wings sparkle in the subdued lighting cast from the moon through the window.

Dougie J. She thought back to the beginning of the day like it was weeks ago and remembered Dougie J had been in the kitchen doorway when Doug was berating her over the bills. She could see in his eyes as he stared at them that he'd seen her hurt. This was his way of trying to make her feel better. Her tears started falling again, but this time from knowing that the one person in her life that truly saw her for who she was, was only six years old.

She held the doll to her chest as she lay back down on the pillow and let the cold plastic warm to her body. With a contentment she hadn't felt in a very long time, she slowly let herself float into sleep.

She dreamed, a restless dream. She dreamed she was a fairy in a torn blue dress, running and running because she couldn't fly. She couldn't fly because her wings were broken and from behind her she could feel the breath of a giant boar chasing her. The boar was breathing loudly and snorting. She was afraid and she couldn't run fast enough and with every few steps she could feel the sharp poke of the boar's tusk on her back. He was going to eat her. She was so afraid because she was lost. She just kept running. She ran throughout the night and as she ran her subconscious reminded her that she had no power, she would be consumed. The giant pig would win out and destroy her.

SECTION THREE

DUPLICITY

People are rarely what they seem,
do what they say or say what they mean.

CHAPTER THIRTEEN

ARCHER'S SECRET

Jodee stood at the kitchen sink ready to wash the breakfast dishes that had been left. She and Doug had overslept and if Archer hadn't called and told Doug their tee time had been changed to nine, they might have slept until noon. The kids had finished eating and had scattered to the far corners of the house, afraid they'd be made to help her if they lingered.

She had awakened with a slight headache and her right palm hurting. It had taken her a moment to remember the night before – the nightmare that had caused the headache she was trying to tamp down and the reason as to why her hand hurt. When she could focus clearly, she had lifted her hand to find she still clutched the tiny plastic Tinker Bell doll and had held it so tightly through the night that it had caused a bruise to form and had left an impression of tiny wings on her palm.

She dropped the doll into a pocket and absently rubbed her palm as she held it under the cool water from the faucet. She stood staring out the kitchen window watching Dougie J and Dayla. They were playing on the playset, rather Dougie was playing and Dayla was twisting herself around and around on one of the swings. Jodee knew Dayla was enjoying herself but only when she thought no one was watching her. An adolescent behavior that Jodee was all too familiar with since both of her two older girls also went through the phase – the I'm-too-old-for-childish-toys-but-still-young-enough-to-wish-I-wasn't   sort   of thing.

She watched her kids, pondering their sibling relationship, and longed for the chance to be outside with them enjoying her flowers, yard, and the green shade of the trees, or maybe take a walk along the greenway outside their fence that paralleled the Mississippi river – a place that always brought her peace.

Her meandering mind returned to her kids when she heard Dayla laugh at something Dougie had said in one of their rare moments of camaraderie. She had to admit she felt a little guilty having given Dougie J the playset for his birthday. It was the most extravagant gift they'd ever given any of the kids and it went to Dougie J. It screamed of favoritism and she was afraid it would distance Dayla from Dougie out of jealousy. But in her own defense, she never wanted the thing, it was all Doug's idea to give it to him.

In the secret thoughts of a troubled mind, it bothered Jodee that their girls always seemed to take a backseat to Dougie J. She knew Doug adored all their children, but everyone in the family knew that Dougie J, apart from being their youngest child and only son, was Doug's pride. He was what Doug referred to as his 'little legacy' and his final chance to help pass on the Warren name. To Jodee, Dougie was simply her baby and the one person that seemed to be able to peek into her thoughts and decipher her feelings. The one man in her life who truly understood her was just a little boy. She sometimes thought being so emotionally attached to Dougie was, perhaps, not normal. She had a connection with him she couldn't explain. She loved all her children the same and loved them with her very soul, but it seemed she could feel Dougie even when he wasn't near her. She could feel his hurts and his wants to the point where it physically affected her; from yesterday's sweet gesture of him leaving the doll under her pillow, she suspected it was the same for him.

Shaking herself free from the doldrums, as her mother liked to call them, she finished rinsing the dishes, wrung the sponge out and turned to wipe down the table. As she turned around she gave out a little gasp, "Oh, Archer, I didn't see you there! You gave me a start."

Checking himself, as if being caught with his hand in the cookie jar, he coughed slightly and turned his eyes to anywhere but Jodee.

"Sorry. Someone left the front door open, so I let myself in. I saw you daydreaming and didn't want to disturb you."

The expression on his face when she turned around, the softness surrounding his eyes, had confused her but had changed so quickly she wasn't sure if she hadn't imagined it.

"It must have been one of the girls," she said, referring to the open door. "How long have you been standing there?" She clutched her free hand to her breast.

"Just a moment or two." He lied. Truth was he'd been standing there quite a while. He had let himself in and when he'd stepped to the kitchen door and saw Jodee just standing with her back to him, he'd stayed quiet and just stood looking at her.

"Oh, well, I hope I didn't do anything to embarrass myself."

"I don't see how that would be possible. I saw you watching the kids and just liked the look on your face. You take on such a gentle, loving look when you look at them."

"Oh, well, uh... I guess it's just part of being a mother."

"Maybe," he said, "but I've seen other women with their children and for some reason, you have a look of pure love. Of course, with a face as pretty as yours it probably comes naturally."

"Uh, thank you," she stammered, trying hard to keep her eyes from their incessant blinking when she was embarrassed. "But I think you're biased. Look at me, I'm totally forgetting my manners. Why don't you sit down and I'll get you a cup of coffee and let Doug know you're here."

"That would be great." Archer walked slowly to the kitchen table, brushing her left arm ever so slightly with his right one. "Don't worry about hurrying Doug though, we have plenty of time."

Not noticing the touch, Jodee explained as she got down a cup. "He kind-of overslept. We had a late night. Have you eaten? Would you like some breakfast?

"No, I haven't eaten yet, but you don't have to go to any trouble, I can grab something at the clubhouse."

"Don't be silly, it's no trouble. I'll make it right now."

Jodee turned away from him and started rummaging the cabinet for a skillet. She was so intent on making Archer's breakfast she didn't notice he'd gotten quiet.

Archer was so intent on watching Jodee move about the kitchen, he didn't care that the talking had stopped. He was contemplating their comfortable silence and how the entire scene could have been right out of a Rockwell painting. With a look of pure envy, anyone watching would know Archer ached for Doug's life. An ache that was becoming more and more painful and more and more obvious.

As Jodee worked, it was Archer's turn to daydream. He sat quietly and relived the moment he first met her, their past, and the whole college mess.

College. He'd been such a boob back then. He shook his head and let his mind drift.

CHAPTER FOURTEEN

A TRUSTED FRIEND

That first year of college had been one of discovery and life's lessons for Archer and Doug, but lessons in life had been the furthest things from their minds. They'd found three areas of commonality from the get-go; they both excelled in sports, both were good looking, and both had an innate drive to succeed. Their drive, however, depended on the road they were on at any given time, and during their freshman year they had instinctively turned down the exciting road of promiscuity.

Unfortunately, some of those roads they'd ventured down had ended up having a few ruts in them. They quickly learned the hard way that even though they were considered adults, they still had to answer to higher powers, and the higher beings in their lives were their parents – by way of the dean.

The two fast-friends had soon decided in the first few weeks of their freshman year that early morning classes were not conducive to their desired lifestyle – late night parties and lots of dates. Weighing the importance of one against the other, they'd decided – as adults – that something had to give. So with a firm hold on maturity, their decision was that girls were their main priority and to sacrifice their classes.

They'd make up for their lack of academic dedication when they became sophomores they agreed.

The university decided before this could happen, however, that these two particular adults needed to feel the sting of the probation paddle. It was their way of slowing down two out of control speedsters.

Academic probation had put a crimp in their sleeping patterns, but it didn't slow them down from following their course. It was a minor bump in the road they reasoned, besides, they still had their financial freedom by way of the credit card applications that so frequently came in the mail, which they applied for with reckless abandon, and they still had the girls.

Six months after they were slowed down by authoritarian speed bumps, the angry letters from credit card companies started accumulating on their doorstep, putting a barrier between them and their dating path. They had maxed out their numerous credit cards and the twenty-six percent penalty they incurred had made their road muddy and hard to travel. It also meant their journey might actually come to an end.

It was during this desperate time that Doug had discovered another talent – his 'natural' charm with the girls. Some dated him because he was cute, some dated him because he was fun, but those with the more maternal instincts wanted to rescue him.

After having his ego stroked by countless women, he had made the conscious decision that the wealthy, privileged girls were more his style. They were the ones that could aid him down his road to success. So, with a little manipulation, and a lot of sob stories, his bank account no longer became a concern. Somehow his dates always ended up footing the bill.

Doug and Archer developed a reputation around campus of being players and their dating choices started petering out. Because of his finances, Doug had had to slow his escapade of female sampling down to only two women – one whose daddy was rich and one who was easy to manipulate because her daddy was absent. In the meantime, Archer had stopped his sampling when he'd gotten involved with a girl with a will stronger than his own and a determination to keep him to herself. He was forced to sit back and watch Doug's back as Doug juggled two girls as different as night and day – Lacey and Eden.

Lacey O'Day's father was a successful lawyer, so in the small college town her name was synonymous with respect and money. She had given Doug fun times and made him respectable with his fellow classmates. She liked to buy him expensive clothes, good dinners, and shiny little gifts. She was a good time with no ties, or so he had convinced himself.

Eden Osgood, the other girl in his whittled down selection, had a Cinderella complex. Her unconscious desire to be taken care of by men fed his ego as she treated him like her knight in shining armor. She was lonely, needy and made him feel like the hero he believed he was by allowing him to save her from the bitter childhood of a neglectful father. Her absent father had caused just enough psychological damage to give her insecurities with men. This had taken a toll on her early in life in the form of possessiveness bordering on obsession. She'd felt that in order to keep the men in her life from leaving her, she had to ensure total control of their time and attention; phone calls at all hours of the day was her norm. Leaving notes on Doug's car asking where he'd been was a regular occurrence. Paying for their dates with her scholarship funds eased her conscience. Showing up outside his classes became a nuisance.

At the beginning of both relationships, Doug had loved the attention from two very pretty girls. If one wasn't available on a certain night, he could always count on the other one to be. It was the ultimate power game of organization and multi-tasking;

stringing two girls along while keeping them from finding out about each other. It was a game he reveled in. After three months of this game though, he started growing tired of both girls trying to monopolize his time.

At the end of the fourth month into his double dalliance he began growing weary. His partying was always being cut short because one of them would always call him, he was missing football games, and he was tired of constantly being on call. If he'd had been paying attention he would have recognized the warning signs. How unstable a vulnerable girl could be and how needy a rich one truly was.

By month five, he was growing angry of always being on alert. Afraid that Eden would show up while he was with Lacey or that Lacey would call while he was with Eden.

He couldn't decide who he preferred. Eden was athletic and prettier than Lacey, but Lacey was fun, and rich. Eden made him feel needed – as a man, but Lacey provided entertainment and kept him from eating at the campus cafeteria. Eden liked to experiment in bed, but Lacey had the respectability he craved.

Unbeknownst to him however, both women had decided that the loose ties tenuously binding their relationship needed to be tightened and went about securing it for themselves – in very different ways.

As his relationship with Lacey progressed, dinner with her family started becoming a weekly Sunday expectance. Archer began running interference with Eden to keep her from asking questions of where Doug went every Sunday. His excuses were growing tiresome, though, because no twenty-year-old college man went home to visit his parents as much as Archer told Eden Doug did. He started telling her that one of Doug's grandparents was sick and was why he went home so often. He soon started running out of sick grandparents, however.

It was at dinner one Sunday night at the wealthy home of his 'no strings' attached princess, he learned just how tight Lacey was willing to bind that metaphorical knot. Feeling things were getting out of hand, Doug had found a way to have Archer invited to dinner hoping to avoid any unforeseen episode with Lacey.

Thankful for Archer's presence, thinking the evening was going to end calmly, Lacey suddenly announced her intentions of matrimony between herself and Doug in the middle of dessert. It appeared she wasn't going to settle for the same carefree lifestyle of dating any longer and had taken one of his declarations of love during sex literally.

It was a night of sex where they'd had a few drinks and she was unusually uninhibited that he had groggily told her he loved her. Of course, he hadn't actually meant love like 'let's get married' type of love. He meant love like 'that was great sex' type of love. He had discovered, very astoundingly, that he could shut up almost any girl from wanting to talk right after sex if he simply told them 'luv ya.' They usually were taken so off guard that they would let him turn over and go to sleep. He always reassured himself that the girls he slept with knew it was said as a compliment. Lacey, however, decided it was a promise of marriage and that she had found her future husband.

Lacey's parents, not entirely convinced of Doug's worth, indulged their daughter's whim but also decided to keep a tight rein on her intended's rope. Being the over-protective parent that he was, Mr. O'Day could see from the pale pallor of Doug's face the truth behind his daughter's statement of marriage – simply, that she was the only one involved in it.

As Doug sat in shock at her sudden news of their engagement, he could feel the knot tightening around his neck.

Mr. O'Day's eyes bore into him while his hands flexed unconsciously around the stem of a thirty-five-dollar wine glass, not unlike a man itching to pull the lever at a hanging.

Lacey continued to tighten her hold on Doug by also announcing that she wanted a quick engagement – six months tops – and chatted on at lightning speed to her mother of what kind of wedding she wanted.

Doug sat at the table in unaccustomed silence while he watched his carefree lifestyle being crushed under the weight of white orchids and lavender chenille. The rope kept growing tighter with every enthusiastic squeal from Lacey and her mother over guest lists and gown designs.

It didn't take long for Mr. O'Day to assess the situation, probably because the sweat that had popped out on Doug's forehead shined like a beacon of panic. What he had deduced very succinctly was that this young man, who had been a guest in his home every Sunday for the last three months, was nothing more than a lothario. He had been keeping his eye on him ever since Lacey had brought him to their home the first time and watched as Doug tried to charm his way through the women of the O'Day family.

Mr. O'Day knew he indulged his daughter, but he hadn't expected to hear her announce her engagement after only a few weeks of knowing Doug, and in such an abrupt manner. Now it was up to him as her father to either squash his daughter's dreams by refusing to give his blessing to this catastrophe of an engagement or make sure Doug did the honorable thing. He didn't want this man-child for a son-in-law any more than he knew Doug wanted to be a husband, but he also knew he wasn't going to let this over-confident little punk use his little girl then toss her aside like a well-chewed piece of meat. He decided he would let his daughter marry this man and then watch him so closely that Doug wouldn't be able to use double-ply toilet paper without him knowing about it. So, in a guise of welcoming him to the family, Mr. O'Day took Doug for a walk to have a 'man-to-man' talk.

During this talk, Mr. O'Day had explained to Doug that he knew his daughter had caught him off-guard with her sudden announcement, but with unrelenting bluntness he warned Doug that if he had any thought of bolting and running from 'this sham of an engagement' and hurting his little girl, he would proceed to end his college career faster than Doug could say lawsuit. Mr. O'Day had known from the beginning what Lacey had been spending on Doug and he let Doug know it.

The threat from his future father-in-law brought the truth of reality to Doug like ice water to the face – that he was viewed as being a kept man. It humiliated him to his core, but he was also painfully aware he couldn't afford to lose this meal ticket. Being young and not knowing how to deal with a very real adult situation, all he could do was hang his head like a whipped dog and mumble false promises. Doug had gotten the message loud and clear and could feel the noose leaving rope burns around his neck.

The announcement of Doug and Lacey's engagement was in the local paper the following week. While Doug had been trying to keep Lacey happy and her father off his back, Archer had been playing nursemaid to Eden. He had run interference and had been able to keep her at bay for over a week. It hadn't been easy but Archer had done it because, secretly, he had envied Doug's situation – two pretty girls vying for his attention and the balls of conning them out of their respective income. Although, this was before Doug was soon to hang for the crime.

Archer had been a willing participant in the ruse because he always hoped he'd be able to pick up some of Doug's confidence with girls and maybe shake lose the woman who currently clung to him like a bur. But, it was Eden's reaction to seeing Doug's picture in the paper – engaged to another girl – that finally made Archer realize that Doug's situation didn't warrant envy.

Eden's reaction to the news was just a shade under normal. Her insecurities had turned a darker shade of crazy and she hunted Doug down like a rabid wolf smelling blood. She was no longer going to be put off. Archer was actually scared of her at this point and told Doug as much. Doug simply blew it off by continuing to ignore her.

After three days of being hounded beyond his endurance by Eden, Doug finally decided to face her and end it. He met her for dinner one evening with the sole purpose of explaining to her that the engagement wasn't his fault, that he'd only dated Lacey a couple of times, and that he had no idea how Lacey could have gotten the idea that he loved her. He had been blindsided but that there was no way he could end it with Lacey without her father destroying his future. As always, Doug made himself out to be the victim. Something he'd become expert at.

By the time he had finished reliving the regrettable circumstances to her, almost coming to tears in the telling, Eden was convinced Doug was being trapped by one of the 'rich bitches' on campus. She secretly decided it was up to her to save him from a fate worse than death.

Doug, needing to explain to his parents about his engagement before they heard it through the grapevine, told both girls he was going home for spring break. So, with a well-thought-out lie and practiced humility, he told Eden he was going home to see his sick grandparent. He didn't tell her which one since he couldn't remember which one was supposed to be sick. She, in uncharacteristic calmness, wished him safe travels.

After he had gotten off the phone to Eden, he had then called Lacey and told her he was going home to break the good news of their engagement to his parents and thought it best if he did it alone since his sick grandparent – he had decided that old relatives was the greatest excuse – couldn't handle too much excitement. She, in characteristic wedding glow, simply told him to tell them hello from her and she was looking forward to meeting them soon.

Doug did go home but he didn't talk to his parents. Instead, he went to football games at the high school, watched hours of TV, and slept. He had convinced his parents that he was home for some much-needed rest and downtime. They didn't question him, after all, their boy was home for spring break instead of off to Cancun or something, and they were just happy to have him home.

While on his emotional sabbatical, he began thinking about the two girls that were quickly trying to ruin his life. He decided he was going to have to dump them both when he returned to school. It didn't matter how rich Lacey was, he would not be trapped by any girl, her father be damned. As for Eden, she was just becoming too crazy, truth-be-told. The fact was that her eerie calmness when he left made him more uneasy than any of her melodramatics. He agreed with Archer, she was a little scary.

Until he could figure out a surefire way to end both relationships, Doug was temporarily enjoying the break and was having fun visiting his old high school buddies at home. It was during a high school football game one night when he noticed a petite blonde sitting in front of him on the stands. She was talking to another girl in a quiet demure voice. After striking up a conversation with her, he'd found out she was a senior and about to graduate. There was something about her, something soft and shy. Her name was Jodee Olson, and he began pursuing her like a man possessed. A man who needed to find a diversion from the nightmare at school and he always found the best kind of diversion was another girl. His single-mindedness never let him consider the fact that girls were the reason he was in trouble in the first place.

Doug spent the rest of his time at home doggedly pursuing Jodee. He found her sweet, funny, and smart. He also discovered the fact that she was just slightly afraid of men, which made her easy to manipulate.

Jodee was so complimented by the attention this college man was paying her, she thought herself the luckiest girl in the world. "A college man, imagine," her friends kept telling her.

She spent every available moment she could with him. By the time he left to go back to school, she was entirely in love.

Doug, thinking himself clever, thought he had found a way out of his dilemma with Lacey and Eden. He would marry Jodee as soon as she graduated by telling both women who were making his life hell, that she was pregnant or something. He hadn't worked out all the details but just knew he'd think of some excuse so he could get out of the mess he was in. He decided he would simply face the music, break up with Lacey and Eden when he returned to campus, and forget the whole thing ever happened.

On the night before he was to leave to go back to campus however, he took Jodee's virginity in a moment of quick passion. She had fallen under the blinding crush of new love when he'd asked her to marry him. For her, it had been quick, painful, and gloriously sweet. For him on the other hand, it had simply been uncontrollable lust, while he tried to tell himself that, yes, maybe he could fall in love with this girl after all.

When Doug did get back to school a couple of days later, the university campus was strangely quiet. People he didn't know watched him as he walked by like he was some kind of oddity. People he did know avoided eye contact with him and walked in the other direction. It had taken him two hours to locate Archer before he could find out why people were treating him like he had a communicable disease. When he finally did find his best friend, Archer pulled him aside and started giving him brotherly pats on his back so quickly that anyone watching would have thought Doug might have been choking on food.

After the initial care-giving rub down, Doug was finally able to determine the reason for all the side glances and whispers. Seems while he was home trying to figure out how to rid himself of his female leeches, his engagement to Lacey had been called off. Before he was able to collapse from relief, Archer proceeded to tell him that Lacey and Eden had finally met face-to-face, or face-to-back to be more accurate.

Archer had found it hard to tell Doug, not knowing how Doug truly felt about his engagement and the fact that his fiancée was seriously hurt and in the hospital. According to the police report, they had found her lying in the park under a picnic table. She'd been stabbed in the back, which had punctured her left lung. The police were holding Eden in jail for attempted murder. The only reason the authorities hadn't tried to contact Doug yet, was they were asked by Mr. O'Day to wait until he could talk to Doug first – as a favor.

The reality of what Archer was telling him slowly sank in and made Doug feel like a lead weight was tied to his neck. They'd done it – that was all he could think at the time – these two girls had done it to him, had ruined his life. They couldn't have left a good thing alone, they couldn't just continue to have fun, a little sex, a few laughs, and then be on their way. No, they had to control him.

Archer continued to explain that once Lacey woke up in the hospital and explained everything, her parents made her call off the engagement. Archer watched Doug as he slumped, thinking he was hurting from the news. His slumping wasn't from the broken engagement; this news was secretly a relief. No, what was bothering him was when Archer told him Mr. O'Day was claiming he was an accomplice. Doug knew Mr. O'Day didn't have any proof that he was involved, but when the news got back to his parents, their shame and disappointment in him was going to be far worse than anything a lawyer could do to him.

As for Eden, when she found out about Doug's secret engagement, she had called Lacey, according to her, 'just to talk.' It wasn't until Lacey had dismissed her as a liar and turned her back on her 'like she was white trash,' that Eden lost control and stabbed her with a pen.

"I've tried to get hold of you for the last two days," Archer explained earnestly. "But no one ever seemed to know where you were."

"I never got any messages," Doug insisted.

"I must have left at least a dozen with Robbie."

"I'm gonna kill him!" Doug all but yelled.

"Anyway, you're in a real mess. Lacey doesn't want to see you, which I think might be for the best. But Eden does."

"I'm not going over to the jail. I didn't have anything to do with this. I never told her to do anything like this and I never told her we were exclusive. This was all her idea."

"You'd better explain that to the cops then."

Doug did explain his side of the story to the cops, deciding it best to leave Eden alone. And, with a written promise to Mr. O'Day that he would never again try and contact Lacey, Mr. O'Day dropped his accusations against him, knowing he didn't have proof anyway as Eden kept swearing Doug had nothing to do with it, as a way to protect him, believing he'd come back to her.

After Eden realized that Doug wasn't going to come back to her, even after everything she'd done for him, she had a slight meltdown. During trial when she saw him in the corridor, she grabbed a guard's gun and started firing in his direction. He ducked, but she had shot an innocent bystander by mistake. She ended up getting the maximum prison sentence for two attempted murders. Some thought it was because the judge was a friend of Mr. O'Day's.

The trial was the talk of the state for eight months. As for Doug, he spent his time between explaining the circumstances to his family, Jodee, Jodee's family, and keeping his nose clean throughout the rest of his college career. It just took a couple of needy, slightly warped, women to straighten him out.

Over time, the humiliation of the situation had worked itself into Doug's psyche and sliced open a piece of his soul, leaving a festering wound of anger and shame. Never being able to completely forget how he was made to feel, his resentment grew slowly over the years and infected his personality. Subconsciously, it was what made Doug decide that never again would a woman have any control over him. He kept this promise to himself throughout his marriage to Jodee.

Archer came out of the very unpleasant past to see Jodee handing him a plate of eggs and toast.

"Are you okay? You were a million miles away."

"Sorry. I'm fine. I was just thinking of the first time we met." He took the plate from Jodee and placed it on the table in front of him like it were fine china.

"Seems like a million years ago, doesn't it?" She walked the few feet to the other side of the table and took the seat across from him.

"Yeah. It does. There sure are some things I wish I could've changed though."

"Really? Don't you think you've had a pretty good life?"

"Maybe. But I *am* divorced."

"Oh, Archer, I'm sorry. I'm being insensitive."

"No. No, you're not. I just married the wrong woman is all."

"Of course, you did. And I believe that one day you'll meet that special someone. I hope you believe that, too."

"I think I have met that special someone already and missed my opportunity." Archer looked up into Jodee's eyes and held her stare.

"You met someone? I had no idea. Can I ask who it is?"

"Who is who?" Doug asked as he came into the kitchen carrying a golf sweater. "Jodee," he ordered, "get me a thermos of coffee. I want to take it to the course with me."

Being saved from answering, Archer dropped his eyes to his plate. An expression of relief, anxiety, and worry crossed Archer's face as if he were secretly scolding himself for his narrowly escaped indiscretion.

Archer reminded himself that Doug was his oldest friend, and as such, he was allowed into the family circle, which was something he needed. But more than that, it was his friendship with Doug that kept him close to Jodee.

"While I have you here, Archer, I want to ask a favor." Doug was completely oblivious to Archer's pale expression. "I have to leave next week for San Francisco to help open a new branch of the bank. I may be gone for a couple of weeks. Do you think you could come over once in a while and check on Jodee and the kids?"

Archer looked up like he'd been given the key to the city, knowing he answered a little too quickly. "Of course. Whatever you need."

"Good, good. I'll rest easier to know someone is in charge of things." Doug didn't seem to notice Archer's instant enthusiasm. For once, Doug's egocentric personality played in Archer's favor.

Jodee knew better than to question Doug's request, insulted he felt she needed a sitter. But in her inner truth, a place she couldn't allow herself to go, she was excited about having the house to herself for a while. Besides, having Archer come over didn't bother her. He was a good friend. Someone she could trust.

CHAPTER FIFTEEN

A SILENT YEARNING

"Jodee, what are you doing down there?" Archer had walked through the house looking for her, getting used to making himself at home. He found her kneeling on her hands and knees in the backyard flower bed with a trowel in one hand, a pot in the other, and dirt on her face.

Looking up at him with pure joy, he thought she was the cutest thing he'd ever seen. "Oh, hi Archer. I'm just planting some daisies. I just love daisies, especially Gerber daisies." She exuded such deep contentment that even being found in old cut-off shorts and a ratty tank top with dirt smeared on her face and arms didn't seem to spoil her mood.

"Well, if you plant any more, we're going to lose you in the foliage." He knelt beside her and surveyed her work. "They do look pretty, I have to admit."

"Don't they though? And tomorrow I'm going to plant some ferns and hostas under the tree in the corner, and some day lilies on the side of the fence."

"I've never seen anyone enjoy plants the way you do." With a longing look and soft voice he said, "You have some dirt on your cheek. Do you mind?" He reached over with his right hand to touch her face, hesitating. He then used his thumb to rub her cheek.

"Oh, gosh, I must look a mess." Innocently, not knowing the movement made her look sweet, she tilted her head to her shoulder in an attempt to remove the soil.

The gesture had trapped his hand between her cheek and shoulder. He marveled at how soft her cheek was and realized it was the first time he could remember ever touching her face. But even with the soft touch of her cheek against his palm, it was the seductive softness of her shoulder on the back of his hand that gave him a quick jolt.

When she realized his hand was caught under her cheek, she looked up slowly at him, a little surprised she wasn't embarrassed. She straightened her head and continued to stare into his eyes.

He moved his hand to her jaw and delicately rubbed the dirt from her cheek. "You didn't get it," he whispered, afraid that any sudden movement might scare her into realizing their close proximity. "Let me help."

"Thank you," she replied in a low murmur.

"No problem." They stared at each other. Hers locked on his by friendship and confusion, his by anticipation and desire.

For one second in time the world had stopped turning for Archer. He swallowed hard when he saw her take a deep breath of air, raising her cleavage above the cut of her tank top.

"Mom, Mom, I got a hit!" Dougie J had run through the backdoor with a baseball in his right hand and his glove in his left, as if the technique helped balance him as he ran.

Jodee and Archer broke eye contact and jumped apart.

Jodee stood up quickly and watched her son bound toward them. "You did?"

"Yeah, I forgot to tell you." Archer looked down at Dougie J with pride. "Our little slugger got a hit today and actually made it to second base."

"Oh, I'm so proud of you, honey," Jodee beamed.

"Yeah, and guess what? The coach said he thinks I'm the mostest proved."

"I think he's just a little excited. He means, the coach thinks he's most improved."

"Well, that is special," Jodee encouraged.

"Yeah. And next week he's gonna let me bat first."

"Wow, maybe next week I'll go with you to the game. I'd love to see how mostest proved you are."

"Okay. Can I call Dad and tell him?" Dougie J asked.

At the mention of Doug, Jodee and Archer simultaneously, and inwardly, squirmed. Both were too embarrassed to ever admit to themselves that a few moments ago when their eyes had met, they'd forgotten Doug even existed.

"Honey, I think your daddy isn't in the hotel right now. But we'll call him tonight, okay?"

"Okay…" Dougie J showed a smidgeon of disappointment as he drew out the word.

"Will he be home next week to see me bat?"

"He'll be home Tuesday night, sweetie, then I think he has to go back on Sunday, so he might be able to make it to your game if he's not too tired."

Turning to Archer, Dougie J asked, "Will you be with me again, too, Uncle Archer?"

"I wouldn't miss it for the world, buddy, if it's all right with your mom."

"Of course, it's all right with me. I don't know what I would have done without you these last few weeks with Doug being gone so much. And I know he appreciates you being here to help Dougie J. The flight from San Francisco to home every week is exhausting him."

"I've had a great time," Archer replied. In truth, it had been the best summer of his life. Doug's trips back and forth had taken more of his time than anyone expected, and Archer had stepped in as the good friend and extended uncle to help. It was a chance to feel the need of family he so desperately wanted. Even if they were Doug's family.

"I hope we haven't taken you from anything important. You just let me know if it gets to be too much." Jodee looked at him from beneath her lashes, afraid he'd see the fear in her eyes that he'd tell them he couldn't continue to help out.

"To tell you the truth, it's been a nice break from practices. And if I have to spend one more Sunday watching clips of our games, I think I'll throw the TV through the window."

Jodee laughed. "We wouldn't want that now, would we? And to show you how much we appreciate it, why don't you come to dinner with me and the kids tomorrow to see their grandparents?"

"I don't know if I should. I don't really know you're parents all that well."

"I'm sorry, I should have been more clear. We're going over to see the Colonel and their Grandma Warren. It's just Sunday dinner and I know they'd love to see you."

Archer was relieved she didn't mean the Olsons. Truth was, he hated her old man. As far as he was concerned, Mr. Joe Olson was the biggest asshole on the planet. He hid his emotions for her dad and piped up, "I haven't seen them since Rob's wedding. Yeah, if you don't mind, I'd really like that."

"That's great. Why don't you drive with us? We're leaving around eleven."

"I'll be here." They stood and shuffled their feet, unsure of how to part. Fortunately for Dougie J, he broke their unease with eager youthfulness. "Mom, want to see how far I can throw my ball?"

"You know I do. Let me see."

Dougie J walked backward a few steps with the seriousness of a major league pitcher. He adjusted his glove in his left hand, took a sideways stance, threw the ball into the glove a couple of times, then with added exaggeration, he pulled his left knee up to his waist, lifted the ball in his right hand over his head, and threw the ball with all his might.

Jodee, Archer and Dougie J all stood and watched as the ball flew over the back fence.

"Wow, did you see that, Mom? Wasn't that far?"

"My, oh my, that was far." Jodee truly was surprised.

"I'll go get it." Dougie J was already headed for the back gate.

"Whoa there, slugger, you know you're not supposed to be outside the fence."

"But, Mom, I don't want to lose my ball."

"I'll go get it for you. I don't want you in the weeds. There's poison sumac out there and the last thing you need is to get into that, you'll itch for days. Besides, as far as you threw it, I'd be surprised if it didn't land in the river," Jodee teased him.

"Ah, Mom," he giggled.

"Why don't I go get it?" Archer hurried to the back gate and swung it open. The back fence of their yard paralleled the cement path that ran behind all the houses down the block and separated them from the wild vegetation that banked the Mississippi river. The ball had landed just a foot over the fence into the grass.

"Here you go," he said with a smile as he brought the ball back to Dougie J. "You better be careful. With an arm like that you could throw it clear across the river."

Dougie J laughed and grabbed his ball, obviously enjoying Archer's teasing. "Mom, I'm going to go show Mikey how far I can throw, okay?"

"All right, but don't be gone long." She watched as her son ran for the house. "Oh, hey," she said. "Look what I found in my flower bed." Jodee tossed the trowel on the ground and fished in her shorts pocket. She pulled out a little Peter Pan doll.

Dougie J had stopped and watched as his mother pulled out the toy. Coming back to stand in front of her, he reached out his hand. "Did you find Tinker Bell, too?"

"No, is she in there too?" Jodee cocked her head and looked down at her son. "What are they doing in my flower bed?"

"That's where they live." Dougie walked around his mother, tip-toed over a row of pink primroses to the base of a tree that stood in the corner of the yard, brushed aside a leaf with his foot and bent to pick up the little green Tinker Bell doll. He held it up to show his mother. "See, they live in the forest and they were sleeping till I got back," he explained.

"Oh, well that explains it then. I'm sorry I disturbed them," she offered with embellished sincerity as she made a slight bow.

"That's okay, they needed to wake up anyway," Dougie explained in all seriousness.

Archer tried not to laugh at the display and hid his mouth behind his hand. "How about the next time I find them there I put them on the windowsill in the kitchen so you don't lose them?" Jodee continued.

"That's okay for Peter, Mom, but Tinker Bell likes to be outside 'cause that's where the other fairies live."

"I see. I certainly wouldn't want to take her away from her friends. If that's where you think she's the happiest, then I'll leave her alone. But for now, why don't you take her in with Peter because I was going to fertilize and we don't want to get it on them, do we?"

"'Kay." He grabbed the dolls and fumbled to get them in his pocket. "Can I go to Mikey's now?"

"Yes, you may go to Mikey's. Be back in time for lunch, though." She barely got the last statement out before he disappeared into the house.

Archer hated to break the family scene he was reveling in, but he felt he was dangerously close to asking if he could move in. "I'd better get going myself."

"Yes, yes, of course. We've taken up enough of your Saturday as it is."

Jodee looked down at the pot she still held and gently cradled it in both her hands, bringing it to rest between her breasts like a mother protecting its young. She bent her head to smell the orange petals.

Archer watched her, marveling at her tenderness. He stood just close enough to her that he could smell the musk from the earth on her skin, the sweetness of the flower in the pot, and the scent of his desire as they mingled together to make his insides ache.

He knew he was in danger of doing something he'd regret so he quickly backed away from her and stammered, "Uh, how about if I come by sometime around ten and we'll stop and get some donuts for the road. Do you think the kids will like that?"

"Yes, that would be great." She looked up, unaware of how her actions were affecting him.

He half ran, half stumbled to the back door, waving a hand at her above his head without ever turning around. "See you tomorrow."

Jodee watched him go through the door. Standing for a

moment staring at the house as if contemplating his sudden haste in wanting to leave. Dismissing it as him simply wanting to get back to his normal Saturday routine, she turned to pick up her trowel and she saw the Tinker Bell doll lying in the grass. It seemed Dougie had missed his pocket. She picked the doll up and decided she would keep the sleepy little fairy next to her for the rest of the day so she could oversee the planting. She didn't want to be accused of mistreating the fairies' home, she inwardly mused.

That was how Lexie found her mother an hour later, talking to a little toy fairy as if she were at a garden club discussing the latest gardening tips.

"Mom, you keep talking to dolls and people are going to think you're crazy."

Jodee chuckled and went back to enjoying her planting.

CHAPTER SIXTEEN

A STRICT MILITARY FAMILY

"There're my little darlings!" Grandma Warren squealed when Jodee led everyone into the door the following day. "Come here and give Grandma a hug," she continued as she made a beeline for her grandchildren.

Grandma Warren called everyone darling. She always smelled of rose water and lotion. Sometimes the smell was so overpowering that Dayla and Dougie J would hold their breath when they hugged her.

Lexie loved the way her grandmother smelled though. She would hug her a little longer than anyone else and draw in a deep breath, as if to implant the smell on her memory.

"Archer, it's good to see you, boy." The Colonel had come up behind his wife.

"I hope it's all right that I came. Jodee invited me and since I haven't seen you since Rob's wedding, I thought I'd tag along."

"You're always welcome, you know that." Grace Warren had interrupted her husband and hugged Archer around the neck, treating him as if he were one of her sons.

The Colonel reached around his wife and shook Archer's hand. He then turned his attention to Jodee, "How's the prettiest girl in Minnesota?" He bent down and hugged her around the waist, giving her a quick, hard squeeze.

"Oh, Colonel, you say that about everyone in the family."
His hugs always took the breath out of her, but she loved them.

"Well, now, that's not true," he feigned insult. "You are the prettiest girl in Minnesota whenever I see you. And then when I see Marcy, she's the prettiest. Besides, you are the prettiest blonde in the whole state. Marcy should just be glad she's a brunette."

"I guess it's a good thing that Mother Warren is a redhead then, huh?" she teased.

"It looks like you've found me out." He put his arm around her shoulder and drew her to his side.

After giving Archer a warm, motherly hug, Grace turned her attention back to Jodee. "Jodee, where's Audra?"

Eager to grab their attention, Dayla chimed in, "She stayed home so she could spend time with Travis," she said in a childish sing-song tone.

The Colonel intervened good-naturedly, "Well, now, she's a young woman and I'm sure she'd rather spend time with her boyfriend than a bunch of old people like us."

Dayla looked disappointed that her news didn't get the reaction she was hoping for. She turned to her grandmother and quickly changed the subject, "Grandma, did you make my favorite cake for dessert?"

"Yes, you know I did. Come on kids, let's go get lunch on the table. Jodee, why don't you and Archer go wait out back with the Colonel until lunch is ready? I know he's been wanting to show you the garden anyway."

"Are you sure you'd rather not have me help you in the kitchen?"

"No, I have my grandkids for that. Colonel, take them on back and I'll call you when we're ready." She turned, and sandwiching herself between her granddaughters, raised her arm and guided them down the hall. "Onward-ho, girls. Doug Junior, you come on, too, and I'll let you fill the glasses. I have a new jug that is just the right size for little boys."

Jodee and Archer watched as the foursome walked away from them like a marching band being led by a drum majorette. Archer turned and saw Jodee smiling. She looked up at him with a blush coloring her cheeks, as if him catching her staring at her children like they were rare gifts on earth made her embarrassed.

"She's so good with them." She looked away quickly, turned and followed the Colonel to the backyard.

Archer stood for a moment marveling at what seemed to be Jodee's one major vice – her children.

A small round patio table with matching chairs and an umbrella had been set up on the grass just yards from the river which served as a peaceful backdrop. Rays from the sun bouncing off the breeze created small waves on the river, making zigzag patterns of miniature lightning bolts that struggled valiantly to strike the shore before they dissipated. The combination of wind and sun had the blue and white stripes of the umbrella blend into the lapping water causing Jodee to feel a slight dizziness as she stared at it, trying to mentally separate the two entities. It put her in a dreamlike state as if she were part of something surreal. It was hypnotic as she tried to make sense of the movement – one against the other.

Becoming a little lightheaded, she sat down at the tiny table and refocused her attention. As she took her seat, it dawned on her that usually when her mind was captured by moments of strange fascination it would make her confused and the panic attacks would overtake her thoughts and made her anxious. But not this time. Why? she wondered. The fact was, as she thought back, she hadn't had a panic attack in several weeks, and no rapid blinking episodes...When was the last time, how long had it been? Then it hit her. She hadn't had an attack while Doug had been traveling. The idea he could be a cause of her anxiety was so foreign to her mind that she couldn't quite grab hold of the possibility, like trying to focus on light particles from behind closed eyelids and not being able to focus on any single one. Her temples started to throb in that familiar way they did whenever she couldn't quite make sense of something. Her breathing started slowly increasing with a suffocating sense of her own insecurities just thinking about it.

Suddenly, like a life preserver thrown to her drowning mind, the Colonel brought her world back to the present, "Jodee, how is Doug doing in California? He sure has been traveling a lot lately."

It was just the interruption she needed – thankfully. Quickly, without missing a beat, she answered him, "He seems to be doing really well. He told me last night that it may take him longer than they'd expected to get the merger finalized so he may have to keep flying out there for a couple of more months still."

She was fidgeting, rubbing her palms against her thighs as if she were trying to clean dirt off them. Her focus may have been brought back to the current moment, but her subconscious was playing havoc with her equilibrium.

Archer was watching her as she continued to furiously rub her thighs. Her eyes had a distant look like someone trying to see a long distance away. She appeared agitated and he watched her with a concerned furrowing of his brow.

She looked over and saw him watching her and quickly stopped fidgeting. She turned away from him and reached for the mint julep the Colonel was passing her. "This looks great. No one can make a mint julep like you, Colonel."

Her transformation from nervous restlessness to a calm, self-contained woman was so quick Archer's expression went from concern to curiosity.

"The secret is you have to break up the mint leaves and then soak them in the bourbon for about half an hour. My dad taught me that when I was just knee high to a grasshopper." The Colonel continued, oblivious to anything that had affected his daughter-in-law or Archer's intent study of her. "Archer, how have you been, my boy?"

Archer answered his question without taking his eyes off Jodee, "Good, Colonel, really good. I've been helping Jodee out with the kids while Doug has been gone."

"Yes, he's been a really big help." Looking straight ahead as if her peripheral vision were blinded by her self-consciousness, Jodee pretended she couldn't see Archer staring at her.

"Good thing it's your off season." The Colonel took a sip of his drink like it was life-saving nectar after days of drought.

"Yes, but I still have practice about twice a week."

"No matter, I know Doug appreciates whatever time you can give." He jiggled his glass of ice and watched the light green liquid swirl in melody to the clinking.

Uncomfortable with Archer scrutinizing her, Jodee got up and walked to the boundary of the lawn. "Colonel, is this your vegetable garden?" she said over her shoulder.

"Yup, been babying that piece of land all summer and barely got a thing to show for it."

Jodee studied the long, rectangular piece of worked plot. There were some vegetables she recognized but most of it was an indistinguishable netting of leaves and new blossoms as if the Colonel had stood back and just thrown seeds to the wind. It was a gallimaufry of vines, bamboo supports, tomato cages, and plants all vying for space. She couldn't quite make out where one plant ended and another began.

"I suppose I should have picked a different spot to plant. One that wasn't so close to the woods."

Jodee silently agreed as she spotted the Creeping Charlie, Witch Grass, and sedges that were encroaching on the border of the garden, and while the trees above let just enough filtered light through the leaves to allow the garden to grow.

Grace, her footsteps cushioned by the soft pliable ground, walked up and stood beside Jodee. She slipped her arm around Jodee's waist and whispered, "Don't you let him fool you none, he doesn't care no more for that garden than the birds and the bees. He thinks he has me fooled telling me he's coming down here to water the garden but I know it's just so he can smoke a cigar and get a beer out of that cooler."

Jodee turned her head and smiled down at her mother-in-law. "You don't mind?"

"Goodness no, a man needs some diversion once in a while. Give him the freedom to smoke a cigar and he gives me the freedom to buy a new dress. It lets 'em think they're in charge." She chuckled as she looked over her shoulder to make sure the men couldn't hear her.

The Colonel and Archer were sitting in quiet friendship drinking their mint juleps and gazing out at the stillness of the day. They hadn't paid any attention to Grace talking to Jodee, but by some unseen connection, her mere mention of cigars had somehow planted a seed in the Colonel's mind from twelve feet away. He reached in his pocket and brought out a cigar, offering it to Archer, "Would you like a stogie, son?"

Before Archer could respond, Grace answered for him, "Oh,

no you don't you two, I came down here to tell you lunch is almost ready. You two come on up to the house now."

The Colonel and Archer turned in unison with wide-eyed surprise, feigning innocence. Taking the cigar back and tucking it inside his shirt pocket, the Colonel acted like nothing out of the ordinary had happened. "We'll save this for later," he said to Archer with a wink. "It doesn't do any good to argue with a woman, son. Besides, it lets 'em think they're in charge."

Archer swallowed his laugh along with a drink from the julep, almost choking in the process. "Yes. sir," he finally said. "I'll remember that."

The lunch was a medley of southern cuisine with Grace's famous potato salad recipe she'd served at every function for the past forty years, ham steak, black-eyed peas and buttermilk biscuits. The whole luncheon was served with side dishes of stories and laughter.

"Lexie, you eat up now, you hear?" Grace told her granddaughter. "You're much too thin."

"Oh, Grandma, I'm not too thin, I just have small bones," Lexie defended. Very quickly adding, "Besides, I came to lunch today just to get some of your dessert."

Jodee was pleased that Lexie was actually eating anything at all.

"Mississippi Mud Pie, yessiree, no one makes it better than your grandmother," the Colonel boasted.

As everyone was finishing their lunch, Jodee took advantage to find out about the other family members.

"How are Rob and Marcy doing, Mother Warren? I haven't had a chance all summer to give them a call."

"Oh, they're doing just fine. I saw them last month when I took Marcy a quilt I had finished for them. I didn't have time before the wedding to get it done."

"They're happy as two pigs in slop," the Colonel added.

"George, that's an indelicate way of putting it," Grace said in a half-hearted attempt to scold him. It was a rare occurrence for Grace to call her husband by his first name, always referring to him as Colonel. "But I have to admit, I think he's right and I wouldn't be surprised if we don't get another grandchild soon."

"Oh, won't that be wonderful," Jodee added. "Children, wouldn't it be nice to have a new cousin?" she asked, turning to smile at three of her own.

"I think it would be great," Lexie squealed. "Do you think it will be soon?"

"I wouldn't be surprised none," the Colonel replied.

"Colonel, how is William doing?" Archer joined into the conversation.

"He's still at Ramstein Air Base," the Colonel answered.

"Is he going to be able to come home soon?"

"Well now, Bobbie Boy is making the military a career, you know." The Colonel was the only one who called his second son by his childhood nickname.

"Who's Bobbie Boy?" Dougie J wanted to know.

"Bobbie is your daddy's younger brother, William. Grandpa calls him Bobbie," Jodee explained.

"I guess you wouldn't remember him, would you, Dougie?" Grace said, looking at her grandson. "You couldn't have been more than three when he left."

"He had just turned three when Bob was deployed."

"Where is Ramstein, Grandpa?" Dayla asked.

"That's in Germany. Way across the ocean."

Everyone could tell that the subject of William was making Grace melancholy, so the Colonel quickly changed the subject.

"So, tell me about this boyfriend of Audra's. Is he the young man we met last fall?"

"Yes," Dayla interjected with a face that looked like she'd just bitten into a lemon. "They're always kissin' and everything."

"He seemed like a nice enough young man, although we didn't really get to talk to him much that day. Do you like him, Lexie?" The Colonel had always been protective of anyone dating his granddaughters.

"He's okay, I guess." Lexie looked down at her plate like she'd just seen a bug run under her ham.

Jodee noticed Lexie's attitude had quickly changed from happy to reserved when Travis was mentioned. As she watched Lexie's gaze go down, she saw the Colonel's eyebrows go up in concern.

Jodee tried to quickly cover up Lexie's change in attitude, leery of why it changed, hoping the Colonel wouldn't start asking questions she wasn't prepared to answer. She needed time to talk to Lexie alone about what she knew of Travis, so she quickly exclaimed, "You know Audra graduates this coming year."

There was a slight pause while everyone tried to understand the shift in the emotional atmosphere.

Grace covered the minute pause in conversation with a question that trailed into a story, "Does she have any plans for her senior trip? I know it's a ways away, but I remember Robbie's senior trip and I tell you, if we weren't a nervous wreck the entire time he was gone. Do you remember that, Colonel? He went down to Ft. Lauderdale with a bunch of his friends and I think it was the longest week of my life. I was just glad he was the last of our children to graduate because I couldn't have handled another week like that."

"Why, what happened, Grandma?" Her grandmother's story

had brought Lexie out of her temporary gloominess.

"He hadn't been gone no more than a day or two when we get a call in the middle of the night. It must have been two or three in the morning. Well, you know any time you get a call at that time of the morning you just know its bad news. I pick it up, half asleep, and Robbie is on the other end of the line and I can tell right away he's upset. I tell you, I never woke up so fast in my life. I start asking Robbie what's wrong but there is so much noise in the background with music and kids yelling and all that I couldn't understand a word he was saying. After about five minutes or so, with me thinking the worst, like he had been in an accident or mugged or some other horrible thing, the phone line suddenly went dead!"

The children were enraptured. "What did you do, Grandma?" Dayla asked excitedly.

"First, I tried to wake up your grandpa but all he did was mumble something about Robbie being a grown man or some other such nonsense and then he went right back to sleep, snoring almost immediately." Everyone laughed as she tried sneering at her husband but instead it came out looking like a pucker of lips that only enhanced the river of deep red lipstick lines.

"I got out of bed and started searching the house for Robbie's schedule, the numbers of his friend's family, but I couldn't remember who he said he was going with. I almost started to call the operator and ask for every hotel in Ft. Lauderdale. I was on the verge of panic and was about to call the Ft. Lauderdale police when Robbie called back. He had moved to another part of the restaurant so I could hear him and was finally able to tell me what was wrong. Turns out, he had lost his wallet and didn't have the money to get back to his hotel. His friends had all left him and gone to a club and he was stranded about ten miles from where they were staying. I could tell he had been drinking, which was bad enough, but when I found out all he wanted was for us to send him more money, at that moment I didn't know if I was more relieved that he was okay or angry at him for worrying me out of a year of my life."

Lexie had come alive with mirth. "And you never even woke up, Grandpa?" she hiccupped with a chuckle, looking over at the Colonel.

"Now don't blame me," he pretended to be offended. "I knew if he was in any real trouble we would have heard from the police. Besides, he always knew that if he did anything wrong that I would've tanned his hide."

"Really, Grandpa?" Dougie J asked with worried eyes.

"Now don't let your grandpa fool you, Dougie. Your grandpa is just a big teddy bear," Jodee said fondly as she smiled at the Colonel.

"Well, I for one was never so worried in my life," Grace exhaled with a breath of relief like the incident had just happened the night before.

"I can just see him half drunk and trying to get back to his room. I know Rob, he was probably trying to hitch a ride with anyone with wheels," Archer laughed.

"Don't you just know it? My Rob is a good boy, but when he was that age, he didn't have a lick of common sense," Grace injected.

"Just be glad he hadn't decided to go to Cancun for his senior trip. If he had called from Mexico in the middle of the night, I might have actually lost a couple of minutes of sleep," the Colonel teased.

"Oh, Grandpa," Lexie sighed heavily, making everyone laugh.

The Colonel looked over at Jodee with a smile as he forked another piece of ham steak into his mouth, "Well, now, Jodee, you know what I'm talking about. Didn't you and Doug go to Cancun for your honeymoon?"

Jodee was busy wiping potato salad from Dougie J's face, listening to the story, enjoying the laughter and not prepared to defend her husband like she'd done for the past eighteen years. She answered the question without thinking, "Oh, no, I didn't go. Doug went to Cancun with a bunch of his friends."

She stopped fussing with Dougie when she realized what she had just let slip and noticed the entire group had gone quiet. She looked up at a circle of confused and frowning faces. "Well, I mean, he'd had that trip planned before we were married," she explained in a rush. "He had just graduated college and with the wedding plans and all he needed some down time, some time to regroup... I totally supported him... And, uh, I understood completely. Besides, he always promised to take me on a honeymoon when we could see ourselves clear, but then the kids were born and his career started taking off and, well, we just haven't gotten around to it yet."

She looked around the table at each set of eyes, all revealing different emotions. Grace was perplexed. Archer sat in stunned silence before quietly saying, "I remember that trip. We had taken it a month after Jodee and Doug were married. No one knew it was supposed to be their honeymoon."

The Colonel's face was slowly turning red with each passing second as the circumstances started taking shape in his mind.

Jodee had never seen him get angry and was afraid he was going to explode.

Lexie finally broke the awkwardness with a stunned question, "Mom, you never went on a honeymoon?"

"No, but like I said, we've just never been able to seem to find the time to go. I didn't really mind though, really," she stammered.

With teeth so clinched it made his jaws look square, the Colonel said in a way that made it feel like an interrogation, "I seem to remember giving Doug a thousand dollars for that honeymoon. Are you telling me he took a bunch of friends and you stayed home?"

"Um, well, Colonel, Doug used that money to help pay off the wedding and put the security deposit down on our first apartment."

"I see. You were so hard up that Doug used it as a deposit for your first apartment and yet he still somehow found the money to go to Cancun without you?"

"George, now's not the time," Grace pleaded.

The Colonel looked sternly at Archer like he stood in proxy for Doug.

Jodee watched the glare the Colonel was aiming at Archer, who looked like he'd just run over the family dog. She was becoming frightened as the Colonel got angrier and angrier by the second. What had she done? She frantically searched her mind trying to find a solution that wouldn't backfire on Doug, and thereby on herself.

Grace saved the moment, and Jodee. "Children," she said, jumping up from the table. "Did you bring your swimsuits? The river is nice and warm. Why don't you go on and get changed and I'll bring some lemonade to you in a little bit. We'll have dessert after you've had a swim."

Dayla and Dougie J shouted in unison, "Yea!" They got out of their chairs so fast Dougie almost knocked his over. They ran to the back bedroom to change.

"Aren't you going to go, too, Lexie, dear?" Grace asked.

Lexie looked between her mother and grandfather, but stuck in that uncomfortable world of adults and children, she seemed frozen to her chair.

The decision to not push her limited boundary into adulthood was apparent as she got up from the table in an unsure fashion and walked slowly away to find Dayla and Dougie J.

"Colonel, why don't you help me clear the table and we'll let Jodee and Archer go watch the children?"

Grace was desperate to stop what appeared to be her husband's transformation from joviality to anger. She started stacking dishes so fast she almost dropped the entire pile. She looked at her husband as they walked into the kitchen. He didn't get angry often, and the fact was, he had hardly ever yelled at their boys when they were growing up, but when he did lose his temper he could become as hard as any father who suddenly finds himself disappointed in one of his children. She'd only seen it once before and that was when William had taken the family car without permission and crashed it into a pole, breaking his arm. She'd had to intervene then, too, she remembered. Grace knew that her husband was not a strict man, that deep down he was really very gentle. And the times he had disciplined their boys could be counted on one hand. But now was another time to intervene. "George," she said under her breath. "Try and stay calm."

Lexie lingered in the bathroom as long as she could hoping everyone was already outside, and that she could get in the river without anyone seeing her in her swimsuit. She walked cautiously by the kitchen door on her way outside and heard the angry voice of her grandfather. She stopped in her tracks and tip-toed to the edge of the door where she could hear and not be seen.

"Now, George, it doesn't do any good to get upset over something that happened almost nineteen years ago."

"Grace, in all my years you know I've never been disappointed in my boys, but this goes beyond anything I could ever imagine Doug doing. I don't care if it was nineteen years ago, I'm so angry I could chew nails."

"Well, what do you think you can do about it now? It will only upset Jodee. You need to calm down, so it doesn't ruin what's left of the day."

"It's going to take me a long time to calm down, Grace. I mean, for the love of God, what kind of man does that... Take his buddies on a trip and leave his new bride at home?"

"I don't know, George. I just don't know. I would have never imagined he would do something like that either."

"The only saving grace is Jodee was so young and so in love she probably never gave it a second thought. Not even thinking it was the height of insult and inconsideration to her!"

"No, George, don't kid yourself, she knew. Every woman dreams of her honeymoon. No, I'm telling you now, she knew and she felt the slight. She's probably felt it all this time and has just kept it so deeply buried that it's become nothing more than a scar on her heart."

Lexie heard her grandfather grunt as if he were in pain. She turned and silently headed back down the hall to the bathroom with the echo of her grandmother's words following her every step, 'a scar on her heart, a scar on her heart.' The thought was too painful for her to deal with – the disappointment she felt in her father, the indignation coming from her grandfather, her ache for her mother.

She walked into the guest bathroom, quietly closed and locked the door, then stuck her finger down her throat and threw up her lunch.

CHAPTER SEVENTEEN

HER FATHER'S LOVE

"Mom, pleeeaasssee!"

"Dougie J, I've already told you, I just don't think we have time to stop by."

They had no sooner stepped out of the Warren's home, after spending a pleasant afternoon at the river, when Dougie J started pleading to see his other grandparents – Papa Joe and Gammy Kate.

"But, gaw, Mom, we're right here in town." It was Dayla's turn to whine.

"They're not expecting us and it's dinner time. I doubt if Gammy has enough food for all of us to just drop by."

"But I want to show Papa Joe my new baseball Grandpa gave me." Dougie was being relentless.

Dayla kept the pressure going with, "We don't have to stay for dinner, Mom. Can't we at least stop by and see them?"

"You know, Archer was kind enough to bring us up here to see Grandma and Grandpa Warren, I don't think he has time to run us all over Minnesota." Jodee felt guilty using Archer as a scapegoat to try and get out of having to see her parents, but she hadn't seen her father since she had broken the snow blower and she didn't want him to humiliate her in front of Archer and the kids.

In unison, Dayla and Dougie turned to look at Archer, begging with the innocent manipulation of children's faces for him to agree.

Jodee knew Archer was between a rock and a hard place. She wanted to be fair and let the children see both sets of their grandparents since they lived in the same town, but she also knew that the visit would be a bad end to a good day. In the end though, it was the pitiful little faces of her children that did him in.

"Don't worry about me. I don't mind dropping in and seeing your parents, Jodee," he said as he turned his face slightly away.

"Archer, really, you don't need to do this." Jodee's tone was pleading as she silently urged him to look at her so he could see the desperation in her eyes.

"It's really no bother, Jodee. Why don't we go over for a few minutes so the kids can see them, and we'll still be able to make it home early."

She had the distinct impression he was lying, but that was it, she was outvoted. There was nothing she could do without making it obvious she didn't want to go and having questions asked. Maybe she was blowing things out of proportion, at least she hoped so. One thing she could be grateful for was she knew her father dearly loved his grandchildren and had never transferred any of his feelings for her to them. She relented with, "Oh, uh, well, uh, if you're sure you don't mind. I guess we'll go for a little while." It took so much effort to say the words she used every last bit of her breath being expelled from her lungs to get it out.

"All right children, we'll go over but we can't stay long, understand?"

"Yea!" came the shouting from her two younger children.

Lexie had not participated in the back and forth. Jodee had

noticed she'd been particularly quiet after lunch. She'd been so animated at her grandparents, and it had given Jodee some hope – hope that her usually reserved daughter had just been going through some teenage phase and was finally outgrowing it. Unfortunately, her feeling of hope did not last long as Lexie was back to her old self within a matter of minutes, ten to be exact, from the end of lunch to everyone meeting down at the river Lexie had once again transformed back into her aloof, distant self.

Hoping she was reading too much into her daughter's quiet demeanor as well, she decided to question Lexie. Maybe she wasn't feeling well. It wasn't something Jodee hoped, but in the deep recesses of her guilty mind she thought it could be a way to get out of the visit to her parents.

"Lexie, are you not feeling well? You've been quiet all afternoon. If you don't feel well we can forget about the visit to your grandparents and take you right home."

"No mom, I'm fine. I'd like to go over to Gammy's. I was just a little tired at the river and I think the sun just took it out of me, that's all. And lunch was so big I got drowsy and I swam too long. You know."

Jodee knew that when Lexie started making excuses, it was her way of withdrawing into herself. It was becoming a habit that whenever she couldn't reconcile something, she would retreat into her own world, as if her thoughts and feelings were in conflict with each other. People thought she was quiet or introverted, but Jodee knew it was her way of needing to be left alone. She found that Lexie feigning tiredness was a great way to stop people from questioning her since it was the most mundane topic of small talk. Jodee sometimes thought her daughter must be the most tired person in the world the excuse was used so often.

It was Jodee's last ditch effort and with forced resignation she said with a reluctant sigh, "If you're sure, then." After another moment of stalling she finished her sentence, "I guess we'd better go before it gets any later."

The look on Jodee's face had confused Archer. Did she want to see her parents or not? Was she thinking about the inconvenience to him or was she thinking about the kids? Was she trying to convince him to take the children or was she pleading for him to say no?

Not understanding any reason besides him why she wouldn't want to see her own parents, he decided to be magnanimous, He wanted to spend more time with Jodee and the children anyway, but he didn't have any desire to see Joe Olson.

Ten minutes later, as Archer swung his truck into Mr. and Mrs. Olson's driveway, he noticed they weren't the only ones visiting for the evening. The driveway was full of cars he didn't know. The one on the street was one he did recognize however, and it made him inwardly groan. It belonged to Brigid. His guard went up immediately. He knew she liked him, but she was a little too forward for his taste. She made him a tad uncomfortable, which is why he had never pursued her. Oh, she was pretty enough and nice enough, but she just wasn't his type. He got the feeling, though, she thought she was every man's type. But the most obvious reason of all why he would never date her was she was Jodee's younger sister. He was not brave enough to admit to himself that Brigid was not the sister he wanted.

"Oh, my, it looks like the whole family is here," Jodee commented on a quizzical note.

"Yea, I can show Kevin my new baseball, too," Dougie

squealed.

"Just remember children, we can only stay a little while." She turned to Archer and apologized. "Archer, I had no idea my sisters would all be here. I'm so sorry."

"Don't worry about it, Jodee. I know you didn't know, and I don't mind, really." Archer found that if he just thought about Jodee it made the lies easier to say.

Dougie J and Dayla bounded from the car as soon as it stopped and ran straight through the front door without knocking.

"Gammy, Gammy, we came to visit," Dougie J shouted as Archer, Jodee, and Lexie followed at a more halting pace.

Katie Olson had been walking past the living room headed for the backyard when the front door banged open. "Oh my, what are youse doing here?" Her surprise was genuinely happy. She stopped in her tracks and held open her arms. "Come and give your Gammy a hug!" She hugged her grandchildren with such force it always made them gasp for air.

"We were visiting Grandma and Grandpa Warren and had to come and see you too," Dayla offered as she gathered air back into her lungs.

"I vas just telling fah-der dis morning how I vish all my kirls could be home and look'it here dey are. Kevin, Sara, come see who's here!" she yelled at her other grandchildren.

Archer was very fond of Katie Olson. He didn't know if it was the way she always seemed happy to see him or her Minnesota niceness with her thick Norwegian accent he found so cute. Although it took him great concentration to understand her, he loved listening to her talk. He found her completely charming and returned her embrace when she addressed him, "Hello, Mrs. Olson. It's nice to see you again."

"Now, Archer, vhat do I huvda ta do ta get you ta call me

Katie?"

The rest of the family came through the backdoor in one big group. He stood back and watched as Jodee's sisters, niece, and nephew all came in, followed by her father.

The yipping and yelling and the jumping up and down by the cousins made such a high-pitched noise it made Archer cringe.

"Oh my goodness," Katie Olson laughed. "I dint expect dis, dun-cha-no. With da noise in dis house you could wake da dead. Why don't da kids go out back until dinner? But youse boyce try and keep from getting dirty."

"Hello, Mother," Jodee said timidly as her mother turned toward her. Archer was perplexed by Jodee's shy demeanor in front of her family.

"Jodee! Dere's my kirl. Joe, look who's here!" Katie yelled as she grabbed her oldest daughter in a hard hug that included a little swaying motion in a kind of loving dance.

Over her mother's shoulder, Jodee watched her sisters come through the door and caught her father's eyes.

"Hi, Daddy," Jodee said shyly when her mother finally let her go. She went to him and gave him a quick squeeze. He gave her a half-hearted pat on the back where only his shoulders touched her and his head was bent back at an odd angle.

Archer noticed this strange encounter as he watched Jodee's face. The off-handed hug by her father didn't seem to bother her. But Archer found Mr. Olson's behavior odd and the non-existent hug insulting, as if any affection shown on his part was made out of protocol and not true love.

Jodee then turned to Nora and gave her a hug with such a look of relief on her face Archer could tell she was happy her sisters were there to cushion the evening.

"Hi, Jodee, where you been hiding?" Nora said teasingly.

"We haven't seen you all summer."

"I'm sorry. I've just been really busy with Doug traveling so much. You know how it is. Is Adam here?"

"No, not yet. He's at his weekly baseball game. Lord knows he can't miss a practice. You'd think he was trying out for the minor leagues the way he's so dedicated to that team. He should be here in a little while, though."

Nora turned to Archer, "Hello, Archer, it's nice to see you again."

"Nora. How have you been?"

Interrupting the greeting, Brigid slid into the room with a roll of her shoulders followed by swerving hips. She squeezed herself between her two older sisters. "Jodee, aren't you going to give me a hug?"

It always surprised Archer when he would see the three Olson sisters together because they looked nothing alike. Jodee was petite with a stylish blonde haircut and the curves of a woman. Brigid had long mousy brown hair that hung to the middle of her back and offset her small frame. She had just enough curves, so a man knew she was full grown. And Nora's hair was short and dark, and she had a more portly body. The thing about Nora was her nose, the tip of it twitched when she talked as if there were an invisible string attached from her upper lip to the tip of her nose. It reminded him of a rabbit. It was hypnotic and Archer would watch it move with every sentence until it started to drive him crazy. He couldn't concentrate on what she was saying from watching her nose constantly bob up and down. To keep from appearing rude, he started staring at her forehead when she spoke.

"Brigid, of course." Jodee gave her youngest sister a tight squeeze then quickly looked down to see what she was wearing.

217

Held together by a blue strip of cloth and a wish, Brigid was sporting a thong bikini so small Archer was embarrassed to look in her general direction. Even though she had a swimsuit cover up on, the material was made of sheer white lace and did nothing to hide Brigid's butt and breasts as the strings worked overtime to keep her inside its confines.

Brigid turned from her sister and addressed Archer. "Archer, how nice to see you again. Is Jodee dragging you around to see the family?"

She walked up to him and with her body pressed solidly against his front, reached up to put her arms around his neck and gave him a seductive hug. Unashamed of who might be watching, she oozed sexual charm that bubbled to the surface like an artesian well seeping through layers of dry earth.

Archer had no choice but to bend down to meet her height and hug her back. Her semi-nudity made him uncomfortable. He didn't know where to look that wouldn't make it obvious he noticed her. He also didn't want Mr. Olson to think he was ogling his daughter. As he gave her a light hug, he was unsure where to place his hands. He wrapped his arms around her middle while keeping his hands bent at the wrist. He held them so high they looked broken. He could feel her breast pressed up against his chest and her tiny frame in his arms, but her build was so petite and her breasts so small it was like hugging Dayla, or any fourteen-year-old who hadn't quite developed yet. But Brigid was not fourteen and she knew how to entice men. She held the hug a little longer than was comfortable for him, and with a sexy lift of her shoulders that even Marilyn Monroe would have envied, pressed herself a little harder against his chest before letting go. No one was paying attention to them so no one but Archer knew of her movement.

Archer quickly stepped back when her hold on him was over. With a gulp of nervous swallowing, that Brigid mistook for desire, he willed himself to look anywhere but at the tiny lace cover up she was wearing and the bright blue string that had found its home in the crack of her behind. He had noticed it when she had turned toward her sisters, but now it was like a beacon, taunting him to look.

Between the shining glare of Brigid's butt cheeks and Nora's twitching nose, Archer didn't know where to look. He decided his safest bet was to finally acknowledge Mr. Olson. "Mr. Olson, sir, nice to see you again."

Joe eyed Archer like a cop eyeing a suspect who was unsure of his innocence. "Archer," was all he said as he held out his hand to be shaken.

Archer got the feeling he had just been found guilty of some unknown infraction. He told himself he was letting his imagination run away with him, but the hard stare from Mr. Olson was making each moment more and more awkward so that soon he couldn't even look at Mr. Olson. He felt he'd been thrown into a pit of thorns with no way of climbing out.

Katie stepped up and saved him from the uncomfortable stare. "Joe, isn't it nice to have all da kirls home? Brigid, go and get some clothes on, now, we have company."

"Oh, Mother," Brigid said with a roll of her eyes. "Archer has seen a woman in a bikini before." She turned and gave Archer a wink, as if to say, 'Mom is so old-fashioned.'

"Never mind dat. We're going to eat soon so you jus' put on some clothes before you come to da table."

"Oh, all right." Brigid turned and began sauntering out of the room, convinced all eyes were on her retreat. Before leaving the room entirely, she turned to her niece. "Lexie, want to come and see my new boots I got for fall?"

"Um, sure, okay." Lexie proceeded to follow her aunt out of the room.

"And I'll let you try on one of my other swimsuits, too." Brigid cooed.

"Jus' dun dawdle," Katie said as she turned to go back into the kitchen. "Dinner is in ten minutes."

Afraid they would be made to stay longer than she wanted to, Jodee quickly spoke to her mother's retreating back. "Mother, we didn't come for dinner. You don't need to worry about us."

"Oh, dun be silly, of course youse are staying."

"Yes, dun be silly, Jodee," Nora mimicked her mother. "I'm sure Archer and the kids are hungry even if you're not."

"It's just that we only intended to stop by for a little while so the kids could see Mom and Dad. I wasn't expecting to find everyone home. What is everyone doing here, anyway? Is something special going on or something?"

"The same reason you're here." A quizzical look drew Nora's eyebrows into a deep frown between her eyes. "Planning our trip to Vegas with Dad. I didn't think you were ever going to get here either."

"Uh, I'm sorry, I don't know anything about a trip to Vegas," Jodee said.

"What are you talking about? We've been planning this for a month. Dad's going to a conference and asked us to go." Nora turned to her father, confused. "Daddy, didn't you tell Jodee?"

"Oh, well, I meant to until I heard Doug was traveling then I knew she wouldn't have time to go." His lie was only slightly less apparent than the uncomfortable situation Nora had put him in.

Archer watched the hurt look on Jodee's face come and go

in a single move. He knew she knew that her father had had no intention of asking her to go. Archer watched as Jodee turned her head and saw her swallow hard.

In an obvious pretense, at least to him, she turned aside as if fumbling for something in her purse and said, "Dad's right, I don't have time to go."

"Don't be silly, Jodee," Nora persisted. "It's not until next month and by then the kids will be in school."

Shifting his weight to his right leg and sticking his hands in his back pockets, Joe glanced quickly at Archer and then down, as if trying to save face in front of him, and replied a little too rapidly, "Well, yes, of course you should come."

"Dad's getting a suite at the Bellagio and we get to stay for free. I keep telling him I can pay for my own room, but he's insisting."

"Well, now, I don't know how many people the room will hold. If Jodee wants to come, she'll have to pay for her own room." Mr. Olson's gaze was suddenly anxious and hard.

"Then I'll stay with Jodee and maybe we can get a suite that connects. What do you say, Jodee? Want to come?"

Watching Jodee's face and the rapid blinking she always started when she was upset or nervous, Archer knew she was trying desperately to figure a way out of the hurt her father had caused. Jodee hemmed and hawed and fidgeted with the end of her hair. Nora stared at her waiting for an answer. Her father suddenly decided his shoes were the most fascinating things he'd ever seen.

Archer watched the interaction between Joe and his daughters. Not believing what he had just witnessed. Two of his daughters had been invited on a trip and Jodee hadn't even been given a second thought. Archer was becoming livid. If he didn't dislike Jodee's father before now, this obvious snub had him despising Mr. Olson.

Archer knew immediately Jodee needed help, so he quickly came up with a lie to help save her, "Uh, Jodee, I don't mean to overstep my bounds, but doesn't Dougie J have a tournament next month?"

"But we haven't even told you what day we're going yet. Maybe it won't fall on the same weekend," Nora reasoned.

"No, but I've been helping to coach the team since Doug has been out of town and he told me he wants the kids to practice as much as possible. And then if their team wins, they could end up playing most of the month."

Jodee stared at Archer, relief brightening her eyes. "Yes, that's right. And we still don't know how much longer Doug is going to have to travel back and forth to California. He thinks it could go well into fall and I can't possibly expect Archer to continue to help out. I'm going to have to take over pretty soon. Besides, someone will have to be home when the kids get out of school."

A little put off, Nora huffed out a reply as if she were blaming Jodee for some offense, "Well, that's too bad. You're going to miss a good time. We're going to go to a couple of shows, go to the casinos, lay out by the pool..."

"What is everyone talking about? I heard the word pool." Brigid regained the attention of the crowd when she walked back in from the bedroom. She had changed from the tiny thong bikini to a pair of tight cut off Daisy Duke's with a strategically placed hole on the bottom part of her left butt cheek, showing she was going commando. A pink cotton blouse, which was missing the first top two buttons, was tied at her waist just above her bellybutton.

"We're talking about Vegas," Nora answered, a little testily.

"That's why I'm trying to get a tan now, so I don't look like a typical Minnesotan. Aren't you coming, Jodee?" Brigid asked.

"Like I was telling Nora, I just can't get away right now, with Doug traveling and all."

At that moment, Nora's husband Adam came through the door. Heading directly to his wife, he kissed Nora on the cheek, then turned his attention to the group and spotted Archer.

With a smug smile at his sister-in-law he asked, "So, Jodee, have you replaced Doug with a new husband?"

"I'm sorry?" Jodee asked, confused.

"Well, why else is Archer here? Has he taken over Doug's duties?"

It was like opening the flood gates of who could torture Jodee the most, Archer noticed, as Nora joined in with her husband, "Of course not, Adam, Jodee can handle two men. Can't you, Jodee?"

"Maybe Doug doesn't even know you're with him. Is that it? Maybe I should call him and tell him what's going on," Adam continued.

Archer stood, too shocked by the innuendo and wondering why no one was telling Adam to shut up.

He looked over at Brigid, who was giggling behind her hand. He looked over at their mother as she walked back into the melee, but she simply looked down at her apron like nothing out of the ordinary was going on. Her behavior was duplicated by Lexie, except Lexie was pretending to suddenly be interested in family photos on the wall. When he looked at Mr. Olson, he sensed an underlying tension as the older man's face got redder and redder and angrier and angrier with each passing second. Good, Archer thought, someone in this dysfunctional family was reacting normally.

"Adam, Doug is perfectly aware of Archer helping me. He's the one who asked him to," Jodee defended herself.

"Oh, come on, Jodee, I'm only kidding. No need to get your panties in a bunch."

"Panties in a bunch," Brigid whispered under her breath as she suppressed a giggle. "Jodee never could take a joke," she added.

This seemed to re-ignite the fire under Jodee that Adam had started. Nora added to her younger sister's insult, "Yeah, Jodee has always been the sensitive type, wah. We never could joke with her that she wouldn't get upset at."

Jodee kept her head down, and as if her eyes had a mind of their own, they began the rapid blinking.

"Well, I think that's enough of everyone picking on Jodee," Archer said briskly.

"Archer, Jodee knows it's just a little innocent teasing," Brigid explained. "Besides, she's always been so oversensitive I was never sure who the baby of the family was – me or her."

"Oh, no, now she's starting that ridiculous blinking she does whenever she gets upset. Maybe we'd better stop before she starts to cry," said the nose-twitcher.

"Jodee needs to learn to take a joke," her father piped up. "She can dish it out, but she can't take it."

"No disrespect, sir, but I don't really see Jodee dishing anything," Archer said as he looked Mr. Olson in the eyes.

Jodee looked up at Archer, surprise showing in her eyes. He could tell by her shock that no one had ever defended her before.

"Everybody jis needs to calm down," Mrs. Olson declared tentatively, looking over at her husband to gauge his reaction to Archer's comment. "Now, who is ready for dinner? Some hotdish and coffee, maybe?"

"Oh, all right, Mother," Brigid said reluctantly. "I'll help you and get the coffee." Before she left the room however, she turned back and addressed her sister, "Jodee, do you want coffee or your usual coffee flavored water with milk?" She must have thought this was funny because she laughed as she followed her mother out of the room.

"What was that all about?" Archer wanted to know.

"Well, you see, Archer, Jodee thinks if you add about a fourth teaspoon of coffee to hot water then she can call it coffee. But then she adds so much milk to it you can't even tell it's coffee," rabbit girl explained.

"Yeah," Adam added. "Then she dunks her bars or toast or whatever she can find in it and calls it dessert. That's how she got the nickname 'milquetoast.'"

Concurring with her husband, nose-twitcher continued, "It was actually Adam who gave her the name, but we all think it fits perfectly. I, personally, think it's kind of clever, but then, Adam has always had a quick wit."

You would, Archer thought.

"Well, I do have to say that I've been told I'm pretty funny. But Nora is the smart one because she's the one who pointed out Jodee's silly habit in the first place."

Archer stood and contemplated this a bit, always amazed at how one person would think another person was intelligent or clever or witty just because they agreed with something they'd said. But this was taking things too far, he fumed, they were making fun of how she liked her coffee like a couple of high schoolers. The whole thing baffled him. They had seemed all right with Jodee individually and had even showed care about her not going to Vegas. But when they got in a group it was like watching a pack of wild dogs circling a wounded deer and tearing at its legs, waiting for it to fall to the ground, and Adam seemed to be the alpha male.

He couldn't take any more. He turned to Jodee, "You know, Jodee, do you mind if we skip dinner? I really do have to get home."

"Oh, please, Archer," Nora said with a smirk. "Are you going to be over-sensitive too? Jodee knows we're just kidding."

"Oh, no, Nora, I understand you all think it's in good fun." His tone was laden with condescension. "I really do have to get home, though. I have practice in the morning, and I know Jodee has to get Dougie J to baseball and Dayla to swim class." Archer couldn't help adding an extra barb for Adam's sake. "You know the schedule of a pro player is pretty strict."

"No. No, not at all. I understand." Jodee reacted so quickly, she almost ran into the wall trying to get to the kids who were still in the backyard. "Children," she yelled, "we need to get going."

"But gaw, Mom, we haven't even eaten yet," Dayla whimpered, coming through the back door.

It wasn't the fact Dayla was arguing with her mother, but her high-pitched whine that had Archer gritting his teeth. He had to keep reminding himself she was just a young girl and so it was expected she might be a little annoying at times, but for some reason Dayla always hit his last nerve. Reminding himself it wasn't his place to discipline her even though his tongue was on the verge of doing just that. And although he didn't think about it at the time, it occurred to him later that Dayla was the only one of the children to complain about leaving. Lexie had simply gone to her grandmother to hug her good-bye, and Dougie J had come in without muttering a single word of complaint.

Katie looked up with defeat in her eyes. "Oh, vell, if ya must. Kids, let me get'cha some bars for da road. Jodee, my kirl, give me a ring later in da week. I miss ya dun-cha know."

Jodee had hugged her mother quickly then started gathering her things as she said, "I will, Mama." As she waited for her kids to say good-bye to their cousins and grandparents, for her mother to wrap up some bars for the road, and Archer to try and make amends with her sisters, she watched as her dad came across the room heading directly for her.

"Jodee, I want to talk to you a minute."

She thought perhaps he was going to say something kind, or apologize, or offer some support for her taking care of the kids on her own while Doug was away. She didn't know why she thought this since he had never apologized in the past, even after he'd slapped her one time when she was fourteen when she had rolled her eyes at him for something, that to her teenage mind, was a dumb remark. He had slapped her so hard it had left her bruised and swollen and then he yelled at her to never show him disrespect in that manner again. It was the only time her dad had ever hit her and she thought he actually felt bad about it, but he never apologized. After that, she had learned to never, ever roll her eyes at him, and it was what had begun the propensity of her uncontrollable blinking. She thought that if she couldn't roll her eyes then she'd blink away her frustrations and wouldn't catch her father's ire. It was just that the blinking had become such an ingrained part of her mental makeup over the years she couldn't help herself any more. Whenever she was in a vulnerable state it was her eyes that gave her away.

After the day her father slapped her, he tended to stay away from her. Instead, he started using subtle remarks and insults hurled at her as a way to discipline her. It was the verbal abuse in place of hitting her that finally started taking its toll. Then her sisters started in and it seemed she had become the family punching bag. Sometimes she wished he had just kept slapping her. But with a lifetime of wishful thinking she answered him hopefully, "Yes, Daddy."

"Let's talk on the porch," he said as he waited for her to follow him out. When she had stepped just past the screen door, he started, "I know you might be needing help with the kids while Doug is traveling, but it's not proper for you to be bringing another man to my house in his place. It's not showing proper respect to me or your husband. And if I ever find out you've been disloyal to him, I'll turn you out. You understand me, girl?"

Jodee's eyes had grown eerily wide as he spoke to her, her face grew pale, her heart rate increased, her legs got wobbly, ringing began in her ears. She could barely hear him chastising her because the ringing kept getting louder and louder, like he was standing on the other side of a large field trying to yell over a noisy crowd.

He continued to berate her, ending with, "I'm disappointed in you, Jodee, I truly am." With that last remark he came to attention like a soldier, eyed her one last time, then turned his back on her and walked back inside.

His words always flayed her alive. Every insult made her feel like she was dying skin cell by skin cell. He had hurled them at her so fast and razor-sharp she didn't feel the cutting hurt until he walked away.

She grabbed hold of the door jamb so she wouldn't sink to her knees and into the abyss of her father's cruelty. His words had stunned her to a point so sharp she didn't know how to react, so she stood by the door dashed of any hope of her father showing her some kindness. Instead she was doomed that he would forever be disappointed in her, no matter what she did. Now he had accused her of cheating on Doug.

Jodee was humiliated when she turned and saw Archer staring at her just inside the door. She wondered if he had heard what her father had accused her of but the look on his face was one of pity. She thought of all the times she had been the butt of their jokes. All the family gatherings, all the holidays where she left depressed from their attacks, all the times she prayed Doug would stop them only to realize Doug was part of it. It seemed the whole family reveled whenever they got together because it was their chance to gang up on her. *Innocent teasing?* Jodee thought. It had never been innocent. Every time she'd ever tried to defend herself, the insults would get worse and the name calling became more personal. It left her feeling like she was surrounded by a firing squad begging for her life. It only made everyone react more aggressively and the 'teasing' got more vicious. She soon learned to just keep quiet, endure the hurt, and pray for it to end. A self-preservation habit she had developed early in her life. As usual though, her body started its familiar tingling, which indicated she was not controlling her emotions as well as she had hoped.

Now, standing and looking at Archer through the screen, she realized that no matter how old she got, she was doomed to forever be stung by her family's words, her father's disappointment and his cruel remarks. Remarks like sharp barbs that would continue to dig deeper and deeper into her skin until maybe, one day, they would simply sting her to death.

SECTION FOUR

CONTRIBUTING FACTORS

Let your guard down or look away,
And life can turn in a single day.

CHAPTER EIGHTEEN

ESCALATED

The trip back to the Warren's was the longest of Archer's life – one hour, thirteen minutes and forty-three seconds. He knew because the second they had left the Olsons Archer was so angry he couldn't bring himself to look at Jodee, so he alternated from the road to the speedometer to the clock on the dashboard. He wasn't sure what upset him more, anger at her family or pain for her.

He also didn't trust himself to speak because he knew once he started, he wouldn't be able to stop. He knew he couldn't rant about her family because he didn't want to criticize them in front of her kids. Fact was, he wasn't even sure if Jodee would tolerate his venting since she seemed to accept their behavior as normal. He knew they had upset her, but except for the habitual blinking, she didn't show it. So, he simply drove and kept quiet and had yearned for the highway to magically propel him forward like a time machine. He needed to drop everyone off, go home, have a drink, and try and figure out what the hell had happened.

Archer pulled into the Warren driveway after the longest drive of his life. He didn't turn off the engine but simply asked, "Are you going to be okay getting inside by yourself? I kind-a need to get home." He waited for the family to get out, anxious to leave, not really waiting for an answer. "I'll wait until you're in the house, okay?"

"No, you don't have to. A light is on so Audra must be home. Thanks for taking us today, I really appreciate it. I enjoyed the day." Jodee was addressing him but not looking him in the eye.

The kids had gotten out and headed for the front door, all of them subdued, even Dayla, as if his bad mood had been an oppressive layer of fog engulfing the interior of the car and had smothered everyone into silence. No one said good-bye as he drove away. It was just as well, he thought.

"You kids go on and get ready for bed now. I'm going to go see how Audra is doing," Jodee ordered softly as they walked into the house, even though they didn't need any prodding and had already headed for their individual rooms.

Jodee walked into the kitchen to check on her oldest daughter, glad she was home before eleven for a change. Instead of finding Audra as she expected, she was met by Toni sitting at the table pushing an empty cup from one hand to the other like a ball at a tennis match. The look on her face told Jodee her day wasn't over.

"Toni?"

"Hi, Jodee, I've been waiting for you. Audra gave me a key; I hope you don't mind?"

"No, I don't mind. Why would Audra need to give you her key, though? Where is she? Is she in her room?"

"Jodee, sit down and let's talk." The inflection in Toni's voice had Jodee's maternal instinct jumping.

"Okay, in a minute, I need to see Audra." Jodee turned to leave the room, anxiety swallowing her courage.

Toni turned in her chair and faced Jodee head-on. "Jodee, wait, I need to talk to you."

Jodee stopped and turned to face her friend. The look on Toni's face was haggard with sadness smudging her eyes.

"Toni, you're scaring me. What's going on?"

"All right, I can tell I'm upsetting you. The first thing I have to tell you is Audra is okay, but she's in the hospital. She has a bad sprain on her left arm and some bruises on her body." Haltingly she added, "And she may have a concussion. The doctor wants to keep her overnight for observation."

"Wait. What? What are you talking about? The hospital?" Jodee clutched her chest. Her breathing became labored, and she swayed as if she were going to faint.

"Jodee, sit down before you fall down and let me explain." Toni stood up ready to guide Jodee to a kitchen chair.

Jodee could feel the panic clawing through her insides like it was on fire. "The hospital... I need to go see her. Wait, what happened? No, tell me on the way. Why didn't someone call me?"

She became disoriented from the pressure of trying to think rationally. Where were her keys? She needed her car keys. Doug, she had to call Doug. Yes, Doug needed to know. Wait, the kids. She needed someone to watch her other children. Lexie, Lexie was old enough. "I gotta talk to Lexie." She couldn't think. Her confusion over what to do was robbing her of any coherent thought. She started turning in semi-circles trying to decide what to do first, like a caged bird prancing back and forth on a perch.

Toni stepped forward and grabbed Jodee by the shoulders, forcing her to stop. "Jodee, stop, she's okay, I just left her about half an hour ago. She's probably asleep right now and I need to explain everything to you. First, I want you to slow down your breathing. Can you do that?"

Jodee was so dazed that Toni taking control seemed to help.

It was what Jodee needed to calm down, someone to tell her what to do so she could focus.

"Yes, yes, I'll do that, just tell me what happened," she insisted as the pitch of her voice grew higher. "Was she in an accident or something?"

"Jodee, Audra was beaten up by Travis."

"What? No, no, that can't be."

"I know you've suspected Travis has been abusing Audra for a while now. Like all abusers he's gotten more violent and this time he went too far. I was on duty when I got the call. I met her at the hospital and waited until she was seen to."

"What did he do to her?"

"Well, now that part is a little more difficult to explain because, well…because Audra won't tell us."

"Wait, what are you talking about? If she didn't tell you what happened, then how do you know Travis beat her up?"

"Because I've been doing this a long time and I know the signs of when a girl has been abused, as do the doctors. Let me explain, okay? I was called out to the skating rink about nine o'clock. The police were called out on a public disturbance but when they got there, they found a girl crying. She was clutching her arm and stomach and covered in bruises. They suspected she'd been assaulted, so they called me because it's standard procedure to call out a Victim's Advocate. It was Audra. She wouldn't tell them what happened but another girl at the rink, I guess she's a friend of Audra and Travis, said they had been arguing. They saw Travis drag Audra outside and around the building. By the time everyone else ran outside to find them, Travis was headed back into the building and Audra was standing by the car, doubled over and crying. Because of the marks on her body, I took her to the hospital to be checked out. She wouldn't confirm anything, and it was a struggle to even get her to agree to go to the hospital. When I asked her what happened she said she fell down in the dark and hit her head on the side of the building."

"What did Travis say happened?"

"Travis said the same thing…that she fell down."

"I still don't understand. If they both said she fell, why do you think Travis beat her up?"

"Because the doctors know, and I do as well, that you don't get injuries like she's gotten from falling down. Her arm shows signs of being wrenched like someone grabbed it and twisted it in different directions causing some soft tissue damage. The bruises on her neck and back are not consistent with a fall, plus, some of them are fairly old. I also think he punched her in the stomach the way she was clutching it."

"Is she okay? Tell me she's going to be okay."

"She'll be fine. She'll just need some rest when you get her home and some understanding. And, she needs to stay away from Travis."

"Isn't he in jail?"

"No, Jodee, he's not in jail and he won't be going to jail. Like I said, Audra won't confirm anything he did to her and without her bringing charges against him, the police can't do anything."

"Then I'll talk to her myself."

"When you bring her home in the morning you can talk to her, and you should, but legally there is nothing that can be done because she hasn't accused Travis of doing anything wrong. Jodee, the only reason I'm telling you what happened in the first place is because she's in the hospital and you're going to have to pick her up in the morning, so I wanted to warn you, but she's going to tell you she fell down. You're a friend and I care about

Audra but she asked me not to tell you and I pretty much shouldn't have, even though she's a minor. But I reasoned with her that, because of her injuries, there was no way you would believe that someone didn't do this to her. The doctors are bound to tell you their theory, too. Do you understand? If my supervisor finds out I treated a close friend differently and didn't keep a victim's confidence, I could be dismissed. In any other circumstance, I wouldn't say a word because of the confidentiality I promise my victims. But if I didn't tell you, you probably wouldn't know Travis had anything to do with it."

"This isn't right. He's going to get away with hurting my daughter?"

"The only thing I can tell you is that you need to convince Audra to break it off with him or bring charges against him or it will get worse."

They stood staring at each other as if their minds could not reconcile the situation.

With a final sigh, Toni said, "Why don't I go with you in the morning to pick her up and we'll talk to her together. Just let her sleep tonight and you try and get some sleep. Things will be better in the morning if you both get some rest. How's that sound?"

"Sleep. Right. It's best if she sleeps. And thanks, Toni, for offering to go with me to pick her up, but I think this is something I need to do myself. If I can't get anywhere with her, I'll call you and have you talk to her again. Right now I need to call the hospital and check on her, then I have to call Doug." She needed to get Toni to leave because she could feel her heart rate increasing, beating in rhythm to her rising panic. She didn't know how long she could hold it together and she didn't want Toni to know of her panic attacks.

"Do you want me to hang around while you do it?"

"No, that's all right, but if you don't mind, if I need to talk to you tonight, can I call you?"

"Of course, honey, anytime. I'll go home now and give you some privacy." She headed for the front door but stopped suddenly when she saw Lexie standing in the hall. The pale look on the girl's face had Toni stopping in her tracks.

"Lexie, are you okay?"

Lexie ignored Toni and turned to her mother. "Mom, is something wrong with Audra?"

Jodee hesitated to answer her, not sure how much she should reveal. Eventually she replied, "I'm afraid so. She's in the hospital and Toni thinks Travis hurt her."

Toni took the chance to find out the truth, "Lexie, do you know if Travis has ever hurt Audra before?"

"No, but I've suspected. Once I saw some bruises on her back and when I asked her how she got them she said I wouldn't understand because I don't have a boyfriend. Is she going to be okay?" she asked, worriedly looking at her mother.

"Of course, sweetie. I'm going to pick her up in the morning and Toni is going to help me talk to her." Jodee's voice was a squeak as she tried desperately to control her anxiety.

"Lexie, Audra is saying Travis didn't do anything, so don't tell her we suspect that he did. If it got out that Travis hurt Audra without a formal charge, there could be legal repercussions. You understand?" Toni warned.

"Yes." With that one simple word Lexie turned and went down the hall and into the bathroom.

Toni watched as Jodee went into the other room to phone Doug and then walked down the hall to see if Lexi needed help. Seeing that the door was slightly open, Toni started to knock when she peeked through the crack of the door and watched as Lexi stuck her finger down her throat and threw up. Stepping quickly back into the shadow of the hall, Toni looked to see if Jodee was in sight and then back into the bathroom to see Lexi sitting beside the toilet. Toni simply shook her head as if deciding Jodee had had enough trauma. She slowly turned and walked to the front door and let herself out as Jodee's high-pitched conversation to Doug followed her out into the night.

"Doug? Doug, its Jodee."

"Jodee, I know it's you, I recognize your voice for God's sake. I was going to call you tonight, but I got in late and realized it was already past ten there and I didn't want to wake anyone up."

"Doug, I need to talk to you."

"I gathered that, Jodee, but let me tell you what I need to say first. I was going to call and tell you I won't be home on Wednesday like I planned. I won't be able to get home until the following Sunday. They have another meeting they want me to go to, then I have two days of training—"

Jodee knew she was taking a chance interrupting him, but her frustration was bubbling up through her throat and finally erupted like a volcano, "Doug, Audra is in the hospital!"

"What did you just say?"

"I said Audra is in the hospital. She has a sprained arm, some bruises, and a concussion. They are holding her overnight for observation."

"What happened?"

"She says she fell in the dark and hit her head on the wall of the skating rink, but Toni thinks Travis beat her up."

"What does Toni have to do with this?"

"Toni was called to the scene as a victim's advocate."

"The police were called. Why were the police called if she fell and hit her head?"

"Because the doctors, Audra's friends, and Toni don't think that's what happened. They say Travis did it to her so I guess someone at the skating rink must have called them."

"Are you telling me that Audra claims she fell and hit her head, but everyone is accusing Travis of beating her up?"

"He did beat her up."

"No, Jodee, that is what everyone wants to believe. I, for one, happen to believe my daughter."

"But Doug, they're saying her injuries are not consistent with someone who fell but with someone who has been assaulted. And her friends said they saw Travis drag her outside and left her crying."

"All that proves is that they had another fight. Jodee, I really can't believe you are bothering me with this. I am in the middle of a very important project and you call accusing a boy of beating up our daughter without any proof. I am worried that Audra is in the hospital, but I believe her when she says Travis didn't do anything. We've known him for years. Now, is she going to be okay?"

"The doctors think so, yes."

"Then you need to handle this. I can't take time out of my day to try and take care of things at home as well as handle the things I need to do here. I am tired of traveling and I want to finish this project. As it is, it looks like I may have to continue to come out here for at least another three weeks."

"But, Doug…"

"No, Jodee, I mean it. Handle it and don't bother me with anything like this again unless you have solid proof that Travis hurt our daughter. And for once, why don't you believe her and

241

back her up instead of accusing her boyfriend of something he may or may not have done. As for Toni, I'm sure she's very good at her job but sometimes I think she sees trouble where there isn't any. Not everyone in a relationship is abusive, you know."

"But Doug, even if Toni is wrong, the doctors can't also be wrong."

"Jodee, I said handle it. God, are you completely useless?" It was a question he'd asked her several times over the years. Jodee knew it was a rhetorical question, but she gave the same answer as always.

"No, Doug," she said in her habitually timid fashion.

"Fine, then I'll call you in a couple to days and check in and by then I expect everything to be under control." As usual, he hung up with a finality that caused Jodee to jump.

She stood in the middle of the room with the receiver in her hand, staring at it like it were a crystal ball and if she stared at it long enough she'd be able to make sense of what happened.

Jodee slowly hung up the phone and walked to her bedroom turning off the lights as she went. In the quiet of her room, she climbed into bed, clothes and all, and decisively pulled the covers over her head to block out the blackness of the situation. Inside the soft cotton cave, she prayed its darkness would hide her from the disorder outside.

It was moments like this when she felt most crushed from the pressure, sinking deeper and deeper into a pit where air was scarce, and where the emotional impact of that moment when she finally hit the bottom would be her undoing.

Oddly enough, if anyone could look into Jodee's soul, it wasn't the cruelty of Doug's words causing the pressure but her own guilt from not stopping what she had expected was going on with Audra. What was it Toni had said? 'I know you've suspected

Travis has been abusing Audra for a while now?' Yes, she had suspected and had done nothing. Toni was right, it was her fault. She was guilty – guilty of being a bad mother, guilty of being weak, guilty of letting her baby be hurt. The guilt began eating away her insides and making her nauseous, like she'd eaten a rancid piece of meat that didn't want to stay down. Doug was right as well, she was useless. She deserved to be rejected by her husband, her father, her children. This thought frightened her so much she came swiftly out from under the protective cocoon of her sheltered cave and took in big gulps of air. The fear of her family totally rejecting her sent a chill through her blood that paralyzed her mind. She lay in the night with the covers pulled to her chin and stared blankly into space.

From an unexplained need, and not knowing how long she'd lain there in that frozen position, she threw back the covers, got up from the bed and walked back through her quiet house to the backdoor and looked out at her garden washed in the glow of a half moon. There was just enough light from the sky to allow her to make out the silhouettes of her flowers bending sadly to the truth of her nature, bowing their heads in sorrow just for her.

She slowly walked out into the night where a chilled breeze blew across her face. Welcoming the attack on her senses, she stood, waiting for the wind to lift her and carry her away. All she had to do was let the panic take her over. Let it devour her. Let the pressure build until her body could no longer hold itself together and her spirit would be weak enough for the wind to lift her, then, with extreme relief, it would be over, and she would be gone.

Clarity smacked her back to reality when a sudden cold gust came out of nowhere and hit her in the face so hard she winced, as if God himself was yelling, "NO!"

Blinking, shaking her head, she too yelled inwardly, No. No, she wouldn't let the panic take her over. Audra needed her. She had to keep herself from floating away!

She looked around trying to think. There had to be a way to keep herself grounded. She saw it, like a buoy in the sea – the playset. At the top of this toy was the little house with a roof and four small walls. It was just large enough to protect her from the spiteful wind, and the roof would keep her from flying away. She half ran to the set, climbed up the five rungs of the tiny ladder and sat cross-legged in the middle of the five-foot square cabin. She felt this was the answer, but to be on the safe side she decided she'd better tie herself down so her body was not carried away between the support beams, over the little knee walls, and lost to the sky.

She pulled her belt from the loops of her shorts, tied it to her wrist and then to the little plastic steering wheel. She laid down waiting for her pulse to return to normal, convinced she was secure enough to be safe. She closed her eyes and focused on slowing down her breathing. She blinked and blinked and blinked until her eyes closed out of sheer exhaustion. She drifted off into a sleep of bad dreams, but at least she slept, curled into a ball with her left arm stretched above her head and her hand dangling from the wrist just like the heads of the sad little flowers watching over her from her garden. The thought of returning to the house and the safety of her bed never occurred to her.

Toni woke from a fitful sleep feeling heavy-headed like she always did after having a case that disturbed her. She stood at her kitchen window drinking a glass of water and trying to wash the distaste of sour human behavior from her mouth. She surveyed her yard as she drank, lost in thought. Her house and the Warren's home were twins of each other except hers sat on a small rise which made it possible for her to see into the Warren's backyard easily. Both houses had the kitchens in the back of the house where the windows overlooked the trees lining the banks of the Mississippi River, like the architects thought it would reduce the monotony of the mundane chore of doing dishes for the women. 'So thoughtful of them,' she thought contemptuously.

She always woke in a mood where she was angry at the world, particularly men, whenever she had to deal with an innocent girl who had been victimized by a man. She knew it wasn't fair because men could be victims too. She sometimes thought that maybe she should quit being a Victim's Advocate before she became too jaded and grew to hate all men.

She drank the water slowly and looked over the good neighbor fence separating her yard from the Warrens, the welcome sight of bright flowers easing her male-bashing mood. Jodee was so fastidious when it came to her flower garden it made Toni envious. The way she was always puttering around it, Toni thought, it could possibly be the one thing Jodee loved as much as her children.

Toni then turned her attention to the monstrosity of Dougie J's playset that dominated the center of the yard. She wondered if Doug was ever going to keep his promise to Jodee and cut off the large branch from the maple tree which scraped the roof of the little cabin. As she stared at the shelter her attention was interrupted from her musings by an unusual sight – a shoe sticking out of the door of the cabin. A shoe that was too large to be Dougie J's.

She set her glass of water down on the counter, tied her robe a little tighter around her waist and walked out the backdoor. She walked around the corner of her house, through the gate in her fence and the three feet it took to get to the Warren's gate. She focused on the blue sandal as she walked toward it, causing curiosity creases in her forehead, something she hated because she was afraid they would become permanent and make her look older than she was – her one vice.

She stood at the base of the ladder staring at the shoe and realized it was Jodee's. She knew because she had seen her wearing them the night before. She reached up above her head and grabbed the toe of the shoe giving it a couple of shakes. "Jodee?" When she didn't get an immediate response, she shook it again, "Jodee, are you okay?"

Pointing the toes being wiggled, Jodee sat up quickly. She reached up to grab her head but was stopped short when her self-imposed tether jerked her left wrist. Looking down, she saw Toni staring up at her and frantically started to untie herself before Toni could see she had tied herself down. She stammered out, "Toni, uh, good morning, I'll be right down."

"Jodee, what are you doing up there? Did you sleep in Dougie J's playset?"

"I, uh, was, uh, just sitting up here last night and must have fallen asleep. I was staring at the stars and got sleepy, I guess." It was as good a lie as any and better than the embarrassment of the truth of her panic attack and the hope of floating away.

"I totally get it. I'm just glad it was a warm night."

"Yeah, me too." She climbed down the little ladder and straightened her hair when the memory of Audra being in the hospital caused a sharp crease across her forehead.

"I'm glad you woke me, Toni, thanks. I've got to go get Audra."

"Do you want me to stay until the kids wake up in case they wonder where you are?"

"That would be so nice. You know, I was thinking that maybe I would like your help in talking to Audra after all. Do you mind if I bring her to your house when I get her home? I really don't know what to say to her."

"Of course. I'll talk to Lexie and explain things and when I see you drive up I'll come over and we'll talk in my house. It will give Audra some privacy. And don't worry, Jodee, I handle these things all the time. We'll get through to her."

"I hope so. I really do because I'm scared to death for her."

Toni had been trying to get Audra to open up for over ten minutes. "Audra, I know this is hard but if you'll just talk to me, I can help. Your mom is worried about you, and frankly, so am I."

Audra hadn't said a word and Toni was getting frustrated – she'd seen it too many times before where the victim would shut down to keep from incriminating the person who hurt them.

"Please, sweetie, we only want to help. Tell me how long Travis has been hurting you." Jodee pleaded. "If I have to beg than that's what I'll do to get you to start talking to us."

Audra finally spoke up, but only to defend Travis. "He didn't hurt me, Mom, how many times do I have to tell you?"

"Audra, I know that's not true. I spoke to your doctors and you couldn't have gotten your injuries any other way. Why are you protecting him?"

"I'm not." Audra's voice had gone from angry teen to whining adolescent. "He didn't do anything. It was my fault, okay?"

"Listen to me, Audra." Toni knew she had to take control of the situation, so she forced herself to distance her emotions from her friend and let her training take over. "I see this kind of thing all the time. You'd be surprised at how many young girls I see every month that are being abused by their boyfriends. You're not alone in this and you'll feel better if you talk about it."

"He didn't hurt me. I slipped and fell," Audra almost shouted.

The rise in the girl's voice was a positive sign to Toni. In her experience, it meant she was willing to fight. Now the problem was getting her to fight for herself and not Travis.

"Okay, Audra, let me tell you something and see if any of it sounds familiar. All you have to do is listen. My guess is when you first started dating Travis, he was the sweetest, most attentive boyfriend in the world, and you thought you were the luckiest girl for him wanting to date you. Then, very shortly after you two became exclusive, he started making subtle little insults to you, maybe telling you he didn't like what you were wearing, that it was unflattering or too revealing and he didn't want the other guys staring at you. It was probably something along these lines, right? Because you didn't want to disappoint him you started dressing to please him."

Audra sat and listened to Toni, subduing her previous outburst. She stared straight ahead as she cradled her injured arm.

"Well, him dictating what you wore was the first sign of him trying to control you. He probably did this in such a sweet, caring way you didn't even recognize what was happening. After he realized he could control what you wore he probably began controlling who you talked to or who you could be friends with. Am I right?"

Audra's eyes shifted from the spot on the wall in front of her in a jumpy look of confusion.

"He probably started accusing you of intentionally trying to make him jealous and hurt him if you ever talked to other boys, even boys you've known your entire life. So, my guess is you stopped talking to many of your friends. Then it started getting worse, didn't it? He began demanding you tell him where you were at all times of the day, you had to always answer his calls, meet him between classes, be on time. This was his way of making sure he controlled your every move. Is any of this beginning to sound familiar?"

Audra shifted her gaze to Toni's face.

"Then I bet you started hanging out with just his friends. If you objected or wanted to see any of your own friends, he'd get physical with you. Oh, it wasn't anything too serious at first, maybe a small slap or a little shove, just to see how much you would take. The problem was you were becoming frightened of him, weren't you?"

Relenting slowly, Audra revealed, "He didn't mean to hurt me. I told you, it was my fault."

"Was it always your fault, Audra, every time he hurt you? Is that what he told you?"

"He didn't mean to hurt me, and he was always so sorry afterward. I shouldn't have made him mad."

"That's what he wanted you to believe, Audra, that it was always your fault. And I'm sure he was sad afterward and it sounded sincere, I bet he even cried a few tears, huh?"

Audra's defenses were beginning to crumble so Toni pushed a little harder. "I'm sure he promised you after every time he hurt you that he'd never do it again, right?"

"He would actually cry." Audra had finally looked Toni in the eyes, tears forming along her lashes.

"But then it would happen again, wouldn't it? And the times started getting closer together as his temper got worse and worse. It probably got to the point where you never knew what would set him off. Am I right?"

"Yes, okay? It's just I never knew what to do. He'd get so

mad at everything."

"Of course he did, Audra. In my opinion, the more insecure the abuser the more they try to control."

"I tried to break it off with him in May, but he said he loved me so much that he couldn't live without me and that if I left him he'd do something drastic."

"He feared he was losing control over you and started using guilt. He wanted you to believe it would be your fault if he did do something drastic. For a while, I bet he stopped hitting you and started being sweet to you again. Just when you thought everything was going to be all right and he felt secure in the relationship again, bam, out of the blue you did something that set him off and he started hitting you *again*." Tony emphasised the word. "You probably didn't even know what it was, but it got worse than ever, didn't it?"

"I knew he didn't like me talking to Ryan, but I had to because we were lab partners. I tried to tell him that, but he got so mad. He hit me so hard I couldn't breathe. That's when I tried to break it off with him."

Jodee was listening to the conversation with her head in her hands, resting her bent arms on her knees and staring at the floor. Toni knew she was probably in such shock she was numb and didn't know how to react. Common for relatives of victims.

Toni continued addressing Audra. "What is happening, Audra, is his violence is escalating and it's only going to get worse if you don't get away from him. The next time, there is no telling what he might do. If you'll file charges…"

"NO! I can't do that. If anyone finds out, I don't know what might happen. He might get kicked off the football team or something."

"Audra, what's more important, your life or his playing football?" It always astounded Toni the length women would go to protect their abusers.

Audra's comment finally had Jodee finding her tongue, "Audra, if you don't press charges against him, I will."

"Mom, no, you don't understand, I think it will just make things worse than they are – if not for him then for me. Please, don't say anything."

"I am going to call his parents and tell them what Travis has been doing to you."

"Audra, your life is in danger. I see it all the time in my job and you have got to stop protecting him and start thinking about yourself. You're stronger than that, I know it. No one has the right to hurt you, no one."

Turning to her mother, Audra pleaded, "Mom, if I promise to break it off with him for good, will you not say anything? Not even to Daddy?"

"I don't know if I can do that, Audra."

Toni interjected, "Audra, if you promise to break it off with him, then what I can do is call his parents and tell them the legal repercussions of what can happen to him if he doesn't leave you alone. And if he does ever do anything to you again, you will file charges. Is that okay with both of you?"

Jodee and Audra looked at each other and nodded.

The three women talked throughout the morning until their stomachs started complaining loudly from hunger. Around noon, Jodee decided it was time to leave.

"We're going to go home now, Toni. Thank you so much." Jodee hugged her friend.

"I'm here if you need me." Turning to Audra, she finished their meeting with what she hoped was something the young girl would think about. "Audra, you are a pretty, intelligent girl and you're not a victim any more. You have the strength and courage to control your own life, remember that. You have the strength and self-respect to not let anyone ever hurt you. It's up to you to help yourself, to save yourself."

"Toni," Audra asked timidly. "Do you think I'm weak?"

'No, Audra. I think at this moment, you're simply confused. But weak – never!"

She hugged the young woman and walked her neighbors to her front door.

Before they could leave, Jodee turned to Audra and cradled her face. "Audra, I'm so sorry I didn't see what was happening. I suspected something was going on but didn't do anything to stop it. I'm your mother, I should have seen you were in trouble and helped you. Can you ever forgive me?"

"Mom, there was no way for you to have known. I kept it hidden pretty well. Besides, you wouldn't know what to do anyway because you've never been abused. You married daddy, the most perfect man who would never hit you. You've never been a victim. God, it hurts to admit that I am."

Audra hugged her mother as Toni watched an uneasy, confused look cross Jodee's face. Disappearing almost as fast as it came on.

"No," Jodee said with a flinch, "your father would never hit me."

This time it was Toni's turn to be confused. The way Jodee reacted to Audra's statement, something was going on with the Warren family, but she didn't know what.

Toni watched as Jodee and Audra walked back to their home, arm in arm. She stood, watching, contemplating, unsettled, unreasonably achy like an invading virus was slowly clawing its way into her gut. 'How far can someone go, to intrude in someone's life, when they're not asked?' she asked herself as she gently closed her front door and went back inside.

CHAPTER NINETEEN

BETRAYED

It was eleven in the morning on a Tuesday. School had started a couple of weeks before and Doug was expected home that Friday, the necessity for his travelling almost over. Archer had called Jodee, distraught. She'd struggled for three weeks from the guilt she'd felt over Audra, feeling helpless and depressed, but keeping her daughter's secret like she'd been asked.

Jodee couldn't turn to Doug with her feelings of inadequacies and was ashamed to let Toni know any more of what a poor mother she felt she was. She'd fought with the anxiety attacks and the fear that accompanied them. When Archer had called her, it lifted her spirits to feel needed by someone.

They were sitting across from each other at the café style table in the kitchen of his expensive but scarcely furnished apartment. She listened attentively to him discuss his ex-wife's upcoming marriage.

"Jodee, I shouldn't be bothering you with this. I'm sorry."

"Archer, don't be silly, you're not bothering me. You can talk to me anytime. You've been here for me the entire summer. You know you can call me whenever you want. I'm just sorry Doug isn't here for you to talk to."

"No, I'd rather talk to you. I need a woman's advice."

"Well, you're one of my dearest friends and you can talk to

me about anything."

"I know and I appreciate it. I just didn't think it would affect me like this. I mean, we've been divorced for over a year and I knew it would happen eventually. After all, she's a beautiful woman."

Jodee reached across the table and took hold of his hand. He squeezed hers affectionately.

"I don't know if we ever really get over a true love, Archer, no matter how long you've been divorced."

"That's the whole thing, Jodee, I don't know if I ever truly loved her. But for some reason, the news of her getting remarried sure hit me hard. God, I feel like such an idiot."

"No, you're not an idiot, don't ever say that. You're one of the sweetest people I've ever known." With her other hand she tried to take the glass of scotch out of his reach he'd been drinking for over an hour.

He watched her remove the glass but ignored it, instead, he took hold of the bottle and tipped it up to his lips.

"You know, it's not so much the fact that she's getting remarried so soon after the divorce but who she's marrying. Chad Nelson of all people. I thought he was my friend. Now I'm wondering if they had been seeing each other before we even split. And do you know, she's still wanting alimony from me." This last piece of information was said between clinched teeth.

He took another swig of scotch, a small amount dribbled down his chin. He wiped it with the back of his hand while still holding the bottle by the neck like it was his ex-wife's throat.

"Don't think that way, it will only drive you crazy." His words were becoming more indistinguishable with every tip of the bottle. Knowing she needed to get him to slow down she asked, "Archer, maybe you should slow down a little on the scotch, its only eleven in the morning. How much of that have you had anyway?"

"I don't know, a little. And the crazy thing is…" he continued as if the conversation had not been interrupted, "I don't even want her back, so I don't know why I'm letting this bother me." He squeezed her hand a little harder. "God, I'm glad you're here, Jodee."

"There's nowhere else I want to be, Archer. And, for what it's worth, I think it bothers you because you're a compassionate and caring man. She was out of her mind to leave you like she did."

Archer looked up and into her eyes, the warmth of his feelings swimming clear even as the scotch clouded his focus. Even through the haze of his drunken stupor, his desire for her was as strong as ever. He got up quickly and walked into the living room to keep her from seeing the lust he was feeling.

She followed him and found him standing with his back to the room staring out the plate glass window at the skyline of downtown Minneapolis. She stood quietly and watched as he bowed his head. She thought she heard a hiccup and wondered if he was crying. She stepped up to him and touched him softly on the shoulder. "Archer, what can I do to help you?"

He sat the bottle on the windowsill and slowly turned to face her. He looked so sad she reached up and hugged him.

Like a child who'd lost his best friend, he put his arms around her waist and buried his face in her hair. They stood that way and she just let him lean on her. Another hiccup escaped his throat from a pent-up tear.

"You don't have to be brave in front of me." She reached up and cradled the back of his head.

He breathed in deeply and smelled her hair. The oxygen,

along with the deep bend of his neck on her shoulder, had an adverse reaction with the alcohol in his bloodstream. He got a little dizzy and clung to her for support. They stood holding each other for a few minutes as she tried to comfort him.

Fueled by scotch, it soon overturned his inhibitions. He lifted his head and met her eyes. Their lips were inches apart. He could feel her breath as she sighed, and her breast pressed against his chest with each intake of air. "I'm not being brave for you, Jodee. I'm trying to be brave because of you."

With a tilt of her head she looked at him confoundedly, "I don't understand."

"Jodee, you have to know how I feel about you." The words were slurred, making his inebriation more obvious.

She stood looking at him, confusion muddling her face. She tried to step back to put some distance between them but with a move that was almost imperceptible, he tightened his arms around her. She tried again to gently push him away.

He looked down at her, into her eyes, those lovely eyes with their gold specks encased in green. His eyes roamed over her face; her forehead, her cheeks, her hair, her lips. Without coherent thought, he bent forward and kissed her. A spark went through his system that no drink he'd ever had could duplicate.

Jodee froze in place as his lips moved on hers, her open eyes staring at his closed ones. She stiffened when he took the kiss deeper and his arms tightened around her waist.

When she didn't back away, Archer took it as a sign of consent. His hands started moving from her waist up her back and he gripped her shoulders, his desire racing his common sense along a bloodstream of alcohol.

His kissing got more aggressive and instinct had her straightening her back even more and leaning slightly backward pushing at his shoulders to get him to let her go.

She wrestled her lips out from under his and tried to speak as he aggressively nibbled at her neck. "Archer—" she forced his name through a throat bent at an awkward angle. She tried to get enough space between them to push harder.

He moved his lips back to hers and started pushing her down to the carpet. Speaking through the kisses, he confessed, "Jodee, you have no idea how long I've wanted this…" She could smell the liquor on his breath.

Fear was causing goose bumps to shimmy up her skin. "Archer, please." She moved her head to the side, but he mistook her pleading for desire and forced her knees to bend until she was on her back on his plush beige carpet, his body heavy on top of her.

"Jodee, I want you. I've wanted you forever." He started groping at her clothes and got his hand under her shirt. He squeezed her breast, his head swimming in alcohol fueled eagerness.

"Archer, Archer, stop." She tried to wriggle out from under him when she felt the buttons on her blouse pop open. Tears started forming behind her eyes, but he couldn't see them for having his head buried in her neck. He never heard a word she said for being so overcome by drunken lust.

"I love you. I've always loved you. Oh, Jodee, I've got to have you." The words were muffled but she heard them nonetheless, disbelief making her draw in deep breaths of air.

Amongst the groping and squirming, he was able to get his hands under her skirt and pulled at her panties. She felt them rip. Her tears clogged her throat as he fondled her. Within a matter of seconds he had both of them naked from the waist down. He pinned her wrist to the floor and used his knees to push her legs apart and entered her roughly.

She swung her head from side to side frantically, trying to understand what was happening. As the inevitable settled in, she resigned herself to the attack. She turned her head to the left and let the tears run down her temple.

She stared at the far wall; at the plaques he'd won from playing hockey. Her mind detached itself from reality. Everything was surreal, in slow motion, as she felt herself floating outside her body and calmly studied the pictures on the wall.

She lay still, crying as he violated her body.

With thrusts that were brutally painful, her sense of self-preservation finally had her swallowing the lump in her throat – she heard herself scream.

Noise… He could hear something but wasn't sure what it was. It was a panicked sound, loud like someone was in pain… Screaming, someone was screaming.

His face scrunched in confused comprehension as his senses started working independently of the alcohol. Blinking his eyes in focused concentration, his mouth stopped ravaging her neck as he looked up.

As quickly as he had started, he stopped. Sluggishly he rose up and looked down at her. It felt like someone had doused him in ice cold water his shock was so great. He watched her head move from side to side in panic, her screaming had him instantly sobering.

She kept screaming, unable to stop the hysteria. She started bucking under him.

"Jodee, Jodee, oh God, Jodee, I'm so sorry."

Her hysteria had blocked her ears.

"Jodee, honey, I'm so sorry. Listen, listen, Jodee, calm

down, I'm so sorry. I didn't mean to hurt you. I never meant to hurt you." As the reality of what he'd done hit his hazy system, he sat back and with a disbelieving stare, looked at his own hands, shame making them unrecognizable.

He realized he still had her pinned down with his knees and jumped back like he'd been hit by lightning, landing on his bare butt between her legs. Crab-crawling hastily backward he tried to put distance between them as fast as he could. He scurried backward until his back hit the wall, his knees pulled tight to his chest, his pants at his ankles, his legs bare.

Jodee had felt his weight come off her and calmed down enough to stop the noise in her head. She lay for a moment, continuing to cry. She sat up rigidly and braced her weight on her hands. She stared at the shock on his face.

Languidly, as if she were doing no more than politely leaving a tea party, she stood up, pulled her skirt down, picked up her ripped panties, grabbed her purse, and headed for the door. "I have to be going now," she said with eerie calmness.

Archer stared at her retreating back, unable to move from his position on the floor. "Jodee, I'm so sorry. I didn't mean to do that. Please forgive me."

"I have to go now," she repeated as she continued to head for the door, never looking over her shoulder or turning around.

"Jodee," he spoke in a whisper.

She closed the door behind her very gently.

Archer heard the click of finality when she shut the door, like a bang from a gun. For several minutes he sat and stared at it, then he fell to his side and curled into a ball. "God... Oh God, what have I done? Jodee, Jodee, I'm so sorry, so sorry." His apology was spoken to an empty room and was repeated like a mantra over and over and over. He stayed on the floor of his apartment until the sun set that evening and begged for forgiveness to an empty room and a woman who couldn't hear him. He laid there until exhaustion overtook him and he fell into a deep, alcohol-induced sleep.

Jodee drove home on auto-pilot. She could feel the soreness between her legs but didn't concentrate on it. When she entered her house, she went directly to the bathroom, ran a tub of very hot water, pulled off her clothes, and slowly climbed in. Bruises were beginning to form between her legs, and she saw droplets of blood run into the water. She bathed herself as if this sort of thing happened every day. No tears, no hysterics, no contemplating what had happened.

Her mind ran in circles. 'Doug must never know. Doug doesn't like it when I'm emotional. No emotion, no emotion,' she said over and over in her head. 'Archer, oh God, why?' She began questioning her own role in the attack. 'I must have led him on. It's my fault. I let him kiss me. I shouldn't have led him on. Doug can never know. Don't cry, don't cry. I must never cry.'

When she was finished bathing and calmed down enough to think, she got out of the tub, toweled off, put on fresh clothes, then dried the tub with her used towel to wipe away any evidence. She gathered up her dirty clothes and towel and walked to the garage. As she passed the laundry room, she dropped the towel into the washing machine and turned it on. She held the clothes in her left hand as she entered the garage and went to her garden tools. She picked up the trowel, and as if she were doing no more than gathering up seeds to be planted, went through the kitchen and into her backyard.

Under the big tree in the corner of the yard, where the ferns curled their leaves in an array of harmony, she dug a hole and buried her dirty clothes.

'Doug will be home on Friday. I'll have to tell him I'm on my period so he won't want to have sex. Yes, that's it. Everything's fine... He mustn't know, he can never know,' she reminded herself.

Her thoughts were calm and rational, but her movements were jerky and she was unsteady on her feet.

When she was finished burying the reminders of the betrayal, she lay down amongst her flowers letting the ferns and Gerber daisies hide her naked shame. Her eyes roamed as her head lay in the dirt and she tentatively reached up, and one by one, pulled the petals of the daisies from their stems. As she watched them flutter to the ground around her, she saw it, laying there, amid the orange confetti was Dougie J's little fairy doll.

Her mind went blank as she picked up the doll. With one hand she held the doll and with the other continued to pull off petals. A wind came up and she watched the petals being lifted into a tiny swirl of dust and wind as they floated away on the breeze. The sky clouded over and a slow drizzle began to fall. She laid there not feeling the cold drops on her skin. She was protected, she could not be touched her fractured mind believed – she was protected by the flowers, the ferns, and the little fairy.

"Jodee, you look terrible. When's the last time you washed your hair?" Nora interrogated her sister like a drill sergeant.

"I don't know."

"Are you sick?"

"No," her answers were spoken in a monotone as she picked at the cuticles on her nails.

"Well, if you're not sick, then what's wrong?

"Nothing."

"Jodee, you're anything but fine. Besides, I can't imagine you looking like this and Doug not noticing." Nora's concern for her sister was apparent from her tone, but there was also an underlying impatience with Jodee's lack of commitment to the conversation. She never had the patience, nor the inclination, to try and drag out a problem, especially when it concerned her older sister.

"Doug just got home last Friday and I've not been feeling well so I was in bed most of the weekend."

"What's wrong, flu or something? You look like you've lost a few pounds and you don't need to get any skinnier. It makes your face look pinched and old. You know Brigid will be here soon and we only have the afternoon to go shopping. Are you going to come with?"

"I don't know, I don't really feel like going out." Jodee was pacing from one end of the room to the other like a wild animal. When she saw her sister's face at her second turn, she walked past her down the hall and into her bedroom.

Following Jodee down the hall, Nora continued to question her, "Oh, for Pete's sake, Jodee, what is it? You really do look terrible." Nora waited no more than ten seconds for an answer before her exasperation got the better of her. "Either tell me now or I'm going to get really angry."

"Okay, I'm sorry." Jodee apologized without turning around. "Don't be angry." When she entered her bedroom, she continued her pacing.

"Jodee, you're really beginning to concern me... Or frustrate me, I don't know which. And stop picking at your cuticles, you're making them bleed."

"I'm sorry," she said again. She then folded her hands over her chest so her nails would be hidden under her armpits and out of her sight. She looked at Nora and said haltingly, "I guess I could use some advice, but please, please don't tell Doug. I'm so ashamed." After another moment of stalling, she finally relented. "Nora, I don't really know how to say this, but, hum, I think… I think I was raped." Jodee dropped her eyes to the carpet, embarrassed by her confession.

"What?" Nora's voice took on an edge that startled Jodee. "By who? No, wait. I want you to sit down and tell me exactly what happened."

Jodee sat down gingerly on the edge of the bed, obeying whatever she was told to do, grateful she didn't have to make decisions for herself. "I think I was raped. I think Archer raped me." Her words were just above a whisper, as if she had swallowed a ball of air that was blocking her voice from surfacing.

"What? Archer? Are you kidding? And what do you mean you *think* he raped you?"

After another moment to swallow her shame along with the air, Jodee proceeded to tell her sister everything that had happened a week ago in Archer's apartment. She only hoped Nora would understand. "…Then I just walked out and didn't look back."

It was the longest ten minutes of Jodee's life.

"Okay, I'm going to ask you something, Jodee, and I want you to think hard. Did he finish?"

"Finish? What do you mean?"

"Did he finish? You know, did he have an orgasm?"

Jodee's mind was slightly blank, confused by the question. "Why are you asking that?"

"Because if he didn't finish then it wasn't rape."

Jodee looked at her sister, her mind spinning from the

memory. "But I told him to stop, Nora, and he didn't. It hurt and he wouldn't stop. He entered me and left me bruised and bleeding."

"It doesn't matter, Jodee. If he didn't finish, it wasn't rape. Oh, I'm sure he might have gotten a little rough or something, but it doesn't sound like he raped you. Do you remember if he finished?"

"I don't remember, but I don't think he did. He just kind-of stopped. I think I was screaming. I don't know. Everything is such a blur. And like I said, I just got up, picked up my clothes and left."

"Well, did he say anything or do anything to stop you?"

"No, not to stop me, but he, uh… He said he loved me. I just…" Jodee was interrupted from finishing her sentence when Brigid walked into the room. She had walked into the house without knocking and had followed the voices to the master bedroom. She had stopped to check her appearance in the art deco mirror that hung at the end of the hall before entering the bedroom.

"What's this I heard? Who said he loves you?" She wanted to know.

Jodee and Nora responded together, "No one," Jodee said quickly. "Archer," Nora answered.

Brigid only heard Nora. She turned to Jodee with an act of swift jealousy, "Archer? Are you kidding me? Archer said he loves you?"

"It's not what you think, Brigid," Nora started to explain.

"Nora," Jodee pleaded. "Let's just drop it, okay?"

The look in Jodee's eyes stopped Nora from relating the entire story to Brigid.

"Drop what?" Brigid asked again, more forcefully.

"Nothing," Nora said reluctantly. "It was just something Archer said to Jodee."

"That he loves her?" Brigid crossed her arms as if an explanation was her due. Finally, she turned to Jodee and said condescendingly, "Jodee, please, you can't really be thinking Archer's in love with you? You obviously misconstrued his meaning. If Archer said he loves you it's because he loves you like a sister. He's only Doug's best friend after all and you've known him forever. Sometimes you can be so gullible. I swear, is the sky purple in your world?" She ended her string of questions with a chuckle and a roll of her eyes.

Jodee sat mute, hurt by Brigid's patronizing attitude.

"Besides," she continued as she gave her makeup one last check in the bureau mirror. "You're not his type." Dismissing the entire conversation as irrelevant, she asked with apparent impatience, "Now, are we ready to go?"

"Yeah," Nora said, heading for the bedroom door. "Let's just drop it."

"You know, I'm still not feeling well," Jodee said quietly. "I think I'll stay home and get some rest."

"What? Do you mean I came all the way out here and you're not even going?"

"Brigid, I think Jodee needs to rest. Let's just give her the day and she'll be back to her old self in no time."

Finally noticing her sister's appearance, Brigid gave in. "Fine," she replied. "I'd try and talk you into going but I'm not in the mood to put up with your depressing behavior anyway."

As Brigid headed out the door in front of Nora, Nora turned back to Jodee quietly. "I'll call you later, okay? The best thing for you to do is just forget about it. It's not important enough to think about so pull yourself together. I won't say anything to anyone, but for Pete's sake, take a shower before Doug gets home."

Jodee watched her sisters leave. With no one to tell her what to do, she did the only thing she could think to do – obey her sister. She slowly walked to the bathroom, intending to do what she'd been told and shower. She had to pull herself together before Doug got home from work. He'd been patient with her so far about not having sex but she knew it wouldn't last.

She stood and stared at her reflection in the large mirror over the bathroom vanity. Her mind wandered as she stared at someone she didn't seem to recognize – a woman with her hair and her eyes, but the face seemed unfamiliar. Her mind was so mixed up she felt like a storm was brewing in her head, the clouds blocking coherent thought with only the sharp shards of obedient dictates that had been pummeled into her by her parents since she was a girl; a wife does not complain, she doesn't whine, she obeys her husband, she does not bother him with petty problems. They had pounded commands into her psyche the moment she'd started sprouting breasts. They were so ingrained into her by the time she'd married Doug she didn't know where her thoughts started and theirs ended. It was one of the things Doug had liked about her, her compliant nature. She knew all of this but as she stood and stared at herself, her survivor's instinct begged for an outlet from the unpleasantness that didn't make sense.

She thought of what Brigid had said, 'a purple sky.' It made her smile for the first time in days.

Her mind became a jumble of rumination from her conversation with both her sisters as she watched the glazed eyes of the stranger in the mirror: 'a purple sky... Must pull myself together... He didn't finish, it wasn't rape. Maybe the sky would rain purple drops... Not rape, not rape, not rape... Mustn't complain, mustn't tell... How beautiful a purple sky would be...

It's not important, I'm not important… Maybe somewhere on the other side of the sky the world is purple, too.'

She smiled at her image and went into her backyard and sat amongst her flowers.

CHAPTER TWENTY

THE BEGINNING OF THE END

Summer had blended into fall with its usual grace of colors, cold air and fading sunlight. Jodee had taken to getting up at dawn to walk the river path behind the houses. She liked the feel of the crisp air on her face that had given her an uncommon strength of will to deal with what she now knew she had to keep secret – a rape that Nora didn't consider a rape. She was trying hard to come to terms with everything that had transpired over the summer; her poor skills of not being able to protect Audra against an abusive boyfriend who she had considered a good kid, another example of what poor judgment she truly had and the inappropriate episode in Archer's apartment. She didn't know how else to refer to it. There were times she found herself barely holding onto the fragile existence of balance between conventional right and wrong.

Archer had been conveniently absent from their home ever since it had occurred. He made excuses to Doug for reasons why he couldn't play golf or come over for dinners. Even though the regular hockey season had begun, she knew he was only making excuses. She was grateful he had the good sense not to come over, whether they were excuses or not. She didn't know how she'd handle herself once she did have to see him again, so she tried not to think about it.

She strolled the path in deep contemplation while a dessert of late cascading leaves in butterscotch yellow, lime green, cherry reds and chocolate browns floated around her. She raised her face to the sky trying to feel their flavors, enjoying the gift of peace that Mother Nature always gave her. She knew she wouldn't be able to stay out on this particular morning as long as she usually did because it was Halloween. She had promised Dayla and Dougie J she would finish their costumes for trick-or-treating.

Before she turned to head home, she took one last gaze up at the blinding whiteness of the sky where the sun was trying to force itself through the ice-encrusted clouds shielding the oncoming storm like a mask. It made her think Mother Nature wanted to participate in the Halloween festivities, too, with a disguise of winter gloom.

Reluctantly, she started walking back to the house. She bent her head and watched her feet crunch the icy frost that had covered the world that morning, hoping the snow would wait until after Halloween to make its appearance. She knew the kids always hated hiding their costumes under heavy winter coats. Dayla was going as the latest movie heroine and Dougie J had traded being Peter Pan for the Captain Hook costume Doug had bought him from the Disney Store in California – Doug thought his son was getting too old to play Peter Pan any more and needed 'toughening up.'

Jodee was thankful the day was progressing quietly for a Saturday. It was with sheer will power she held back the memories that constantly plagued her mind, but for these few hours she was going to let the complicated task of finishing Halloween costumes keep her busy. She sat at the kitchen table where she could see Dougie J out the kitchen window playing on his playset. Doug was in the living room watching hockey. Lexie was in Audra's bedroom doing some sisterly bonding, and Dayla was behind her rummaging through the refrigerator for an afternoon snack.

"Mom, can I have an orange soda?"

"I suppose so, but first can you take Dougie J his jacket?"

"Can't you just tell him to come in and get it?"

"Dayla, if you want me to finish your costume you'll do as I ask without questioning me. I'm up to my elbows in glitter and if I move now it's going to get everywhere. Do you want the belt to go with this thing or not?

"Yes," Dayla said with a pout on her lips.

"All right then, take Dougie J his jacket. It's right here on the back of the chair." Dayla made a pretense to object by slightly stomping her feet as she went out the door.

Jodee made an order at her retreating back, "And make sure he puts it on."

Dayla walked to the end of the playset and stood at the base holding Dougie's jacket. Looking up at him she ordered, "Dougie, Mom wants you to put your jacket on so come down and get it or I'm coming up."

"I'm not Dougie, I'm Captain Hook." He was inside the little cabin of the playset steering an imaginary ship. "This is my ship and you can't come up less I say so."

"Dougie J, I mean it, come down and get your jacket."

"No, Captain Hook don't need no jacket."

Dougie watched as his sister made a move to climb the ladder with his coat. He backed away and drew the little plastic sword that came with the costume. "Hold or I'll strike you down."

"Gaw, don't poke that thing at me. Come here and get this."
Dayla was at the top of the ladder watching her brother swing his
sword.

"Rrrr," Dougie J growled in his best imitation of a pirate.
"You're the crocodile that ate my hand." He held up his right arm,
his hand inside a cup that sported a plastic hook on the end. He
climbed up on the knee wall of the cabin. "You can't get me." He
balanced himself on the ledge and scooted over to the support
beam. Earlier in the summer he had discovered that if he climbed
up the frame surrounding the little cabin, he could reach the large
beam the swings hung from, hoist himself up, and then climb
onto the pitched roof of the cabin. There was just enough
decorative woodwork that he could get a firm foothold allowing
him to climb to the top.

"Dougie J, get down from there," Dayla scolded as she
jumped down and again ran to the front of the set.

Dougie had braced his feet on both sides of the pitched roof
as he tried to gain his balance. He pulled the plastic hook from
his waistband where he'd put it in order to climb up. He put his
hand back inside the plastic cup attached to the hook, and said in
his best pirate voice, "You'll not get my other hand, crocodile."

"Dougie, get down or I'm going to tell Mom." Dayla waited
a heartbeat. "I mean it."

"Oh, gosh, you're so mean. Okay, I'll come down," His
mischievous grin did not match his response. "I'll come down
but I'm going to swing down from the branch."

"Don't be stupid, Dougie. You can't swing down from the
branch. Gaw, you're so obnoxious."

"Can too, watch." Dougie J bent down and scooted
backward until his feet hung over the edge of the roof. Slowly
scooting backward, he grabbed hold of the lattice work and slid

down one of the frame studs. With one arm wrapped around the stud, he gained his footing and started walking across the large ridge beam supporting the swings like a gymnast on a balance beam. Halfway across, he reached up and hooked the branch that hung above the pitched roof of the cabin with the plastic hook on his hand. Giving a tug, he pulled the branch toward him, preparing to swing to the ground.

He took a step forward putting weight on the branch. Quickly, with very little effort, the hook separated from the handle inside the plastic cup. Dougie J teetered on the beam trying to regain his balance but for the small amount of morning frost that hadn't hampered his footing until then. He slipped, holding onto the handle of the hook and trying desperately to grab the branch with his other hand. Dayla watched Dougie wobble. Then, as if in slow motion, he slipped off the beam, letting out a little squeak, and fell hard onto the frozen ground. Still holding the handle of the plastic hook in his hand, he lay crumpled at her feet, silent, still.

It took Dayla a stunned second to realize what had happened. "MOM!"

It was the chilling cry of a child that only a mother can interpret. Something was wrong… Something was terribly wrong!

Jodee jumped up from the kitchen table, fear raised goose bumps over her flesh as she ran to the back door, where she froze.

She saw Dayla standing at the base of the playset, crying, looking down at Dougie J's crooked, unconscious form. Chills ran down her body.

"He's not moving, Mom! He's not moving."

"Doug!" Jodee screamed as she ran out the door. "Doug, call an ambulance!"

They said he sustained an intra-axial hemorrhage resulting from a traumatic brain injury. The doctors worked for hours trying to relieve the pressure on his brain. He died in the ER at seven fifty-two p.m.

The only evidence that any of it affected Jodee was the whiteness of her face and the emptiness of her eyes. She listened to the medical jargon, the doctor's sincere apology upon her son's death, saw the nurse pull the sheet over his face, and watched Doug break down. She did not cry, she did not get hysterical, she did not respond to the doctor's questions.

As Doug ran to his son's body, draped himself over the hospital bed and sobbed, Jodee stood where she was in the middle of the emergency room – still and unmoving.

The doctor stood and eyed her, wary of her response until he watched her slowly, slowly slide to the floor in a faint. She crumbled into a smooth, flowing puddle from the shock dissolving her bones.

Jodee woke to shouts and crying and people milling around. She was lying on cold, white sheets and saw her family in hysterics.

She heard the doctor say to her mother, "We gave her a mild sedative. She's had a severe shock and she fainted. When she came to, she started hyperventilating. We thought it best before she passed out again and hurt herself."

She heard Doug shouting at the doctor, "What do you mean you couldn't relieve the pressure on his brain? Isn't this a hospital? Isn't that what you do?"

Somewhere in the recesses of her mind she knew the questions were coming from a hysterical man who didn't know how to handle his grief except to shout and ask questions.

She saw her daughters gathered in a circle, embracing each other and crying.

She watched her sisters try to console her mother, and their children.

She listened as her father yelled, "What the hell was he doing standing on top of that damn playset. Who was supposed to be watching him?"

Jodee lay, watching her family, as calm as if she were seeing a movie on a screen and watched everything play out, detached from her emotions.

With little recognition, she felt her hand being squeezed. She let her eyes roam down her prone body and saw Toni standing next to her, holding her hand.

"Jodee... Jodee, thank God. You've been asleep for quite a while, and I was beginning to get worried. I'm so sorry. I'm so, so sorry. I heard the call for an ambulance over the police radio and came as soon as I could. I'm here for you, whatever you need." Jodee watched tears fall down Toni's face, not comprehending why.

Jodee saw Toni's lips moving, heard her speaking in a sort of mumble in her head, but she couldn't make out their meaning.

Her eyes roamed back up and across the room, the noise from everyone making her head pound. It took a moment for her mind to function. Everything was so confusing. She stared at Doug who continued to yell at the doctor. *Why?* she wondered. What was it? It was something important, she could feel it, but what? She stared perplexed.

Slowly, with painful clarity that tore her soul in two, she began to scream – she screamed and screamed, thrashed and cried and screamed.

The doctors sedated her again.

SECTION FIVE

THE WELCOMING MADNESS

Mothers are all slightly insane.
- J.D. Salinger

CHAPTER TWENTY-ONE

DOUGLAS ARTHUR WARREN, JR.

Once the sedative had worn off, the doctors and nurses stood around her with needle in hand in case her hysteria began again. Her father approached her with a look that confused her, his eyes were red and swollen – he'd been crying – but his voice had the hard edge she was used to. He looked her in the eye and told her she needed to relax, as if the mere authoritativeness in his voice would induce her to calmness, yet she could see the underlying pain in his eyes.

"Dougie J's in a better place now," he said. "God has taken him home."

Home... In a better place, it was the only thing she heard. For a moment her spirit jolted as she thought her father had just told her Dougie J was okay, he was just at home. She jumped up from the bed, getting entangled in the sheets, stumbling, but finally shedding them she started marching across the room, intent on getting to her son. By the time she reached the door, everyone had deduced what was happening.

Someone stopped her as the automatic doors of the hospital slid open. They gently grabbed her shoulders, she didn't remember who, but it made her angry to have someone stopping her from leaving when she knew Dougie J was at home.

Hunched and tense she informed her would-be captor, "Let

go of me. I have to get home."

Very slowly and softly, the voice behind her head explained, "Jodee, Dougie J isn't at your home, that wasn't what your dad meant. He died. Do you understand?"

She turned swiftly and looked Toni in the eyes. Toni had let Jodee turn around while keeping both hands on her shoulders.

"What are you talking about? He's safe at home, Daddy just said so." The incomprehension in Jodee's eyes had the doctor taking a step toward her with a worried expression on his face. Toni raised her hand to stop him.

"Give her a minute."

Jodee saw the doctor from the corner of her eye, a strange being in a white coat hovering like an apparition. She then looked at her family standing around staring at her. Everyone's faces were an odd tint of blotchy reds, whites and pinks of a kind of eerie disease – her father, Doug, her sisters, her mother, her daughters, her in-laws.

She turned her eyes on Doug. "Doug, what is Daddy talking about?"

The room remained stunned into silence. She looked from face to face waiting for someone to answer her.

"Answer me, damn you!" she yelled in uncustomary forcefulness.

Toni gave her arm a slight squeeze. She turned and watched Toni's dark eyes shimmer with a look of pity.

"Jodee, honey, he died, remember?"

"How can you just blurt it out like that? How mean can you be?" Audra shouted at Toni.

"I know it seems cruel, but I'm trained that by being straight forward, it leaves less chance of people being confused when someone dies. Like your mother is now," Toni explained.

"Well, I still think it's mean. Of course Mom knows Dougie J is gone."

Jodee was watching the exchange of words, but comprehension was impossible. *Remember? Do I remember what?* She had looked around the room but didn't see the gurney where they had covered his broken little body.

Her mother stepped over and took hold of Jodee's arm. "Jodee," she said just above a whisper, "ya gotta be strong now. The doctor wants to keep ya overnight and possibly keep ya sedated, but if ya can be strong we can take you home. They can give you something to help you sleep but at least youse'll be with family. Is that okay? Do ya want to go home?"

Jodee had watched her mother walk tentatively toward her and take her arm like the very touch of her would cause her pain. She looked down at her mother's trembling fingers as they held onto her bicep, but she couldn't feel it. Her eyes registered the contact, but her mind couldn't understand why the nerves had shut down. It was elusive – unreal, untouchable, senseless. "Mama?" She pleaded for her mother to tell her things were all right, to clear up the confusion, to tell her Dougie J was okay. But it wasn't what she did.

"Be strong fer me, sweet kirl. You have to be strong for the kirls. Stay calm and let us take ya home." Katie Olson rubbed her daughter's arm like she was brushing lint from her sleeve as tears ran down her face like silent rain.

Be strong. Everyone was telling her to be strong. *Stay calm.* Why was everyone so concerned about her being calm? She would stay calm if they would simply let her go home and get Dougie. She was getting impatient with the lot of them for keeping her from leaving. *Fine*, she thought. *If staying 'calm' will have them letting go of me, then I can stay calm.* She was determined to do what they asked just so they'd let her go home and get her baby. She just didn't understand why Doug wasn't fighting just as hard to go home as well. Didn't he understand their six-year-old son was home alone? 'Why did he leave him at home by himself, anyway?' she thought angrily.

With the urgent need to get to her child, she strengthened her resolve, pulled her arms from Toni and her mother's fingers, and said to the room with a firm look on her face in a demanding no nonsense voice, "I have to go home now."

"I don't think this is a good idea," Toni said. "She needs to stay and be watched."

"I agree," the doctor chimed in.

Ignoring them all, Jodee walked toward the exit sign of the hospital and stepped into the frigid blackness of the Halloween night without waiting for anyone to follow her.

Her family had watched her leave, perplexed at the change in her behavior. Finally shock jolted them into action. Toni raced after her first.

"You just leave her be," Mr. Olson said sternly to Toni. "She wants to go home and that's what we're going to do. We're going to take her home so she can be with family."

"I have to protest this action," the doctor reiterated. "There's no telling what she might do when she starts truly comprehending what happened. Right now, she's in a state of denial."

"I think we know what's best for our daughter," Mr. Olson argued.

"Mr. Olson, please. She thinks Dougie J is at home. What do you think is going to happen when she realizes he isn't?" Toni pleaded.

"Just never you mind. Now, everyone gather your kids and let's get Jodee and Doug home. Let her get some sleep." Mr.

Olson acted like a general in charge of everyone and headed out the door to follow his daughter and drive her home.

The others soon followed as they shuffled in a death march to their cars. Audra drove her dad and sisters home as the rest of the family, not knowing what else to do, drove away with pain burning their hearts that they knew would never heal.

The funeral was held in the local Lutheran church. The Warren family arrived in a black Towne car provided by the funeral home. Jodee had been living off valium in a coma-like stupor for five days while her sisters handled the arrangements of where her son would be laid to rest.

During the week that followed, moments of lucidity peaked around the corners of Jodee's mind to remind her that Dougie J wouldn't be coming home. Then, just as quickly, it would duck back into the darkness of welcomed denial and disappear into the phantasm of a world she wanted desperately to stay in. Her family had floated around her like cartoon characters – noisy, animated wisps of color that had no real substance. Doug fielded phone calls that came in almost non-stop. Her mother and mother-in-law cooked and reheated food like a country preparing for doomsday. Her daughters walked in and out of her line of vision with such varying degrees of emotion it made her head ache. Her father-in-law stayed in the backyard, hunched against the cold inside his coat. Her sisters gave orders and made plans like drill sergeants, and her dad... Her dad simply sat in a chair in the corner of the living room saying nothing at all. Nothing made sense. Nothing was real, and yet, she waited for Dougie J to walk in the room wearing his favorite Peter Pan costume and telling her he was going in the backyard to let Tinker Bell play with the other fairies. That's where she wanted to be, with the fairies in their carefree world of magic and no heartache. More than once, someone in the family had caught her in the backyard sitting on the frozen ground and staring at the tree that had killed her son. Or, at least what was left of the tree.

The following morning, after the accident, Toni had been woken by the sound of yelling. When she looked out her kitchen window, she had been shocked to see Doug Warren standing in a pair of flannel pajama bottoms, house slippers and an open robe exposing his bare chest chopping away at the trunk of the tree with an axe. The temperature was in the mid-teens, but he didn't seem to notice. He just kept yelling, "You killed my son! You killed my son!" As he frantically tried to destroy the tree.

Toni had grabbed a sweater and ran to the Warren's backyard just as Jodee, who had fallen asleep somewhere inside the house, came running out barefoot in her rumpled clothing. She threw herself against the tree and wrapped her arms around the trunk.

Toni heard Doug shouting, "Jodee, get away!"

"No, you won't take this tree. Dougie loves this tree."

"Jodee, this tree killed our son, I'm taking it down. Now, get away from it!"

"No, you'll break Dougie's heart."

Exasperated with her denial of their son's death and feeling she was intentionally prolonging his pain, he stared into her moist eyes and shouted, "God, can't you get it through your head? Dougie is dead!"

The pain of his words was as hard as a slap. Jodee stopped breathing and simply stared at Doug. "What?" she whispered.

"Dougie J is dead, damn it. And this tree killed him." Doug's chest was heaving with exertion and his face was strained from grief and anger.

"No, no he's not. He's inside in bed," Jodee said calmly.

"Jodee, get it through that thick skull of yours, he's gone."

"Noooo," the screaming seemed to fill her head. "You're a liar! Dougie J is asleep and he'll want to play when he wakes up."

The grief had finally consumed Doug. His tone was menacing like he wanted to punish someone and make them hurt as much as he was hurting. Jodee was the closest victim. What he said had Toni stopping in shock as she slowly approached her friends.

"You killed Dougie. Maybe it wasn't the tree at all, maybe it's your fault."

"Doug," Toni intervened forcefully. "Stop it."

"Stay out of this, Toni. It's none of your business." The hatred in his eyes had her stop in her tracks.

Turning back to Jodee he continued his assault. "If you had been watching him you could have stopped him from getting on top of the playset…"

Toni waited as Doug stopped in mid accusation as he finally heard his own words. He turned from the trunk of the tree and stared dumbstruck at the playset. A slight breeze blew the limb of the tree that scraped the upper beam and Doug looked up. The top part of the little plastic hook Dougie J had been playing with was still hooked over the branch, the toy he had bought Dougie himself – hanging from the branch his son had tried to swing from, the branch he had been told to trim back for months. The whole scene taunted his culpability.

With slow jerky movements, Toni watched Doug's body visibly slump. His head hung in dejected misery, being too heavy for his neck to support any longer. Ignoring his wife's raw gasp of pain, he slowly turned around and walked back into the house, dropping the axe in the middle of the yard.

Jodee slid to the ground with her arms still around the tree, his accusation stabbing her guilt, making her grief bleed. She slid to the ground letting the bark scratch her face.

Toni ran over to Jodee and tried to pick her up off the ground. "Come on, honey. Let's get you inside."

Jodee let out a sound like an injured kitten.

"He didn't mean it, Jodee. He's just upset. Please, Jodee, let me get you inside. You've scratched your face. Let me get you inside and wash it up."

Jodee slumped limp in Toni's arms as she stared at the slammed door Doug had just entered. His words rained down on her head like sharp shards of ice as she whispered, "My fault, my fault, my fault."

Toni was able to get Jodee to her feet but listened to Jodee's litany of self-incrimination and knew the hard impact Doug's words would have on Jodee's fragile emotions. She watched Jodee's eyes go from a watery blue to the stare of an empty shell.

Jodee's behavior gave Toni pause. She'd seen a lot of grief in her job and she knew people handled death differently, but Jodee's grief seemed to go from the center of her heart right to the marrow of her soul.

Toni had never seen anyone react to a death like Jodee had. In that moment they had walked into the house after the ride home from the hospital, Jodee had gone from the front door directly to Dougie J's room, without a word or a tear, she laid down on his bed, covered herself with his blanket and began to sing a lullaby. Her voice had been so strangely sweet, as if she were singing quietly to her sleeping son, it had frightened Toni. And over the rest of the week she did not get better.

She stayed by Jodee's side for the entire week. Now waiting for her to climb out the Towne car, she was genuinely concerned about her friend.

For Jodee, it was her turning point. With cold-blooded resolution, her mind decided it was time to leave and take with it the frayed ends of her sanity – leisurely, maliciously, gleefully.

When the car stopped at the church Jodee stayed in the car. It was one of the days where the antidepressants, the only medication Doug would allow the doctor to give her, had overpowered her sense of peace and left her mind seeped in reality. She hated those days, and on this day, this particular day, she did not want reality because this was the day they were going to bury her son. In the deepest part of her being, where sanity teetered like a top, she knew if she thought of them putting Dougie in the ground, her mind would simply stop her heart and she would die. Maybe that wasn't such a bad thing, she reasoned. Sometimes, when she watched the sun sink at the edge of the world like it too were being laid to rest, she wanted to die, to simply lie down with the sun and let the universe fade to black.

Toni had stepped up to the car when she hadn't made a move to get out. Opening the car door, Toni reached her hand in, "Jodee, honey, you want to get out of the car?"

Jodee looked over at her friend. 'She looks so pretty in her gray and black sweater,' she thought. The pills let her mind meander through shifts of normalcy and dreams, and it relaxed her. As if she were talking to one of her children, she replied motherly, "Toni, you should come in out of the cold. Come, sit down with me."

With gentle authority, Toni went into advocate mode. "Jodee, let me help you into the church. Your family is waiting for you."

Jodee looked over at the door of the church where her family stood. "I'm not really up for service today. Do you think people would like to come over to the house for punch and cookies afterward?"

Toni stood bent at the waist staring at her friend. Her hand staying outstretched. Pulling herself from her temporary silence, she responded carefully, "I think the service is going to be nice and I know your family would like to have you there."

Jodee noticed her mother wringing her hands and looking in her direction with a worried face. Jodee looked at her mother as if she didn't recognize her. She took a shaky breath of air into her lungs and the tearful bubbles popped softly inside her eyes as the memory returned and brought her from her stupor. Looking back at Toni she admitted, "Toni, I can't do this." The tears started flowing down her cheeks in endless streams.

Before Toni could react, she was grabbed by the waist from behind and moved aside by Mr. Olson.

"Jodee, you're holding up the service. You need to walk into the church with the family. You stop this now, you hear? I don't want any tears. You gotta be strong for the girls." It was said firmly, but with a hint of compassion. It was as close as her father had ever come to being understanding. He wasn't very good at it. "I know this is hard but try and take comfort in knowing Dougie J is with God now. And though we can't understand His reasoning, we should be grateful Dougie will no longer feel the pain of this world."

Toni looked over at Mr. Olson, eyes wide from the shock of his words. "Mr. Olson, I don't think that's what she really needs to hear right now."

Reaching into the car and taking Jodee's hand in uncustomary gentleness, he replied to Toni's concern. "We appreciate your help Ms. Cavallo, but as her father I think I know what's best for her. She needs to be with her family at this time."

Keeping hold of Jodee's hand, he pulled her out of the car with just enough forcefulness that Jodee had to comply.

Toni watched as he walked Jodee up the steps and into the church, stunned into immobility by his actions. She eventually followed them into the church and stood at the back of the room.

A woman Toni had never met came up and said, "I'm sorry for my brother, he means well but he can come across a little harsh. He's just hurting so much right now. That's all."

"It's all right," Toni replied, "I understand. I guess he feels I'm interfering."

"Perhaps for now it would be best just to keep your distance."

"Perhaps. I understand when a grieving family asks for privacy that it's something that needs to be respected."

"Just for a little while, dear."

"Of course, but I'm letting you know now, as Jodee's friend I will be checking up on her in the coming weeks, except, of course, when Mr. Olson is around."

The woman patted Toni's arm and turned to find her seat.

Toni continued to stand, never taking her eyes off the Warren family. Studying them as if they were a case study for odd behavior.

Jodee had sat through the sermon, stiff-backed and dry-eyed. She had crawled inward, inside herself to forget the pain and numb herself to the words the minister spoke. He spoke of sorrow, indeterminate sorrow. Who's sorrow she didn't know because hers was so deep it was eating a hole through her chest. 'Sorrow,' she pondered, 'what a strange word.' How inadequate a word that is supposed to describe a pain so deep it hurts to live.

She looked around letting her thoughts continue to wander,

marveling at the colors in the stained-glass windows and listening to the sniffling of people around her. Far away, somewhere in the distance, she felt a slow sharp pain in some part of her body. It was a physical pain that worked itself slowly through her emotional state. She couldn't focus long enough on it, however, to distinguish between the emotional or the physical pain she was enduring. She looked down from an instinct of survival to locate the feeling. She saw it, there in her lap. She was squeezing the fingers of her left hand in a death grip with her right. The tips of her left fingers were white, and the diamond from her wedding band had turned sideways and was digging into the soft thin flesh of her middle finger. Blood had started to form in the small puncture marks caused by the gem. She looked at her finger quizzically, she could see the damage she was causing herself, but she couldn't seem to feel it; 'interesting,' the thought came unwillingly into her mind.

She was brought out of her self-mutilation when the minister asked everyone to stand and pray and Doug lifted her by her elbow.

She stood as she was instructed to do, but she did not bow her head. She could hear people reciting the prayer, the noises coming from their mouths, but the words had no meaning. She was lost in the movement of their lips. 'How odd that people's lips have to move in order for humans to talk.' If she watched close enough it became hypnotic; and yet, it irritated her senses. 'Stop!' her head screamed. 'Stop that annoying movement of your faces. Don't you know how ridiculous you look? The silly way your faces contort when you talk. Why don't you stop? You all look so stupid!'

The minister finished the sermon with, "If anyone would like to come to the gravesite, please follow the procession. We will then say one final prayer for Douglas Arthur Warren, Junior and let the Lord take this sweet child into the kingdom of heaven to sit by his side."

The mention of her son's name, and what was going to happen to him, brought Jodee's head snapping to the front of the room like a bullet. The minister's words had finally penetrated her muddled mind, her eyes started the stressful blinking that had been missing from her personality since her willful dismissal of her rape, and with one quick inhale of breath, she fainted.

CHAPTER TWENTY-TWO

A WANTON REALITY

A week after the funeral, Jodee's lack of sleep had her staring out at the backyard as the sun peeked its light over the roof of the house. A fresh snow covered the ground, its white iciness smooth and shiny as pulled taffy. Standing with an old gray shawl wrapped around her shoulders like a withered fairytale character, she stared at the playset, the instrument of destruction that had killed her baby. It was blanketed in the purity of snow trying to convince her of its innocence. But it was a contradiction. It wasn't innocent, not by a long shot, she mused. It killed and caused pain and laughed at her by the clanging of the chains from the swings and the slide that resembled a tongue, mocking her. She could hear it; she could feel it. The longer she stood there being taunted by its mirth, the angrier she became. She started to shake, feeling the anger begin at her feet and working its way up her spine. She had to stop it, she decided firmly. Stop it from enacting more harm on anyone in her family.

She threw off the shawl, walked into the garage and grabbed Doug's hammer and stomped back through the kitchen to the backdoor, pulling the door open with enough force it hit the far wall with a thud. The snow snuck its way into her bedroom slippers as she marched to the playset. Raising the hammer over her head, she brought it down with a blinding crash on one of the support beams, again and again until Doug stopped her and yanked the hammer from her hand. Without a word, he simply looked at her with a shake of his head, turned and went back inside the house, leaving her as stranded as her emotions.

After that, the days fused together one into the other until they stretched into a darkened tunnel of melancholia. Weeks dragged into an endless journey of sorrow and unbearable pain that stabbed like a constant jab of needles from the inside out.

Christmas had come and gone with little fanfare. No one expected the holiday to happen, but her father demanded the family celebrate all together with dinner and prayers – no exceptions, "It's Christmas after all and we must show our respect to the Lord," he insisted.

During grace, Jodee had bent her head in customary fashion but instead of praying she cursed God under her breath for his cruelty.

The following day, she woke with such a pounding headache she knew it was her punishment for disrespecting God on His most holy of days. She lay in bed and asked for forgiveness until the headache made her fall asleep.

The turning over of the new year was Doug's way of expecting life to return to the routine of daily life, as if the time for grieving had been allocated to two months. The sympathy he had shown up to that day, and pain he endured, was dismissed along with the passing of the year.

He stated one night as gently as he could, "He's gone, Jodee, and we need to move on. You have three other children who need your attention. We'll always grieve but thinking about him is just continuing the pain. I can't endure thinking about him or it's going to kill me. I feel it's time to move forward and we try and get back into a normal routine, for all our sakes."

The words may have been said gently but Jodee heard hateful bitterness and blame and the unrealistic demand that she forget her son. She heard his options with ruthless finality to either abide by his wishes or catch his wrath.

Even with the shock of Doug's dictate stabbing her heart she knew she had no other options but to obey him. If she disobeyed her husband, she would be breaking a vow and would garner God's wrath. He might punish her by taking another one of her children, she feared irrationally. She would obey if by no other means than pretend life was normal.

As the days flowed endlessly on, she tried to reconcile her guilt with her grief and pretend things *were* normal – like the rest of her family had seemed to do. She watched and wondered in perplexed turmoil as her family moved forward with inexplicable continuity, the way someone might accept the passing of a beloved pet. Dougie J's absence had become just another aspect of life.

In her grief-induced state this was what she saw, and it became a resentful reality.

In order to hide the disappointment she felt toward her daughters' callous attitudes, and her disgust with Doug's nonchalance, she tried desperately to disguise her feelings under a cover of normalcy. She had been warned by her father that crying was unacceptable; that God had His reasons for taking her son and crying was not showing true belief in His will. Her mother acquiesced with her father, and her sisters were uncomfortably absent. She was expected by everyone to go on with life like nothing was wrong, to not talk of Dougie J as she was prone to do, to not show grief, to not remind anyone of their loss.

The weeks passed one into the other, endlessly,

monotonously. The weight of the pretense getting heavier with each concealed emotion. Sometimes, while trying to maintain the daily routine that Doug expected, the weight bore down on her with aching cruelty and her mind would slip into the past. Her daylong façade became so tangible at times she'd forget Dougie J was gone and call his name during the chaos of getting the kids ready for school, or seeing to their individual needs and wants, or just saying goodnight to them – her memory was constantly taxed under the burden.

It was February, she woke from a fitful sleep and disturbing dreams to a sense of bewilderment. She lay in bed trying to gather her thoughts while a feeling she was forgetting something important hummed along her nerves – was it a dream? Did the kids need a gift for school or something? Had she forgotten something Doug wanted her to do?

Without the luxury of gathering her thoughts, she was forced out of bed by the shouts of Lexie and Dayla arguing, Doug up and demanding a clean shirt, and Audra standing at the kitchen counter separating her mother's daily dose of medicines while doling out instructions to her. The doctors had loaded her with so much medication she stayed numb most of the time. The urge to remember what she knew she'd forgotten went around and around in her head until she was dizzy.

Knowing she was expected to stay on task with morning routines, she set aside the frustration of her faulty memory until the house was quiet and she could concentrate more fully on it. She instead started addressing the problems at hand.

"Dayla, Lexie, please stop shouting, I can't hear myself think."

"But our class is rehearsing for a Valentine concert next week and the teacher wants us to come dressed like we're going to the actual concert. I don't have a red sweater and I asked Lexie if I can wear hers and she got all stingy and said no."

"It's my sweater and I'm wearing it this weekend. I don't want you to get it dirty."

"Mom, tell her to let me wear it." Dayla's whining was like nails on a chalkboard.

Audra ignored the melee to inform her mother, "Mother, listen, you have to take the blue ones at noon. Can you remember that?"

Doug's deep, demanding voice added to the pounding of the chaos, "Jodee, where's my blue shirt and matching tie? I'm going to be late for work."

"Mom, are you listening? You have to keep on schedule. The doctor said to make sure and not miss a single day."

"Yes, Audra, I hear you. Dayla, find something else to wear. You have a nice pink blouse, wear that. Doug, the shirt is in the laundry room, I just ironed it and haven't put it away yet. I'll get it for you in just a sec. Girls, hurry up, you're going to be late for school. Lexie, don't you dare take that sandwich out of your bag, you are going to eat more than an apple for lunch, do you hear me?"

Jodee moved from counter to table to laundry room, from kid to kid handing out pieces of toast, homework and lunch sacks, her feet and hands hurried in their movements. Frustration of her unsettled memory bore a hole in the back of her head hard enough she was sure she could feel her nerve endings spasm.

Dayla made one last attempt to get her way, "You never take my side!" She slammed the pantry door with her final word.

The noise of the sharp snap of wood on wood from Dayla slamming the door was enough to snap the cord that had been holding Jodee's false attempt at normalcy intact. As if she'd just remembered what was missing, she stated suddenly like she would on any morning before the accident, "Oh, for Pete's sake, where is that boy?"

She walked to the entrance of the kitchen and shouted down the hall, "Dougie J, honey, get out of bed and come and eat your breakfast."

Like a loud boom of thunder, everyone jerked to a stop and fell silent under the electric current palpable from raw emotions.

Jodee turned to see everyone staring at her in stunned dismay, the tension a tangible entity, wondering why they had all stopped and gone quiet. She looked at each one of them in turn as their looks brought back to what she'd done. Dougie J wouldn't be coming to breakfast, she remembered painfully. Like he had died the day before, her heart seemed to stop beating and she grabbed the doorframe to keep herself upright. For one sweet moment in time, she had forgotten, life had been normal. 'Dougie J is dead, Dougie J is gone, he's gone, he's gone...' Her temples began to throb from the continuous litany. Her knees locked in place to support her from crumbling to the floor.

The silence in the room bit like January cold, unrelenting and inescapable. Doug looked at each of his daughters in turn and saw confusion in Lexie's eyes, tears begin to form in Audra's and shame in Dayla's. Like a disciplinarian who'd had enough, he finally broke the silence with an angry outburst. "Damn it, Jodee, we've talked about this. What is it going to take to make you stop torturing us by calling Dougie J's name?" The words were spewed with needless venom.

"I... I forgot," Jodee explained in stunning apology.

"I don't know what else to do, Jodee, I really don't. I feel like you enjoy reminding me he's gone. You have to stop this. It isn't helping anyone. I swear to God if you don't stop, I don't know what I'm going to do."

"I'm… I'm sorry," she pleaded.

"Well, I don't have time to deal with this right now," Doug answered, looking at his watch. "Oh, great, now I'm late for work. In the meantime, Jodee, I want you to take your medication. Pray, read, do whatever you need to do to pull yourself together today. We'll talk about this tonight when I get home."

Doug turned to his daughters and instructed, "Girls, gather your things together and get to school. Your mother needs some time alone."

Doug's dismissal of her feelings pushed the proverbial knife of resentment deeper into her wounds and brought back crippling reality. She looked to each of her daughters as they stared at her with expressions so full of hurt, she looked down to make sure she wasn't actually bleeding.

Deciding the matter was closed, Doug walked furiously out of the house as he tied the tie around his neck like he was angry at his own throat. "I'll grab something at the office."

She had been grateful in the last couple of months with Doug's atypical kindness and patience with her, but it seemed that time was over and he was gradually returning to the hardened personality she was used to. His anger at her slip was proof.

Jodee stood rooted to the floor, a withering weed, as Lexie and Dayla, forgetting their squabble, quickly raced past her, grabbed their backpacks like relay racers, and ran out the front door. In unison, they shouted their goodbyes without ever looking back.

Audra, left alone with her mother in the kitchen, dropped the last of her mother's medicine into the pill case and quickly followed her sisters out of the house, forgetting her coat on the living room chair in her haste to leave. "Mother, take your pills. Gotta go."

Jodee watched her family's anxious need to escape her presence and shuddered in unexpected horror – she'd forgotten again. She'd forgotten her son was gone and for a few moments she'd been happy. Life had been like it was before he'd been taken away. She cursed God under her breath and then felt guilty for her sin.

She stood inside the doorframe; numb, broken, hollow. The silence of the house reverberated against her skull and her mind shut down tight like a locked freezer, a black chasm of emptiness. She didn't know how long she stood still, but when she finally moved her knees ached from being frozen in place. Unsure what to do, she let need take control and followed it into Dougie J's room. She carefully pushed the door open where it had remained closed since his death. Walking to the middle of the tiny room, she turned in slow circles as if searching for him. The minutes passed as her thoughts tumbled over one another, not unlike dried tumble weeds scraping her consciousness raw, her skin tingling from the sensitivity.

'They want me to forget him,' she convinced herself. 'They all want to pretend he never existed. They want to take him away from me. Doug blames me.' The grief-stricken thoughts fought for supremacy as they battled to be at the forefront of her mind. 'What if they wished I wasn't here either? They were in such a hurry to leave, what if they wish I didn't exist any more because I cause them pain.' This thought brought stifling fear. She struggled with the thoughts as they spun in her head. 'I can't forget,' she cried inside, 'but I can't remember either or I'll lose my girls. They're afraid of me, I saw it in their eyes. I'll change, please God, I'll change,' she prayed outwardly, pleading at the ceiling. 'Just please don't take my girls away too.'

With unparalleled courage, she made a silent vow to herself she would have to bear the pain of Dougie's death in solitude. She would have to choke on the rock of tears she'd been forced to swallow and closet her emotions, or the loneliness of missing him would be carried over into the nonexistence of all her children. The earnestness of the thought made her eyelids begin to flutter until after a few moments she was blinking so rapidly the objects in the room turned into a quick moving flip book.

The pressure from the minutes of blinking made her head pound. Needing an aspirin, she walked back to the kitchen, slowly so as not to bump into the walls. Reaching for the cabinet above the sink she lowered her head to ease the pain when she saw the medication Audra had separated. She looked at them with hatred. 'The pills. It's the pills that're making me forget.' She gathered them up in anger and squeezed her hand tight, choking them from existence. 'Never again,' she swore.

With the pills squished in her hand, she searched for a place to hide them, hide them where no one would ever find them. Flushing them down the sink never occurred to her.

With single-minded purpose, she walked back into Dougie J's room and stood still, trying to think. She scanned the room like a spy would scan a room on the best place to hide a bugging device. A flash of yellow on the floor caught her attention as if it had been tugging on her pant leg. Peeking around the entrance of the closet she could just make out the front end of a toy truck. She bent down and picked up Dougie J's favorite dump truck. 'A dump truck, how apropos,' she mused. She took the pills, which were beginning to dissolve in her hand, and deposited them in the bucket of the toy. She then gave it a little shove and let it roll to the back corner of the closet and set his snow boots in front of it.

No more would they be able to make her take those horrible pills that made her forget.

The antidepressants worked themselves out of her system with irritating slowness, but with each passing day she could feel herself getting closer and closer to her son. She began to feel invigorated by the jumble of her thoughts because there was no clear focus in one direction to allow for forgetfulness. She was convinced it made her feel alert and more in tune with the world than she'd ever been in her life. So, when everyone left for the day, she'd go to Dougie J's room and stay for most of the day, coming out just in time to carry on with the façade of the nonexistence of his death.

Paranoia was a feeling she wasn't familiar with and she refused to admit it was taking hold. She remembered a poster from her high school days, 'It's not that you're paranoid, they really are out to get you,' and she took this saying as truth.

'No one understands me but you, Dougie J,' she said one day to the room at large after a very trying morning, hoping to fill the emptiness that was quickly becoming a part of her.

By week three, she could tell the pills had completely worked through her system. Her emptiness began to consume her like God had taken a big scoop and hollowed out her heart, leaving her with just the outer shell of her humanity. In the natural progression of endless routine, the habit of her new reality had her mind slipping between the torn pages of necessity and need. Each morning she would wait with forced patience for everyone to leave so she could retreat into Dougie J's bedroom, hide her daily dose of pills, so Audra, who monitored them each night like Nurse Ratched, wouldn't find them, then spend the rest of the day close to her son. Before the end of the day, she would inspect the room for any imperfections. She'd go over every corner, obsessing over every speck of dust, or wrinkle in his bed – wrinkles she herself made when she'd forget and sat down on it. Her own carelessness would then have her frantically trying to smooth out the imprint, rubbing the coverlet over and over until tears would form in her eyes from frustration.

Weeks after Doug's dictate, she escaped into Dougie J's room for her daily habit of correcting the flaws of life that seemed to reappear each night as if by magic. The feeling that came over her was not one of satisfaction this day, though, but one of trepidation. She stood in the middle of his bedroom immobile in her modified reality trying to identify the cause of her uneasiness. From the corner of her eye she caught a movement. Looking up, she saw an image in the mirror above his tiny dresser – she saw her reflection. No, she saw *a* reflection. It felt strange because the person looking back at her copied her every move; and her eyes… She had pretty eyes, she thought, but they were empty – eyes green as mold but with an endless darkness in the pupils like a bottomless well. She didn't recognize the person and it began to frighten her as the woman constantly stared back at her duplicating her every move.

Jodee bravely looked into the face of this stranger feeling she should know this woman, yet not recognizing the structure or the shape of her face. She watched the eyes blink and blink until it maddened her, agitated that it was so familiar a face yet so far away in a tentative realm. Temporarily forgetting the tidiness of the bed, she sat down on the edge, slowly, like the bones in her legs had melted away. She stared at the eyes in the mirror. The empty emotion of the stranger scared her and she wanted to slip out of sight from this person who would not take their eyes from hers. She slid down the front of the bed in an almost

300

imperceptible move and let her body sink to the floor, hoping if she did it slowly enough, this unnamed person wouldn't notice she was suddenly out of sight. When her butt hit the floor, her body decided to continue the journey until she was lying flat on the floor, secretly hoping it would open up and absorb her in.

In self-preservation, she turned to her side and curled into a fetal position hoping the mirrored person would get bored and eventually leave. She stared straight ahead of her into the darkness under the bed and into the lonely existence of her suffering. The loneliness was stifling, trapped inside her chest with a pressure so intense it made her nauseous.

Was it minutes or hours later? She didn't know, but the shadowed shape looking back at her from under the bed gradually caught her attention. She unfolded herself and tilted her head, trying to solve a complicated problem. She reached under the bed and grasped the figure; the shape was familiar and comforting. Pulling it out and opening her hand, she recognized Dougie J's Peter Pan doll. Squeezing the tiny doll in both hands she held it to her breast like a starving person holds a piece of bread while giving thanks. It was a link, a link to her child! Her mind slipped a little further into a make-believe world of rightfulness.

'Where is Tinker Bell?' she wondered.

"Did you leave Tinker Bell outside by herself again, Peter?" She spoke to the doll, expecting an answer. When none was offered, she got up and said to the world at large, "Well, we must go find her then, mustn't we?"

In the backyard, she kneeled in the icy crust of frozen ground while the sharp ridges of winter dug into her knees. Her hands became scratched and bloody from rooting through dormant growth. She knew somewhere in the back of her mind she should go inside and get a pair gloves, but finding the tiny fairy took priority over her own comfort, so she simply ignored the nagging pains.

She dug amongst the dead brown twigs and hummed to herself while keeping an eye on the Peter Pan doll she propped up against a tree. The earth had the comforting smell of old dirt and stale sunshine and made her wish she could dig a hole to bury herself in its warmth.

"Tinker Bell, where are you?" she asked in a sing-song fashion. She knew the ethereal being was encased in the protective home of her mother – the nature that hid her.

"Don't be afraid, I'm your friend. And Peter Pan is here. Are you with your family? What are their names? Willow, maybe, or Sage?"

The temperature dropped gradually, unnoticed, as Jodee hummed and dug. The morning slid into afternoon as she crawled on her knees around the perimeter of the fence, searching. The sun began to slide down toward a peaceful sleep, and a thin veneer of sanity patched together her wanton reality.

CHAPTER TWENTY-THREE

BLINK

Toni entered her house with a sigh of relief. She closed the door against the cold, threw her coat over the end of the couch and stood for a moment just to enjoy the quiet. She'd returned from a weeklong advocate training session in St. Paul. It was an annual class she had to attend to keep her training up to date, but they were always exhausting. She'd had to put work on hold and hadn't talked to family or friends in over a week. She needed her daily can of Dr. Pepper.

The sound of the pressurized pop from opening the can of soda always gave her an excited anticipation, not unlike an alcoholic anticipating that first taste of vodka before the bottle is opened. She figured if she had to have an addiction, soda wasn't the worst one she could have.

She stood at the kitchen counter enjoying the drink and peering out the window to her backyard, not looking at anything in particular. She lifted the can to her lips and eyed the muted colors of winter out her back window, glad the week was over. Her mind was busy trying to decipher the myriad of information she'd consumed from the training while her body campaigned for a soft bed by sending fatigue warnings to her neck and back.

She lowered the can from her lips and sighed with pleasure as she shifted her weight to lean her hip against the kitchen sink.

The slight shift in position had her notice a movement of purple from across the fence next door. It took her eyes a moment to send the message to her brain of what she saw. She placed the can on the counter and leaned closer to the window for a better look.

Next door, in the Warren's backyard, she saw Jodee crawling on her knees in the dirt, appearing to be searching for something.

Toni's brows came together in the deep furrow of concern. She watched Jodee for several minutes before noticing her hands and the knees of her pants were caked in mud and her bare arms red from being coatless in the frigid winter weather. "Jodee, what are you doing?" she asked into the air as if her friend could hear her. She watched for a few more seconds before saying aloud to the empty room, "And, is she... Is she talking to herself?" She didn't notice the irony of her comment.

Pushing herself away from the window, she grabbed a sweater hanging by the back door and walked out to investigate her neighbor's strange behavior, ignoring her body's tired complaining.

She let herself in through the gate of Jodee's yard and stood watching her friend continue to crawl around on the ground. "Jodee?" she said hesitantly, holding onto the gate as if needing an escape route.

Not getting an answer, she carefully walked a little further into the yard. "Jodee, honey, what are you doing?"

Toni watched as Jodee continued to search and dig with her hands, ignoring her questions. She finally walked over to where Jodee had stopped, seemingly interested in a particular spot in the dead garden. Looking down at the top of Jodee's head, not able to see her face, she listened in surprised worry as Jodee talked quietly to herself.

Toni reached down and placed her hand on the top of Jodee's head. "Jodee, are you okay?"

Jodee looked up with a slow cock of her head, looking at Toni like a child holding onto a secret. "Hello," she simply said, a smile barely curving the corners of her mouth. Her eyes had a faraway look in them, seeing something Toni couldn't see.

Toni realized something was wrong and it put her system into instant alert mode. "Uh, hi," Toni said uneasily, squatting down next to her friend. "What are you doing?"

"Shhh," Jodee said, putting a dirty finger to her mouth. "You'll scare them."

"Sorry," Toni said automatically. She watched as Jodee brushed frost from the dormant root of a dug-up tulip bulb. Taking a chance, she asked, "Uh, who am I going to scare?"

Toni sat back on her haunches and waited patiently for Jodee to answer. When she knew no answer was coming, she asked again, "Jodee, um, who am I going to scare?"

"I have to get the snow off their home so when they wake up, they'll have a pretty place to live. It's almost spring you know."

Toni was becoming more scared with each passing second. Something was terribly wrong with her friend. The hair on her arms raised in goose bumps of fear.

"Whose home, honey?"

"The fairies of course. They're sleeping for winter but come spring they'll be up and flying and will want to have a beautiful garden to live in."

"Uh, okay. Um, what makes you think there are fairies in your garden?" Toni asked, trying not to sound alarmed.

"There are fairies everywhere, silly. But right now, I'm looking for Tinker Bell. I found Peter Pan in the house alone and

I know Dougie J always put her outside so she can be with her friends. I think she got disoriented and got lost. Fairies sleep in the middle of leaves and flowers to stay warm in the winter and I'm trying to find her so she can be with them again."

Not knowing what to do Toni reached over and lightly touched Jodee's shoulder. "Uh, can I help you find her?"

Jodee pulled the bulb away and said with an indrawn breath of air, "Oh, no, no, you don't know what to do. You have to be very careful or you can hurt them."

"Okay, okay," Toni reassured her hurriedly, pulling back her hand. "I won't touch them, I swear. I'll let you do it. Okay?"

"Okay." Jodee went back to cleaning the brown tuber.

"Jodee?" Toni began, "If I let you keep the flower will you come inside? You're freezing."

Jodee ignored Toni's question as she worked diligently on the mud around the bulb.

Toni, her fear turning to worry that something medical might be wrong with her friend, crawled in front of Jodee and sat back on her heels. Carefully raising her hands to Jodee's face like she was confronting a skittish colt, she gently placed them on Jodee's cheeks and raised her face until their eyes met.

"Jodee, honey, why don't you come inside?"

Jodee's answer had Toni grow rigid with worry.

"Why do you keep calling me Jodee?" she asked, the confusion clear in her eyes.

"What?" Worry escalated to a higher level of fear.

"Why do you keep calling me Jodee?" she repeated. "My name's not Jodee."

"Oh… Uh, okay. What do you want me to call you?"

"You can call me by my fairy name. Every fairy has a name that reflects their personality. Didn't you know that?"

306

"No… No, I didn't know that, I'm sorry." Toni spoke softly, afraid any loud noise would frighten Jodee away. Carefully she asked, "So, what is your fairy name?"

"Silly, you know what it is."

"I'm sorry," Toni said carefully. "I guess I forgot. Can you tell me again?"

Without looking up Jodee answered matter-of-factly, "Blink. My name is Blink."

"Doug, it took everything I had to get her back inside the house. She was freezing and didn't even seem to feel it." Toni had stayed with Jodee until Doug had gotten home. "She needs to go to the hospital."

"Where is she now?" He wanted to know.

"She's in the bedroom with Audra. She got home from school just as I was able to clean Jodee up and get her in bed. Her clothes were covered in mud and her hands were actually bleeding from digging around in the dirt."

"I don't understand. You said she was looking for a Tinker Bell doll?"

"Yes, I guess it used to be Dougie J's. But Doug, she wasn't looking for a doll, she actually thinks Tinker Bell is alive and that there are other fairies living outside."

"That's ridiculous. You must have misunderstood her. I'm sure she was simply getting started early on some gardening and found the doll outside. You must have thought she said she was *looking* for a fairy."

Toni was getting angry at Doug's condescending attitude and she didn't try to hide it when she replied in an equally condescending tone, "I did not misunderstand her, and I resent you saying so. And I certainly am not imagining her cut and frozen hands. Why would she start planting flowers in twenty-degree weather, anyway? Tell me what that's about."

"I'm not trying to insult you, Toni, it's just you know Jodee has been under a lot of stress and I think you might be reading more into this than there really is."

"Really?" Toni said sarcastically. "Well, I certainly didn't imagine it when she told me her fairy name is Blink."

"Uh… Well, no, maybe not. I don't know what that's about."

"She needs a hospital, Doug," Toni said a little more calmly.

"No. No, she doesn't. I'm not taking her to a hospital where they'll try and convince me she needs a psychiatrist or something. I will not have people talking about us like that."

"What?" Toni was truly confused. "You won't have people talking? Doug, this isn't about what people might say, it's about Jodee's mental well-being."

"I know that and that's not what I meant. Listen, I'm just a little beside myself right now but I'll take care of it. I don't want you to worry about it, okay?"

"Doug, I'm used to dealing with people who are grieving but this is beyond anything I've ever seen. This is beyond grieving, it's like Jodee has disassociated herself from reality."

"No, listen," he insisted, "I'm sure it's not as bad as you're making it sound. She probably just missed a dose of her medicine. I'll ask Audra to check into it since she's been keeping track. In truth, I think because of your job you see trouble where there isn't any."

"Really? Well you think whatever you want, but at least let me help you with her. I'm truly worried."

"I know you are, but like I said, I'll take care of it… um, her," he corrected. "Now, I hate to be rude, and I appreciate you finding her, but I have to ask you to go so I can see about her."

Toni was dumbstruck by Doug's dismissing her like she was a bothersome servant. Turning abruptly on her heel, she jerked her coat off the back of the chair and headed for the front door. "Fine," she said, not trying to hide her anger, "but I will be checking on her tomorrow."

"That will be fine, and I appreciate you looking in on her when I'm at work, but I assure you that by tomorrow she'll be her old self again."

Toni reached for the door handle and stopped. Turning around to face Doug she said, "Oh, and by the way, you can tell Blink," she made quotation marks in the air, "I found Tinker Bell. She was under the tree in the middle of the yard under some leaves. I kicked her up after I went back outside to get the Peter Pan doll she left. I put them both on the kitchen table, if she asks."

Toni walked out of the house without waiting for a response from Doug. She'd known the Warrens for years, but it was the first time she'd ever seen a side of Doug she didn't like. She always considered him a people person because he had the ability to make whoever he was talking to feel like they were the only person in the room. But this Doug seemed more concerned with himself than his wife, more worried about what other people might say, more, well, more callous and self-absorbed.

SECTION SIX

SHATTERED

And then the mind let go and peace followed.

CHAPTER TWENTY-FOUR

TINKER BELL VANISHES

Jodee swore she could hear the tiny buzzing that always came right before they appeared. Her reality let her believe that any second, dozens of fairies would start to dart around the rainbow that hovered on the brink of her sanity. She could even feel the twitching in her back that let her know her wings were trying to grow in. If only her family would just leave her alone.

For weeks everyone had watched her like she was an anomaly in a zoo. Dayla walked around her with a cautious look on her face that resembled a frightened deer looking for an escape route. Lexie stayed in her room and wouldn't come out even to eat. Audra watched her every move like a prison warden, forever counting her pills.

On her more lucid days, Jodee could feel the change in the air. Doug had been more volatile than normal. especially since his run-in with Toni. She'd noticed he wasn't as careful about what he said in public to her as he used to be. If not for the girls' presence, she knew his desire to smash something would transpire into physical destruction. She could tell he was trying to keep himself in check around them but figured it was just a matter of time. When they were alone, his anger turned into spiteful accusations or warning threats: 'Jodee, I can see right through your crazy routine and you'd better snap out of it or else… Jodee, you're doing this on purpose to gain sympathy. Don't you think I'm hurting as much as you over Dougie J? You're being very selfish… Jodee, I'm fed up with your self-pity, you're embarrassing me in front of my friends. Archer won't even come over any more. He uses the excuse that he's in the middle of hockey season but we both know the real reason…' Jodee this, Jodee that, Jodee, Jodee, Jodee. God, she was beginning to hate her own name.

Audra had begun watching her as she took her pills, not allowing her to leave the kitchen until she watched her swallow them and even following her into the bathroom.

Jodee hated the emotion-killing pills, they made her feel sluggish and sleepy. Her mind couldn't function, she couldn't feel, she couldn't live. When she took the pills, the fairies didn't appear and the purple hue surrounding the clouds faded away into the gray sadness of the winter sky. And she knew that if anyone found out about the fairies, they would do something to make them disappear. The fairies were her secret, her friends. So she wouldn't tell anyone. Not her family, Toni or the doctors.

She had found a way to fool Audra though and keep from swallowing the mood-altering poison. She started paying attention to when it was time to take the medicine and made sure to always beat Audra into the kitchen. She would make sure to grab a white plastic cup, one of the little opaque ones they'd gotten once when a carnival was in town. Then, when Audra handed her the pills and watched as she put them in her mouth, she would swallow a small amount of water to show she had actually swallowed something, but she'd hold the pill under her tongue and very surreptitiously spit the pill into the remaining water. When Audra was praising her for being a good little pill popper like she was some four-year-old, she'd quickly dump the rest of the water down the drain, pills and all.

Everyone thought she had finally resigned to taking the nasty things and started to comply with their whims of changing her, but she had them all fooled. Oh, sometimes she got stuck into actually swallowing the medicine, like the time Lexie was washing a stick of celery at the sink and by the time she could get water in her cup the pill had dissolved under her tongue, but those times were few and far between.

Spring had decided to hide behind the white skirt of winter, afraid in its infancy of showing independence. The sky maintained its color of Minnesota gray which obscured any feelings of rebirth and made loneliness the lead actor in nature's production.

Jodee stood at the kitchen window watching the approaching dawn, feeling the usual anticipation she knew would come with seeing the first glimpse of shimmering wings on the remaining snow that told her the fairies were awake. She had found Tinker Bell on the table the day Toni had visited her and knew this tiny fairy was a lifeline to Dougie J. So, she kept the doll in the pocket of her sweaters, or her robe, or her jeans at all times.

Her routine had changed since Toni had found her in the garden, she'd had to hide the fairies existence from doubting eyes, as well as her own fairy personality. It was a fine patina of illusion she preferred over the more painful reality of life.

Her family seemed afraid of the changes in her, so she knew she had to keep this fragile world to herself. Since that day, she began forcing herself to wake up before Doug every morning in order to close the backdoor. The door she would get up just after midnight to open to let the fairies' come in to warm themselves before they went back outside to play – midnight under the moon was the fairies' most active time. She didn't know how she knew this; she just did. She figured it was her innate spirit coming forth.

The first morning Doug had awoken before her, he'd discovered the door open and the temperature in the house dropped by twenty degrees. He'd gotten so angry at her he threatened to nail the door shut, warning her that if she didn't 'straighten up' he'd have her committed, gossip or not. After that, she started setting the alarm clock at eleven fifty-five every night and putting it under her pillow so Doug couldn't hear it when it went off. She'd get up when the alarm sounded, go into the kitchen and crack the door open by setting a small rock on the floor, return to bed and set the alarm again for five in the morning, in time to get up, close the door again and warm up the house before Doug got up at six.

Things seemed different this day, however. It was six-forty in the morning and Doug hadn't yet come into the room, the girls were still asleep, the house was quiet. Not wanting to think why this was, she opened the door again and stood in front of it letting the frigid air cool her blistered soul and cleanse her of troubled dreams – dreams of Dougie J calling her as he flew with fairies just out of reach; dreams she had night after night, dreams that confused her and made her head hurt.

She stared out at the yard as the glitter in the snow mesmerized her. The twinkling sparkles seemed to be talking to her in some silent musical song. The pain from her dreams started to fade so she walked a little farther out the door, her mind snagging on the possibility that maybe the dreams weren't dreams after all, but a reality only she could understand. It was the fairies, she realized. The fairies that glittered in the snow trying to calm her. They knew of the dreams her mind rationalized. They were trying to help her, telling her Dougie J was safe and with them. They'd take her to him if she'd only follow.

Pulled by their brilliancy, she followed the tiny glittery lights with her eyes across the Palomino-colored yard to where it fell over the fence, through the gap in the wilted winter shrubs down to the pale blue of the river that she could just see through the bare growth of the tree branches.

A sudden gust of wind blew through the door and brushed the hair across her face. She mistook the light breeze fanning her ears for the voices of the fairies calling her – the musical buzzing slaked the suffocating pressure of the house – beckoning her. She slipped out the door toward the lights flitting across the river, knowing they were skating on top of the water and calling her in the whisper of the breeze. Walking across the yard, she continued outside the gate, crossed the running path and headed into the morning shadows of the tangled brush and twigs that rimmed the bank of the river.

The ground was soft from the wet morning dew and melting snow, unaware that her only protection from the lingering winter was thin terry slippers and a robe, she walked blindly on, concentrating on the shimmering lights. Knowing the fairies were leading her to Dougie J, she hurried her pace.

Her robe snagged on the burs of a sumac causing her to trip on an above ground root. She pulled the robe roughly from around her legs. Irritated it was hampering her journey, she took it off and left it dangling from a branch. She had to hurry because she knew that fairies were forever evanescent.

Thankful for the freedom from the now discarded robe, she made her way faster toward the river as cruel fingers of leafless branches scratched her face and arms, the muddy water soaking through her slippers.

Walking forward, intent on her quest, she never looked back

to see the soft blue robe fluttering in the wind amongst the dried leaves. She also never saw the tiny Tinker Bell doll fall from the pocket of the robe to be forever buried under those same dead leaves.

Lexie awoke at seven fifteen in the morning. It was early for a Saturday, but it was going to be an important day and she was anxious about the outcome. Today was the day she was telling her parents she wanted to live with Grandma and Grandpa Warren, for the summer at least.

Her grandparents weren't going to be at the house until noon to help her explain her reasons for wanting to live with them, but she was too excited to stay in bed. Since her little brother's death the house had felt confining and cold. Her parents hardly talked, Audra was always at some school function, and Dayla was still young enough to be a royal pain. She knew in order to conquer her eating disorder, because she knew she had one, she had to escape the trauma of home in order to deal with the emotional reasons behind her illness. She had spoken to the school nurse and read brochures. She knew it was an illness, but it was one she was determined to cure on her own. First though, she had to take care of the emotional upheaval that was causing it in the first place.

She walked into the kitchen ready to deal, once again, with the lost look in her mother's eyes; the look which made it too painful to live at home any more. It was that constant tortured look that made her feel sorry for her mom but want to hide from her at the same time. She missed her brother more than she could ever have imagined so she could comprehend to some extent what her mom and dad were going through. Having one less traumatized person in the house would only help, she

318

rationalized.

Walking into the kitchen, the cold air hit her senses, causing her to take a sharp intake of air. Looking around, it took a moment to see the reason why – the backdoor was standing open. She froze in place, more out of confusion than concern. She walked slowly to the door as if she was afraid something was going to jump out and say 'boo.' Instinct told her something was wrong as freezing air sucked stability out the door along with the warmth. The hair on her arms started rising unexpectedly from an innate fear.

"Mom?" she called tentatively.

Letting her eyes follow the sound of wood banging against metal, she watched the back-gate swing lightly open and closed. Thinking the wind had caused the latch on the gate to pop open, she quickly scanned the back yard out of natural curiosity. As she stood looking out at the empty space of morning, an uneasy feeling nestled against the nape of her neck and kept her from closing the door against the cold.

Audra walked into a cold kitchen, still half asleep. Wrapping her robe tighter around her middle she stopped midstride to scold her younger sister, "Lexie, what are you doing? Close the door for Pete's sake. It's freezing in here."

Lexie responded to her sister without turning around. "Audie," she asked, using her pet name for her sister, "is Mom in her room?"

"No. I just passed their room and Dad told me to tell mom to put the coffee on. Why?"

"Because she wasn't in the kitchen when I got up and when I came in the door was standing open."

"Wait, what?" Lexie could hear the slow panic begin in her sister's question. "God, do you think she went outside again?"

"I don't know but she's not in the backyard either. What do you think we should do? Should we get Dad?"

"No. Let's look around first and make sure she isn't just in another part of the house. You check the office and I'll look in the garage. And close the door before Dad gets in here or he's gonna freak."

Lexie proceeded to obey her sister when, not knowing why, her eyes scanned the dark recesses of the mesh of branches she could see over the fence. A flutter of blue that seemed out of place on that gray morning caught her attention.

"Wait, Audie, wait," she said stopping her sister before she could leave the room.

"What is it?"

"I see something in the woods."

Walking to her sister's side, Audra asked, "Where?"

"There," she replied as she pointed in front of her. "Look over the fence."

Like two sentries standing side by side, the sisters gazed at the slither of blue that hung on a brown branch thirty yards away fluttering like a forsaken flag.

As they stared at the soft baby blue, trying to determine what it could be, a glint of sun caught the blonde movement of a head farther between the twigs and branches.

"Oh, God, Lexie, look!" Audra exclaimed with alarm in her voice. "Look in the water. I think it's Mom!"

Lexie followed her sister's outstretched arm and pointing finger. "It is mom! She's in the river. We gotta tell Dad!" she cried as she started to turn.

"No, wait," Audra commanded, stopping her by the arm. "You go next door and get Toni. I'll go get Mom."

"Why? We should tell Dad first."

"No, believe me, if he sees her in the water he is going to completely flip out. You weren't here when Toni found her outside digging in the mud and I thought dad was going to go ballistic. We're going to need help dealing with him when he finds out about this and help with Mom when we get her in the house. Toni will know what to do and maybe Dad won't get so angry with someone else in the house."

"Okay, but hurry, there's no telling how long she's been in the river," Lexie said as she ran to get Toni.

CHAPTER TWENTY-FIVE

THE TRUTH IS COLD

It had been two hours since they had dragged Jodee out of the river. Toni sat in an armchair of the Warren living room drinking hot tea willing the warmth to return to her body as the icy cold of the Mississippi water persisted in permeating to the marrow of her bones.

The morning events had set off a disjointed mound of chaos. Audra had called her grandparents, they in turn called another family member who then called another until the group had escalated into a full-blown intervention.

Toni watched from the outer fray as the Warren and Olson families faced off in a heated circle as they discussed Jodee's fate like bidders at an auction.

Katie Olson: "Where is she now?"

Audra: "She's in bed, Grandma. As soon as we got her out of the river, we put her in a tub to warm her up and put her to bed. She was freezing."

Joe Olson: "What the hell was she doing in the river?"

"We don't know. All she said was fairies were taking her to find Dougie J."

Nora: "Fairies? What are you talking about?"

Lexie: "Mom said she saw fairies on the water and they were leading her to Dougie. She kept saying her name was Blink."

Grace Warren: "Oh my God, she's lost her mind."

George Warren: "Now, Mother, let's not think the worst."

Nora: "Who the hell is Blink?"

Audra: "It's the name she said the fairies gave her."

Brigid: "Great, now she's a fairy. I think that pretty much says she's losing it."

Katie Olson: "She's probably jist needs more medicine."

Doug: "Oh for God's sake, forget about the damn fairies. It's something she's been talking about for months. Ever since Dougie J's accident she's been carrying around that stupid Tinker Bell doll he used to play with. I should have thrown it away a long time ago. I didn't know she was going to start talking to it."

Nora: "Obviously she needs a hospital."

Brigid: "Or a looney bin."

Nora: "Oh, nice Brigid, way to be sensitive."

Audra: "Aunt Brigid, I don't think Mom needs a 'looney bin,'" she said gesturing with air quotes, "but I do think you might be right. I think she needs professional help."

Nora: "She should be in a psych ward for evaluation if you ask me."

Doug: "Now hold on just a minute. Listen, I don't care what anyone says, no wife of mine is being admitted to some insane asylum."

Nora: "No-one said anything about an insane asylum. God, what year are you living in? We're talking about a hospital. And you can't tell me after this morning that it's not what she needs."

Lexie: "Dad, please, Mom is sick, she needs help."

Grace Warren: "Doug, honey, I know this is hard but if they hadn't found her when they did, she could have frozen to death, or drowned."

Audra: "By the time we found her, she had walked clear up

to her waist. She didn't even seem to be aware of the cold."

Joe Olson: "Doug may be right. He is her husband after all. Besides, you always feel better when you're in your own home."

George Warren: "And who's going to watch her? Isn't this the second or third time she's done something like this?"

Katie: "I'm sorry, but my Jodee don't need no doctor telling her she's crazy. She jist needs time to figure things out, dun-cha-know. She's grievin' and a little alone time will do her good."

Lexie: "Grandma, she was *in* the river!"

Audra: "That's right and she was literally shaking by the time we got her out. In fact, if it hadn't been for Toni I don't know if we could've gotten her out by ourselves."

As if on cue, everyone turned and looked at Toni.

Audra: "Toni, don't you think Mom should go to a hospital?"

The question brought Toni out of her wary watchfulness. "Yes, I do, if for no other reason than to be checked out for hypothermia."

"But as a victim advocate, do you think Mom needs a psychiatric hospital?"

"I'm not family, it's not my place to say one way or the other. But as her friend…"

Interrupting, Doug said, "That's right, she's not family and she doesn't have a vote."

Toni turned quickly and looked at Doug. Standing up, she stood directly in front of him, derision darkening her eyes. "Your right, Doug, I don't have a right to say anything, but as I was saying, as her friend I care about her and I think she needs more help than a regular doctor can give her."

"Listen, Toni, I appreciate you being there when you were, but this really should be discussed in private. I don't mean to be rude, but maybe it would be best if you left us alone for now. This

324

just isn't your field of expertise."

Toni was shaking on the inside. Doug's condescending tone had anger working itself up her legs into her neck. *Jerk*, she thought. 'And, if he says 'listen' one more time I'm going to deck him.' She knew it was a habit of his, but habit or not, she knew he used it as a way to get attention from everyone around him just by commanding them to 'listen.' It certainly seemed to work with his family at any rate.

Audra: "Dad, Toni is our friend!"

George Warren: "Doug, son, I think we're all fine if Toni stays. We can use all the help we can get."

Nora: "Oh, for Pete's sake, Doug, stop being so mule-headed. And you are being rude. Toni already knows everything so what will it hurt if she stays? She may have insight into things we don't." Nora plopped down in a chair with ceremonious decisiveness, as if her word was final.

Speaking to the group, but staring at Nora, Doug said, "Fine, she can stay. But listen everyone, I appreciate you trying to help but Jodee'll be fine. They just need to increase her dose of medicines, that's all."

Toni clinched her fist at the word 'listen,' screaming in her head and biting her tongue to stay quiet.

Nora challenged her brother-in-law. "I think it's a little more serious than a few pills. Besides, you know as well as anyone how fragile Jodee has always been."

"Listen, I'm her husband and I think I know what's best. I mean, can you imagine what my boss would say if he found out Jodee was admitted into a hospital for psychiatric reasons? I'd never be promoted again."

"What? Did I just hear him right?" Toni looked shockingly at each member of the family, waiting for someone to respond.

Ignoring Toni, Joe Olson said, "Now, see there. We need to think of Doug's work. Do we really want to risk his job over this?"

George Warren: "Now hold on a minute, we need to think about what's best for Jodee, even if it means her going into a hospital for a while."

A lull momentarily quieted the room.

Dayla walked to Doug and put her arms around his waist. "Daddy, is Mom going away?"

"No, Dayla, your Mom is not going away."

Grace Warren: "See what you all have done. You're upsetting the children." She went to her youngest granddaughter and wrapped her arms around her.

Brigid, stretching her back as if the whole ordeal exhausted her, said with a tired exhale of breath, "Has anyone thought that maybe she's doing this just for the attention?"

"*Excuse* me," Toni bit out with sarcastic disbelief.

Like a politician speaking before her constituents, Brigid placed her hands on the back of a chair to speak. Everyone stopped talking and turned to look at her, as if immense wisdom was going to spew from her mouth, "I just think everyone should stop coddling her. I mean, I know how hard this must be for her, losing Dougie J and all, but it was months ago. Don't they say that time heals all wounds? If we all stop jumping every time she decides to act a little nutty maybe she'd stop doing things like this."

Anger caused goose bumps to rise on Toni's skin.

Katie Olson, interrupting quickly. "Brigid, dear, this isn't something you can jist let go of."

"Oh, for the love of Pete, Mother, I know that. But you have got to stop babying her."

"Brigid, you don't know what you're talking about. Jodee needs a hospital. You know she's always been the weakest of the three of us," Nora stated with authority. "But even so, I can't believe you think that she's going to get better in a few months after losing a child."

"I didn't say that. I'm just saying…"

Doug: "Okay, okay, everyone, let's just calm down."

Grace Warren: "You all know that Dougie's birthday is in just a few weeks. What do you think she's going to do when that day rolls around?"

The family went silent as Toni watched the expressions change on individual faces one by one.

Joe Olson: "We don't need to think about that now."

Brigid: "I think we just don't let her focus on it when the day comes and wallow around in self-pity."

Toni, bristling, took a step toward Brigid. She was stopped in her tracks by Doug's next statement.

"Brigid has a point. Maybe we need to stop over-reacting with every change in Jodee's behavior. Besides, has everyone forgotten that Dougie J was my son too? I also lost a child if you'll remember. You don't think I'm also hurting? I mean, there are days I can barely get out of bed for the pain, but I have other responsibilities that I have to consider. I don't have the luxury of sleeping away half the day or wandering off to reflect. I have no choice but to go on."

Grace Warren, releasing her hold on her youngest granddaughter, lunged for her son. "Oh, baby, you're right, we've completely overlooked that fact."

George Warren: "Son, we're sorry. We know you're hurting too."

Doug, "Yeah, well…" He bowed his head in a sheepish

327

manner.

Toni watched Doug's transformation in amazement as he laid his head on his mother's shoulder like a shy little boy.

Suddenly, like everyone had just been invited to Doug's pity party, the whole family turned their attention to him.

Brigid: "Oh, Doug, I don't know what we were thinking. This must be so hard for you." She placed her hand on his back and rubbed it in small gentle circles.

Joe Olson, walking up to the huddled trio said, "Doug, my boy, I know Jodee can be a burden. What can we do to help?"

"Dad, I'm so sorry," Audra cried as she ran to her father's side. "I forgot how hard this is for you, too."

Lexie joined her sister. "Daddy, I'm sorry, too."

Dayla ran to be included, squeezing herself between her grandmother and her dad.

"Doug, my boy, we all miss him, you know that." George Warren placed his large hand on his son's head like a preacher offering solace.

"Doug, ya know Jodee's gonna be okay. Dun you fret none."

Nora relented her initial assault on her brother-in-law. "Dad's right, let us help."

Toni watched in stunned silence as the family gathered into a large group hug of bodies and tears as they crooned over Doug.

Doug, raising his head so he could be heard, answered Nora in the most pitiful voice Toni had ever heard. "It just helps to know I have family I can lean on. You don't know what it means to me that you'd all drop everything at a moment's notice just to come and listen to my problems."

'Oh, for the love of…' Toni thought.

George Warren: "Well, that's why we're here, son, and I think we have a solution."

Grace Warren: "Yes. Now, don't get upset, but we want to take Lexie for the summer. I think it would be good for both her and Jodee. And, she would be one less person you would have to worry about."

"What? Why? When did you come up with this?" Doug stammered.

"Well, Lexie called us a few weeks ago and asked us if she could. We think it's a good idea."

Doug turned his attention to his middle daughter as he disentangled himself from the mass of family. "Lexie?"

"Daddy, I want to do this."

"Doug," his father explained, "there's a clinic up around us that we want to put Lexie in. It's an eating disorder clinic that we think can help her. She wants to do this and I think it's very mature of her. We'll even pay for it."

"Eating disorder? She doesn't have an eating disorder. She's a little thin, I grant you, but it's not a disorder."

"Daddy," Lexie said, bending her head in shame, "I passed out at school last month."

"What? Why didn't I know about this?"

"With everything that's happened, I didn't want to bother you and Mom with it. I had them call Grandma Warren when it happened."

"Doug," his mother said, "we've known about Lexie for a month or so now and we've been talking to her school and think this is the best solution."

Lexie continued for her grandmother. "I've talked to a counselor at school and I know I have a problem. Grandma and Grandpa said I could stay with them and I can go to the clinic on an outpatient basis if you'll agree. I want to get better, Dad. I need this."

Audra, "Dad, I think that's a great idea. I've known she's been throwing up for months now, but I'm ashamed to admit I haven't paid much attention to her from trying to keep up with Mom's medicine and school and college applications and all."

Doug, "Wait, everyone just hold on, you're saying Lexie is what—anorexic or something? And that you've already talked to the school and a clinic? Why the hell wasn't I told?"

"We didn't want to add any more to your plate, son. Since Dougie J's funeral, the whole family has been in turmoil. We have a chance to take some of that worry from you, if at least for now and through the summer."

The room went quiet as everyone waited for Doug to answer.

"Well, I suppose," he started, "but school isn't out yet and if she's as sick as you say…"

"I'm not sick, I just have a small problem," Lexie interrupted fiercely. "I just want to talk to a counselor."

"Okay, okay, fine. If she wants to go and you've already talked to her school about it, then I assume it would be best if she went right away. Shouldn't she have gone before now?"

"Because it's taken us this long to get her scheduled and figure out all the logistics," George Warren explained.

"And my teachers have already said I can finish off the last month of school and finals by mail."

"Well… I guess I don't have much choice if I want you to get better, do I?"

"Uh, excuse me," Toni said, "but don't all of you think that maybe Jodee should be part of this decision."

"Jodee?" Doug said her name like she was a foreign being – unfamiliar and distant. "Jodee can't even take care of herself right now. She certainly can't make this decision."

Audra, speaking quickly, "Dad, I also want to leave for the

summer. I want to get a summer job at the Mall of America. That way I can make money for college and Mom won't have to worry about me being underfoot either."

Brigid: "I've already told her she can live with me."

"God, I feel like I'm losing control of my family. Is there anyone else who's made plans without asking me?"

Toni watched Doug hang his head in a show of sadness as his family oooed and aahed over him.

"No, son, we're just trying to help. We know how hard this is for you."

"What about Dayla?" Doug asked. "I have to work, and I just don't think Jodee is capable of watching her."

Toni could have sworn she saw a spark in Doug's eyes at the prospect of not having to deal with his kids for the summer. It was like a light bulb materialized over his head from the glow on his face.

Dayla, as if on cue, transformed from the sad, scared three-year-old of minutes before to an exuberant teenager. "Dad, I also want to go somewhere this summer. There's a language camp up in Bemidji I want to go to with Amanda. And then her mom asked if I could go to South Dakota with them for a couple of weeks."

"Well, I don't know…" Doug looked to be thinking but Toni could tell he was thrilled with the news of having all his kids gone for the summer. She watched his self-pitying head-dangling with disgust. Any second she expected him to kick the toe of his shoe against the carpet and say, 'golly gee, poor widdle me.' She slightly shook her head, amazed at how blind everyone seemed to be to his charade.

Nora said, "And after she gets back from South Dakota, she can stay with us for the rest of the summer. That way she can spend some time with her cousins. I'll even pay her to babysit. It will really help me out. Is that okay with you, Dayla?"

"Yeah, that would be great," Dayla exclaimed.

Joe Olson, "Well, it's all settled then."

Toni stood stock still, watching the whole scene play out like a drama in a play. 'All settled?' Toni thought furiously. 'Had everyone forgotten the main reason they had gathered, which was to decide what to do about Jodee? Is this what it's always been like for her? Being ignored? Her needs taking a backseat to Doug's?' She watched as the family broke apart and started jabbering excitedly about their individual plans. Doug had come alive under the family's attention, like all the cares of the world had been taken off him.

She was about to shout at the whole lot of them when a small hiccup to her right caught everyone's attention. Jodee stood in the shadow of the hall, eerily white in its darkness.

Wide-eyed, she choked through a wall of unshed tears, "You're... You're taking my children away?"

Toni ran to her side as Jodee stumbled into the room.

Everyone turned in surprise, their smiles frozen in place from their shared guilt.

"Jodee, what are you doing out of bed?" Doug scolded.

Desperate, Jodee reached for Doug like a starving beggar, "Doug, don't let them take my kids away."

"Jodee, baby, they aren't taking the girls avay. They're just gonna have a couple of veeks with family so you can rest."

"Momma, no. Please, don't let them take them. I need my girls with me."

Mr. Olson, walking up to his daughter, told her firmly, "Jodee, I think we know what's best for you. You really haven't been yourself lately and having some quiet in the house will give you time to get better. Now, you need to stop making a scene and get back in bed."

Jodee fell silent and stared blankly at the short stout man in front of her like she didn't quite recognize him.

Toni watched emotions drift across Jodee's sad hazel eyes as she weighed the consequences of obeying her father or arguing. Holding her by the elbow, Toni saw a hurt in Jodee's eyes like none she'd ever seen in any victim she'd ever encountered.

She knew the second Jodee made up her mind. Pulling her arm from Toni's hold she ran to Lexie and wrapped her arms tightly around her daughter's shoulders.

"Lexie, Lexie, baby, I'm so sorry you're sick. I didn't know. I'm so sorry. Please, baby, please don't leave me. I'll be better, I promise."

"Mom?" Lexie stumbled backward. "Mom, it's not you," she said as she tried to pry her mother's arms off her shoulders. Lexie looked up, help and fear written in her pupils.

Audra ran to her sister. "Mom, Mom... Let go, okay?" Audra whispered into her mother's ear as she gently loosened her hold. "Lexie isn't leaving forever, just for a few weeks. Grandma and Grandpa Warren are going to help her."

Jodee switched her attention from Lexie to Audra, "Audra, you don't want to leave me, do you? Can't you get work around here somewhere? The Mall is so far away. When will I ever see you?"

"It's only forty minutes away. I can come home on my days off and it will allow me to make money for college. You remember, don't you, that I'll be leaving for college in the fall?"

"College?" Jodee tasted the word as if it was an unknown flavor.

"Jodee... Jodee, ya need to calm down, everybody is jist trying ta help," Katie Olson said, the stress always causing her accent to thicken.

"No they aren't, they're trying to take my kids away. Just like they took Dougie J away. They took him away and I can't find him."

A collective gasp sucked the air from the room. The family backed away from Jodee like she had a contagious disease, leaving her standing alone in the middle of the room.

"Jodee," Nora stated bluntly, "Dougie J wasn't taken away by anyone. He died."

"What?" Jodee looked at her sister with pure hatred in her eyes. "What did you just say?"

The look had Nora back further away and clutch the closest person to her.

"Answer me! What did you just say?" Jodee shouted.

"Jodee, stop this! Stop it this minute!" Doug yelled.

Jodee stopped immediately and cowered next to Toni the way someone would from being whipped.

Wrapping her arms around Jodee's trembling frame, Toni studied what had just happened, taking in the scene in its entirety, she was seeing the truth of this family for the first time: Joe Olson's officious demand, Brigid's blunt cruelty, the whole family physically distancing themselves, Doug's harsh tone.

A thought passed through Toni's mind like lightning, so fast she wasn't sure what it was – something important, something vital, something that explained everything, something that washed over her and made her blood cold. Before she could concentrate and try to recapture the moment, Dayla spoke.

"Mommy, are you okay?"

Hearing Dayla's timid voice brought Jodee to attention. Running to her daughter Jodee knelt in front of her like a parishioner at a religious alter. Grabbing both of her hands she cried, "Oh, my baby, you want to stay with Mommy, don't you?"

Dayla turned her confusion to her father. "Daddy?"

"Jodee, get back to bed this instant. You're scaring her," Doug ordered.

Toni went to Jodee and bending over her, took hold of her shoulders. "Jodee, please try and stay calm. I promise, no one is going to take the girls from you. I won't let them. They just want to go someplace new for the summer and have some fun. Don't you want them to have fun?"

Jodee looked up at Toni without ever moving her head, her eyes independent of her face, giving Toni an eeriness she'd never felt before.

"Fun?" Jodee asked.

"Yes, that's right. They just want to have some fun for the summer."

Jodee pulled away from her daughter. "Yes, yes, that would be nice. They need to have some fun." Standing up Jodee brushed her robe down like it were a gown made of delicate chiffon. Clapping her hands together she looked around the room and said at large, "Well, we'd better get you packed, hadn't we?"

Walking to the hall closet, Jodee opened the door and said, "Dayla, don't forget to pack your swimsuit. And Lexie, you should take a sweater. You never know when it'll get cold. Oh…" She chuckled. "Remember that time it snowed the end of June. That was a sight, wasn't it?" Jodee continued to rummage through the closet where the winter coats were kept, mumbling to herself with her back to the room.

Dayla, still standing with her hands outstretched as if her mother still had hold of them, said to her father, "Dad, what is she doing? I'm not going till after school is over."

"Dayla, hush," Audra scolded.

After a few moments of letting Jodee look for a swimsuit in a coat closet, Brigid stepped up and said firmly, "This is exactly what I've been talking about. Everyone needs to stop enabling her. Jodee, you stop pretending to be nuts this minute. You know damn well that school isn't out for another month."

"Brigid, stop. We don't know what this could do to her," Toni demanded looking at Jodee's back, watching as it stiffened.

"Oh, for pity's sake, she's only pretending. She knows perfectly well what's going on. Jodee, turn around and look at me."

Jodee turned slowly, looking at her sister with a parka in her hands.

"Now, you admit this minute, in front of God and everyone, that you've been doing all this just to get attention. Personally, I think you've always been jealous of the attention I've always gotten and want people to feel sorry for you and this is the perfect opportunity to get it."

"I don't understand," Jodee said. "What opportunity are you talking about? Is something happening?"

"Oh, for the…" Brigid gritted in frustration. "Of course something is happening. You using Dougie J's death to get attention."

Jodee's face whitened even more and with a sharp intake of breath she whispered, "Dougie J," and slumped to her knees on the floor.

CHAPTER TWENTY-SIX

BRUISES BEHIND THE EYES

Toni stood outside the closed door of Jodee's bedroom waiting for Audra to bring a sleeping pill. They'd been able to get Jodee back to bed after a lot of convincing that her girls would be fine, but as Toni stood waiting she could still hear the family's rapid debating coming from the living room reminding her of a murder of chattering crows.

Doug: "See what I've had to put up with?"

Brigid: "I'm telling you she's only doing it for attention. Do you know I had to take the day off to come here today? I do have a job, you know. And not one person has even mentioned my promotion to Floor Supervisor."

Nora: "It's not an act, Brigid. I've always told her she wasn't strong enough to handle four kids, or to raise a boy for that matter. She's just too weak."

Joe Olson: "It's just one more time that she's caused trouble. I'm not blaming her, mind you, but we need to focus on getting this family back to one piece and keeping Doug's job secure."

Doug: "Listen, it's been hard enough around here without Jodee going to pieces. Why, she hasn't cooked a decent meal in months and just last week I had to iron my own shirts. And do you know I haven't been able to get Archer over here to play golf in I don't know how long. I know it's because he doesn't want to be around Jodee and all her moping. You don't know how hard it is to get through the day without breaking down in tears over my son and I just can't handle that and Jodee breaking down, too."

Audra's presence at the bedroom door disrupted what Toni considered was the most inconsiderate bunch of caterwauling she'd ever heard. The insensitivity of the entire family was building a pressure of pure anger in her chest. Her father was a brute, her mother a mouse, her sister Brigid totally self-absorbed, Nora was an anomaly – kind behind her back and completely unsympathetic to her face, and Doug was just completely narcissistic. No wonder Jodee always seemed to be walking around in a haze.

Interrupting Toni's thoughts, Audra looked into Toni's eyes and asked, "Is Mom going to be okay?" She handed Toni the sleeping pill.

"I don't know," Toni said.

The two women left the noise of the family outside the bedroom as they walked farther inside and closed the door firmly.

"It looks like your mom may not need another pill for a while. Looks like she's asleep. One may be enough for now."

"I'm going to sit with her awhile in case she wakes up. She usually doesn't sleep very long and then I'll be able to give her the pill anyway if she needs it."

"I think that's a good idea, but let's hope one is enough."

A couple of minutes of silence elapsed before Toni stated, "You know, I do think your dad should let her see a doctor."

"I think so too, and I'll talk to him. I think he would just rather have her here at home is all."

Jodee mumbled in her sleep, "My girls, they want to take my girls."

"No, honey, your girls are fine, and Audra is here to help."

Opening her eyes slightly, Jodee turned her head to look at her oldest daughter, and said, "Audra, I'll be good. I'll take my medicine. Please don't leave."

"Mom, I know you'll be good but I'm only going to college. You remember, don't you?"

"College? You're going to college?"

"Yes, and I need to make some money for expenses. I need to get a summer job."

"A summer job? Oh, well, I think that's a fine idea. I'll help you find one." The words were dragged from her lips as once again her understanding of the situation slipped deeper under her emotional exhaustion. Her eyes started to droop, leisurely drawing down a curtain over the hollowness in their depths.

"I think she's going to go back to sleep. Why don't we leave her alone?" Toni said.

Leaning over her mother, Audra gave her a kiss on the cheek.

Toni, standing on the other side of the bed, watched Audra linger over her mother's face, her hair falling to the side exposing a green and blue bruise at the bottom of her neck.

Holding her anger in check, Toni walked to the door of the room willing Audra to follow.

As Audra reached for the doorknob, Toni stopped her by leaning forward and quietly whispered into her hair, "I saw the bruise on your neck. Did Travis do that to you again?"

Audra turned so abruptly Toni had to jump back so that their faces wouldn't collide.

"A bruise?"

"Yes, on your neck."

"Oh, it must be an old one."

"Audra, I know what bruises look like and that one is not that old. I thought you had stopped seeing Travis," she whispered fiercely.

"I did… I mean, I did for a while but we kind-of got back together a few weeks ago."

"I see. And he's still manhandling you."

"No. I mean maybe just that once about a week ago, but he didn't mean to do it. He'd gotten in trouble at work and was in a bad mood and I was pushing him to go to a party. It was totally my fault. I should have just let him calm down a little before I asked. He just grabbed me a little harder than he meant to, that's all."

"Audra, that isn't all. I told you how abusers work. They always make it feel like it's your fault. I thought you were going to break it off with him."

"I did, but he was so sad and he kept calling and asking for another chance. It was just that one time, I swear. He promised he'd never do it again if I'd get back together with him."

"It's never just one time. There will always be another time and other reasons and they'll always be your fault. Don't you understand?"

"He's not like that. Maybe other guys are like that but not him. He's changed."

"No, honey, he hasn't. He may be good to you now, but what about the next time he gets mad or blames you for something that went wrong?"

"You don't know him. I tell you, he'll never do it again, he promised."

"Fine, I hope you're right. But, please, if he ever does hurt you again will you at least tell your Mom? Knowing she's needed may help her emotional well-being."

"No way. Why would Mom understand? She's barely holding it together as it is. Besides, she's never been with anybody but Daddy and he's never raised a hand to her. She can't possibly do anything. But I'm telling you, it won't ever happen again."

"Okay, but remember, Audra, I did promise I'd turn him into the police if he ever physically…" The word physically dragged slowly from Toni's lips making her halt her tirade mid-sentence. An answer to a question she'd never thought to ask flitted through her mind too fast for her to capture it. But it was there, again, lurking as she asked herself, 'what is it? What am I missing?'

Perplexed by Toni's sudden halt, Audra asked, "Toni? Are you okay?"

"What? Oh, yes. Anyway, like I was saying, if he ever physically hurts you again, I will turn him in, and I mean it."

"He won't, I promise. Can we just drop it now?"

"Yes, I'll drop it for now, but God only knows what can happen when you're in an abusive relationship. It's up to you to decide when to save yourself, and if you don't do something about it, I'll have to intervene."

"Okay, I swear it won't happen again. I think I need to go see if a decision has been made about Mom, okay?"

Giving a sharp nod of firm authority, Toni let Audra walk out the door. Lingering behind to get control of her emotions, Toni had her back to the bed and didn't see the troubled expression crossing Jodee's face as the words of their conversation seeped into her anguished dreams.

After a few moments of calming herself down, Toni decided to leave the room so Jodee could sleep when she heard a sudden intake of breath. Turning, she saw Jodee's glazed eyes trying desperately to stay open and her hand lift in silent beckoning.

Walking back to the bed she took Jodee's uplifted hand. In a voice stronger than she looked, Jodee said, "It's my fault, you know. It's all mine."

"What is, honey?"

"Everything," came the determined whisper. "Dougie J's death, Lexie, Audra, everything. Even Dayla hating me."

Toni squeezed Jodee's hand with both of hers. "That's not true. Lexie and Audra are fine. Don't worry about them. Dayla doesn't hate you. And no one is to blame for Dougie J. Why would you think that?"

A slice of silence fell inside the room. Toni could tell that fatigue was fighting for power over Jodee's will to speak. Just as Toni thought Jodee had fallen back asleep, she said, "I know…it's my fault…Doug said so. I should have… I should have watched him closer… Doug blames me." Another bit of silence followed as she seemed to be gathering her thoughts. "You know, they always said I wasn't strong enough to raise a son. I guess they were right."

Toni's back stiffened from disbelief. "It wasn't your fault, Jodee. Do you hear me? It was an accident. Doug said what he said out of grief, nothing more."

In a semi-state of sleep and guilt, Jodee murmured, "No, it's my fault. Doug always said I was a pathetic mother. But, God, why did it have to be Dougie J? My baby…" she whimpered as tears rolled down her cheek.

Toni watched as Jodee's eyes closed again, her heart breaking for her friend. She stood over Jodee hoping the sleeping pill had finally taken full effect, but after only a small spell of silence, Jodee once again broke through the strength of the drug with eyes staring dreamily into a world only she could see. "Can you find Tinker Bell for me? Tink will know what to do."

Tamping down the worried panic building inside her chest,

342

Toni simply answered, "Tinker Bell? Uh, sure, honey, sure. I'll find her for you."

"Can I ask you something, Toni?"

"Of course, you can ask me anything."

"I heard what you said to Audra. Will you please help her? Save her from Travis. Save her from herself." The words were barely audible, but they took Toni aback.

Trying to keep her emotions hidden, she replied to Jodee's request, "I'll keep an eye on her but it's you she needs. You're the only one I think who can get through to her. Jodee, you just get better and you save her, okay?"

Jodee had once again found the strength to look up and directly into Toni's eyes and said, "I don't think I can, I'm not physically strong enough. Like you said, only God knows." Her eyes fluttered closed once again.

Toni stayed bent over her, staring at her face, distraught by what she'd seen in Jodee's eyes before she fell asleep – pain, extreme pain and hopelessness. Suddenly, in the silence of the room while she watched Jodee sleep, the answer she'd been looking for popped into her head like a bullet to her temple.

The word had Toni tripping over her thoughts; 'that's it! Oh, my God, all these years of living next door and I never knew. Jodee was never physically abused. Jodee has been emotionally abused, and probably verbally.' She could see it all so clearly: the subtle put downs and insults, the negative labels, the undermining of her confidence as a wife and mother – it was all there. First by her father, then by Doug, both demanding obedience. A mother who looked the other way and two sisters with their own issues. One with the obsessive need to be the center of attention and the other with her passive-aggressive personality.

Mentally beating herself up, Toni sat down on the edge of the bed and berated herself for her own stupidity. 'How could I have missed it? All the years of knowing Jodee and Doug and I never recognized it. I've been trained to recognize the signs and I didn't see it.'

Toni mused over the past years as she hung her head thinking as memories flashed by like an old movie projector on high speed. 'All these years of thinking the joking at Jodee's expense was just that – jokes. But to Jodee they weren't jokes. She had taken them seriously and hid the hurt behind gentle smiles and little chuckles to protect the illusion of a perfect life.'

Toni's thoughts mingled together in a chaotic mess as her relationship with the Warrens tangled with her advocate training:

- Distance yourself so you don't become personally involved. How do you distance yourself when the victim is so close?
- Watch for domestic violence, there will be physical signs. How can there be physical signs when the abuse is emotional?
- Victims will wear long sleeves and dark glasses to cover bruises. There were never any purple marks marring Jodee's arms and legs, there was no need to wear sunglasses to hide black eyes.

Toni sat and felt ashamed feeling she had failed Jodee and her work. Like a record stuck on a scratch, the question went around and around in her head; 'How do you recognize emotional abuse when there are no physical signs of it? How did I miss it? What did I miss?'

Turning her head, she looked down at her friend when she felt the shadow of Jodee once again staring at her. A glazed look of eerie non-recognition in her eyes. She turned over leisurely and finally fell into a deep sleep.

Unexpectedly, like the needle on that flawed record jumped over the groove, all of Toni's questions were answered with that one brief glance in Jodee's haunted expression – it's in her eyes!

There, behind Jodee's eyes, was the emotional trauma of hurtful words, belittlement, insults, and non-support. In one quick moment she had revealed the abuse she'd been living with her entire life hidden behind a façade of normalcy. Deep in the silent well of Jodee's eyes was the truth that Toni had failed to see. Jodee's life of criticism and put-downs had branded her with a permanent mark of worthlessness.

Toni then realized that there were physical signs after all. It was the bruises behind her eyes – these were Jodee's scars.

With renewed determination Toni stood up and said aloud to herself, "I have to help her, and I know just who to call."

CHAPTER TWENTY-SEVEN

BEYOND A PURPLE SKY

The decision had been made against some of the family's better judgment; the girls would visit friends and relatives over the summer and Jodee would stay home, supposedly to recover, but Jodee knew it was to avoid any embarrassment to Doug. Doug had spoken and his word was final. Jodee didn't mind staying home anyway. It was the one place she felt close to Dougie J.

The day the girls' all left for their summer plans, Jodee had had no say as she watched them leave. Deep in her heart, where instincts played catch with reason, she knew it wasn't permanent, but it made her feel empty, nonetheless.

To add to the emptiness, Doug found reasons to stay away from home longer and longer. Secretly, Jodee was glad when Doug didn't come home right after work, but she knew it was wrong to feel that way, so she fought daily to push the guilt down and hide her inner betrayal.

With no one home to hear him and act as a buffer, Doug's insults had grown more blatant and loudly vocal: 'You look like hell. Why don't you take some pride in yourself and clean yourself up?' or, 'This house is a mess, you can't even do that right any more… You're the reason we don't have any friends. No one wants to be around you… Your stupidity amazes me. No wonder the girls left. I don't want you calling them, either. Just leave them alone and let them have some fun being away from you... I expect to have sex on schedule. Don't think this act of yours is fooling me for a minute. And I don't want you to just lay there like a dead fish any more, either. I'm a man and I have needs.' Then, the final blow, 'I'm sick to death of you moping around. If you want to walk around half-dead then go ahead, but don't expect me to be here to pick up the pieces.'

On days when Doug left early with the threat of staying late at work, she would stay in bed for hours lying still and calm, letting the mattress consume her as the cotton batting engulfed her in a shroud. Surrounded by synthetic feathers she would allow herself to sink ever deeper into the confining fabric of the sheets, unnerved by the thought of disappearing into its folds.

For days at a time nothing would change as sleep eluded her and the routine of the minutes turned into the drone of the hours, which turned into the monotony of the days. As the days melted one into the other, her mind would glide effortlessly into the sweet peace of imaginary worlds. The only thought that kept her from being sucked under was getting her daughters back. She would remind herself that she had to stay in the here and now as her inner self fought with her exterior existence. Until the day Doug told her the truth of the girls' leaving.

"The girls aren't coming back, you know." The statement was said in such a matter-of-fact way it took Jodee a while to comprehend what he said.

"What?" she asked.

"That's right. Audra is going straight to college as soon as summer is over. Lexie is thinking of staying with Mom and Dad next year so she can continue her treatment."

"But... What? No. No one told me. What about Dayla, she's supposed to be home next week?"

"Don't be stupid. I'm telling you now, aren't I? And Dayla, well, of course she'll be here for school, but I decided to let her continue to stay with the Fergusons for the rest of the summer. Your parents think it would be a good break for you and I agree. You need to stay home and pull yourself together."

"But, Doug…"

"Jodee, stop right there, the decisions have been made. By the way, I let Toni talk me into taking everyone on a vacation before school starts. That should be enough."

Her children's absence caused an edginess in Jodee that she filled with obsessive cleaning. She'd prove her worth to Doug, she vowed.

While sleep eluded her, she scrubbed the grout in the kitchen tile on her hands and knees until her knees were bruised. The spots in the living room carpet by the front door grew into imaginary dark smudges that wouldn't come out no matter how hard she washed them. She thought the walls were dusty so she used a step ladder to dust them from top to bottom, at one point scraping the paint off because it would not come clean. There was no end to the emptiness and no end to the dirt she constantly saw about her.

Fatigue finally made Jodee give in to the filth. Besides, she reasoned, no one was around to care anyway. To fill her days, she began to count the hours until the beginning of the school year and the vacation Doug had promised that would bring her girls back – one-thirty in the afternoon, only ten and a half hours left in the day to go, only twenty-seven days needed to pass, and on and on she went until the fidgeting made her lose count.

Three weeks into her isolation, Jodee stood and stared out the kitchen window into the bluish haze of a July fog while condensation rolled down the panes like tears. The house was warm but she was cold down to her core, the loneliness seeping through her pores had her hugging herself against the ache. She felt chained, a prisoner shackled to bolts in a wall unable to move very far yet still seeing life go by and not being able to be a part of it.

Unmoving, she stared out into the yard until the sun evaporated the sweat from the window and replaced it with raindrops as a summer storm galloped its way across the sky. Stepping to the back door, she opened it and let the rain pelt her face through the open mesh of the screen door. She could see the flowers in the yard bow their heads from the heavy drops as if seeking an audience with a queen, and the leaves on the trees fluttering as though they were applauding her appearance.

Quietly, from far away, she could hear the wind calling her name – a low, soft whisper of moaning – long and hypnotizing. Remembering she had once again forgotten her pills, she convinced herself she'd take them later and ignored the nagging pressure to obey the doctor's orders. She just wanted to follow the sound of her name.

She stepped out the door and into the rain letting it anoint her head and baptize away the sins of her existence. She stood quietly until the rain finally abated and the wind no longer had to fight for superiority – drenched but clean.

She stood in the middle of the yard feeling the colors of the garden tingle across her skin. It stimulated her senses and made her want to drape herself in its essence: the purple of the hydrangeas brought a vanity to her head, the velvet red of the roses made her chest swell, the blues of the pansies calmed her, the yellow of the lilies tickled her, and the Gerber daisies – her favorite – made her want to fly.

She wanted to lie down amongst the colors and find silence from the voices punishing her skull while the shadows of the trees wrapped around her like a security blanket swaddling a baby. Reality was once again sliding smoothly from her grasp and she relished the feeling.

As the crisp warm wind blew into her domain, dainty dandelion seeds floated across the grass and into the air and she marveled at the effortless way they took flight. It dawned on her then that it wasn't the wind calling her name but the fairies whose purpose in life was to protect her. It wasn't seeds crossing her view but the glimmering of wings flying toward heaven. They were back!

She watched in fascination as the seed-like fairies drifted by her, their fuzzy wings catching the light. There was an urge she couldn't explain, she knew she had to protect the fragile little fairies from the thorns of the bushes, believing they were too light to fight where the wind took them. She could see them flapping against a blade of grass or leaf trying to free themselves. Without realizing it, she walked faster and faster trying to catch them as they played hide-and-seek with the shadows. When they fell to the ground she crawled after them and gently cradled them in the palm of her hand. Picking them up she would lift her open hands to the sky and wait for the wind to once again lift them to flight.

Looking up, she saw the sky darkening into shades of purple and gray – the rain wasn't over. Her mood changed swiftly as she watched the white clouds struggle to stay pure. There were too many contradictions capturing her attention and it began to give her a headache: the swift flight of the fairies moving faster and faster away from her, knowing the rain would drown them when it came; the urgency to follow them contradicting the need to stay within the confines of peace among the flowers, the heaviness of the shadows breaking up the fragility of the light… It all started disturbing her composure. She had to get away. She had to let the fairies lead her beyond that darkening purple sky.

Jodee watched the seeds float over the fence of her back yard toward the front, and she followed them, picking an orange daisy as she went. Turning the corner of her house, a flash of light blinded her eyes making her squint. The cross on top of the church steeple a half mile away caught a spark from the sun making it gleam like a beacon, capturing her attention. Stopping in her pursuit, she stood fascinated by the gleaming symbol. The steeple, she hadn't noticed it in months. She knew immediately it was where the fairies were going – to the church, where Dougie J was. She blessed them silently under her breath and started walking.

Two blocks from her house she stopped and glanced back, unsure if leaving was right. But as the sun filtered through the lingering fog it bounced off the white aluminum siding of the house and darkened the windows, reminding her of black eyes staring from a too white face. The skylight above the door gave the face a broad nose and the door itself was a wide mouth leading to the throat of a beast that devoured souls. She turned and kept walking and never looked back, certain what she was doing was right.

Keeping the cross in sight, Jodee walked around houses, avoiding cars, crossing streets. The whiteness of the sky melded the steeple into a two-dimensional impression of reality, she would stop and contemplate it, confused, and with her head tilted like a child trying to understand adult terminology, she panicked and started walking faster until it made sense again.

Toni looked down at a sleeping Jodee lying on top of the soft mound of dirt of Dougie J's grave. Her face was covered with a large daisy. She had followed Jodee to the cemetery.

Luckily, Toni had decided to work from home that day and had been at her kitchen window drinking coffee and watching the rain fall when she saw Jodee step outside into her own backyard. She'd been watching Jodee for three weeks, ever since her girls had left. Every chance she got, she would look out her window into the Warren's backyard hoping she wouldn't see Jodee lying in the dirt again talking to invisible woodland creatures.

Doug had told Toni in no uncertain terms that he didn't appreciate her interference, so she had watched over Jodee in secret.

Toni had stood and watched Jodee stand in the rain and chase something around her yard. She wanted so badly to rush over and pull her back into the house and out of the rain but Toni had been careful over the last few weeks not to do anything that might appear as if she were disobeying Doug's orders. She knew that Jodee's fear of any kind of disobedience from anyone would be perceived as disloyalty and would scare Jodee back into her isolated hell.

After the incident in the river, Doug had taken a board and nailed it across the back gate so Jodee couldn't get out of the backyard. Toni was grateful he at least had done that.

When Toni saw Jodee start down the street, she slipped out of her house and followed safely behind her, worried about her friend's safety. It was several blocks before it dawned on her where Jodee was headed. Toni watched her enter the cemetery gates and head directly to the row where she knew Dougie J lay.

Standing outside the fence, Toni watched Jodee stare down at the little grave for half an hour. After a while, Jodee had laid down on top of the tiny mound and fell asleep.

The tears in Toni's eyes blurred her vision and she waited until she was calm enough to go to her friend and give her the aid she needed.

Toni bent down and touched Jodee's shoulder. "Jodee, honey, you need to wake up now."

Jodee opened her eyes and let herself be rolled over. "Oh, hi," was all she said.

"Hi."

Jodee sat up and took in her surroundings. "Gosh, however did you find me?" She picked the flower off her chest where it had fallen. "I was hiding behind this daisy. You're very good at finding fairies."

Toni kept her expression neutral, getting used to Jodee's meandering mind. "I saw the flower moving and knew it had to be you."

"Oh, well I'd better be more careful, huh? You can never tell when there are dangers about. I could've been eaten by a bird or something."

"Yeah, you're going to have to be more careful. You know, being this far from home you could have gotten lost."

"No worries about that. I could have just flown back with my friends."

"But what about the wind or rain, what if they'd been too strong for you to fly?" Worry was beginning to cause Toni's chest to tighten, Jodee's separation from reality usually didn't last this long.

"Oh, well then I'd just go underground and follow the elves." The mention of elves was new. Toni turned her eyes away so Jodee couldn't see the fear in them.

"Well, let me help you this one time, okay?"

"Okay, I guess that'll be all right. You know, elves live in tunnels. They're tiny so they fit. It's how they get around."

"No, I didn't know that."

"Sometimes I wish I was an elf because when the flowers all die there is no better place to be than underground."

With her arm around Jodee's shoulder, Toni halted in her steps at the statement. After a few moments of musing she said, "You know, I think you're right. There is no better place than underground."

CHAPTER TWENTY-EIGHT

THE CHOICE OF FREEDOM

Toni cornered Doug as he stepped from the car. She walked up to him without the pretense of polite salutation. "Doug, I hear you decided to take the family on a vacation before school starts, after all."

Trying unsuccessfully to hide his irritation, he stood for a moment with his back against the open car door facing away from Toni. Straightening his shoulders slowly, he turned around to face her as she approached. He had pasted on a fake smile that didn't fool Toni for a second. With a smile that didn't go any further than his mouth it reminded her of the Joker from a *Batman* movie.

A little too jauntily he said, "Well, hello Toni. How are you tonight?"

Ignoring his pseudo .friendliness, she said, "Fine, thanks. Anyway, I heard from Audra that you plan on taking the family on a vacation."

"Yes, that's right. I gave your suggestion some thought and figured it was a good idea. Why?"

"Well, if you don't know where you're going yet, I thought I could help you out. I have some friends in Washington State that own a B and B. I was talking to them last night and they were telling me that they're always a little desperate for customers by the end of the summer because the tourists start leaving to get their kids ready for school. You'd be going at just the right time. I think I could get you a couple of rooms super cheap, you being friends of mine and all, probably more than half off. And where they live is absolutely beautiful, green trees, hiking, boat rides, right on the coast… Something I think Jodee and the kids would love."

"I haven't made any plans yet, no. Where in Washington State is it?"

"It's a place called Kokanee Bay, right next to Canada. I've been there and it's gorgeous. And at the end of summer you might even see whales migrating. There are islands all around that you can tour, a cute little tourist town for shopping, and some great restaurants."

"That does sound nice, but I don't know. Listen, I think the girls would rather go to Disneyland or something."

"Oh, I know, I know, but Audra and Lexie are a little too old for Disneyland, don't you think? Besides, you know how Jodee loves nature. It would also give the girls a chance to see the most northwest tip of the country, maybe even go into Canada. And I know they'd love to see whales."

"That's true. You say I can get your friend's place half off?"

"Maybe even more than half off if I vouch for you and they know for sure you're coming."

"It does sound nice."

"Just wanting to help," Toni said.

"Okay, I'll take it. Listen, tell them we'll be there the middle of August, around the fifteenth."

"Great, I will. You're going to love it."

Dayla had been the first to come home, but after a summer of traveling and being indulged she had developed an attitude of worldly superiority that only a fourteen-year-old can master.

"Gaw, Mom," she said on the second day home. "You need to stop bugging me. I have friends to call before we leave on this stupid vacation, so I need some privacy."

Lexie came home next. She walked around the house trying to avoid everyone and looked at her parents in a manner of non-recognition. At dinner time, she asked for a piece of toast. When Doug ordered her to eat more, she responded with, "Mom isn't eating. If she doesn't eat why should I have to?"

She then stomped away from the table, went into her bedroom closing the door with a definite bang, and stayed there. During the day she would come out of her room long enough to shower, drink juice and water, and then retire back inside her room. Jodee's attempt to connect with her was met with the statement, 'nothing's changed.' Sometimes she mixed it up with 'Nothing's changed with me or with anything else,' but her answer always started with the empty word 'nothing.' On her third day she snapped at her mother to stop asking, "Nothing ever changes around here. I just want to get this trip over so I can return to Grandma and Grandpa's."

Audra was delivered home at the end of the week by Travis. Jodee had watched her emerge from his car with a sunken heart. Not wanting to cause an unhappy homecoming, she simply hugged her daughter and watched as Travis helped himself to a soda from the fridge as if he was a member of the family.

Once back in his car he gunned the engine until Audra stepped outside onto the pouch. Leaning over the seat, he yelled out the passenger side window that she'd better remember to call him. Audra nodded and waited for him to speed off down the street. Seeing her mother behind her, Audra simply walked past her into the house and held up her palm at face level in a way that said, 'Don't bother me, I don't want to talk about it.'

In the privacy of their bedroom, Doug reprimanded Jodee that it was her fault Lexie still wasn't eating, that Audra wouldn't confide in her, and said Dayla wasn't excited about their vacation because of her. "All your moping and crazy behavior has everyone on edge. I'm not even sure if anyone wants to go on vacation with you," he berated.

Jodee had been excited to have her daughters' home, but secretly she didn't want the vacation to Washington State anyway. It was just too far away from Dougie J. Who would watch him? So after Doug made it clear no one wanted to be around her, she left the girls alone and spent the days in their backyard among the flowers and ferns, digging, replanting – hiding.

The owners of Hearth and Home Bed and Breakfast were Bill and Vera Miller. They welcomed the Warren family on their arrival like old friends at a reunion. The couple looked more like brother and sister than husband and wife; both were smaller than average, Bill not standing more than five foot four and Vera a good four inches shorter with the same color of dark green eyes. The one prominent difference was Bill had short curly gray hair and a round boyish face, whereby Vera's hair was black as tar, cut straight across at the shoulders, with a face so heart shaped her chin was almost comically pointed. Their small statures gave people the misconception they were meek, but once meeting them, the fact was learned quickly that they were both bold and straight forward – they had no nonsense types of personalities.

The Miller's B and B sat on the south end of Kokanee Bay overlooking a small inlet that was fed by the southern waters of the Strait of Georgia flowing from Canada. It was built in the Victorian style with a porch that wrapped around three sides of the house, a turret with a white shingled peak, and an upper deck on the third floor with an iron railing that resembled a crow's nest on a ship. The lawn was wide and green sloping down to a small rocky beach that cradled a white gazebo and a worn wooden dock that reached out to sea like a beckoning arm.

Doug had opened introductions to the Millers with a statement that booked no argument. "We're here on vacation but mainly for my wife to get some rest. I hope you understand if she appears unsociable, but I think it's best if she spends some time alone to recuperate."

The Millers acquiesced to his request with a silent stare of ambivalence.

So, while Doug golfed and the girls roamed the town and beaches, Jodee wandered the grounds of the B and B always feeling the eyes of the Millers on her. She didn't know if Doug had told them to watch her, but to hide from their prying eyes she began exploring deeper and deeper into the woods surrounding their house. Almost daily she ventured farther and farther with each walk she took.

On the fourth day of the vacation, Doug cornered Jodee inside their room before going down to breakfast. "Jodee, I know you had plans to go with the girls today to some Farmer's Market, but I want you to stay here. I want you to be rested for this afternoon because we're taking a boat tour to an outlying island to some kind of heritage center and dinner. The local Nooksack Tribe is putting on a show or something. Listen, I want you to be at least somewhat coherent enough to enjoy it. I'm spending too much on this vacation for you to go nuts on me again and do something foolish that will embarrass me." Looking in the mirror, he adjusted his collar as he continued roughly. "And make sure you take your medication. You've started that ridiculous blinking again and it needs to stop. I thought you'd quit doing that."

He walked out of the room with authority – confident she would obey.

Jodee watched as her family got in the rental car and headed toward town right after breakfast that morning, to shop or visit a museum, she didn't know what. She didn't feel abandoned, she didn't feel sad, she didn't feel anything. She thought that the blinking Doug had scolded her for had given her a headache, but as she watched the car head down the hill and turn the corner the pain vanished along with the red glare of the brake lights.

She waited until the car was completely out of sight, turned toward the side of the house that was protected by the woods and disappeared along a narrow dirt trail.

Retreating into the solitude of the thick forests, she savored its calmness. A quiet thin aura of mist surrounded the pine trees like moist smoke. She crouched every so often at the trunk of a tree and let the wisp of coolness drift around her. She let her thoughts go dormant and allowed whatever feelings that floated to the surface to overtake her.

Sitting against a large trunk, she thought she heard footsteps behind her. She turned and peered through the dense forest. Seeing no one she dismissed it – it was the forest watching over her she reasoned. The noise and eyes she convinced were always around her and were nothing more than the elves who lived in this part of the country spying on her.

She got up and walked farther into the shelter of the woods. She knew the fairies had not abandoned her as she went deeper and deeper into unknown territory, unafraid. Tinker Bell may have never been found back home, but she knew the little fairy was still protecting her somehow – they had a network... A fairy network. She chuckled to herself at the joke.

Jodee hiked along the grass-strewn trail until pine needles and new growth camouflaged its contour. She could feel the air around her – wet and cool from the dew on the plants. The day was crisp and sweet like peppermint on the tongue. The sporadic light coming through sparse openings in the forest ceiling mesmerized her. The olive, chartreuse and bold green of the leaves flirted with the blue of the sky.

Half a mile from the B and B, she came to a circle in the forest, a tiny mountain meadow that looked like it had been cleared for a winsome cottage. The grass was short, mid-calf height, with tall clumps of clasping pink monkey flowers molded together with yellow fiddlenecks and the remaining remnants of nodding onions. The grove of trees surrounding the mini meadow stood like tall wooden soldiers ready to protect the area from harm. She circled the plot slowly, not wanting to tarnish the freshness of the grass or trample the sweetness of the flowers. At the western edge, she heard the ocean as rebellious waves smelling of fish and salt slammed against the shore. She looked up through the interstice of trees to see its endless wonder not more than forty yards away. Turning toward the water, she made her way carefully over fallen branches and around the sticky hairs of turbulent grass until she stood on the closest spot of open beach.

Letting the scene before her unfold as if she were watching a drama on a stage – the waves crashing like cymbals, sun beaming off the water in floodlight fashion, sea birds singing in a choir – she stood transfixed waiting for the climax. Then, when she thought the story was at its apex, she saw the clouds part and a ray of sun, brighter than any light she had ever seen, burst through onto the scene below. Bright red, yellow, orange beams flowed down from a large white cloud split perfectly down the middle as she waited, knowing the lead actor, God, would descend.

Becoming impatient for Him to make his entrance, a feeling of quiet unrest started to consume her. Entranced, she walked toward the light, eager to feel God's presence the moment His feet touched the ground. She headed to the ray. Keeping her eyes on its brightness for fear it would disappear if she looked away, she walked until the cold of the ocean nibbled at her ankles and made her look down, breaking the spell. When she looked up again, the cloud had closed in upon itself and the light was fading into muted colors of prosaic wash. It made her want to cry – she had missed her chance.

As if on cue, a lone pelican screamed above her and flew out to sea, startling her at the sound. She looked up and watched it fly toward the horizon – a horizon that seemed so near she could almost touch it. She knew then it wasn't God's intention to ignore her, instead He was showing her the freedom that beckoned just on the edge of the world – a world maybe not even a mile away. A mile she knew she could easily swim.

She could feel the freedom pulling at her as if a rope were tied to her breast and was slowly, firmly tugging her forward. Her chest and arms ached from the pull. Her mind wandered beyond the spray of ocean. All she had to do was walk out into its depths, a slow walk in a straight line to freedom – freedom from the pain, the loneliness, the burden of obedience. She took a step forward, then another, following the beauty into a crystal world of fairies and peace calling her.

"Mrs. Warren?" Bill Miller walked up to the edge of the

water, fishing pole in hand. She was thigh high into the surf. "Mrs. Warren," he said behind her, catching her attention. "You gotta be careful this time of year. The water can be strong with undercurrents."

From a distance, eons away, she could hear his voice behind her. Looking down slowly, reality came back with a harsh slap. The weight of the water tugging on her pants and the goose bumps freckling her flesh surprised her. She looked back at Mr. Miller, an apparition born from the sand. Blinking in confused awareness of her surroundings, several seconds passed as she mentally shook her head clear. Giving a shy little chuckle she said, "Oh, silly me, I, uh…was just so caught up in the beauty of the water I guess I wasn't thinking."

"Yeah, that can happen," he said matter-of-factly. "You better come on outta there though before you lose your footing and get completely drenched."

"Yes, of course." She treaded carefully out of the water letting her thoughts thaw in unison with her skin.

"Would you like me to walk you back to the house? I'm done fishing for the day." Bill Miller had walked into the water and took her hand, helping her the last five feet out of the ocean.

"That would be nice. I guess I lost track of time. What time is it anyway, do you know?"

"It's almost two," he said without looking at his watch.

"Oh, my. My family will be back soon. I'd better go and get ready. We're going on a boat tour."

"That's what I hear."

They walked in silence a few moments until the awkwardness of his closeness made her uncomfortable. Looking sideways at him, she asked casually, "Do you fish around here often?"

"Whenever I get the chance." He was a man of few words.

"Oh, well, my husband likes to fish. Maybe I'll tell him about this spot."

"Best fishing is out at sea. Fact is, I'm going fishing out there later this afternoon. I've got a buddy with a boat. Wouldn't be surprised if I saw you out there."

"Oh, maybe I'll look for you."

"Yes, you do that. I'll be keeping an eye out for you, too." There was an underlying tone in his voice she didn't understand.

They continued their walk in silence. Jodee watched him from the corner of her eye, his right hand holding his pole that was slung over his right shoulder. Occasionally, he took her elbow with his free hand to help her over beach debris.

Bill Miller reached into his shirt pocket and pulled out a granola bar. "Would you like this?" he asked. "I noticed you missed lunch."

Looking at the bar, she refused it with a little revolted shudder, "No, thank you. I'm not really hungry. I think I should save my appetite for dinner tonight."

Putting the bar back into his pocket, he walked beside her, slowing his steps until he was a foot or two behind her, relegating himself to her bodyguard who was forbidden from getting too close.

Jodee walked ahead of him. Every so often, she'd risked a glimpse of him from the corner of her eye as she pretended to look out at sea. For being on the small size, he was an imposing man, yet somehow he was beginning to make her feel safe.

Becoming uneasy with their positioning, she stopped and turned to wait for him to catch up to her. "I hope I didn't disturb your fishing."

"Naw, I wasn't having much luck anyway."

Turning as he caught up to her, they continued walking side by side. His presence enveloped her in a warm breeze of security chasing away the chill. She found their silence comforting, not unlike an old friend who knew her secrets, making conversation unnecessary. Trust in him came easily so that when he stopped to tie his shoe, she stopped with him. He lay his pole on the ground and as she stood patiently waiting for him to finish, she stared at the top of his head, his bent shoulders, the pole on the ground. Liking the colors of red and yellow stripes that circled the brown rod, she followed the shiny string creeping itself up along its sleek body as it wrapped around itself ending at the hook snagged firmly in the end ring. Never once did it occur to her the fact that the pole lay alone on the sand – there was no tackle box, no net, no fishing gear of any kind.

CHAPTER TWENTY-NINE

A SLOW DESCENT INTO SANITY

Having cleaned up from her walk in the woods, Jodee sat next to Vera Miller in one of the many rocking chairs that had been strategically placed around the porch to provide privacy. Waiting for her family to return, the women made small talk like two old friends. Their conversation had no real direction, yet within the hour they'd spoken, Jodee got the feeling Vera Miller had delved into her life without ever having asked a direct question. It didn't feel intrusive but comforting. She felt the woman had a true interest in her.

Hearing the car approach, Jodee stood up and went to the rail of the porch. As the car came to a stop, she watched her girls exit the car in a flurry of noise and excitement. Forcing a smile across her lips, she addressed each one as they approached, "Hi, Dayla, did you have fun?"

"Yeah."

"What did you do?"

"Stuff."

"Like what?"

"Just stuff."

"Okay. Can I have a hug then?"

"Not now, Mom. Daddy bought me a new dress for tonight. I want to put it on." She ran past her mother and let the screen door slam behind her, her footsteps echoing through the house as she ran up the stairs to their rented room.

Jodee flinched as the door slammed. To hide her embarrassment as Vera Miller watched, she tried to defend her daughter. "I guess she's excited about her new dress. Teenagers, right?"

Turning quickly away as Lexie came up the stairs toward her, Jodee said cheerfully, "Hi, honey, did you have a good day?"

"I suppose."

"What did you do?"

"Went to some museum and walked around town."

"Did you go anywhere special for lunch?"

Slowing her pace up the porch steps Lexie answered the question snappishly, "No, Mom, I didn't have anything special for lunch. Did you?" With a direct look into her mother's eyes, as if challenging her to a duel, she brushed rudely past her and followed her sister into the B and B.

Jodee dropped her head, sucking in a painful gasp of air. With her eyes closed she held the air in her lungs until the pain screamed at her to exhale. Hoping Mrs. Miller hadn't heard Lexie's rudeness, Jodee risked a glance up through the bangs that hung in front of her eyes.

Vera Miller sat rocking in her chair looking at Jodee with a stoic expression.

As Jodee dropped her eyes again, Audra ran by her in a rush. Thankful for the interruption, she turned quickly to her oldest daughter who continued down the opposite side of the porch away from where Mrs. Miller sat.

"Audra, where are you going?" Jodee yelled after her.

"I have to call Travis," Audra said. "It's almost four here and I told him I'd call him by two Minnesota time. My phone died and I gotta reach him before he leaves for work."

Audra's unthinking admission had Jodee straightening her back as she watched her daughter head toward a small parlor at the farthest end of the house. "Can you excuse me, Mrs. Miller? I think I'll go see about my daughter."

Vera Miller nodded and switched her attention to Doug who had gotten out of the car and was walking slowly toward the house. Mrs. Miller stood up and walked to the far end of the porch as if the most important thing in her life at the moment was to straighten the cushions in the other rockers and pluck dead flowers from hanging baskets. At the far corner, hidden in the shadow of the eave, she turned to watch him.

Having been preoccupied with folding a local informational brochure, Doug had sat in the car until he had gotten it the way he wanted it. Because of his need for order, his slow departure from the car had him missing the comments of each of his daughters to their mother. Vera Miller watched him stop for a moment and stare in the direction of his wife. Upon seeing Jodee go after Audra, he shook his head in two sharp jerks from side to side and said something inaudible through clinched teeth. He then continued into the house without seeing the proprietress of the B and B as she faded deeper into the shadows.

Jodee stepped into the parlor as Audra dialed the phone. "Audra, can you put the phone down, please? I want to talk to you."

"Not now, I have to get hold of Travis."

"That's what I want to talk to you about."

"Mom, please, this doesn't concern you."

"It very much concerns me. I thought you had broken it off with Travis."

"Please, Mom, not now. He's going to be so mad if he

doesn't get my call."

"Is this really how you want to live, Audra? Being afraid of Travis and every mistake you make?"

"I told you, he's changed. He hasn't touched me since we got back together."

"And you think he never will again? You remember what Toni told you, abusers don't just stop," Jodee said.

"I told you Travis has changed. Besides, what would you know about it? Daddy's never raised a hand to you. In fact, he's never even raised his voice to you."

"I, uh… What?" Audra's comment made Jodee's mind go temporarily blank from buried memories. Dark and forbidden thoughts began to slither to the surface of her mind like a virus.

"I said," Audra reiterated, "you're married to someone who wouldn't hurt a fly. You know nothing about it."

Like a door of brilliant light opening inside her soul, Jodee's life came into sharp focus in the split second it took for Audra's comment to penetrate the substance of her existence. Her entire life had all been boiled down to one fine point – no one knew.

Jodee stood in shocked stillness letting the truth wash over her. 'No one knew.' The words kept repeating themselves in her head. Her daughters didn't know, her sisters didn't know, her parents didn't know – or didn't care if they did. The revelation made it hard for her to breathe.

Staring at her daughter, Jodee watched as Audra's impatience with the phone made her fidget with worry.

She had done this to her, Jodee realized, she had made her daughter a replica of herself. Awareness hit her hard as the virus poisoned her blood with the truth. Trying desperately to draw in air, Jodee let it sink in; that Audra was right in one way, that Doug had never raised his *hands* to her. Instead, he used harsh insults and cruel words said in secret and behind closed doors to hurt her, eventually breaking her down into a weak and submissive puddle, cowering in fear of his disapproval – just like her daughter was doing.

Watching Audra pace with fear of Travis' possible reprimand, Jodee thought with self-hatred how her daughter was wrong about one thing, she did know about abuse.

She had done this to Audra, to all of them, she thought with a shameful heart. She had taught them it was all right to be in a submissive position as long as the person they loved was happy – their needs, their wants, their own happiness didn't matter.

Her head felt like a vice was squeezing her temples as blood seemed to drop from her chest to her feet draining the life from her. This was the legacy she would leave her girls. Stark realization effaced her life and withered basic hope.

Audra's words came at her like a scalpel slicing wider the wounds of her truth, "I'm sorry, Mom, but you really wouldn't understand and I'm not a little girl any more. I think I know what I'm doing."

"Audra," Jodee said, trying desperately to regain her focus, her mind racing faster than her words as she expertly hid her feelings behind the mask of complacency she had been taught to master. "There are other ways you can be hurt other than just physically."

Having turned her back to her mother, Audra continued to ignore what was being said as the phone rang on the other end.

"I don't need you to protect me any more, Mom," Audra said distractedly. "...Come on, come on, come on," she muttered under her breath to the phone urging it to connect.

"Audra, please, listen to me." Maternal instinct had fought through the blackness of her self-awareness and she reached for the button on the phone to end the call.

As quickly as Jodee's maternal determination burned through her self-disgust, Audra quickly snuffed the flame. "Mom, stop," Audra scolded, grabbing her mother's wrist before she could end the connection. "I'm not your little girl any more. In a couple of weeks, I'll be going off to college and I have to learn to do things my way. I'm sorry," she said as the distant ringing of the phone changed to a muffled 'hello.'

"Travis, just a second," Audra interrupted herself, releasing Jodee's wrist and covering the mouthpiece with her right hand. "Mom, I have to take this. Please, just leave me alone. I'm a grown woman now. I don't need you any more."

Turning her back to her mother, Audra answered the call, "Travis. Yeah, I can talk. No, it was just my mother... I know... I'm sorry I'm late but it's only by a few minutes. Please don't be mad..."

Jodee withdrew her hand as the final stab of Audra's words punctured her heart. So, this was it – her daughter had made her choice. 'Because of my weakness,' Jodee said to herself, 'it's too late to save my child.' She let the poison ride up and burst through her skin. 'I did this.' Backing out of the room she stumbled through the door. Her skin tingling, the familiar anxiety started at her feet and grew until the panic settled in her chest. Her breathing became erratic, her skin clammy. She felt herself disappearing... Shrinking... Shrinking down into the splinters at her feet to become one with the burnished wooden floor.

Bent over at the waist, she waited for the earth to swallow her. Taking great gulps of air, somewhere in the faraway distance she could hear Doug yelling impatiently, "Girls, hurry up or we're going to be late for the ferry. Jodee, get Audra off the phone and get in the car."

Jodee stood at the rail of the boardwalk watching tourists pass beneath her on the beach. At her back, the dock bore the pounding feet of vacationers as the sharp screech of hungry gulls sounded overhead while the sun simultaneously heated the top of her head. In front of her, the occasional scrape of moored boats fought the ocean wind knocking them against the dock.

Below her, she watched the waves wash away footprints of the people from the wet impressionable sand as if the owners were nothing but mere apparitions. It amazed her how easily they could be swept away. They strolled by so carefree, unaware their very existence was disappearing behind them. It was surreal as she watched small quiet waves rush back and forth to shore erasing these vulnerable creatures – alive… Dead… Alive… Dead. 'They are so vibrant,' she thought, 'yet their lives can be taken away so effortlessly,' just like her son's. Life was so out of perspective.

A young boy below her caught her attention when he squealed in delight at having found a shell. She watched him pick it up and hold it to his ear as wonder crossed his face. She knew he could hear the hollowness of the wind inside it but like her, it was vacuous, spiraling down into an endless cavern of empty regrets.

"Jodee," Doug snapped, "pay attention. Here's your ticket." He thrust a small rectangular piece of paper into Jodee's limp palm. She looked at him, but recognition was slow in coming, the texture of the paper in her hand unfamiliar and odd.

Ignoring the emptiness behind her eyes he continued, "I'm going to go round up the girls. The ferry leaves in ten minutes. I'm giving you five to be on it. Do you understand?"

As if the whole world obeyed him, the horn of the ferry

reinforced his order blasting loudly with his final word as he turned away.

Following his command like the good wife she'd been molded to be, she mingled with the crowd across the dock and onto the rocking sway of the ferry as Doug disappeared into a nearby store.

Controlled by the masses, she allowed herself to be pushed past the gate onto the deck of the ferry. Obediently following the lead of the other passengers, she absent-mindedly handed her ticket to a deckhand who punched it and handed it back – never looking up at the faces passing by him.

Jodee walked slowly down the length of the ferry, past the large enclosed passenger cabin that held rows of benches and tables, a snack bar and the restrooms, until she reached the bow. Dropping down onto a metal box that read 'Life Jackets' in large red letters, she leaned against the shadowed wall below the window of the bridge. The metal box was cold through her thin slacks. A chill skidded up her spine but went unnoticed as she pulled the hood of her jacket up over her head to block the sun from her eyes.

The boat rocked gently, lulling her into a rare serenity. Leaning her head back against the salt-worn paint of the cabin, she closed her eyes. Minutes later, she heard the soft scraping of the boat as it pulled away from the dock.

People milled around talking loudly against the breeze that blew their words out to sea, taking pictures, and roaming the ferry in a rush of excitement. Jodee sat quietly with a detached air of solitude waiting for her family to cross her path so she could join them in their illusion of a happy vacationing family.

After several moments, like an animal sensing its offspring, she looked up to the upper deck. Seeing Lexie and Dayla leaning over the rail, Jodee saw Lexie point to a spot in the distance and heard her over the din of the crowd. "Look out there, I think I see a whale. Where's Mom? She should see this."

Jodee's heart jumped with a small smidgen of encouragement as she raised her hand to yell up in answer. Before her words could make it past the hopefulness in her throat, Doug gave a quick flick of his hand as if ridding himself of unwanted trash, dismissing Lexie's question and diverted the girls' attention with, "Forget about your mom for now and just enjoy the scenery."

Jodee's hopefulness turned once again into her familiar feeling of worthlessness as she watched her family disappear from the rail above her.

Over the ferry's loudspeaker the captain welcomed his guests aboard the *Blue Mermaid Ferry*. The trip, he explained, was half an hour to the indigenous island of the Lummi Tribe. With a short history lesson of the region, he then gave instructions that the Lummi Heritage Center closed at nine and the last ferry back to the mainland left at nine-fifteen sharp; whoever wasn't on board at that time would have to wait until morning. He finished with a practiced thrill in his voice. "…And keep your eyes peeled, folks. It's migration season for the whales so I wouldn't be surprised if we saw some on this trip. We have calm waters today, so everyone sit back and enjoy the ride."

Ten minutes passed as Jodee waited for her family to find her. Resigning herself to the fact that they weren't looking for her, she gathered her strength to go and find them. Rising, she walked along the waist high bulwark down the starboard side of the ferry, passing people without really seeing them. Her fellow passengers, intent on their own goals, ignored her, making her believe she was invisible.

Reaching the stern of the ferry she stood a moment and stared at the water below her, the airy clouds above her. She became transfixed by the small fishing boats angling for distant islands.

There was one small boat that seemed to be following the *Blue Mermaid* like a duckling after its mother. Becoming slightly sick from watching the bow of the boat jump with each wave, Jodee turned her attention to the water beneath her and its mysterious darkness.

Letting the depth of the ocean overtake her, she stood transfixed. The sun, sinking warmly at her side reflecting rays across the water as droplets sprayed the surface and turned them into liquid glitter.

Letting her mind slip into that world where peace abounded, she once again saw fairies where light should have been. She watched as the sun filtered between the waves lapping against the hull, breaking up the water while the forward motion of the ferry drove the iridescent creatures farther out to sea. Worried she would lose them, panic started rising in her as she followed the thousands of flickering lights with her eyes as they rode the waves and bobbed teasingly, reaching for her.

A strong urge to join them overtook her, making her ache. The need for serenity lured her deeper and deeper into its silent depth; each descending wave ripping reality along its bias with slow, consistent tears.

"Ladies and gentlemen," came the captain's voice again, "we have whales off the port side. We'll be stopping the boat so they can pass. If everyone will look to your left, you'll be able to see them as they breach."

The sudden thrill of excitement coming from the other passengers escaped Jodee as the ferry came to a slow stop. She continued to stare into the water as the boat listed slightly to one side from the frantic movement of people scampering to port like excited mice.

Ignoring the thought of seeing the majestic animals, Jodee stood transfixed, feeling a pull she couldn't explain. It was there, she knew, in the deep darkness below, the tranquility she so desperately needed.

The fairies vibrated on the surface of the water as if telling her it was okay – it was her time. Without taking her eyes from their sparkling presence, she quietly lifted herself up on the rail and swung one leg over the side.

Straddling the six-inch piece of wood, she let the natural sway of the boat rock her like a child's rocking horse. Taking a moment to look up at the horizon one last time, she ignored the little duckling fishing boat quickly coming up behind with its friendly waving passengers, and casually lowered herself over the side.

Being on the starboard side, the ferry rose higher above the water giving her added coverage as her body hung down. Clinging onto the rail with her fingertips, the natural weight of her body stretched down until her feet dangled into the water. Feeling freedom, she calmly let go and slid quietly into the coldness of the ocean without a splash.

The frigid water sucked the breath momentarily from her lungs but bobbing up like a cork she arched onto her back and spread her arms like Christ on the cross. Jesus had sacrificed for her sins, she reasoned, she could do no less for her own children. Giving a slight push on the hull with her feet, she glided gently away from the ferry.

Looking up at the sky, she let the beauty of the shadow-laced clouds lull her into a sleepless calm. Ignoring the icy water soaking through to her skin and dragging heavily at her clothes, she accepted the waves lapping at her face and chest, as a form of baptism that purified her life of self-perceived sins – the sin of letting her son die, her incompetence as a mother, the love she once held in her heart for Archer, her subconscious hatred for her father… Her contempt toward Doug. All these were her truths and her failures – failures she never allowed herself to acknowledge yet now bombarded her with clear precision as each wave swept over her and cleansed her.

The coldness burrowed stingingly into her pores, setting her spirit free while a leisurely acceptance of the truth licked the edges of her tormenting guilt.

A slow rumble sounded under the water echoing against her ears as the ferry restarted its engines and slowly started moving again, its wake pushing her farther and farther away from its safety. With a clarity born of despair, the need to surrender overtook her. Telling herself it would all be over if she just took a long cool drink of water. She marveled at the simplicity of it.

Releasing the breath from her lungs like she was kissing the wind, she let her body relax and sunk slowly under until the water engulfed her. Beneath the surface, she could just make out the blurred images above, the bright blue sky, the sparkles of the sun on the water.

In her mind's eye she could see her family as they sailed away – Doug garnering attention from other passengers, befriending them with his wit and charm yet oblivious to her whereabouts; Dayla craving her father's approval at her own detriment, Lexie slowly letting herself starve in some sort of rebellion that even she didn't understand; Audra on the cusp of womanhood, focused on a young man who was so much like her father it was frightening. For the first time in Jodee's life she could see it all so plainly as the water made everything come into focus clear as glass.

The ocean surrounded her as she continued to sink, her mind racing with past memories and current truths. Her lungs began to scream for air as she let herself settle toward the bottom in a synchronized rhythm of colors that bounced off the surface above. One simple sip was all she needed, but she continued to hold her breath. She finally closed her eyes against the glitter of the fairies swimming on the surface.

She was at death's door. The door was still closed but she was close enough to it to see the blackness of its surface, feel the roughness of its texture. The feeling was like none she'd ever had – smooth ebony with a tangible yearning that made her want to reach out and grab the handle and open the door. As she descended closer and closer to the final turn of the handle, memories played over and over, disjointed in their speed, frigid in her mind.

Above her she heard the high whine of a fishing boat's engine. Opening her eyes, she watched a shadow pass over her, blocking out the filtered sun. In a blink the fairies were gone, only a cold darkness remained – a darkness that suddenly frightened her in its perpetuity.

As she descended deeper into the unforgiving Pacific, her thoughts continued to clear. It was all making so much sense, the water was washing away the pain of her insanity so she could finally breathe over the intensity of it. But breathing was something she couldn't do as she sank deeper and deeper with greater and greater speed.

All at once, the reason for her being came into focus – her daughters, life… Living. Clarity struck her thoughts as fast as lightning bolt. 'What am I doing?' she thought with long forgotten lucidity. 'How can I leave my girls to the likes of men like Doug and my father?'

As reasoning filtered into her nightmare, she realized she wanted to live. Startled, she drew her knees toward her until she was upright underneath the water. She started clawing for the surface. Panic blurred her reasoning, the art of swimming escaping her. Flailing, her clothes tangled around her pulled her down faster, the ocean refusing to give up its bounty.

'NO!' Her mind screamed. 'I can't let this happen. Not now. I have to live. I have to survive.' She tried climbing the watery walls with frightened enlightenment, frustrated as it glided through her desperate fingers like silk on silk.

She clawed and kicked, trying to reach the surface. She was so deep... Her clothes so heavy... Her lungs so exhausted. Her mind silently screamed for help as her lungs burned for air.

With one final desperate push, she stretched her arm up and kicked viciously. There, above her – life. She could feel it. As her fingertips pushed past the cover of her approaching grave into the open air, her starving lungs prematurely anticipated the taste of oxygen and gulped greedily. In shock, water began pouring down her throat, freezing her lungs.

Her body reversed its position and started sinking again.

Hopelessness swarmed her as water filled her body. With an acceptance learned from a life of strict obedience, she relinquished to the inevitable. With one arm still raised above her in a natural pose of helplessness – she sank.

With despair smothering her lungs, she watched through half-dead eyes a hand reach below the surface grappling for her own outstretched offering. Convinced it was the hand of God, she relaxed into languid repose, giving in to salvation.

The icy ocean settled inside her body like a rock as it slowly drowned her sluggish mind. Death watched her eyes flutter as it pulled simultaneously at her feet. Above her, God's mighty hand played tug-o-war with her arm. She could feel their strength in equal measure and relinquished her fate to them.

Letting her eyes close, along with her starving lungs, a strange warmth overtook the cold inside her as she relished sleep.

Before death could claim her entirely, the last of her mind was semi aware of God giving her arm one last hard pull.

No, not God, but someone. Someone was pulling hard on her arm. But the suction from her body's weight and the heaviness of the ocean above her was only serving to force the water deeper into her throat.

As life raced through her mind and pulled her into darkness, a wisp of a final thought escaped her mind as she was jerked into unconsciousness – 'so this is sanity.'

EPILOGUE

Saving Jodee wasn't just out of compassion, it was out of fairness. After everything that had been taken away from her, someone had to give her something back.

It took a long time for her to open up about her life with Doug and to accept that her father's cruelty wasn't her fault. But even with all the verbal and emotional abuses these two men doled out to her over the years, it was Audra telling her she was no longer needed that finally broke her.

After Bill Miller pulled her from the ocean that day, he and Vera hid her from the authorities by moving her to friends who specialized in special cases of abuse. Then they nursed her through the breakdown that had been lurking under the surface for months.

Toni watched over the Warren girls from a distance, as a promise she'd made to herself. After Travis had put Audra in the hospital again, Toni was finally able to convince her to file charges. Doug could no longer ignore anything was happening by blaming Jodee for over-reacting. He had to face it head on. He was by her side when she went to court against Travis. That was one thing in his favor.

Lexie's anorexia got worse until she ended up in the hospital under supervision and counseling. It is not anything that has ever really gone away for her, and she battles it daily, punishing the personal demon that took away her mom.

Dayla had to grow up fast when Doug no longer took the

time to coddle her against the self-perceived unfairness of her mother. Like it had been a perverse game to thwart his wife, he grew weary of Dayla's whining when Jodee was not there to play.

Dayla had to give up too. It took a long time, but she eventually grieved for her mother, tip-toed around her father, and matured.

Archer. Well, Archer just stopped hanging out with Doug at all. Doug had prodded him several times saying he needed a friend, but Archer slowly slid away. He was seen occasionally giving interviews after a hockey game, but there was something missing, a kind of deadness behind his eyes.

As for Doug, Jodee's disappearance garnered him pity and the attention he always craved. He dated often, and a lot, but he came to realize that it was Jodee who had kept him grounded – at least, that's what he told anyone who would listen. In reality he realized something he would never admit; with Jodee gone there was no one to blame for his failures, no one to control, no challenges, and a life without challenges turned into an empty life.

And Jodee, for months her sanity floated in and out of existence like autumn leaves tossed in a storm. She had wanted to hide – from herself, from life, from God. Unknowingly, she had found a way.

But one day, when no one is expecting it, the clouds of self-persecution will part and she will walk through them to be stronger than she has ever been. She will emerge to show everyone a bright, secure individual. She will return to Minnesota to collect her daughters, turn and walk away with the courage to never look back, to not feel trapped, and to walk onward in freedom. The kind of freedom that will give her an inner light even the fairies will envy. And on that day, she will finally be able to say to herself and the world, "At last I'm free."

Printed in the USA
CPSIA information can be obtained
at www.ICGtesting.com
JSHW020914211023
50613JS00001B/3